The Fragment of
Water

By Ben Hale

To my family and friends,

Who believed

And to my wife,

Who is perfect

The Chronicles of Lumineia

By Ben Hale

—The Shattered Soul—

The Fragment of Water
The Fragment of Shadow
The Fragment of Light
The Fragment of Fire
The Fragment of Mind
The Fragment of Power

—The Master Thief—

Jack of Thieves
Thief in the Myst
The God Thief

—The Second Draeken War—

Elseerian
The Gathering
Seven Days
The List Unseen

—The Warsworn—

The Flesh of War
The Age of War
The Heart of War

—The Age of Oracles—

The Rogue Mage
The Lost Mage
The Battle Mage

—The White Mage Saga—

Assassin's Blade (Short story prequel)
The Last Oracle
The Sword of Elseerian
Descent Unto Dark
Impact of the Fallen
The Forge of Light

Table of Contents

The Chronicles of Lumineia...4

Map of Lumineia...8

Prologue: Shattered 9

Chapter 1: Dakorian 16

Chapter 2: Eternal 23

Chapter 3: A Troll's Bounty 30

Chapter 4: Dangerous Prey 37

Chapter 5: A Mysterious Message 43

Chapter 6: Cloudy Vale...50

Chapter 7: Ancient Visitors..57

Chapter 8: Breached..64

Chapter 9: Heth 72

Chapter 10: The Cat's Eye 81

Chapter 11: Outlanders 89

Chapter 12: The Lost Temple 96

Chapter 13: The Hidden Chamber 103

Chapter 14: The Invited 109

Chapter 15: The Titan Chamber..116

Chapter 16: Assassin Council 123

Chapter 17: The Bloodsworn 131

Chapter 18: Lost to the Deep 138

Chapter 19: Churning...146

Chapter 20: The Ear 152

Chapter 21: The Strange Master 160

Chapter 22: King Numen 166

Chapter 23: The Dark Dwarf...174

Chapter 24: Stormwall 181

Chapter 25: Beacons of Light 188

Chapter 26: The Broken Crown 196

Chapter 27: Burned 202

Chapter 28: Lira's Gate 210

Chapter 29: Renara 217

Chapter 30: An Unexpected Ally 223

Chapter 31: The Fragment of Shadow 231

Chapter 32: Father of Guardians 238

Chapter 33: Brothers United 245

Chapter 34: Willow 253

Chapter 35: A Royal Request 260

Chapter 36: Seeking Wylyn 268

Chapter 37: A Daring Plan 277

Chapter 38: Draeken 285

Chapter 39: A Dragon King 292

Chapter 40: Adversaries 299

Chapter 41: Draeken's Power 306

Chapter 42: Divided 314

Chapter 43: A Brother's Request 320

Epilogue: Light and Shadow 325

The Chronicles of Lumineia 328

Author Bio 330

Prologue: Shattered

Elenyr Elsheeria exited the tunnel and surveyed the view. The shelf of rock she stood on overlooked a wide valley, cut by twin streams that fed a sprawling lake. Spring was in full bloom and flowers dotted the ledge, finding purchase in patches of soil. The sun rose in the east, casting the view in vibrant light.

"Are you ready?" she called back into the tunnel.

A young man advanced from the shadows, his expression confident, his eyes wary. Dark haired and dark eyed, he conveyed an imposing air that suggested slumbering power, yet none but Elenyr and Alydian knew the truth of his identity. He slowed and raised a hand to block the glare. A ghost of a smile crossed his face as he advanced to the center of the shelf and turned a slow circle, taking in the scenery.

"I didn't think it would be so bright," he said, his tone soft, as if he feared to disturb the sense of wonder.

"Dawn is always bright," Elenyr said. "And beautiful."

She watched him, curious to see how he would react to his first time outside. He seemed content to take in the view, looking first to the flowers and then to a hawk that soared above. The expression reminded Elenyr of when she had first seen him, not when he was born, but when he was created.

A guardian.

She shuddered and looked away, recalling all the devastation the mighty guardians had wrought. Creatures and men, infused with raw liquid magic, had lost their minds to the madness of power. Mal had been one such boy who'd survived the charm, but his forging had been unique, leaving him with not one guardian magic, but five. More stable than the others, the power had nevertheless warped his mind until

Alydian had ripped the magic from his flesh, restoring the boy's mind and body. But the magic had been part of him too long, and instead of dissipating, it had taken a part of its host, and coalesced into a new being, one who knew its own identity.

Draeken.

"You're worrying again," he said. He turned and raised an eyebrow.

"You may not be my son, but mothers worry," she said. "We can't help it."

"Isn't this why you kept me in the catacombs of Verisith for so long?" he asked, "because you were worried I could not control my magic?" His voice carried a hint of a challenge.

"Your flesh is born of magic," she said, and then offered a faint smile. "Even if you look like a man."

"I don't know what I am," he said.

"You are Draeken," she said, as if that was an answer.

Draeken raised his hand and watched the flesh fade to water, the sinews and bones changing to a crystalline blue. Then he morphed it to fire, which licked at his fingers and wrist. He grimaced, but not in pain, and the fire turned to the purplish color of mind magic. Then it faded to the darkest of nights, the shadow magic, before turning bright yellow, the magic of light.

"I don't know what I am," he said again, softer than before.

"Do you remember what I said a year ago?" she asked. When he didn't answer, she did. "I said that I'm still figuring out who I am as well."

Elenyr advanced to stand with him, and raised her own hands, which faded to ethereal. She felt the breeze stop pressing against her skin and pass through, as if she wasn't there. Then she let her entire body phase to ethereal and dropped into the stone.

The rock was dark, to her eyes resembling a dirty window. Contours of stone, cracks, and soil were all visible as spots, but the rest

10

was transparent. She willed herself several feet forward and rose again on Draeken's opposite side, rising and returning her body to flesh.

"You know how to control your power," he said, his voice touched by envy.

"Not yet," she said. "Need I remind you that I was once an oracle? I could manipulate *every* magic. Now I am this."

Elenyr recalled the moment she'd forsaken everything to become the Hauntress, including her considerable magic. It had given her a chance to save her daughter, but never imagined she would become an ethereal warrior, one free of the ravages of time.

"In time you will know your identity," she promised.

"How?" he asked, an edge creeping into his voice. "I'm a being of magic—with a mind of a man."

"You are not so different from the rest of us," she said with a small smile. When he looked to her she motioned north. "Take my daughter, for example. It took her nearly a century of life to understand her role as oracle, and now the world is changed. She is the high oracle and the other bloodlines have been extinguished."

"So?"

"Every choice we make shapes our fate." Elenyr placed a hand on the boy's arm. "Identity is not given at birth. It must be discovered."

Hope kindled in his eyes. "So I must discover who I am?"

She nodded and squeezed his arm before withdrawing to the tunnel. "And we start today. The first step in using one's magic—"

"—is knowing one's magic," he said. "I know, you've said it many times."

She grinned and swept a hand to him. "Remember, this is not the training room, where distractions are minimal. Here you will have to contend with the sounds of life, the brush of the wind, and an abundance of light. Keep a firm leash on your magics or they will overpower you."

11

He nodded and cast the rising sun a last look before turning to face her. As they'd practiced, he drew in a breath and closed his eyes, centering himself as he prepared to use his magic. Elenyr watched as energy began to crackle on his arms.

One year, that's how long she'd insisted they stay in the catacombs beneath the ruins of Verisith. In that time he'd learned spells that took mages decades to master, and still his talent grew.

She'd pledged to teach him, but a thread of fear seeped into her thoughts. Such power had a price, and she had no idea what his price would be. If he could not control the roiling power, what would he become?

The question had haunted her, driven her to teach him discipline. At first he'd resisted, but over the last year a bond had grown between them, and she considered him akin to a son. Yet still the fear remained.

Draeken cast a fire entity first, shaping a human out of flames that stood at his side. He stood tall, his boots burning the grass at his feet as he gazed into nothingness, a massive sword coalescing on his back. Then a water entity joined them, its body forming with arms and legs, the fingers coiling around a staff weapon.

An entity was a frequent charm used by mages. It lacked a consciousness of its own, and merely served the will of the caster. Elenyr thought of an entity as an extra appendage, one that required constant focus to maintain. Entities were frequently cast with weapons or tools, but Draeken's entities always carried the same weapons.

"Why does the water soldier always have a staff?" she'd asked once.

Draeken had shrugged. "That's what it wants."

Mind magic joined the others, forming a man of pure purple light. It was the only entity that never appeared with a weapon. Draeken smiled in triumph as the third soldier appeared at his side. Then he summoned the fourth.

"Shadow will be difficult," Elenyr cautioned. "Do not forget the amount of light."

"I know," Draeken said as a person of shadow took shape.

It was smaller than the others but no less solid, a dagger and a whip coiling away from its hands. Shadow magic was regarded as the weakest of the all the magics, and dissipated at the first touch of any light. Yet Draeken's shadow entity held its form even in the face of a rising sun, an enigma Elenyr had yet to comprehend.

Elenyr watched Draeken's face as he worked to cast the last soldier of light. His face was fixed, his jaw set in a determined line, the light flowing from his fingers and shaped into the body of a final entity.

The rule of entities was constant. The larger they were, the harder they were to cast, yet here Draeken demonstrated the control of a master, as if it was easy, as if he was born for it. Again Elenyr felt the spark of fear.

The soldier of light took shape and raised its head, looking about, a smile on his face. Like the others he had a weapon, only his weapon was a curved blade without a handle. Like a shard of light, it could be thrown and returned with ease, or used up close. Draeken's smile turned to triumph as the final soldier took its place.

"Well done," Elenyr said.

"I told you I could," he said, his dark eyes sparkling with victory.

"Hold them together," Elenyr said, watching his face. "You must stay focused or—"

A hawk screeched, the sound close and grating. Draeken glanced its way, the distraction causing the soldier of light to brighten. He fought to control it, but the entity continued to brighten, swelling with light and power.

"End the spell!" Elenyr warned, but Draeken jerked his head.

"I can hold it!"

But he couldn't, and Elenyr saw what was coming. Unable to prevent it, she phased to ethereal as the soldier of light became blinding, and Elenyr braced for the detonation. Draeken's shout of anger, of desperation, sent a shudder into the rock at Elenyr's feet, and suddenly the soldier of light began to change shape.

The light darkened, but not with power. Instead it darkened to flesh and clothing, the magic gaining a solidity as Draeken poured himself into the entity. Elenyr's eyes widened in shock as the entity of Draeken . . . *became* Draeken.

Her gaze flew to the youth but his body was evaporating like smoke, his expression one of horror and fear. The five entities leached Draeken's flesh from his body, stripping his essence, draining him away until he was gone. All five of the entities gained the same solidity as the first—until one Draeken was replaced with five.

"Draeken?" Elenyr asked, her voice uncertain.

"What happened?" Water asked.

"I still feel like it's me," Fire said, his voice the same, yet tinged with irritation.

Light marveled at his fingers, his eyes bright with amusement. "I didn't know I could do this."

"I shouldn't be able to," Shadow said, a smirk playing on his face as he examined his new skin.

"What is happening?" Mind asked, turning to Elenyr.

Their voices were all the same, as if a single mind had fractured into five fragments. Elenyr stared at them, shocked to silence. She'd studied magic for nearly nine hundred years, but the guardian charm was relatively new, and untested.

Before she could respond, Light began to shimmer. He grimaced, the pain spreading to the others as each gained a matching expression of terror. They groaned in unison and their bodies began to flicker, like a candle about to go out.

"*Help me!*" they cried.

Elenyr took a step forward but a blast of power from Fire scorched the ground and he doubled over, groaning in agony. All at once they

14

dropped to their knees, power leaking from their bodies. Their collective scream rent the dawn as the magics burned bright—and detonated.

The blast cracked the stone and burnt the flowers to ash. It passed through Elenyr's ethereal form, a superheated wave of power that ripped great chunks of rock free of the ledge and sent them tumbling to the valley below.

Elenyr sprinted forward and found Draeken where Mind had stood. He lay on the ground, his hand gripping his stomach, his fingers white. He looked up at Elenyr with desperation in his eyes.

"What am I?"

Elenyr knelt and held his hand, burying her fear beneath a smile. "We'll find out together."

He nodded before his eyes fluttered and his consciousness failed, leaving Elenyr on the devastated ledge. She stood and looked at the scorched stone and the fires licking at the rock, and wondered again what Draeken would become.

Chapter 1: Dakorian

Lira advanced through the forest, pulling her cloak tighter to ward off the chill. The sun had set hours ago and the second moon had risen, bathing the trees in dim light and revealing the native vegetation.

Veins of green light pulsed in the trunks and limbs, the treeblood visible only at night through the thin membrane of bark. The liquid trickled upward, feeding the mushroomlike leaves, each glowing beneath the silvery light.

She heard a faint footfall and slowed, glancing into the darkness beneath the trees. The forests of Grenedal were renowned for their beauty, but she vastly preferred the trees of Lumineia, her home.

She drifted off the path, wrapping her cloak around herself just as a lumbering figure appeared on the ridge ahead. The creature stood at nine feet, its body layered in bone armor that grew from its own flesh. More bone wrapped around its head, forming two serrated horns that pointed downward.

Dakorian.

The soldier scanned the trees, his blue eyes passing over Lira where her shadow cloak bent the light, hiding her in darkness. She couldn't resist a faint smile. The Krey Empire may have been vast, but none knew about Lumineia, or the magic its people possessed.

He carried a giant, bladed hammer, the favored weapon for dakorians. The weapon had a hammer on the front with a sharp, curved blade on the back. It gathered energy from every impact, and the energy could be discharged in devastating blasts.

He hefted its bulk as he turned about, sniffing the air. Then he grunted and turned back before descending from view. Lira waited until she was certain it was clear and then crept to the crest of the hill. From the vantage point she looked down on the small gathering.

More dakorians hefted curved plates of metal, placing them to form a towering arch. Lira scanned the workers and spotted no humans, their absence noticeable. Within the Empire, mankind held the lowest caste, the slaves to the krey. Dakorians were the warrior caste, and abhorred manual labor, yet here they were, building what was obviously a Gate, the size of which would connect beyond Grenedal.

Lira worked her way around the exterior of the camp until she spotted a trio of krey talking at the corner of the camp. Thin and wiry, the krey resembled humans in size, but their white skin and luminous purple eyes set them apart.

As the aristocratic caste of the Empire, the krey owned everything, even the lives of their slaves. Of the three krey supervising the construction of the Gate, one had a red band around his neck, indicating fifth tier, while the other two had blue bands around their throats, the swirling purple marking them as second tier. Royals.

Lira's scowl deepened. Royals of the second tier were related to the empirical line, and never ventured out of their gilded cities. For one to come here, to an unpopulated corner of Grenedal, suggested they wanted their actions hidden from the Empire.

Then the krey turned and Lira sucked in her breath. She'd hoped for a backwoods transfer of illicit goods, but Wylyn's presence could mean only one thing. They'd discovered Lumineia. The presence of a Gate meant they intended to reach the secret world.

Lira grimaced and reached to her back, where two triangular weapons were strapped beneath her cloak. The idalians were originally krey weapons, but a friend had added magic, making them far more than simple throwing weapons. Easing them free, she scanned the camp once again, and spotted a sphere placed close to the nearly completed Gate. The gravity sphere was large enough to power the Gate, and destroying it would give Lira time to gather help from the other Eternals.

She had no illusions about the coming fight. Dakorians were bred for combat, able to stand against hundreds of humans with their bare hands. Even with her magic, battling four patrols of twelve would be suicide.

Gripping the idalians, she stepped free of her cloak and darted into the night. She reached the first sentry and cast strength, her body filling with power. Her muscles throbbed with the augmentation and she sucked in a long breath, resisting the urge to strike until she was close.

When she was just feet away she leapt high, sending the blade spinning into the trees. Enchanted to fly in patterns depending on how it was thrown, the weapon twirled up and came down, digging a blade into the neck of a dakorian. The soldier groaned and slumped to the earth, the *thud* of his body alerting those nearby.

Lira summoned the blade and it flew back into her hand. She dived into the trees again, but the nearest dakorian spotted her and barked an order. In seconds the entire patrol plunged into the trees, hunting.

"I want them alive!" Wylyn shouted.

Lira relinquished the strength spell and cast agility, then leapt into a tree and kicked off a branch, bounding off the mushroomlike leaves. Two dakorians appeared beneath her, one slamming his hammer into the tree, spilling green blood down the trunk and forcing it to withdraw its limbs. Lira jumped free and caught a branch of a neighboring tree, flipping back to the ground. Then she ducked behind a tree and wrapped herself in her cloak. The dakorians charged into the trees and spread out, using scent to track her. Marked by the three serrations on his horns, the officer jerked his head back to camp.

"Get the Gate active. There might be more."

Lira twisted and heaved one blade and then two, the angle of the release sending them in different directions. One flew high, nicking a tree trunk, the other striking two dakorians standing close to the tree. They braced for the blow and retreated a step, the blade bouncing harmlessly off their bone armor before spinning back to Lira. But the wounded tree lashed out, its limbs flailing like giant clubs, bashing the two dakorians. Bone cracked as one was knocked into a second tree, while the first fought the tree, bringing its hammer to bear, hacking the limbs until they withdrew to the trunk.

18

The distraction created a gap in the line of soldiers and she sprinted through the breach, charging into the camp. Her sudden appearance drew the eyes of every dakorian, and a second patrol charged at her, the captain hurling his hammer.

She leapt into a flip that carried her over the weapon and landed on her feet, but the dakorians were quick to surround her. She swept her hands wide in defeat and one strode to her, wrenching the weapons from her hands and tossing them away. Then the soldier sneered.

"It's only a human."

"A human that killed one of mine," the first captain said, striding from the trees. He motioned to the rest of his patrol that were carrying the body of the one she'd killed. "She is more formidable than she looks."

"With these?" the second captain snorted, picking up one of the idalians and breaking it on his knee. He tossed the pieces away like they were trash. "She has luck, that is all."

Wylyn and the second royal stepped through the ring and approached Lira, coming to a halt well out of reach. Lira's eyes flicked to the companion, and recognized him as one of Wylyn's younger sons, a krey named Relgor. The two regarded her for several moments, their eyes taking notice of her clothing, her demeanor, and finally settling on the empty earlobes.

"You are not owned," Wylyn said.

"I have always been free," Lira said, eliciting rumbling laughter from the dakorians.

Relgor cocked her head to the side. "What brought you here, slave?"

Lira remained silent. Slaves were taught to bow their head to krey, but she held the gaze of a royal, an act punishable by instant death, usually carried out by injection of the earring all slaves wore. Relgor's eyes darkened with hatred and he drew a short blade, but Wylyn raised a hand.

19

"You did not come here of your own accord," Wylyn said. "I suspect you were sent here by another."

Wylyn's voice was warm and inviting, but her eyes were cold and haughty, the legacy of being taught that she was a supreme being. Lira didn't flinch or speak, but her eyes flicked to the Gate.

Noticing the motion, Wylyn's purple eyes narrowed. "Who sent you?" she demanded.

Lira remained silent, gauging the circle of dakorians, and the other two patrols just finishing the Gate. If she acted too early she would be surrounded. Too late and the group would get through the Gate.

"You're uglier than most royals," she said, and then smiled.

Dakorians sucked in their breath and several stepped forward, instinctively raising their hammers, all itching to punish her for her words. Wylyn simply glared at her, black darkening her eyes to indicate hatred.

"In all my life I have never been spoken to in such a fashion," Wylyn said, her voice soft, dangerous. "To hear it from a slave is all the more surprising. I do not see fear in your eyes, and trust me when I say, by night's end, you will beg to be my slave."

"Permit me to kill her," Relgor said, his voice eager.

Lira looked to the second captain. "Royals *love* to hear their own voice. Do you ever tire of it?"

The dakorian snorted, but the touch of amusement in the sound caused Wylyn to glance his way. He lowered his gaze and shuffled his feet. The third krey, the one from a fifth house, stepped forward and stabbed a long finger at Lira.

"You *dare* to speak to a krey in such a manner?" he snarled. "We should cut out your tongue."

"I'd still be prettier," Lira retorted.

Another gasp and the second captain dropped his hammer to thud on the ground. "Your death will silence you." Lira glanced his way and noticed the four serrations on his horns, making him the high captain of the group.

"Tardoq," Wylyn said, "finish the Gate." She then glanced to the first captain, the one she'd fought in the woods. "Kill her, and make it painful."

The dakorian reached for her and grabbed her arm, dragging her away from Wylyn. His grip was an iron shackle, the bones clamping onto her shoulder so she could not escape. He leaned down, his voice like stones grinding against steel.

"It's always a pleasure to break a woman's bones . . ."

Wylyn motioned to the second patrol and they returned to their work, connecting the power source to the Gate. As it activated, purple light seeped from the sphere and a mirror flickered to life within the arched gate. Lira winced and realized she was out of time.

"Do you miss Skorn?" she called over her shoulder.

Wylyn whirled. "Stop." She closed the gap in quick strides until she could glare into Lira's eyes. "What do you know of my husband?"

"That he and his brother disappeared three sentenia ago."

"That fact is common knowledge," she snarled, her purple irises spinning with red.

"I know that two brothers wanted to tinker with the race of man," Lira said. "And rumor has it, they succeeded. But how are we supposed to know, given that the two brothers never returned?"

"You know of my father?" Relgor demanded. "Speak, or I will have your skin flayed from your bones."

"I know he sought to change the race of man."

Lira held Wylyn's gaze. Wylyn stared at her, the fury of her eyes fading to a calculating cold. Lira could almost see the thoughts churning in her mind, wondering how a simple human could know such a dark secret.

21

To alter the genetics of a slave was forbidden across the Empire, and one of the few crimes that merited an execution for a krey—even a royal. If a krey or a dakorian had spoken those words, Ero and Skorn would see their entire houses put under the most intense scrutiny. If the accusation was found to be true, both would be executed in public.

"On what grounds do you make such an accusation?" Wylyn asked.

Lira glanced to the Gate, which was nearly complete, and then turned back to Wylyn. "Because I was one of those changed," she said.

Drawing in her breath, she gathered her magic and cast a strength charm, her magic seeping into her bones and muscles. As Wylyn's eyes widened in shock, Lira turned to the dakorian holding her arm and struck him in the chest, sending his large body tumbling like a stone thrown across a lake.

Chapter 2: Eternal

The dakorians froze in disbelief, all their vaunted training unprepared for a human with such might. Before they could recover, Lira surged into a sprint. Calling on her second magic, she summoned the wind into an air blade, a gust coalescing into a blade thinner than parchment, yet sharper than steel.

Racing for the line of dakorians, she dropped her strength in favor of agility. Tardoq charged, swinging his hammer down on Lira with a bestial roar. She slipped aside and leapt upward, casting an air stone.

The block of air was the size of her boot, and it solidified beneath her sole. She stepped on it and leapt again, casting a second, allowing her to ascend a thin staircase fashioned from stones of air.

Shouts of surprise rang out as she sprinted upward, dancing across nothingness as her boots landed on floating stones. She raced above the dakorians, charging for the gravity sphere connected to the Gate.

"Kill her!" Wylyn shrieked.

She was already outside the ring of dakorians and the soldiers by the Gate raised their hammers. Activating the energy within, they aimed and fired, the weapons sending bolts of power in her direction.

Dakorian training was legendary, their aim flawless. But Lira summoned a wall of spinning air, the magic turning solid to deflect the energy bolts in every direction. Dakorians ducked as the bolts impacted the ground, the trees, and their own ranks. One soldier was too slow and it slammed into her chest, tearing a burning hole in her bone armor and sending her to the ground. Trees ignited, the fires spreading as the forest released a keen of anger, the branches flailing.

"*KILL HER!*" Tardoq bellowed.

But Lira leapt through her own shield, the air turning clear as she passed through and landed on another air stone. The dakorians converged on the gravity sphere, forming a wall of bone flesh. Lira leapt higher and hurled her sword, morphing the blade into a spear that arced high into the air. Energy bolts leapt towards the spear but passed through the soaring weapon.

Lira curved the spear's flight, arcing it around the formation of dakorians to strike at the back of the gravity sphere. She clenched a fist just as it struck, the weapon turning solid and plunging into the energy source, piercing the heavy shielding with a screech of metal.

Purple energy flared from the hole and spilled outward, the mirror beneath the Gate flickering in response. Then the purple light began to brighten, the breach building with power, the purple light sparking and igniting small flames.

Lira rolled into a flip and dropped agility, augmenting her strength as she fell forty feet and struck the ground. Rising to her feet, she whipped her hands outward, casting two air blades, and turned a circle, ready for the group to flee.

"Through the Gate!" Wylyn screamed. "Before it collapses."

Lira blinked in surprise. They had less than a minute until the gravity sphere detonated, shredding the area. It would be difficult for the entire group to depart with their supplies, especially with Lira to fight. She'd thought Wylyn would flee and make another attempt, giving Lira time to gather more forces.

Wylyn shouted to the first captain, who had risen to his feet. Cracks marred the bone platting across his chest and rage filled his eyes. Picking up his hammer, he barked an order and the rest of his command closed the gap, charging around Lira's dissipating shield. One of the dakorian patrols charged from the opposite side, closing her in a trap.

The fourth captain and his soldiers hurled the containers of supplies through the Gate, the materials disappearing from view. Others dived into the mirror, all while Tardoq guarded the three krey on their way around the raging battle.

With strength active, Lira wielded her twin air swords, deflecting the hammers that came at her from all sides. She tried to leap into the air but a hammer swung above her head, forcing her to drop back to the ground.

She twisted to avoid a downward strike and rolled up the hammer, driving her air blade through the bone armor and into the dakorian's chest. It groaned and retreated, but another was quick to fill the hole.

Helpless, Lira watched Wylyn and Relgor circumnavigate the battle on their way to the Gate. Wylyn smirked, her expression one of triumph. Then Lira growled and struck the ground, sending a blast of air in all directions.

The dakorians didn't fall, but they slid backward, giving Lira room to jump. This time she didn't use air stones, and instead pulled the wind to aid her. She leapt into a high flip, soaring over the ring of dakorians and landing outside the circle of foes. Then she sprinted for the Gate.

The remaining dakorians converged on her and she dived to the ground, ducking under the swinging hammer and twisting, slicing her blade across a soldier's knee. Roaring in pain, he went down and she deflected the next blow, the hammer bouncing off her sword and plunging into the ground, the impact powering the weapon.

Lira reversed her grip on her sword and leapt, punching the dakorian in the face. He stumbled back, dazed by the blow, giving her a straight line to Wylyn. Dropping strength, she cast speed, and felt energy course into her body.

She charged forward, moving so quickly the remaining dakorians could not stop her. Just feet from the Gate, Wylyn glanced back and spotted Lira. Her eyes widened, but Tardoq stepped between them and lunged. His hammer came down on Lira but she was moving too fast, and she drifted to the side—into Tardoq's fist.

On instinct she lifted her arms, bracing her forearms against the blow and wreathing her skin in wind. The blow cut deep, the spines of bone drawing blood and knocking her brutally to the dirt. She rolled and came up, raising both swords to catch Tardoq's hammer as it landed upon her.

The impact sent her to one knee. She'd dropped speed in favor of strength, but Tardoq was still stronger, and she strained to keep the hammer at bay. Other dakorians converged on her but Wylyn barked an order and they veered into the Gate, disappearing from sight. The others followed, and Wylyn stepped to where Lira was pinned.

"I do not know where you draw such power," she said. "But know this, I intend to possess every living thing in Lumineia."

"You have no idea what you face on the other side," Lira growled. "A handful of dakorians will be no match for what you will discover."

"You should not be so confident," Relgor said with a sneer. "For your home is not what you imagine."

"It does not matter," Wylyn said, glancing at the gravity sphere. It trembled and sparked, the sphere close to the catalyst within. She sneered at Lira. "Soon I will own everything you thought to protect, and all your people will call me master."

"Mother," Relgor said, his expression uneasy as he glanced to the shaking gravity sphere.

"Go," she barked, and he disappeared into the mirror with a scowl at his mother.

"You think to control Lumineia?" Lira strained to keep Tardoq at bay. "The races of our lands have power greater than I."

"You are merely human," Tardoq spat, grinding her deeper into the ground. "No amount of power will prevent you from being a slave."

Wylyn issued a dark laugh as the last of the dakorians disappeared from sight, leaving just Tardoq, Wylyn, and the red-banded krey, who stood next to the Gate, her expression uncertain.

"You may have destroyed my gravity sphere but I will build another," Wylyn said. "And when I unleash the might of my house upon Lumineia, I will have vengeance for those who killed my husband."

"He deserved his fate," Lira snarled.

The gravity sphere gained an ominous whine, and Wylyn retreated to the Gate. "Make sure she's dead, Tardoq."

"With pleasure," the large captain said.

He rotated the hammer and swung the handle at Lira, but she rolled backward and sent a gust of air into her feet, sending her skidding away from the blow. The hammer crashed into the ground, sending a plume of soil into the air, the impact adding light to the runes in the hammer, indicating it had gained more power.

Lira rolled to her feet and motioned to the second idalia. A swirl of air picked it up and sent it hurtling toward Wylyn. The woman grabbed her companion krey and yanked her in front of the spinning blade. The second krey screamed as it pierced her chest. She fell to Wylyn's feet, dying just steps from freedom, her body rolling through the Gate, taking the idalia from sight.

Wylyn smirked at the miss and stepped back, disappearing from view into the mirror. Tardoq whirled and, in three great steps, disappeared as well, leaving Lira alone in the clearing with the bodies of those she'd slain. She looked to the gravity sphere and it was rising off the ground, the casing of the sphere cracking and spilling light.

Too far to reach the Gate, too far to reach the forest, she did the only thing she could. Gathering all the air around her, she spun a circle and struck the ground, summoning a tornado with her at the center. The air sucked her skyward as the gravity sphere detonated.

The shock wave ripped the Gate to shreds and obliterated the nearest trees. The dead dakorians were crushed in the whirlwind of dirt and storm of power. It expanded upward, devouring the tornado as she rocketed upward, the wave reaching for her boots like the jaws of a beast.

Then suddenly it sucked backward, drawing every speck of metal, dirt, and flesh it had caught, compressing all of it until it was no more than a ball the size of a dakorian skull. Its power spent, it dropped into the scorched bowl it had created, striking the blackened stone.

The explosion had sapped the power of the tornado and Lira fell, tumbling back to the earth. She righted herself and sent a gust from her hands and feet, landing just feet from the steaming ball of compressed rock.

The base of the bowl was scorched with fire, purple flames licking at the remains of power that had splattered the walls. The trees above flailed or shrank into themselves, green blood dripping from their trunks and limbs. Fire burned amongst their branches.

Breathing hard, Lira looked to where the Gate had stood and extinguished her swords. Anger pooled in her stomach at the failure. For thirty thousand years the Eternals had protected Lumineia, hidden it from the eyes of the Empire. Now she'd allowed Skorn's wife and son, with a force of dakorians, to reach her homeland.

She reached to her cheek and tapped the signal embedded on her jawbone, mentally connecting the message to Ero. It took several seconds, but a faint click signaled he'd answered, his voice as calm as ever.

"What did you discover?" Ero asked.

"Wylyn was here," Lira said. "She made it through a Gate with four patrols of dakorians and her son, Relgor." She then added what Wylyn had said about summoning her house army.

Ero sighed and Lira imagined him hunching his shoulders. "Return to Lumineia using the usual methods and meet me at the Vault. We'll travel from there together."

"You want me to come home?" Lira asked in surprise.

"Wylyn will move quickly," he said. "And the other Eternals are scattered on other assignments. I'll need you to hunt Wylyn."

"I do not know the region," she said. "Not anymore."

"I have some allies in mind," Ero replied. "They are not Eternals yet, but they have the potential to be so."

Lira winced at the disappointment in his voice. "I'm sorry I failed."

Ero grunted. "A breach was inevitable. But we must move quickly before everything we have sought to protect is destroyed."

The link ended and Lira turned a circle, gazing at the destruction that remained. She'd protected Lumineia from threats far and wide, but had not been home in millennia. The prospect elicited a spark of fear, and she wondered if it would still be home.

Chapter 3: A Troll's Bounty

Elenyr watched the caravan work its way north. It had been several decades since she'd visited the unclaimed lands of the northwest, but they hadn't changed—patches of trees in rocky soil, the uneven ground rising and falling into hills and gulleys, each more treacherous than the last.

Home to giant and goblin tribes, as well as outcasts from throughout the kingdoms, the region was dangerous to all visitors, and the trade caravan was no exception. Heavily armed guards rode on top of the wagons with mounted crossbows for additional support. Cavalry from Griffin flanked the slow-moving wagons, the soldiers wary. The caravan leader had even collected a handful of fire dwarves for protection. Marked by their red armor, they'd been contracted to help ensure the delivery of the goods to the rock troll lands on the Fractured Plains.

"They came prepared," Water said from beside her.

Elenyr looked to the fragment. He looked much like he had the day he'd fractured for the first time, albeit now he was an adult. His dark hair was a little long, giving him a rakish look, and his dark eyes still harbored the same power. Yet now there was a measure of control, and a playful smile crossed his lips.

"Do you know what today is?" she asked.

He raised an eyebrow. "The end of summer?"

"No," she said. "It's the day you were separated from Mal, the day you were born."

"Really?" he asked. "How many years ago?"

"Five thousand," she replied. "Give or take."

He grunted in amusement and used water in the air to conjure a mirror. "I look good for my age," he said, raking his fingers through his hair.

"You think?" Elenyr replied with a snort.

"You don't look a day over nine hundred," he replied.

This time she laughed, but the sound was tinged with regret. Five thousand years. She still had difficulty comprehending the passage of so much time. In the beginning it had seemed normal, each day flowing into the next. But as the years faded she'd watched her daughter, Alydian, grow old and eventually die, her daughter taking her place, and the next generation rising.

Without flesh to wither, Elenyr had become ageless, as Draeken had become ageless with his power. Time flowed differently for them. She frowned, wondering if she'd made the right choice the day Draeken had split into five fragments.

That day on the ledge she'd decided to train each fragment separately, afraid the sheer volume of power would consume Draeken. And so she'd asked him for a sacrifice, to retreat into the Dragon's Sleep while Elenyr took time with each of the five guardian fragments.

At first, she'd intended on taking each for a year, but it quickly became apparent that more time was required. Elenyr had worked through the standard training of mages, and then guided the five fragments through advanced training. Eventually she began taking them out into the world so each could use their magic to help the races of Lumineia.

Time had bled away, and when the fragments needed rest she returned to Verisith and ventured forth with another. She'd kept them separate from Draeken, hoping to give each the chance of self-mastery before they became one. She'd expected complaint, but the fragments did not seem inclined to be whole, and she suspected they shared her fear.

"Do you think they're going to be attacked?" Water asked, motioning to the caravan.

"It's likely," she said. "Bartoth likes to attack caravans in The Ranks."

She would never admit it, but she liked Water best. He was amusing and clever, quick with a smile and wit. But what made him her favorite was his sense of honor, a sentiment that appealed to her past as an oracle.

Although Fire was the strongest in pure power, he was impulsive and angry, necessitating the most time in training. Elenyr guessed she'd spent nearly a thousand years just with him, and he was still volatile.

She wished she'd worked with Shadow more. He was thoughtful and intelligent, with a mischievous side that reminded her of a young boy. Whenever they'd traveled to the Deep and visited Dark Elf lands, he was her companion. Light was, as expected, bright and carefree, frequently necessitating a reminder of the weight of their tasks.

Of the five, Mind was the one she feared. At first he seemed the weakest, his only magic that of memory. But she'd come to suspect that he hid his power, pretending his control was less than it was. He was ambitious and methodical, and even after centuries of traveling together, she wasn't certain she knew him. While the others trained with magic, he trained with weapons, and was a true weapons master.

"Do you think Bartoth will be strong?" Water asked, still watching the caravan.

"He's a rock troll," Elenyr said absently, still lost in thought. "But rumor says he has body magic as well."

"At the inn, one man said he snapped a sword in two, with his bare hands."

Water seemed eager to fight the troll, but she knew it was because he despised Bartoth's legacy of bloodshed. There was nothing Water hated more than a brute, especially one that used might to inflict harm on the innocent.

She frowned, recalling the last time the fragments had merged. Each attempt to merge into a single being had ended in disaster, but one or two could merge with Mind to become a less powerful Draeken.

When they did, Draeken possessed only the personality traits of the fragments.

"How much is the contract?" Water asked.

"Does it matter?"

He nodded. "Shadow likes to collect coins from the different kings. He wants one from the current monarch."

"Five hundred gold," Elenyr said with a shrug.

It was a princely sum, but gold mattered little to either of them. They had a fortune stored from the first millennia of work, before they'd switched identities. Although the line of kings didn't know it, they'd been using Elenyr and Draeken for many generations to aid in quelling unrest, hunting bandits, and even preventing wars. Elenyr and the fragments used personas to hide their identity, and only a handful of Elenyr's trusted friends knew the truth about Elenyr and Draeken.

"Will we ever succeed to unite as Draeken?" Water asked.

The fragment's somber tone revealed he'd been considering the question for some time, and his brow knit together in doubt. Elenyr stepped out of the shade of the tree and came to his side, placing her hand on his arm to offer comfort.

"I'm confident you will," Elenyr promised.

He nodded, but his expression remained uncertain. Water's gaze was on the trade caravan, but he looked beyond it, his normally serene expression troubled. Time had less meaning for them, but Draeken wanted to be whole, and she recognized the approaching time when she would have to permit Draeken to be himself.

After all this time she knew the fragments were still drawn to each other, as if they wanted to be one, but she could not say why they still struggled to be whole. Her heart ached for them. The fragments were her family, her friends, her sons.

"What would you like to do after we deal with Bartoth?" she asked, attempting to steer the conversation to the future.

"The rock troll fortress," he said, nodding emphatically. "I'm the only one that's never been to Astaroth."

"Then we will have to visit," Elenyr said with a smile.

The region west of the unclaimed lands was the rock troll domain, the wide plateau broken by countless canyons and ravines. Forged for combat, the trolls were without peer on the battlefield, their very discipline leading to less need of outsiders, which made Bartoth such an anomaly.

The troll had been raised like any other, but unlike the rest of his people, he reportedly possessed body magic, a skill common only among the barbarian tribes of the south. Already nine feet tall and layered in muscle, Bartoth had sought the crown. His bloody rise ended when the entire populace had rebelled and exiled him to the unclaimed lands. That was ten years ago, and he'd set himself a small empire by destroying trade caravans. Even giants feared him, while the outcasts of every race had quickly flocked to his lair, a stronghold hidden in the snow-capped mountains of the deep north.

"We could return and attack him in his fortress," Water said, a smile on his face.

He fidgeted, growing restless as they continued to wait. Elenyr couldn't blame him. Much like Fire, Water always wanted to move, to advance. They'd visited Bartoth's fortress twice, but Elenyr was leery of attacking such a redoubt. In physical form Elenyr could be harmed, and every fragment of Draeken had been hurt before. Attacking a few thousand bandits in a well-fortified cave would not be wise, even for them.

She considered recalling the other fragments, but they were all on other assignments, some important enough she did not want to risk them not being completed. No, she and Water would need to deal with Bartoth.

"Patience," Elenyr said.

"Mind said you'd say that," he said glumly.

"Oh did he?" Elenyr asked with a smile.

"He thought we should all come together and eliminate Bartoth's lair," Water said. "They would not be able to stop us if we were united."

"But would you be able to control your magic as Draeken?" Elenyr asked.

Water nodded, but there was doubt in his blue eyes. "You still think we are not ready?" he asked.

He set his jaw in a firm line, as if challenging Elenyr to disagree. She recognized the influence of Fire and realized she could not keep them apart much longer. Perhaps she had already delayed them too long.

"I think you are ready," Elenyr said.

"Really?"

Elenyr nodded and motioned to their camp. "Let us return to Verisith and speak to the others. Unless . . ."

"What?" he asked.

"If we leave, that caravan will be slaughtered."

She feigned doubt but a hint of a smile crossed her face. Water began to laugh and pointed an accusing finger at her, sending a spray of water into her face.

"Are you trying to manipulate me?"

"I'm just showing you the options," Elenyr said, wiping her face and flicking water back at him.

"We stay," Water said with a nod. "But only because you're right."

Elenyr felt a tremor in the ground and looked to the caravan. It was deep in The Ranks, the region named for the rocky towers that resembled ranks of soldiers from a distance. The spring runoff had eroded the gaps between them while leaving the twenty foot towers, a near labyrinth of connecting corridors, dead ends, and hidden grottos. Summer had just started and water trickled through shallow creeks, with numerous patches of water hidden amongst the stone towers.

The caravan had entered the Ranks an hour ago, following the marked road that gradually ascended to the rock troll territory. A gap in the Ranks allowed Elenyr to spot the top of a wagon, where a few minutes ago a soldier had stood at a mounted crossbow. Now the man was slumped on the wagon.

"I do not think we will have to wait long," Elenyr said.

Water turned to the caravan just as a plume of smoke rose from between the rocks and distant shouts rang out. Elenyr and Water exchanged a look and without a word leapt down the slope.

Chapter 4: Dangerous Prey

Water sprinted forward and summoned his magic from a nearby stream. It flowed up and around his body, becoming a giant wheel that picked him up and carried him down the slope, the vehicle accelerating, bouncing over rocks and brush. It reached a small cliff and sailed over, blasting through the branches of a tree before impacting lower down.

A smile split his face as the wind whipped against his tunic, the sheer speed eliciting a burst of excitement. Even after centuries of training and practice, the use of magic never grew stale, and each use was as exhilarating as the first time he'd felt the spark of power at his fingertips.

A flicker of green caught his eye and he glanced to the side, spotting Elenyr gliding in ethereal form. She had her cowl drawn over her features, her cloak billowing behind her. Her sword hung low in her hand, the metal glowing green like the rest of her form. In the flesh she was bound by the constraints of her body, but in her ethereal form she moved by will, and she veritably flew, easily keeping pace with him.

He grinned at the sight, realizing just how fearsome she must look to those they hunted. She was the Hauntress, her fearsome reputation now a legend that grew with every telling. Many regarded her as a myth, others swore she hunted oathbreakers and killers, that she was the very hand of justice.

"Stay focused," she said. "This is not for your amusement."

"Doesn't mean it can't be fun."

"Killing is never fun."

"Even when they need killing?"

"That sounds like Shadow."

"He's the one that said it."

Beneath her cowl he spotted a faint smile. "The moment they slaughtered their first victim, they accepted their fate today," she said. "Remember, we are here to exact justice, which can have as much heart as mercy."

Water wondered how mercy could be part of justice. They were there to kill the offenders, to end their lives because it needed doing. Some of the other fragments enjoyed killing bandits, but Water merely enjoyed the combat. The killing was a distasteful necessity.

"Focus, Water," Elenyr said. "You strike the left flank, I'll handle the right. Then we'll wrap around the caravan and come together on the opposite side. Try to stay unnoticed for as long as you can."

They veered apart and Water rolled his wheel into The Ranks, diving into the patchwork of shadows beneath the pillars of stone. Water was approaching the caravan from the north, and he caught glimpses of the line of wagons.

The first and last wagons were on fire, the flames licking into the wood and the bodies above. He recognized the tactic to trap the caravan on the road between two flaming barricades. Then he spotted a figure kneeling on top of a pillar and rolled up the side, extinguishing his wheel as he reached the top. His momentum sent him soaring up above the crossbowman aiming at the caravan.

Water landed behind the man and he clenched his fist, casting a spike of water just as the man turned. Punching once, he drove the spike through the man's back and kicked him over the edge. His scream was brief, but drew the attention of the two neighboring men, both armed with crossbows. They rose and swiveled, shouting for aid as they took aim at Water.

Water flicked his wrist and the spike turned into a whip, which he sent snapping at the nearest, the whip coiling around his neck. Water yanked him off the pillar. His body slammed into two pillars on his way to the ground, his makeshift armor clanking on the stone, the sound mingling with his screams.

Water turned to the second but he'd already fired his crossbow, the bolt digging into Water's chest. He grimaced in pain and yanked the bolt free, blood spilling down his tunic before water covered and healed the wound.

The surge of anger was swift and harsh. Water sent his whip at the man, catching his leg and pulling him toward the drop. He shrieked and dropped his crossbow to claw at the smooth stone, but Water pulled him off the lip and sent him plummeting below. Just before he landed on his head, Water felt a tinge of remorse and pulled, swinging him into the stone instead. His helmet struck the rock and he went still, and Water lowered him to the ground.

Water scanned The Ranks before jumping to a neighboring tower and then used a burst of water to leap to the next. Three more and he'd reached the edge of the road. Coming to a halt, he surveyed the caravan.

Half the cavalry was dead, the other half struggling to fend off a horde of goblins, humans, and orcs. The soldiers on the mounted crossbows fired as fast as they could reload, their volley keeping the attackers at bay.

Water caught a fleeting look of a rock troll on the opposite side, his giant body muscled and tattooed. His war cry sent the handful of cavalry scurrying backward as he hefted an enormous hammer.

Water yearned to fight Bartoth, but he couldn't let the caravan soldiers die. He cast a crossbow out of the ambient moisture in the air and armed it with slivers of water. Then he took aim and unleashed the needles.

Streaks of water plunged into the attacking ranks, burying into flesh and bone, filling the canyons with renewed screams. Water cast a gremlin to hold the crossbow and then stepped off the ledge, dropping thirty feet into the midst of battle. His sudden appearance sent the nearby men and orcs scrambling backward, and he took full advantage.

He cast his favorite staff and sent it spinning around him, the blade forming on the end just as he reached out and sliced across an orc's chest. The blade cut deep and Water spun past the dying orc, already sweeping the staff across the next. Four fell before the group of attackers recovered, and by then Water was moving too fast to stop.

Swords, spears, and axes reached for him but he flowed around the blades, sending the staff into a dizzying spin, the blade becoming a whirling arc that cut deep. The weapon hardened further, becoming sharper than steel, cleaving through metal and wood, bone and armor. Unprepared for the sudden assault, the bandits scrambled to flee the dangerous blade.

Ending the spin, Water raised the staff and plunged it into the earth, sending water exploding outward. The liquid engulfed their feet and hardened, the creeping ice rising to their waist and arms, holding their struggling forms in a ring of ice.

The remnants of Bartoth's forces on the north side of the caravan fled, retreating into The Ranks. Avoiding the burning wagon, Water leapt between two wagons and turned toward the sounds of combat.

A giant appeared between two pillars, a trail of dead defenders in his wake. He swung his enormous maul, cleaving an entire wagon in two, spilling gold to the earth. His eyes gleamed with excitement and he roared in triumph, just as Elenyr exploded from the rock tower like a ghost. She streaked by, her sword slicing across his throat before her body disappeared into another stone pillar.

The giant's eyes darkened in surprise and shock, and then in death. The large body collapsed onto the wagon he'd broken, the bulk of his body crushing wood and trapping the gold anew. Satisfied Elenyr had the battle in hand, Water darted into the Ranks, intent on reaching Bartoth first.

—A great hammer swung at his head, nearly taking it from his shoulders. On instinct he ducked and slid forward, whirling to face the towering rock troll. Armored in steel plates, the troll twirled his hammer in a lazy spin.

"Water mage?" he asked.

"Something like that," Water said, unable to resist the smile as he recast his staff.

"That won't do much against me," he said with a snarl, and smashed his hammer against the stone wall, sending fire bursting across the weapon.

Water retreated a step and set his staff into a spin, eyeing the flaming maul. Normal weapons hurt, but fire cut into his very essence. Mistaking his reserve, the rock troll sniffed in disdain.

"And you thought you could stop me."

Bartoth charged, swinging the hammer into a rock pillar. Fire exploded from the impact, cracking the stone all the way to the summit. Water retreated around another pillar and used the staff to leap, rebounding off a small ledge to come at Bartoth as he appeared around the corner.

The bladed staff came down across the troll's helmet, slicing through the steel with the sound of glass on metal. Water carried the strike all the way to the ground, cutting into the chest armor for several feet before he landed and darted away.

Bartoth paused and removed his helmet to reveal a cut along his cheek. He bared his teeth in a smile, twisting the tattoos that spiked across his features. Tossing the helmet away, he pointed the hammer at Water.

"First time a whelp like you has made me bleed."

"Won't be the last."

Bartoth snorted and clenched his fist. Brown light glimmered on his form and Water recognized the use of body magic, enhancing the troll's already mighty strength. Releasing a roar that rattled the stones on the ground, he charged and swung his hammer.

Forced to retreat, Water dived into the maze as the hammer struck a pillar, blasting a hole in the stone and cracking it to its base. Stone ground on stone as it began to teeter, and then fall, the sound lost in another explosion as the hammer blasted into another pillar, smoke billowing from the impact.

In the confines of the Ranks, Water was at a disadvantage. He sprinted deeper into the pillars of stone but Bartoth kept pace, his boots thudding on the ground, the sound rumbling like approaching thunder. Water tried to cast his wheel but there was not enough moisture in the air, forcing him to stay on foot.

"You think to flee, little mage?" Bartoth snarled.

The hammer came down on Water and he spun, using his staff to deflect it aside. It impacted the ground, sending bits of flaming stone sizzling into Water's body. He growled and veered hard to the side, avoiding Bartoth as he leveled another tower, this one crashing into a neighbor and sending them both to the ground in a grinding of stones. The path grew narrow and Water slipped through, hoping to gain space, but Bartoth cast agility, and like a giant cat he leapt and twisted, rebounding off tiny ledges to circle the tight gap and land in front of Water.

Water brought his staff up and knocked the hammer aside, and then lunged. For several furious seconds hammer and staff crashed into each other, with both taking wounds. Water attacked the troll's legs and cast a whip, snapping it in his face before feinting high and plunging his staff into the ground. The circle of ice spread outward but the troll leapt into the air and struck the earth, shattering the ice and knocking Water into another gap.

He tumbled between two pillars and into a cave, but before he could escape the troll appeared the opening. Water retreated as the troll charged, sprinting to the end of the tunnel and the circular cave beyond. Above, a small hole allowed light to spill into the cave, illuminating Water as he turned to face his opponent.

"You're trapped," he snarled, hefting his flaming hammer so the flames illuminated his bloody features.

"There's just one problem," Water said. "The trap wasn't for me."

Bartoth entered the cave and straightened. The troll's eyes widened as he looked beyond Water to see the pond in the back, where the runoff had gotten trapped. Water smiled and called on the wealth of power.

Chapter 5: A Mysterious Message

Bartoth growled and charged, and Water retreated onto the pond, his boots walking across the surface as if it were stone. Then he summoned water from the deep pool and erected walls of water, filling the chamber with a dozen barriers, the light reflecting off them and hiding Water from sight.

The rock troll charged into the edge of the pond, smashing the walls as he sought for Water. The waterfalls continued to flow upward, filling the holes made by the hammer and splashing across the ceiling.

Leading with his hammer, Bartoth swung his weapon through the final waterfall—but Water was not there. Water passed through the pond and rose at his back. He plunged the staff blade through Bartoth's armor, digging into his flesh.

The rock troll whirled, sending the hammer at Water's skull, but Water dropped into the pond and willed himself around the rock troll, again rising at his back. This time Bartoth was waiting for him, and his hammer came crashing down on Water, shattering him into drops that fell into the pond. Bartoth stared at the spot where his foe had stood, and then to the waterfalls that remained flowing upward.

"You think I'm that easy to kill?" Water asked.

Bartoth looked up and found Water standing above him, the waterfall feeding his form—and a quartet of other figures. Each looked like him, right down to the blue tunic and dark trousers. Water smiled, the expression matched across his summoned companions. Then he pounced.

The five figures leapt and attacked, using the waterfalls as cover to strike the trolls' flank, driving him back. One leapt right through a waterfall, plunging his staff into the troll's armor. Snarling, the rock troll leapt, attempting to leave the pond, but a new waterfall rose up to hem him against the cave wall. With blood dripping from a dozen wounds, he wiped at his face and retreated to the rear of the pond.

"I'm not going to die at the hands of a whelp," he spat.

"It's not like I'm giving you a choice," Water said, perched on top of the nearest waterfall as his minions advanced. "And it's only fitting, since you've killed so many."

The troll smirked and kicked off the wall, using the momentum to spin a full circle, the fire hammer exploding through the minions, shattering each until it blasted into the wall. Smoke and fire filled the cave, darkening the chamber.

Water reached for more magic but the hammer burst from the smoke, forcing him to dodge. Bartoth was right behind his hammer, his magically enhanced body allowing him to leap high—with a second hammer in hand.

Too late to evade, Water saw the smaller hammer coming for him and raised his staff, bracing for the impact. The blow struck the staff in the center, breaking the weapon and striking him in the chest. Fire burned through his tunic and into his body. He cried out and fell, and the waterfalls plummeted back into the pond.

Pain seared through him, and Water drew on the pond water to cover the wound, drawing on its power to heal. He stayed underwater, hidden from view. Anger and pain mingled, rising into fury.

He stood and found Bartoth standing at the entrance to the cave. Water thought Bartoth would flee, but the rock troll began to laugh, the sound filled with menace. Water pulled from the pond, shaping a pair of soldiers with matching staff weapons, spreading them out in order to flank the rock troll.

"You are no normal bounty hunter," Bartoth said. "Who are you?"

Water hesitated, the question impossible to answer. He was neither a man nor a mage. Even as a guardian he was part of a whole, even if he now thought of himself as separate. He scowled and dodged the question.

"Who I am doesn't matter."

44

The rock troll's eyes lit with understanding. "After what I've seen, I believe I already know your identity."

"What matters is that I'm here to exact justice for your crimes."

The rock troll chuckled. "Many have said that, but you are the first I believe. Unfortunately, I have no desire to see what lies after death, not when we stand on the cusp of such momentous events."

Water scowled. "Of what do you speak?"

"You have no idea the foe you face," the troll said. "Watch your back. I'm certain this will not be the last time we fight."

Bartoth heaved his hammer into the ceiling of the cave entrance, blasting the stone into pieces that fell into the opening. Smoke and rock tumbled from the ceiling, sealing the opening and leaving Water inside. He drew from the pond and raised himself on a finger of water to the opening above, but by the time he escaped the chamber, Bartoth was gone.

Water's impulse was to follow but he guessed the troll had used speed. That and his knowledge of the terrain would make him nigh impossible to locate. Grimacing his distaste, Water turned and threaded his way through The Ranks to the caravan.

The path was strewn with rock and fallen stone towers, the vestiges of Water's battle with the powerful rock troll. He fought a surge of irritation, and he wondered what the troll had meant about momentous events.

Despite his irritation, he was proud to see so many of the soldiers of the caravan had survived. The battle had been challenging, more so than recent conflicts, and he found Elenyr near the caravan. She saw him approach and turned.

"Bartoth?" she asked.

"Gone," he said.

"He got away?" she asked in surprise.

45

He rubbed the still painful wound on his chest. "He's clever, more so than I anticipated."

The engagement with the troll had been a test of his magic. It was not until they were inside the cave that Water had realized how dangerous Bartoth could be, but by then, the troll had seen his impending death and retreated. Still, the contest could have resulted in Water's death, a fate few had come close to accomplishing.

"We should go after him," Water said. "You can track him better than I."

"He knows the terrain," she said. "So we'll have to pick up the trail later."

Of the seven wagons, only two were intact. The rest were either damaged or destroyed entirely. The fires had been extinguished but three of the wagons were smoking husks, steam rising from the blackened wood.

Half the guards were dead, their bodies laid out next to the wagons, a cloth covering their still forms. Many more of Bartoth's minions had perished, and their bodies were treated with less respect, heaped in a pile a short distance into The Ranks.

Wounded cried out in pain as healers worked over them, attempting to close their wounds so they would not join the dead. Elenyr grimaced, the expression one of regret. Water had seen that look after many battles, when the woman missed her magic of healing.

"We already did what we could for them," Water said.

"I know," she replied. "But I wish we could do more."

That one statement exemplified Elenyr, and Water felt a surge of pride for his companion. She was as much a mother to him as anyone could be, and she taught compassion with her deeds far more than her words. She would gladly trade her life for even these nameless soldiers, a sacrifice Water didn't know if he could make.

The caravan leader noticed them and hurried over. "You have our gratitude," the woman said, wiping dirt and blood from her face before motioning to the wagons. "Without you I fear we would all be on our backs." Her smile was tinged with fear and awe as she looked to the Hauntress.

"Most of his followers didn't survive," Elenyr said.

"Rumor says he has more forces in a secret fortress in the north," she replied.

The woman was a soldier, that much was evident. She had a lean body and a sword on her hip, her eyes firm despite the losses they'd suffered. Griffin trade caravans were always led by a soldier of Griffin, and she had the bars on her shoulder to mark her as a captain.

"We'll see what we can do," Elenyr said. "But Bartoth will retreat and regroup his forces. You should be safe for the rest of your journey."

A man groaned nearby and the captain darted to him. As she cared for the wounded she looked up to Elenyr. "Bartoth is not dead?"

"He escaped," Water said. "But we'll find him."

The woman spat into the earth and then turned her full attention to the wounded soldier. Recognizing it was time to depart, Water and Elenyr left the soldiers to deal with the aftermath of the battle.

"Now can we go after him?" Water asked when they were out of earshot.

"What irritates you so?"

"Something he said," Water said, and shared the rock troll's comments. "It was almost like he recognized me."

"His words imply he is part of an organization," she mused. "Perhaps one that stands against us."

Water had not noticed that, but realized Mind would have caught the implication. Mind had the gift of intelligence, and abruptly Water missed his fragment brother. How long had it been since they'd fought together?

"He's more dangerous than we thought," Elenyr said. "The longer we delay, the more innocents will fall to his hammer."

"Then we should act quickly," Water said, eager to finish the fight. "Do we not know the location of his fortress?"

"For now," she said. "But after today he will feel vulnerable, and may not return there."

Elenyr glanced over his shoulder and frowned. Water turned and noticed a bird dropping to them, aiming directly at Elenyr. Colored a dingy brown, it was small and oddly angular, its wings sharper than seemed natural. It dropped to Elenyr and alighted on her outstretched arm.

She loosened the message attached to the bird's leg and the creature flapped away. Water watched it go, a frown creasing his forehead. Normally he could sense blood in living creatures, the water inherent to their bodies. But the bird had no moisture inside its frame, almost as if it was a machine . . .

"It appears we have a message," she said.

"And they found us here?" Water asked, still watching the bird. "How?"

"The bird is tied to a specific recipient," she said. "It can always find me, anywhere on Lumineia."

"It doesn't have any blood," Water said.

"It wouldn't," she said absently.

Water turned and found her reading a small piece of pure white parchment. The message was small, and he craned his neck to read it. In short, looping handwriting, the brief message was cryptic.

We have been breached.

Water looked to Elenyr in confusion, but she seemed to understand the message. She stepped to where a few flames licked at a piece of wood. Then she lowered the parchment into the flames and watched it crinkle to ash.

"We must go," she said, turning away from the caravan.

48

"For Bartoth?' he asked.

"No," she said. "Another matter is more urgent."

"Who has been breached?" Water asked.

Elenyr paused and met his gaze, her expression the as sober as he'd ever seen. "We must hurry."

"Wait," Water said, catching up to her. "Who sent that message?"

Elenyr sidestepped the question. "An old friend," she replied. "One who does not seek an audience lightly."

"Why does he want to meet us?" he asked.

"I suspect he has a favor to ask," she replied.

"Another bounty?" Water asked, glancing in the direction where Bartoth had disappeared.

"Not likely," Elenyr said.

Elenyr's features were tight with worry, implying their visitor was not as friendly as she described. Water tried to recall the last time someone had visited their home and, aside from Elenyr's descendants, only a handful of treasure seekers had ever found the ruins.

"Come," Elenyr said. "We must summon the others and return to Verisith."

Water fell into step beside her, a smile spreading on his face. Although he had no idea who would be arriving in their home, he sensed that whatever lay in store would bring a change to their life. He hoped it would finally allow the fragments a chance to prove they could be Draeken.

Chapter 6: Cloudy Vale

Elenyr and Water took their journey south, through the mountain passes and into the heart of Griffin. The nation had been gradually expanding its borders for centuries, claiming any lands not under another banner. Their greed had not gone unnoticed, with the rock trolls, the elves to the south, and the Azure people on the islands all resisting the expansion. For their part, Griffin claimed the rise in population necessitated the growth, a not entirely untrue assertion, even if it was not the whole truth.

Riders, wagons, and full caravans filled the breadth of the highway, gradually digging ruts in the fine stonework. Military transports moved north to join the growing army attempting to clear the unclaimed lands, while merchants carried spices from the new northern villages back to the middle cities.

Water didn't mind the crowds and was always fascinated with the multitude of entertainers who flocked to the road. They were always looking to earn coin from the harried parents that wished to distract their children.

A juggler walked with a caravan of merchants, causing the children to laugh and giggle as he attempted to twirl daggers, the blades nearly impaling him as he feigned instability. Farther down a bard sang while he reclined on the back of an open wagon, allowing his horse—which apparently knew the way—to drive. His song was low and inviting, an advertisement for an upcoming performance in a northern fort, a fact he mentioned after every song.

But this time Water kept glancing at Elenyr, who was unusually quiet. She, too, enjoyed the road, even though she'd mentioned that she no longer felt part of the kingdoms she'd sworn to protect. Water fleetingly wondered if she had grown weary of helping those who did not know her identity.

That thought reminded him of what Bartoth had asked. Others had wanted to know his identity, yet in light of how much time had passed, Water found himself unsettled. After so much time, shouldn't he already know?

"Bartoth asked me who I was," Water said, watching a captain bark at his troops to stay in formation. Some of the men were talking to a pair of noble daughters riding nearby, and they straightened at the command.

"And you think I can tell you?" Elenyr asked. "Do you remember what I said when you first separated?"

"That I would choose who I wanted to be," he said, grimacing at the painful memory.

"We choose our own fates," she said, and nodded to a woman riding next to her husband.

The woman watched her two children scamper about, a small smile on her face. Dressed in homespun clothing and astride an aged mount, she was obviously a commoner, yet there was something serene about her that inspired envy.

"I cannot choose my own," he said. "Because I'm only a fragment."

"Perhaps," she said. "But even a fragment has a choice in its fate."

She pointed to a man who was slumped in his saddle, dozing as his horse picked its way north. His white hair tugged in the breeze, his fine clothing shielding him from the morning chill. Two guards rode with him, both watchful, wary.

"A minor noble," Elenyr said. "He was likely raised for his role, yet fragments of his identity call him in other directions. Perhaps he enjoys singing, or weaponry, and both shape him into the man he has become."

Water noticed the sword on his hip. Many nobles wore a blade, as much for ceremony as for protection, but this man's sword was well cared for, the hilt a fine workmanship, yet not for show. As he rode by, Water noticed the calluses on his hands and realized he still trained, revealing why his belly did not extend like many nobles.

Her reminder that others had fragments to their identity brought a smile to his lips, and the confusion dissipated. He spotted a dwarf with a wagon of mechanisms, each designed to entertain and delight. Traveling south, likely to Stormwall for the summer games, he permitted the children to insert coins into the mechanisms, bringing them to life, the mechanical soldiers rising to duel each other.

Children were present, but so were adults, all finding entertainment in the monotonous journey. Water glanced to Elenyr and she smiled and nodded, giving him permission to join the crowd.

The journey passed quickly, and despite his earlier doubts he was no longer discontented. Elenyr still brooded, but Water quickly grew distracted by the many children migrating to the northern villages with their families, where the promise of a new frontier awaited.

He cast small cats of water and they stood like men, fighting with tiny swords. The children giggled and laughed at the comical display and Water drank in their laughter, the combat and battle in the north long forgotten.

Passing Terros, capitol of Griffin, they continued south, the road growing less traveled yet more diverse. Elves journeyed into Griffin, carrying enchanted light orbs, clothing, and weapons, while Griffin exports of ore and food made the return journey. Fewer families were present and Water was forced to find entertainment with a traveling bard, who was well into his stock of Dwarven fire ale.

They reached the elven forest of Orláknia and turned south, departing the highway for the smaller roads. As always, Elenyr avoided the location where Dawnskeep had once stood. During her time as an oracle, the fortress had been her home, but the Mage Wars had left it destroyed, with the four other oracle bloodlines extinguished. Water still remembered when townsfolk talked of the war, but now the tales were relegated to legend. The city had been covered with earth shortly after the war and the forest had reclaimed the region. In recent decades the elves had built a new capitol on the site, and the city of Ilumidora glowed on the horizon. Elenyr still avoided it, and Water assumed her memories were not so easily buried.

The road grew progressively rougher as they worked their way to the southern border of Griffin, the crowds fading until they were alone, and the road was little more than a path through the trees. Shortly after, they reached a large cliff, the edge of the towering mountains that separated Griffin from the barbarian strongholds.

Elenyr reached the cliff and her body phased to ethereal, allowing her to pass through the solid rock. Water turned his body to liquid and stepped to a small stream trickling from beneath the cliff, his body flattening, allowing him to pass through the smaller aperture.

On the opposite side lay a tunnel with no egress to the outside world, one of the forgotten entrances to the ancient city of Verisith. From there, they traveled deep into the mountain, rising to a secret refuge just north of the ruins.

Several side tunnels split off, leading to the city, but Elenyr and Water ascended a long corridor to a separate location. Water grew excited at the prospect of home and skipped ahead, stepping through an arched opening into the hidden refuge of Cloudy Vale.

Like a cup held in the hands of a mountain, the tiny refuge was just a few hundred feet across. Fed by a spring, a well of water flowed up in one corner, while a small grouping of trees grew next to the pond. With sheer rock on all sides, the outpost had the sky for a ceiling, the few scattered clouds touching the peaks.

A handful of structures were cut into the rock that circled the space and contained Elenyr's private home, and the fragment's quarters. The rest of the refuge had training spaces and benches for quiet reflection, the flowers adding to the tranquility.

All of the buildings had been built by the Verinai before their fall. Draeken was the last of the Verinai, and from what Water understood, he was grateful there were no more survivors of the powerful guild. On the north side, a new staircase ascended the cliff, rising to a tiny overlook between two mountain peaks. The overlook provided an unbroken view all the way to the distant elven forests.

Water hurried forward and waved to Fire, who stood on the training grounds, battling a trio of his own soldiers. With a flaming sword in hand, he dispatched them with vicious blows before turning to Water and nodding.

"Your water steed found Shadow and me in Herosian," he said. "Fortunately, we'd just finished our assignment. How was the bounty?"

"Bartoth got away," Water said.

Fire frowned. "I should have been the one to go."

Fire's voice was a perpetually low growl that elicited fear in many of those he met, but Water knew him to be determined and forceful, when he didn't fall to his temper. He was also slightly larger than the other fragments, and his protective instincts made him behave like an older brother. He cast a dagger of fire which he sent winging to the portal just as Elenyr emerged.

She caught the blade before it pierced her eye and frowned. "Fire," she said in disapproval, "we've talked about this. Striking a friend is not friendly."

Fire smiled and inclined his head. "Yes, mother."

Elenyr would normally respond to such a comment by firing the dagger back to Fire, but she tossed it away and strode to her quarters. Fire frowned, obviously confused, and approached Water.

"What happened?"

"A mysterious message," Water said. "No idea who it's from."

"What did it say?" another asked.

Shadow appeared at their side and formed into flesh, obviously listening the whole time. Although they all looked like Draeken, Shadow was shorter than the rest, his dark hair seeming to be darker, and his smile more mischievous. If they were a family, he would have been the youngest brother.

"That we've been breached," Water said.

"That's it?" Fire asked.

"Must be important," Shadow said, and then glanced to Water. His eyes widened in surprise and he looked beyond them both, to the entrance. "Do you think the message came from him?"

Water whirled and tripped, slamming into the ground. Fire too, was on the ground, and both glared at Shadow, who faded to darkness and flitted away, leaving his laughter to echo in Water's ears.

"Sometimes I want to kill him," Fire growled, breaking the band of shadow that had bound his feet together.

Water sliced his bonds with a knife of water and stood. "Have Mind and Light returned?"

"Light's playing on the cliff," Fire said, motioning to the top of the peak. "Who knows where Mind is. Let me know when you find out who the message is from."

"When did you start being curious?" Water asked with a smile.

"Never," he replied, his lips twitching. "But I smell an approaching conflict."

"It might be here sooner than we think," Mind said.

Water turned to find Mind striding toward them. Slighter of build than the rest of them, he seemed forgettable at first glance. Then you saw his eyes, and the simmering intelligence that lurked within. All the fragments had the eye color of their magic, and Mind was no exception, the dark purple a striking hue.

All the fragments acknowledged Mind as the leader, and when they were Draeken, he was the only one conscious. Of the group, Water liked to think of Mind as the oldest brother. On his own, Mind spoke softly, his words articulate and intentioned. When they resorted to the Dragon's Sleep to rest, Water wondered if he ever truly slept, or if he merely plotted.

"You think someone is coming here?" Fire scoffed. "No one knows this place exists."

"The oracle does," Water said, thinking of Senia.

"And apparently two more," Mind said.

"How would you know that?" Fire asked.

In answer, Mind turned to the entrance and waited expectantly. Water glanced between him and the entrance, attempting to sense the approaching forms. Mind looked to Fire, who'd cast a pair of fire daggers in his hands.

"Our visitors are not the type to throw daggers at," Mind said.

Fire grunted and extinguished the blades. The next moment two figures appeared in the entrance and came to a halt on the threshold, looking about in interest before meeting the eyes of the trio in the center.

One was of medium build and clad in a regal cloak. His white hair made him look old but his features were flawless and strikingly handsome, as if he'd never aged. His blue eyes pierced Water to the core.

The second couldn't have been more different. She wore dark, fitted armor, the pattern uncommon, her blonde hair pulled back and tied. Her eyes were also blue, albeit sharper, more seasoned. A warrior. She carried no visible weapon, but Water sensed a power within.

Elenyr appeared on the balcony of her home. "Ero," she called, "welcome to Cloudy Vale."

Chapter 7: Ancient Visitors

Elenyr phased to ethereal and dropped through the balcony to alight on her porch. Then she strode to greet the newcomers. She motioned the three fragments to join her, and watched them carefully, gauging their reactions.

Fire seemed on edge, sparks on his fingers, while Mind was as reserved as ever, his dark gaze calculating. Water looked eager, his eyes flicking to the newcomers and back to Elenyr, obviously wanting to understand their arrival. Elenyr's gaze settled on Ero. She hadn't seen him in ages, not since she'd refused his offer to join the Eternals.

"Ero?" Fire muttered to Mind. "She can't mean . . ."

"Water, Fire, Mind, this is Ero and Lira," Elenyr said. "And before you ask, this *is* the Ero you know from history."

"The one from the Dawn of Magic?" Fire asked, his expression incredulous. "That was three sentenia ago."

"You are not the only one free of time," Ero said, a small smile on his lips. "I take it this is Shadow?"

He turned and looked to Shadow, who now stood behind Lira, examining her profile. A slight shade of pink touched his darker features before he withdrew to stand with the others. He nodded a greeting.

"Were there not five fragments?" Lira asked.

"Light," Elenyr said with a nod. "He's probably off playing."

"He does that," Shadow supplied, staring at Lira.

Water was staring as well, but Elenyr couldn't blame them. The woman was stunning, her skin a shade darker than most, her eyes a slightly different shape as well. Both gave her an exotic look that matched her unfamiliar accent.

"Where are you from?" Water asked.

"Here," she said, a smile on her features.

"You're as old as he is," Mind guessed, motioning to Ero.

"Not quite," Lira said with a laugh. "But much older than you."

A peeling laugh echoed inside the refuge and Elenyr turned to see Light streaking down a nearby peak. Like a diamond tumbling down the steps, he glittered, his face flushed bright as he plummeted down the slope.

Astride a sled crafted of pure light, he leaned one way and then the other, guiding his mount down the patches of snow, bouncing over the stone and boulders. Falling fast, he reached a cliff above the small pond and went free.

In a graceful arc he spun, flipping several times, his laughter growing louder before he dived smoothly into the pond. Light filled the water, shining from his body before he climbed to the bank and stepped free, a wide smile on his face.

Shirtless, he revealed a muscular torso on a lean figure. He sucked in his breath and his body shimmered, the light heating and burning off the moisture. Then he noticed the group watching him and his eyes widened. He darted forward, so quickly he reached them by the time Elenyr had drawn a breath to speak. He leapt into the middle and greeted them, his words tumbling from his mouth in a rush.

"Visitors? From where? And you didn't summon me?" he glared at Mind before turning to Lira. "Well you're beautiful."

"You're not so bad yourself," she said, her eyes flicking to his upper body.

"Will you put a shirt on?" Water asked, obviously embarrassed. "It's our body too, you know."

"Sorry," Light said.

He darted to their home, his body moving faster than seemed possible. Excited as he was, he would not be able to control his magic, and in seconds he returned dressed in a bright blue tunic. He smiled and joined the group, his expression dimming a little when Mind glanced to him, his features laced with disapproval.

"As much as I would love to speak with you all," Ero said dryly, "time is not our ally. Elenyr, may we speak in private?"

"Of course," Elenyr said. "This way."

Elenyr motioned towards her home, a recessed building with only the porch and the balcony visible, along with a handful of windows in the cliff face. The visitors nodded to the five fragments and then followed the path of crushed white stones to Elenyr's house. Elenyr waited until Ero and Lira entered her home and then turned to the fragments, and folded her arms.

"I know you are excited," she said, "but I need you to wait out here."

"She's captivating," Shadow said. "Don't tell me I'm the only one who saw it?"

"Do you need to ask?" Mind replied, a slight smile on his face.

Elenyr suppressed a smile. For Mind to admit he was attracted to the woman was unusual, and she didn't want to embarrass him. She gestured to Shadow, her voice gaining a warning edge.

"No eavesdropping."

"You think I would do that?" Shadow asked, raising his hands.

"Yes," Elenyr said, and then smiled. "I need you to trust me, and wait out here."

She looked at each in turn, waiting until they nodded. Then she looked to Mind, who held her gaze, his expression thoughtful. Eventually he nodded and she knew he would obey. With a nod of gratitude, Elenyr turned and joined Ero and Lira in her home.

Stepping through the front door, she strode into the main hall of her private quarters. Originally intended as a training hall, the large chamber was open to the second floor, where several doors looked down on the main living area.

Couches and chairs were positioned throughout the space, which could have accommodated twenty, yet hadn't had more than six in ages. Paintings of castles and oracle descendants adorned the walls, while a painting of Alydian hung above the mantle, her smile one of joy, a baby girl in her arms.

The moment Elenyr stepped inside her smile faded. "How bad is the breach?" she asked.

"Skorn's wife and son are here," Lira said.

Elenyr's heart sank. She'd hoped it was just a random krey that had discovered Lumineia, but this was worse. Wylyn knew about the Eternals and wanted to destroy what they protected. If she succeeded in revealing Lumineia to the Empire . . .

Elenyr shuddered. "When?"

"Nine days past," Lira said.

Elenyr shook her head. "How did this happen?"

"She has been searching for Skorn since his disappearance," Ero replied. "And wants vengeance upon me. Unfortunately, she did not come just for me. She intends to open a Gate to her house, and bring her army to take the people of Lumineia as slaves."

Elenyr frowned and glanced at Lira. "Does she have such an army?"

Ero sighed, his shoulders hunching. "She does."

"You must find her," Elenyr said.

"That will be a challenge," Lira said. "As you know, the Eternals protect Lumineia, but few have lived here in many years. None know the current world, and we need a guide."

"One that knows about the Eternals," she said, realizing what Lira meant. "You want me to help."

"You and Draeken," Lira said. "Wylyn has come with four patrols of dakorians, and enough weaponry to stop even you."

"The fragments are not ready," Elenyr said.

"It's been five thousand years," Ero said.

"I know," she said, "and they are just now controlling their magics."

"Why has it taken so long?" Lira asked.

Elenyr felt a surge of irritation, as if the woman doubted Elenyr's ability to teach. "You think you could do better?"

The woman shook her head. "I mean no disrespect. But is he not a mage?"

"No," Elenyr said. "He is a guardian." She motioned east, to where the ruins of Verisith continued to decay. "The guardian spell was meant to create a powerful protector. But it granted too much power, and the magic consumed the wielder, frequently within months of their creation. The longer they remained conscious, the quicker they fell to madness.

"Draeken should have fallen to madness ages ago," she said. "And if that had occurred, it would have been my duty to destroy him. Instead, each fragment has spent millennia learning to control their own magic."

"They are all fragments of a single being?" Ero asked.

"They are," Elenyr said. "As fragments they are powerful guardians, but when they are one . . ." she shook her head and looked away.

"No mother thinks of her children as ready for war," Ero said. "Nevertheless, he seems ready."

"Not as Draeken," she said. "They have spent nearly the whole of their lives apart, and as Draeken they cannot control their power."

She recalled the last time Draeken had been whole. The merging consciousness always left Mind in control, but the power was still too much, and the scars from the attempt had taken years to regrow. There was still a blackened section of rock on the cliff from the combat, a legacy of when Draeken had burst back into the five fragments.

Ero nodded as if he'd expected the answer. "We do not know Wylyn's location or plan, so perhaps it's best you separate, with Lira to join your ranks."

"Her?" Elenyr asked, raising an eyebrow.

"I'm capable in a fight, I assure you," she said.

Elenyr's first impulse was to reject the idea. But Ero's point about motherhood was too accurate to dismiss, and Elenyr realized just how much she'd sheltered Draeken. As she considered the prospect she looked back at the last century, at the rising sense of impatience displayed by the fragments. On the most recent journey Water had not displayed his usual lightheartedness, and she realized she'd been remiss in her duty. Perhaps joining this endeavor would be a final test to see if the fragments were ready to become Draeken.

Elenyr looked to Ero. "Do you remember when you asked me to be an Eternal?"

He offered a faint smile. "Shortly after Alydian died. I remember you refused, and said you had not fulfilled your duty to Draeken."

"Are you asking us to be Eternals?" Elenyr asked.

"Perhaps," Ero said. "But all Eternals must prove themselves, for much is at stake. In you I have no doubts, but Draeken is another matter. Do you believe he is ready?"

Elenyr sighed and looked out the window, to where the fragments still stood talking. Shadow was absent, and despite his avowal, was probably listening by now. As an oracle, Elenyr had known she would only ever have a daughter, so to have sons was a privilege she'd never anticipated. A tightening in her chest accompanied her next words.

"He's ready to find out," she said.

Ero nodded in gratitude and turned to Lira. "Although you are the Eternal, Elenyr must lead this endeavor."

"Why?" she asked, obviously surprised.

"She knows the people, the kingdoms, and the fragments. You know our enemy."

Lira obviously didn't like being relegated to a supporting role, but she nodded, her features tight with disappointment. A flicker of self-doubt was also present, and Elenyr wondered if there was more they were not saying.

"We shall begin the hunt tomorrow," Elenyr said, and raised her voice. "Shadow, would you please summon the others?"

There was an impish laugh and the shadow behind the shelves flitted out the window. "Of course," he called.

Ero turned to Lira. "I wish I could stay, but there are other Eternals in danger, and other threats that must be quelled."

He said his farewells and then pulled a pocket mirror into view. It activated at his touch and flowed into a mirror that blocked the fire in the hearth. Nodding to Lira and Elenyr, he stepped through the glass and the mirror faded from sight.

Chapter 8: Breached

Elenyr stared at the empty wall, her thoughts distant. Then she turned and strode to the rear of her home, where a door led to her personal archives. After a moment's hesitation, Lira followed her inside.

Books lined the chamber, rising for four levels. Alcoves dotted the space, while the center of the chamber contained a large fireplace. The chimney rose through the center of the room, the large hearth cold and dark. On a raised section of floor around the fireplace, couches sat with tables and desks for study.

"You have more books than a king," Lira said.

Elenyr nodded absently as she ascended a staircase to a small archive set at the back of the room. She frowned as she sought among her only tomes that spoke of the Dawn of Magic. Many of the archives in Lumineia had material that spoke of that time, but most of the books had been written by historians many years after. She was one of the few with books and archives actually written by witnesses.

She carefully lifted a large tome down from the shelf and carried it to the desk near the hearth. As she opened the cover, the fragments filed in, and Fire gestured to the hearth, sending a current of flame to ignite the wood.

"Thank you, Fire," Elenyr said.

She leafed her way through the pages, her fingers brushing across the air magic that protected the parchment from damage. When she found the right page she turned to Lira and the fragments.

"The krey have discovered Lumineia."

The fragments exchanged a look, and Mind frowned. "How many?"

"Wylyn, Skorn's wife, and Relgor, her son, have come with four patrols of dakorians," Lira said.

"We know what they are," Mind said, motioning to her archives. "What is her goal? She wants the truth of her husband?"

"Hardly," Lira scoffed. "The krey are not known for their love. She wants what he and Ero created, the wealth of this world."

"And we are to stop them?" Water asked.

"We are," Elenyr said, and pointed to the book. "The challenge is in finding her."

"Surely they will be noticed," Shadow said.

"They will," Elenyr said. "The dakorians resemble rock trolls in size and shape, while the krey resemble the race of man."

"Their greatest weakness will be their pride," Lira said. "They view the people here as slaves. They will not be able to resist killing, without regard to age, race, or station. We should be able to follow the destruction to locate them."

"Find them and kill them," Fire said, folding his arms. "Sounds simple enough."

"These are unlike any foes you have faced," Lira said. "Just one dakorian can destroy a legion of men."

"We are not normal men," Shadow said with a smirk.

"I hope not," Lira said. "Because you have no idea the threat you face. The krey have technology you cannot imagine, their weaponry beyond anything you possess."

Mind scowled. "You underestimate us."

"You underestimate your enemy," Lira said.

"We do not know our enemy," Mind said. "That is why you are joining us, is it not?"

65

Lira held Mind's gaze, a frown creasing her features, but Elenyr nodded her approval. Mind had a gift for perception, and intuition. When others saw what lay before them, he saw what lay ahead. Still, the slight tension between Mind and Lira did not bode well, and Elenyr considered who to send with the Eternal.

"Guardian or man, the dakorians will slaughter you all," Lira said. "And if they open a Gate to Wylyn's home, she will be able to bring her entire army."

"How many?" Mind asked.

"Many times the population of Lumineia."

Light, who'd been playing with a dagger of light, looked up in surprise. "Surely there cannot be that many."

Lira folded her arms. "That's just her house guard. If she brings the armies of the allied houses, the number will be far greater."

"So why has she not opened a Gate already?" Mind asked.

"Gates come in several types," Lira said. "The smallest of which connects to a single exit. The largest can connect to other worlds, and that is what Wylyn and Relgor will seek to build. I destroyed their gravity sphere, so they will need a source of power. They will also need a specific mineral that all Gates are built from."

As Elenyr listened, a plan began to take shape. They needed answers from across the kingdoms, and the faster they discovered Wylyn's location, the better. But who to send with who?

"So we know what she wants," Fire said. "Let's stop wasting time and go find her."

"We must hasten," Elenyr said, nodding to herself as she mentally selected the groups. "Light, can you give us a map, please?"

"Of course," Light said.

Light dismissed the knife he'd been twirling and stepped into the center of the group. The chamber darkened as he pulled on the illumination to create a globe of light in their midst, the light bending and twisting into a map, the contours of the islands displayed in intricate detail.

The great blue lake was a shade darker, the rivers connecting to its banks. At Lira's request, Light added script, the letters showing Talinor to the south, Griffin to the east, and Erathan to the west. The dwarven realm was shown in the mountain of the northwest, while gnomes, orcs, and trolls lived in the north. The reclusive barbarians lived in the southeast, the closest neighbors to their current refuge.

"It's beautiful," Lira remarked, causing Light to flush.

"It's nothing," Light said.

Elenyr strode around the map and pointed to the western kingdom of Erathan. "Water and Light, I want you to go to Erathan. Find the Ear. If anyone knows where Wylyn is, he will."

"You don't want to see Jeric yourself?" Water asked, his lips twitching into a smile.

"No," Elenyr said.

"Who's Jeric?" Lira asked.

Fire grinned and pointed to Elenyr. "He's the one that fell in love—"

"Fire," Elenyr said, her voice tinged with warning, "that's enough."

Elenyr looked between them, but the amusement on the faces of the fragments brought a frown to her own. Shadow put his lips together like a kiss. Elenyr's irritation mounted, and she stabbed a finger at Lira.

"You'll find out for yourself," Elenyr said to Water. "Lira is going with you."

"What?" Water asked, his smile disappearing. "Why? I mean, I'm happy to have her with us . . . but we can, I mean . . ."

"I don't mind," Light said with a broad smile.

Shadow drifted close to Elenyr and lowered his voice so only Elenyr could hear. "Nice deflection."

67

Elenyr hid a smile and turned to Water. "While the three of you go to Jeric, I'll travel with Mind and Fire to Herosian. If reports have come in of strange outlanders, King Porlin will have heard of it."

"One group to find out what the people know, one to find out what the nobility has heard." Mind nodded his approval. "What about Shadow?"

Elenyr turned and stepped to the open book she'd retrieved. Summoning Light, she pointed to the small map on the paper and Light nodded. Pointing to the floating map, he added pinpricks of light across the surface. No more than a dozen, they were placed in every region and land, even the unclaimed continent and the Dragon's Teeth to the south.

"These mark the only known Gate sites," Elenyr said. "Each is a place where Wylyn and her companions could have arrived."

"There's not too many," Mind said. "Why don't we just search them all, pick up the trail from the source?"

"Lira?" Elenyr motioned to the map. "Care to answer that?"

"Because this is not complete." Lira stepped forward and pointed to one Gate location out to sea. "As is their custom, the krey built hundreds of Gate sites throughout the region, allowing them to instantly travel to their various outposts. In their war, many were lost, while others were destroyed."

"So she could have arrived anywhere," Fire rumbled, folding his arms.

"Fortunately a map was created near the close of the Dawn of Magic," Elenyr said. "The map should reveal the location of all the Gate sites that survived. It was kept in the archives of the first elven queen until it was stolen by the Thieves Guild. It hasn't been seen since."

"You think they still have it?" Shadow asked, his eyes lighting with anticipation.

Elenyr nodded. "That is my hope. While the rest of us seek Wylyn, Shadow will go to the Thieves Guild and attempt to find the Gate map."

"Why do we need it?" Fire asked. "Surely she will not stay where she arrived."

Lira shook her head. "You're thinking like one who is hunted. But the krey view themselves as superior beings, and Wylyn will not wish to sleep in the dirt. Many of the Gate outposts would have the luxuries of a krey structure. She and her son would be loath to abandon them for a bed in a human inn."

"Pride will be her undoing," Mind said with a satisfied nod. Then he frowned. "Would one of the Gate sites have a source of power for the Wylyn's Gate?"

"Not one of sufficient power," Lira said. "To Ero's knowledge, all the gravity spheres large enough for a World Gate were destroyed in the Dawn of Magic."

"There is one problem with my assignment," Shadow said. "The Thieves Guild is currently in turmoil. A rival guild has arisen, one with more brutal tactics. Answers will be difficult to gain in such a conflict."

Elenyr regarded Shadow, measuring the excitement on his features. She'd sent him alone before, but did so with caution. Of the fragments, he was the most prone to mischief, and an extended assignment alone could lead to disastrous results.

"Shadow," Elenyr said, "can we trust you on your own?"

"Me?" Shadow feigned a wounded expression. "What have I ever done to merit such doubt?"

"Dozens of examples come to mind," Fire said with a laugh.

"It's true," Water said, his tone apologetic.

"I'll go with him," Light exclaimed.

Elenyr shook her head as Mind did the same. "No," he said, his lips twitching in humor. "I don't think we need to deal with the damage the two of you would cause."

Shadow laughed and acknowledged their doubt with a bow. "I'll find the map."

"Without intrigue?" Elenyr pressed.

"You wound me," Shadow said. "But I swear any intrigue I am involved in will be necessary."

Light laughed lightly. "All intrigue is necessary. Isn't that what you like to say?"

Shadow smirked, and Elenyr sighed. "Shadow . . ."

"Fine," Shadow said. "I promise to not be fun."

Elenyr doubted his oath, but there was little that could be done. She needed Water to speak to Jeric, and if he encountered Wylyn he would need help from Light and Lira. She would send Fire or Mind with Shadow, but she would need both if she encountered the krey. Realizing she would just have to trust Shadow, she turned to the others.

"Time is against us, so hasten your journeys."

"What do we do when we find Wylyn?" Mind asked.

"We regroup," Elenyr said. "And then we strike."

The fragments nodded in turn, and Light extinguished the map. As they departed, Elenyr turned to the fire crackling in the hearth, trying to shake the sense of worry. Draeken's fragments were her family, and she was sending them to war. She turned when Mind appeared in the doorway. A glance revealed that he was alone.

"Why are you worried?" he asked.

Elenyr wasn't surprised he understood. Mind always seemed to know what people were feeling, even if he didn't use his magic to see their thoughts. Elenyr regarded him for several moments before pointing to him.

"Do you worry for your fragment brothers?"

"Sometimes," Mind said. "But they are quite capable."

"Worry comes quicker when you have lost one you love," Elenyr said, passing a hand over her face.

"And you think we might lose?"

"A mother's fear," Elenyr said. "But you should rest."

Mind crossed the space and ascended to join her. Flashing a faint smile, he reclined on the couch nearby and closed his eyes. "I think I'll rest here tonight."

Elenyr smiled, grateful for Mind's intuition. Since Ero's arrival she'd felt a tremor of fear, but as she listened to Mind fall asleep, that worry gradually faded. The threat might be dire, but she had faith in her sons.

Chapter 9: Heth

Water, Light, and Lira took their journey north, using the tunnel to reach the elven forests. From there they traveled west through the pristine lands of the fair race. Lira seemed content to ponder her own thoughts while Water cast surreptitious looks at the beautiful woman. Light didn't bother hiding his attraction, and openly stared.

Water had seen many attractive women, but none like Lira, and he fidgeted every time her gaze flicked to him, his chest growing warm. He knew Light was equally enamored, and found himself annoyed by his lack of reserve.

Water hadn't slept much the night before, his thoughts dominated by the upcoming assignment. He'd hoped to be sent with her, and had been pleased by the chance to go. Still, Light's actions left Water feeling decidedly embarrassed.

"Do you always stare?" Lira asked Light.

"Only at one so beautiful," Light said.

"*Light*," Water groaned. "Have some reserve. Not that you're not beautiful, I mean, of course you are, but, just—"

"Very smooth," Light said with a laugh, causing Water to flush and look away.

"Can I ask you a question?" Lira asked.

"Anything," Light said, and Water shook his head in irritation.

"How long have you been alive?" Lira asked.

"A little over five thousand years," Water said with a shrug. "You?"

"I was born in the time you know as the Dawn of Magic," she said.

"Did you see the war?" Water asked, raising an eyebrow. "The one that destroyed the krey?"

Lira's features tightened with regret, and Water wondered what she had endured. "It feels like another life, before I became an Eternal."

"What made you ageless?" Light asked.

"An accident," she said. "My brother and I were playing in an abandoned home of the krey and activated one of their machines. From that day forth we stopped aging."

"And your brother?"

Lira's features darkened. "The krey killed him."

"I'm sorry," Water said.

"We all have reasons we fight," she replied.

Water stole a look, measuring the woman's regret. Then Light spotted a beam of light coming through the trees and darted to it. Even in physical form he could move fast, and reached the beam in a single breath. He shaped the light into a magnificent steed, and then crafted a second. Leaping onto the back of one, he rode back and presented the second to Lira.

"A beautiful gift for a beautiful woman."

She eyed the enormous horse and shook her head. "I prefer to walk."

Water hid a smile. The creature had the body of a horse but the head of a wolf, the hybrid a disturbing combination that inspired revulsion and fear. To avoid sparking a panic, Elenyr had forbidden Light from using the strange mount in public.

"Nonsense," Light said, and the horse ducked under her legs, lifting her astride its back with ease.

"I'm afraid you don't have much choice," Water said with a smile.

Lira looked down to find the reins flowing into her hands. She reached out and touched the animal's neck and it turned, revealing the wolflike jaws. She did not flinch from the hybrid animal.

"And why are you spared from riding such a beast?" she asked.

Water snorted and stepped to the stream and drew from the water. "I have my own method of travel," Water said.

"You don't like the strange horses?" Lira asked, her lips twitching.

"His wolf steeds are disturbing," Water said.

"Only to a few villagers," Light said. Then he cocked his head to the side. "Or perhaps all of them." He smiled and patted the wolf head. "But I think they're beautiful."

Water pulled from the water, fashioning a wheel large enough to surround him. Then he crafted a reclining seat and climbed inside. His smile was smug as he spun the wheel, sending mud splattering into his wake.

"Try to keep up."

The wheel churned and he sped away. Light laughed and slapped his steed, his mount bursting into motion. Fashioned of pure light, both horses barely touched the ground, their passage a glittering streak of gold as they flitted through the forest.

Water heard Lira's gasp and smiled, pleased they'd managed to disconcert the woman. Then he spotted Light rotating in his saddle. The fragment crossed his legs and faced backwards, staring intently at Lira.

"You're staring again," she said, but there was a smile on her face.

"Are you with anyone currently?"

Water shook his head in disbelief. "You have to excuse Light. He has problems controlling his impulses."

"I do not," he said indignantly. "Hey look, a hawk!"

He leapt off the horse and caught a branch, using it to launch himself into the air. Catching the hawk's claws, he brought the startled

74

bird back to the ground, where he alighted on his horse. Holding the screeching animal, he smiled proudly.

"Have you ever seen a hawk before?"

"She lived here for decades," Water groaned, wishing he was alone with Lira. "Of course she's seen a hawk before."

"Oh," Light said, releasing the bird. "What about—"

"Why don't you tell me about Elenyr," Lira asked.

"What do you want to know?" Water asked.

"I know she used to be an oracle," Lira said. "How did she become . . ."

"The Hauntress?" Water supplied.

Water slowed his wheel so he was next to Lira and launched into a description of how Elenyr had become the Hauntress, the tale filling the journey as they skirted the southern end of the elven lands and entered the plains of Talinor.

Filled with an endless vista of thigh-high grass, the plains stretched beyond the horizon, and the trio reluctantly returned to walking so their passage would not be noticed by the farmers tending to their homesteads. By nightfall they reached Herosian, a sprawling city with a massive castle at its heart.

Streams wound their way through the city on the plains, passing through the upper steps to reach the slums that lined the exterior of the city. Taking the lead, Water led them to their favorite tavern in the city, The Oracle's Respite.

Reportedly built by Elenyr's daughter as a favor to a friend in the war, the glittering structure had become a legacy of the building of Herosian, and many vied for space in the inn. The current owner knew the fragments well, and gave them a room in the attic. The space was small and little used, the window allowing them a stunning view of the city.

Darkness fell and, with it, Light's energy. Collapsing into the soft bed, he wiggled in pleasure. As Light slept, Water talked to Lira deep into the night, enjoying the break from Light's antics. When he finally reclined on his own bed, he found himself picturing Lira's beauty.

He woke with the dawn when Light bounded to the window, breathing in the light like it was a morning meal. Water groaned and threw a pillow at the fragment, but Light was unfazed. Lira yawned and rose.

"Do you always need to sleep at night?" she asked.

"When it gets dark he gets tired," Water said.

"I can explain for myself," Light said indignantly, and then turned to Lira. "When it gets dark, I get tired."

"That's what I said," Water said.

"I said it better." Light sniffed and reached for his tunic, pulling it over his shoulders.

They descended to the tavern and ate a quick meal, then departed into the city. Water watched Lira gaze about the city in interest, and answered her questions about its occupants and history.

Herosian, known as the Jewel of the South, had swelled with people from throughout the kingdoms. Rock trolls, gnomes, and dwarves from the north were present, their appearance eliciting whispers and sneaking looks from the children, but not outright fear. Dark elves were also walking among the populace, their presence welcomed by the open-hearted kingdom.

Shop windows contained every exotic tool, toy, or weapon, with storefronts managed by all the races. To the scorn of neighboring kingdoms, King Porlin had opened Talinor's borders to all, granting unprecedented access.

Dark elf chefs cooked giant gorthon fish, the beasts larger than a full-grown bull. People gathered to watch the flesh sear to gold, the more wealthy purchasing a meal. Across the street, stone masons carved statues and intricate beams for the richer homes being built on the eastern steppes.

The noble's houses were richly adorned with banners, fine stone, and elven wood, demonstrating the wealth the kingdom had gained from the merging of peoples. Even the soldiers came from various races, with a dwarf captain riding with a pair of humans and a gnome.

Water loved Herosian because magic was always present, with excited students in the robes of their school following their professors. He spotted a pair of young elven maidens, both talking animatedly as they cast an entity out of water, one that resembled a young man. He was obviously one they both favored, but their magic was insufficient to do more than create his form. As they walked by, Water added a burst of magic to the entity, and the boy abruptly winked and leaned in, kissing the startled elf.

"I didn't take you for mischievous," Lira said, as the girl all but swooned in the arms of the entity.

"That would be Shadow," Water replied. "But that doesn't mean I don't enjoy a little fun."

Departing the city, they made their way to the far western border of Talinor and crossed the great Blue River to reach the kingdom of Erathan. Younger than the other kingdoms, the kingdom of Erathan had fractured from Talinor shortly after the Mage Wars. Known as a haven for the outcasts of the other kingdoms, it had gradually filled with the dregs of the other kingdoms, with crime rampant and murders common. King Deedis, a former assassin, had ruled with an iron fist, using fear as his principle weapon until his son had taken the throne. King Numen had followed a more honorable path, and the kingdom had improved significantly under his rule.

Foregoing the road and the longer route it would require, they worked their way through the forest, circumnavigating several villages on their way to Heth, the capitol city of the kingdom. After two days they stepped through the tree line and Water lifted his gaze to the Giant's Shelf. A thousand feet high, the cliff extended east and west, a massive barrier that separated the southern and northern regions of Erathan.

Two great waterfalls cascaded down the massive cliff, slamming into the pool at its base and sending plumes of mist rising into the evening air. Water smiled at the sight but resisted the urge to leap across the water and play in the falls.

"Heth," Water said, pointing upward.

The fortress clung to the cliff between the two waterfalls, a strategic position that prevented attack from above or below. Built into the crags that split the cliff, the city extended to the summit above.

Powered by the waterfall, a pair of ascenders climbed the cliff, and the trio boarded a boat that took them to a platform between the two waterfalls. Water paid for their passage, and then paid more to board the ascender. Several others were already present—a trio of swarthy thieves and a pair of city guards. The thieves stood clear of the soldiers, but one sauntered over to Lira.

"What's a pretty thing like you doing coming to Heth?" He leered and reached up to touch her cheek.

A dagger appeared in her hand, the tip poking his hand and drawing blood. "I wouldn't," she said mildly. "Not if you wish to keep the limb."

The man recoiled and retreated to his friends, who guffawed at his expense. Water enjoyed the spectacle, and hid a smile as he watched the thief nurse his pride. Then the thief glanced to Light and scowled at the blatant grin.

"Is something amusing?" he demanded.

"You don't have a chance with her," Light said.

The thief whipped his sword from its scabbard and leveled it at him. "And you do?"

"Of course," Light spoke as if it was obvious. "I'm more attractive, smarter, better dressed, stronger . . ."

As he enumerated all the reasons why Lira would be more attracted to him, the man stared, his face turning bright red. Water managed to keep his smile in check. The soldiers looked on in amusement, unperturbed by the sword pointed at Light.

"And I smell better," Light finished. He sniffed and wrinkled his nose.

"It's true," Water said with a laugh.

The man flushed and swung his sword, but Light slapped the tip of the sword free of the man's fingers. It tumbled over the edge, the weapon flashing in the sun before it plunged into the lake below. The man stared at his empty hand and then up at Light. His companions caught him and dragged him back before he could do anything rash.

"I'll gut you for that," the man growled, straining against his companions.

"That's enough, Dalton," one of the guards said.

The ascender reached the top of the cliff and came to a grinding halt, revealing a city illuminated by bright lights. Dalton spit at Light and then stomped off, his companions trailing in his wake.

"You've made a dangerous enemy," the guard said as he stepped through the city gates, "but it was worth the show."

Light shrugged as if he'd already forgotten the encounter, and Water found his attitude refreshing. Light rarely took such a situation seriously, and if the man was foolish enough to return, Water had no doubt that Light would be the victor. Still, making an enemy in Heth was not the wisest course.

He hadn't been to Heth in decades, and it had grown in his absence. The buildings were new, even if the streets were not clean. Even the people were better dressed, and Water wondered how much was due to King Numen's leadership. He stepped to the nearest cart that smelled of sugar and bread.

"Sweet bread?" he asked Lira.

"Of course," she said.

"Fire cloaks!" Light said, bounding away.

Water shook his head, but a smile spread on his face as Light eagerly examined the wares of a dwarven shop. Water had to drag him away to the city walls. The gates were unguarded, and they passed through a small knot of dwarves and a pair of women too into their drink. Even though it was daytime, fires adorned poles and buildings, the colors enchanted with an array of colors.

"Light," Water said, "we're not here to visit. We need to find the Ear."

"The Ear?" Lira asked. "I thought his name is Jeric."

"It is," Water said. "He's an elf that's been around for ages and done everything. Started out as an adventurer before spending time as an assassin, which lasted until he grew tired of killing. Then he became the guildmaster for the Thieves Guild. He's bounced from one life to another until he got bored wrangling sharks and set up shop here. Now he owns part of the city."

"The governed part," Light said.

They'd left the main throughway behind and the area turned seedier. The streets were packed with people from throughout the kingdoms, garish light playing across their features. Merchants were everywhere, all guarded by at least two sentries. Disorganized and winding, the streets seemed to lack any planning, and ended and started at random points. Then the group passed over an invisible line and the streets were abruptly clean, the roads straightening out and pointing to a large structure at the edge of the Giant's Shelf. Part of the building actually leaned over the drop.

Caustic music came from within an inn where hundreds of young men and women sought entry, a pair of timid looking guards barring the way. Exotic and multifaceted, the curved walls shimmered with magic, the light dancing and inviting as the sun set on the horizon. Shaped like a cat climbing over the edge of the cliff, the structure's jaws opened to receive the patrons.

"Welcome to the Cat's Eye," Light said. "Now watch your back."

Chapter 10: The Cat's Eye

They threaded their way to the front of the crowd, drawing several curses as they shoved past those waiting to get inside. Water merely smiled and cast his staff blade, one that spun ominously. They retreated.

The trio reached the guards, who took one look at Lira before permitting them inside. The room was packed with dancers, the bards standing on a stage in the corner, bellowing songs that would have made Elenyr cringe. Then Water saw Lira look to the floor, her eyes widening. The back half of the structure extended over the thousand-foot drop—and the floor was glass.

"Who would build something like this?" she asked.

"Someone like him," Light said, pointing to the elf.

Ear sat at a private table on a balcony overlooking the tavern. A short flight of stairs led up to the room and was blocked by another guard, a troll rather than a human, his wide frame barring the steps with ease.

Light strode to the steps and looked up at the troll. "We'd like to see Ear."

Hearing his name, the elf poked his head around the guard's shoulder and spotted the three of them. His features lit up with excitement and he waved them through. Eager to see him, Water ascended the steps and greeted the elf.

"Water," he said. "It's been too long. And you brought Light?"

Lira leaned over to Water. "He knows about you?"

The elf spotted her and a flicker of disappointment crossed his features, followed by admiration. "My friends, your companion is lovely, but it was another beauty I had hoped to see in your midst."

81

"You still favor Elenyr?" Lira asked, and glanced to Water. "I got the impression your relationship had ended."

"How could I not still favor her?" the elf said, flashing a roguish smile. "She has more secrets than the stars."

"Do they really call you the Ear?" Lira asked.

The elf cringed. "A moniker I can't seem to shed. But I admit it has a certain crass truth to it. Please, call me Jeric."

"You've done well for yourself, Jeric," Lira said, motioning to the tavern.

Jeric's eyes sparkled with delight. "They said it couldn't be built, that it would fall within a year." He winked. "That was thirty years ago."

Water motioned to the tavern. "I see the popularity hasn't waned."

"There are always youths wanting a place where they can pretend the problems of the world do not affect them," he said. "I merely provide such a location."

"Can we talk somewhere more private?" Lira asked as the music picked up, a trio of bards screeching an unholy tune, their sound magic shaking dust from the ceiling.

"Of course," he said, motioning to a doorway at the back of the balcony.

He guided them inside and shut the door, partially muting the sounds coming from the tavern. Then he motioned to the comfortable seats before sitting behind his private desk, placing his boots on the surface.

"What do you need?"

"Information," Lira said. "A dangerous group of outlanders have come to our shores. We seek them."

Jeric frowned and examined her anew. The carefully worded statement gave no detail as to Lira's identity, yet Jeric abruptly smiled and stood. He stepped to a small cabinet made of elven cedar and withdrew a bottle. Pouring a small glass, he returned to his seat and raised it to her.

"It's always a pleasure to meet an Eternal."

Lira's eyes narrowed while Water burst into a laugh. "How did you know?"

"The accent is ancient, and her features are not Talinorian or Griffin-born. Besides, when you come asking about a distant land, that can only mean one thing. Someone unwanted has come to Lumineia." His eyes gleamed with excitement.

"You know a great deal," Lira said.

Jeric chuckled at her wary tone. "You have nothing to fear from me, my beautiful guest. And rest assured, Elenyr has not informed me of the Eternals, nor have her companions. That is one secret I figured out on my own."

Water noticed an air blade forming in Lira's hand and reached out to put a reassuring hand on her arm. She didn't look his way, and her grip merely tightened on the blade. She had the look of one used to being hunted, one who killed to protect her secrets.

"You expect me to believe you figured out the greatest secret on Lumineia . . . on your own?"

"The clues are present for those who know how to read them," he said, his eyes sparkling with mischief.

Water abruptly realized Jeric had green eyes, not the usual blue of his race. The trait had likely been gained from a human in his ancestry, the individual probably the source of his cunning, another attribute not common to the fair race.

Jeric seemed to notice the woman's tension and waved it aside. "Rest assured your secret is safe behind my lips. They do call me the Ear, not the Mouth."

"They'll call you dead if you speak of the Eternals," she said.

"Do you know what we seek?" Light asked, obviously unaware of the tension.

Jeric nodded. "Perhaps, but I fear there must be a cost."

"We have to pay for the information?" Lira asked, raising an eyebrow. "I thought you were a friend."

Jeric's eyes settled on her, a ghost of a smile on his features. "All information has a price."

"We have coin," Water said.

"Not this time," Jeric said, reclining in his chair. "This time it will cost you a different form of currency. A favor."

"I don't like debts," Lira said flatly.

"This one you can pay by night's end," he said.

"Oh?" Water asked, intrigued. "What else do you know?"

His smile widened. "Do we have a deal?"

Water looked to Lira, and the woman reluctantly nodded. "You have yourself a favor," Water said.

The elf leaned back into his chair and gestured north. "At the northern border of Erathan lies a temple to the god Ero." His lips twitched as he said the name, as if he knew the secret. "This particular temple was built during the Mage Wars, but has since been abandoned."

"And what makes this temple special?" Lira asked.

"This one was built atop another structure," he said. "A more . . . ancient one."

"A krey building?" Light asked, leaning forward in his seat.

"Indeed," Jeric replied. "And rumor has it, two months past, a strange light burst from the temple and shone into the sky. When a group of hunters gathered their courage to enter the temple they found it undisturbed, and none could discern the source of the light."

84

"I don't understand," Light said, clearly enthralled. "What was it?"

Jeric's eyes glimmered with excitement. "I think it was an invitation."

"Someone *invited* Wylyn?" Water asked. "How?"

"As to that, I cannot say," Jeric said with a shrug.

The revelation was shocking, and left deeper implications that Water found disturbing. Who on Lumineia knew of the Krey Empire, let alone how to send an invitation? For some reason he thought of Bartoth's comments about what was coming. Light began to pace, flitting from one side of the room to the other, his words tumbling from his lips.

"Who is he? A man? A krey? Perhaps it's a Verinai like Draeken— or even a guardian—or one of the dakorians Lira has spoken of—I would like to see one—"

Water ignored Light as he pondered the news, his thoughts still on Bartoth. Had the rock troll known the foe they would face? Is that what the troll had meant? Then he noticed Lira, who continued to watch Jeric, a small frown on her face. Jeric endured the scrutiny, his easy smile unfazed. Then he swept a hand to her.

"Answers are gained by asking questions, my lady."

"What else do you know about this temple?" Lira asked.

"Ah," Jeric said, his eyes lighting with interest. "You ask the most important question. The temple is old, yet few understand that the original structure was discovered during the Mage Wars. The one who found it was the very woman the people curse as the mother of guardians, Guildmaster Elsin herself."

Water blinked in shock at hearing Elsin's name. The woman had created the guardian charm, and been mother to Draeken's original host. In his youth Water had learned a great deal about the woman, and found little to like.

"The guildmaster of the Verinai was obsessed with the ancient race," Water said.

"You think the secret was passed down?" Light asked, his tone excited. "Or perhaps someone discovered how to activate the beacon?"

"But why?" Lira asked. "Who here would summon such a foe?"

"A mystery that begs an answer," Jeric said, settling back into his seat.

"We can find out when we find them," Water exclaimed, rising to his feet. Light was already at the door.

A muffled shout came from the other side of the door and the music came to an abrupt halt. Light glanced back to Water and Lira, both on their feet, and noticed Jeric still sitting calmly. Water motioned Light aside and swung the door open before cautiously stepping out on the balcony.

The atmosphere of the raucous tavern had changed, with the youthful commoners and nobles flooding out the door, swerving to avoid a group of hulking figures that had entered. They were the size of rock trolls and wore cloaks, but the horns on their head marked them as distinct.

"It appears we have guests," Water said.

Light clapped in excitement as he realized who they were. "Lira!" he called. "Look who has arrived!"

She cast her sword out of air, the blade glimmering as it hardened. "Dakorians." She spat the word.

Hearing their conversation, the leader turned and pointed a hammer at Lira, the head sparking with power. His sneer sent the remaining spectators scurrying out the door. The bards left their lutes and drums, abandoning them for the safety of the outside.

"The slave," the dakorian snarled, "I did hope we would meet again."

"Tardoq," she drawled. "I killed your kind the last time we met. Care to join them?"

"This time we are ready," he growled.

"And I have friends," she said, motioning to Water and Light.

Lira stepped to Water's side and he felt a thrill in his chest. "I think you'll find that Lira and I—"

"Greetings," Light said eagerly. "Do we get to fight? I would love to see what you're capable of. Your hammer is stunning! Can I keep it when you're dead?" He laughed as if embarrassed. "Of course you wouldn't mind, you'll be dead!"

Water groaned as Light veritably bounced in excitement, and wished it was just him and Lira. Tardoq glared at Light, confusion flickering in his eyes before he directed the hammer at Jeric.

"You are the one they call the Ear?"

"What does an elf have to do to shed a name?" he said with a sigh.

"We wish to know—"

"I know," he said. "You want to know about the one who invited you to this world."

Light looked to him in surprise and the elf grunted in irritation. "Of course I knew they were coming. That's why I replaced my guards with nervous folk that would flee. No need for extra bloodshed."

"You *wanted* them to come?" Lira asked.

"Of course," Jeric said. "I can smell adventure and you reek of it— if you would pardon the saying."

Tardoq frowned and looked between them, his confusion turning to anger. "If you know what we seek, tell me now before I—"

Jeric laughed. "There's no need for threats. What you seek lies in a temple six days north of here."

Water blinked in surprise, but Lira's eyes nearly burst from her skull and she rounded on him. "Why would you tell *them?*"

"It wouldn't be much of an adventure without a foe," Jeric said.

"He has a point," Light said.

"No he doesn't!" Lira snapped. "You don't help the enemy!"

Jeric frowned. "Is this a bad time to inform you that I'll be coming with you?"

"No you're not," she growled.

"I do have that favor," he said, almost apologetically. "And I'm afraid I must insist."

Water didn't know whether to laugh or scowl, and settled on a snort of amusement. It appeared Jeric had orchestrated the entire encounter, right down to providing the dakorians with the truth.

Tardoq stared at them as they argued, his anger mounting. Then he flicked his hammer to his soldiers. "Your squabbles mean nothing to me. Now that we know, there is no reason for you to live."

Lira continued to glare at Jeric, but Water cast his staffblade. His tone was apologetic as he said, "I'm sorry, Lira, but I agree with Jeric."

Lira released an explosive breath, anger twisting her features, as if she regretted her choice in companions. Once again Light danced, his curving blade appearing in his hands. He spun it into a blur, making the dakorians shift into a defensive stance.

—the door burst open and Dalton, the thief from the ascender, entered with a handful of swarthy thieves. "I told you that you were going to pay . . ."

He came to a halt when he viewed the standoff, his followers shifting in fear. Water caught his eye and smiled. "Are you here to join the fight?"

"Er . . ." The man retreated a step, and then another. "Perhaps this time I'll forgive the slight."

He turned and fled, and the other men followed. As their footfalls echoed into silence Jeric's quiet chuckle of anticipation filled the empty tavern.

"Let the games begin . . ."

Chapter 11: Outlanders

Tardoq threw his hammer, the weapon blasting the railing into kindling and striking Light's chest. He caught the weapon, the force of the blow carrying him through the wall, across Jeric's office, and out the exterior wall.

Water cast a glance at Light's disappearing form, but the fragment's laughter indicated he was not injured. Then Water turned and leapt the balcony rail, coming down with his staff onto the floor. The blast of ice expanded outward, momentarily trapping the nearest dakorians.

The soldiers smashed their hammers into the ice, but Lira used the moment to cast a quartet of air stones, allowing her to sprint by the nearest soldier. Her sword flicked down, cutting deep into the joint between neck and skull. The dakorian snarled and aimed his hammer, unleashing a blast of energy at her fleeing form. She ducked, and it blasted a hole in the wall.

Water instinctively realized that there were too many, and the dakorians would herd them together and use their superior strength to crush them. They needed space, so he sucked the moisture from the glasses still on tables and burst it asunder, spreading mist throughout the room. The dakorians, Jeric, and Lira were all engulfed in the fog.

Light burst into view and landed in the midst of the dakorians, swinging his stolen hammer with abandon, his gleeful laughter reverberating off the confines of the structure. The dakorians were spread out, and Light's sudden appearance threw their ranks into chaos.

"Kill him!" Tardoq barked.

But Light was too fast. He flitted between the hulking forms with shocking speed, evading the hammers as he swung his own. A knee shattered and a dakorian went down. Bones of a hand snapped as Light brought his hammer down on the handle of another weapon.

Water grinned at the fragment's damage, but had problems of his own. Four surrounded him, and he used the mist to hide his body, making it appear as if he were approaching on the left when he feinted from the right. Then he used the fog to launch himself into the air, allowing him to strike at a third dakorian behind. His target growled in pain and struck back, but Water retreated, and the mist swallowed him from sight.

Water caught a glimpse of Jeric. The elf wielded two hilts, both with magical weapons extending from them. One was a sword while the other had become a hammer, both crafted of hardened aquaglass.

Jeric leapt to a surviving table and flipped over a swinging hammer, flicking his hammer out to chip the bone breastplate of the wielder. Then he morphed the sword into a whip, snapping it into the dakorian's face, making him flinch. Throughout it all, Light's laughter echoed in the confines of the tavern.

"Will you stop laughing!" Lira bellowed.

In the middle of the tavern, Lira fought with ferocious strength, batting the hammers aside before evading a crushing blow from another dakorian. She leapt high and stepped on a sudden platform of air, using it to leap over the dakorian and drive her sword down his back. He cried out and whirled, but she lunged, driving her shoulder into the dakorian's waist. Weighing more than a bear, he nevertheless soared across the space and struck the window at the back of the tavern, shattering the glass.

Water saw the opportunity and sprinted to the dakorian at the back wall, striking his blade into the dakorian's chest. The blade didn't pierce deep, but the force of the blow drove him through the broken window, where he plummeted from sight with a fading roar.

"Perfect timing," Lira said with a smile.

"I live to please," Water said.

But the victory had a price, and mist seeped from the opening in the back wall, allowing the dakorians to see them. Water charged before they could trap him on the back wall and swung his staffblade. The dakorians lacked his speed, but they adapted quickly, trapping him in a ring of flesh. He ducked a hammer blow, the weapon passing inches above his nose, so close he could feel the crackling energy in his teeth.

The tavern shuddered from the battle, the weight of the conflict cracking beam and wall, damaging the lights imbued into the material and casting the battle in flickering light. The dakorians seemed unimpaired by the dimness, their hammers flying with precision.

Water dropped to the floor, landing on a sled of water drawn from the lingering mist. Then he sent a burst of power from his feet and shot through a gap between two dakorians. They shouted in alarm and converged upon him, expertly changing formation and attempting to close the trap again.

He reached the wall and rolled to his feet, using his momentum to sprint up the wall and reach the rafters above. A hammer came for his skull and crashed into a beam, splintering wood and filling the air with dust.

One of the dakorians leapt and grabbed a beam, the roof groaning from his weight as he levered himself up with an agility that belied his large frame. Water brought his bladed staff down upon the soldier, but the dakorian raised his hammer to block, fighting while hanging halfway from the rafters. The fight allowed the other three dakorians to ascend into the network of beams that supported the roof.

"You do not fight like brutes," Water exclaimed, slipping through a pair of angled beams and swinging his weapon at the hand of a dakorian. Because of the beams, the soldier did not see it coming and it sliced across the fingers, drawing blood.

The Dakorian grunted in pain at the broken fingers and switched his hammer to the opposite hand, easily wielding it from the left. Abruptly another dakorian appeared behind Water. Weaving through the beams, the soldier swung his hammer with such force that it blasted through the thick beam, narrowly missing Water's skull as it struck a second beam, bending a metal bracket.

Water danced away from the groaning supports to a more sure footing, catching another hammer on the shoulder. He winced, the blow knocking him through a gap and almost to the floor.

"Are you trying to kill me?" Light demanded from below.

"*Yes!*" a dakorian snarled, furiously trying to land a blow on the fragment of light.

Water saw the fourth dakorian leap to the nearest beam and swing his hammer. The soldier barked an order and the group bashed their hammers into the supports around Water. Wood groaned, metal screeched, and sections of the roof began to sag as the supports were removed. The upper roof, supported by beams extending to the walls, remained mostly intact, but the entire framework beneath was beginning to sag, taking Water with it.

Water sought to escape the ring but the dakorians had surrounded him and were attempting to bring the entire section of ceiling down. Water then hurled his staffblade like a spear at the nearest dakorian, the blade slipping through a gap in the beams to plunge into his chest.

"If you wish to take the roof down," Water said, his voice gaining an edge, "perhaps I should return the favor."

"As if you could," the dakorian snarled. Reaching down, he snapped the rod in half and tossed the piece away.

Anger rose within Water and he drew upon it, reaching for the beams above his head. Like most human structures, the roof contained tubes that captured rainwater, feeding it to the kitchens below. Directly above Water was the reservoir, and Water pulled on its power. The dakorians hesitated when they saw a sprinkle of water come through the cracks, the stream quickly swelling into a torrent.

"You want me to fall?" he asked, his voice darkening. "We go down together."

He shaped the water into a spinning blade, the material spitting with power that cut into the beams. Then he expanded the blade, the weapon accelerating its spin, the blade slicing a scorching line through the beams it crossed, expanding outward as he continued to spin. White hot, the water carved through the wood as it accelerated, and the wood split.

With a growl, Water released the spin, cutting all the beams. Severed from their moorings, the interior supports collapsed in a crash of groaning wood. The four dakorians cried out as they fell, the beams falling underneath and upon them, their sheer weight snapping bone. The metal brackets snapped, becoming shards of broken steel, and cut through one of the dakorians, leaving him bloodied.

Water landed in the pile of beams and cast a shield above his head, grunting as four of the beams landed on top of him. A glance revealed one of the dakorians pinned but alive. The other three managed to extricate themselves as Water stepped from beneath the beams and picked his way to the pinned dakorian.

"You shouldn't challenge what you do not understand," Water said.

He cast a spike and plunged it through the pinned soldier, the weapon piercing the bone and heart beneath. A final snarl escaped the soldier's lips as Water held the gaze of the trio that had sought to trap him, who growled at the kill and charged, driving him toward the back side of the cavern. Water's feet left stone as he retreated across the glass floor.

Abruptly Water was aware of the raging battle being waged in the back of the tavern. He spotted Lira fighting three at once, her expression worried. She, Light, and Jeric had all been driven to the back section of the structure. Then Water noticed it was not just the walls that were cracked.

It was the floor.

Seeing the cracks, Light sucked the illumination from the room and added it to his dakorian hammer, casting the tavern into flickering patterns of shadow. The weapon glowed to life, the light becoming blinding as the sun charm continued to build. Water saw what he intended and shouted a warning.

"Light! Don't!"

His features illuminated by the hammer, Light spun the hammer in a circle and brought it down on the glass floor. The empowered weapon detonated in a blast of light. Glass shattered as a trio of dakorians caught on the floor scrambled for the back wall. Water, Lira, and Jeric did the same, catching the back wall as the floor disintegrated. Other dakorians lunged for the safety of the front side of the tavern, most succeeding, but

93

one failed. He cried out as he fell short, his body bouncing off the cliff before tumbling to the lake a thousand feet below.

Clinging to the back wall, Jeric grinned. "Well done, Light."

"ARE YOU MAD?" shrieked Lira.

"We were trapped," Light said with a shrug as he clung to the back wall. "This gives us an advantage."

"He's not wrong," Water said.

Water sucked in his breath as he looked at the fall. Wind coming off the cliff gusted into him, buffeting him where he clung to the back wall of the tavern. With many of the supports damaged, the wall swayed side to side, and he could have sworn he could hear it cracking.

He fastened himself to the wall with threads of water, the threads turning into spider legs. He then swung free so he could engage the nearest dakorian, also clinging to the wall. The soldier snarled and swung his hammer, breaking one of the spider legs. It quickly reformed and Water plunged his staff into the wall, using it to pry the dakorian free, but the foe gripped the wall and refused to break. The wall did, however, and an entire section of paneling came free, the dakorian tumbling through the gaping hole that had once been the floor.

Lira glanced uncertainly at the drop and then cast a trio of stepping stones out of air. She danced across the gap and struck one of the leading dakorians, drawing blood from his shoulder. She then retreated. The dakorians lined up along the edge of the cliff. Two dakorians remained on the back wall, but both were out of reach.

"You fight well," Tardoq said. "But you're still just human."

"Will you say that when I kill you?"

Tardoq's sniffed, and then his order sent a chill into Water's stomach. "Take out the walls."

The dakorians turned their weapons on the remaining walls. Hammers crashed into the supports, blasting the thick beams to splinters. The beams cracked and groaned as the walls gave way, the roof cracking and crumbling. Water caught a glimpse of Tardoq's smirk before the back half of the Cat's Eye came free, and dropped down the cliff.

Chapter 12: The Lost Temple

Lira looked on in horror as half of the tavern came away, taking her and her companions with it. The dakorians leapt for safety, catching the hammers extended by their companions. Lira's back pressed into the ceiling of the tumbling structure.

The back wall, a section of roof, and the two side walls tipped down, striking the cliff. The impact snapped the remaining supports and set the structure into a spin. As they hurtled for the lake below, the spin forced her to grip the wall with all her strength or risk soaring into the broken glass of what had once been the floor. Fear gripped her, the emotion blocking her desperate attempts of magic. But Light's delighted shout flared her anger.

"You're supposed to kill *them*!" she roared. "Not *us*!"

"What do you mean?" Water asked, sidling up to her.

With his spider legs of water attached to the wall, he wrapped his arms around her and pulled her free. The spider legs began to spin, allowing Water to slow their rotation. Her vision settled, and the structure spun around them.

He looked upward and launched them through a hole in the structure, taking them to open air. The back half of the tavern flipped below them, Light leaping into the air with golden wings holding him aloft. Jeric jumped to the cliff, landing sideways, his boots sticking to the stone.

Water morphed his spider legs into a needle that encased them both. She braced for the impact with the water but was supremely conscious of Water's body pressed against hers, his strong form holding her tight.

The broken tavern smashed into the lake in a plume of water—and the needle knifed through, diving deep, the length of the enchantment slowing their passage. Water smiled as they came to a halt deep in the lake, safe inside the cocoon of water.

"Light was right," he said, obviously enjoying the escape. "We needed to escape."

"I could have saved my own life," she snapped.

She drew her sword and sliced across the bubble, drawing a deep breath as water filled the pocket of air in a rush of bubbles. She lashed the air to her feet and used it to propel herself upward.

She breached the surface to find Light hovering above, large wings of light bound to his shoulders. Lira's irritation turned to shock when she looked up and spotted Jeric on the cliff—walking down the vertical surface like it was flat ground. He picked his way past a particularly rough patch of cliff and then noticed her.

"I'll be there in a moment!" he called, stepping over a crag and continuing his descent.

Her anger returning, she turned and used a burst of air to streak across the surface to the eastern bank. When she reached it, she stepped free of the water and turned to the cliff. Even with the distance, she spotted Tardoq standing in the broken opening. Then he and the other dakorians departed.

Water ascended from the depths, propelled by his own magic, while Light landed next to them, his features bright with excitement. Seconds later, Jeric appeared astride a wave of water, which deposited him in their midst.

"Well done, my friends," he exclaimed, dusting off his arms. "This journey is going to be one for the ages."

Lira drew her blade and placed it on the elf's chest. "If you *ever* help the enemy again, I'll kill you myself."

The heat in her voice did not faze the elf. "You wound me, my dear lady. But I shall adhere to your demands."

"You're all wet," Water said. "Do you want me to dry your clothes?"

She gripped her fist and air blasted her garb, pulling the moisture from her clothing and armor. Then she stabbed her sword toward the cliff where the dakorians had stood moments before.

"They know where we're going and have the lead," she growled. "And after the conflict we caused, the guards are not going to let us use the ascender to get up the cliff."

Light yawned, seeming to abruptly realize the sun was setting on the horizon. "I could fly up in the morning?"

"No," Lira said. "We're going around."

She stomped away from the group and made her way east, not caring if anyone followed. When she heard only two sets of feet coming from behind, she glanced back, annoyed to see that Jeric walked without making a sound. Of course he did.

Ignoring them, she plunged into the forest of Numen and walked through the night, not stopping until they reached the great Blue Lake. Massive and sprawling, the lake was large enough that ships took weeks to cross, and it contained islands at its center, home of the Azure people.

A rough road clung to the edge of the Giant's Shelf, ascending to the plateau above. But fatigue had finally overcome her anger and she made camp a few hours before dawn. All were obviously tired but Light was practically asleep, walking along with his eyes closed. Even Jeric looked tired, and the group overnighted in the trees near the road.

Sunrise came with a shout from Light. Lira groaned and cursed the fragment that was worse than any rooster. He laughed and soaked in the sun, rousing them all like they'd been sleeping for weeks.

"You get used to him," Water said.

"Blasted sunrise," she muttered.

He grinned, and she reluctantly rose. Rubbing sleep from her eyes, she avoided looking at Jeric and then retrieved a morning meal of dried fruit from her pack. Light noticed her irritation and dropped to her side.

"Why are you so sleepy?" Light asked, his voice bright with anticipation. "The dakorians are miles ahead of us and we need to hasten!"

"We're only behind because of him," Lira grumbled, casting Jeric a baleful glare.

Jeric ignored the comment. Packing his things, he bounced to his feet and clapped Light on the back, his eagerness as grating as the fragment's. Water yawned and looked down at Lira, his expression one of concern.

"Do you need more sleep?" he asked.

"*No*," she said.

She rose and gathered her things before striding onto the road. Light's exuberance gradually bled into her and by noonday she found her irritation was gone. Her suspicion remained, and she cast several glances at the mysterious Jeric.

"I'm flattered by your attention," he finally said, his lips twitching, "but I already favor another."

She jerked her head. "You do not seem to regret the loss of your tavern."

"I was already restless," he said. "And you gave the Cat's Eye a fitting end."

"And you just left it behind?" she asked. "Just to risk your life with us?"

"We are all given a single life," he said ruefully, "yet I was blessed with a desire to live more than one."

"They said you were an assassin?" she asked.

"I have been many things," he said. "None hold my fancy for long. A tavern owner sounded like a pleasurable way to spend my final years, but I gradually grew envious of the tales I heard."

"And you are determined to make this journey more dangerous?"

His smile was one of anticipation. "A sunset is most vibrant when it is about to expire."

Lira scowled at him but did not respond. The elf represented an enigma, one she guessed would not be solved by her. Of all the characters she had encountered in the conflicts she had fought, her current companions were the strangest.

As they journeyed north she found herself studying the fragments. She could not deny their attractiveness as Draeken, but they were fragments of a single personality, and each was unique. They were undeniably brothers, a family, yet also parts of a whole. It was a disconcerting concept.

Ever optimistic and impulsive, Light was almost chaotic in his behavior, one moment pointing to a soaring bird, the next leaping off the ground to soar at its side. Yet despite the lack of reserve, he displayed occasional outbursts of anger that revealed a streak of darker impulsivity.

Water represented a distinct contrast. While Light had the attention span of a child, Water possessed a more seasoned happiness. Quick to smile and laugh, he also expressed doubts and occasionally irritation. She knew little of the other fragments, but Water seemed to possess a sense of honor more than his brothers.

At first, Lira had thought the fragments to be simply expressions of a single personality trait, but the more time she spent with Water and Light, the more she realized they contained a full range of consciousness, albeit some attributes came in smaller quantities. She wondered if the smaller traits had been learned under Elenyr's tutelage.

They passed a grave next to the road, the simple placard fastened above signifying it had been a beloved daughter. Light paused, his entire body going dim when he saw the grave, and abruptly he added a burst of light to the inscription, brightening the sign so the child would not be forgotten.

"A touching tribute," Jeric said.

Light flashed a sad smile before a butterfly distracted him and he was off again. Unnoticed by any except Lira, Jeric plucked a flower from a nearby grove and deposited it on the grave. Then he turned and hurried to catch up.

Lira disliked the quandary the elf presented. He was obviously a wanderer, one that never ceased in his quest for the new and exotic. Lira wondered if his choice to join their group had been predetermined, or if he'd decided in the moment. All she knew was that his unpredictable nature made him dangerous, and she disliked the prospect of him at her side.

The group journeyed north, through the forests of northern Erathan. Lira set a blistering pace and, where possible, they accelerated their journey with the fragments' magic. She rotated her magic between hearing and sight, wary of encountering the dakorians. Aside from a few scattered villages and merchants, they encountered no one except a caravan of dwarves traveling south who spoke of strange outlanders.

When they parted ways with the caravan Lira nodded. "The dakorians might already have found the temple."

"Indeed," Jeric said.

Lira clenched her jaw in irritation at Jeric's obvious enthusiasm. How could the man sound excited upon learning their foes were gaining ground? It rankled that he insisted on accompanying them, and she had yet to decide if he was a threat that required elimination.

"They will need a source of power," Lira said. "A strong one."

"Like magic?" Light asked.

"Perhaps," she mused. "I doubt they can find an intact gravity sphere here, so I'm not sure how they intend to power a Gate."

"Why do you suppose they are seeking the beacon?"

"I came to you for aid," Lira said, motioning to the fragments. "Perhaps they are doing the same thing, and looking for a guide."

"What sort of magic creates a Gate?" Jeric asked.

"You do not already know?" Lira asked.

The elf smirked at her tone. "I am a collector of information," he said. "I do not claim to know everything."

"Just the important bits," Light said with a laugh.

"There are several types of Gates," Lira said, "ones that connect in both directions, small ones, large ones, even those that only permit certain things to pass."

"How intriguing," Jeric mused.

Lira frowned, abruptly realizing she was giving information to an individual she could hardly trust. In the Empire she was always on guard, but since arriving on Lumineia she'd lapsed her focus. She could not afford to forget her purpose. Changing the subject, she focused on the approaching temple.

The trees gradually thinned as they neared the plains that marked the border between the dwarven kingdom and Erathan. Her rising tension was not shared by her companions, who displayed emotions from anticipation to outright excitement.

They reached the edge of the forest, where a small hill formed a sentinel that seemed to hold the forest from growing into the grasslands. The sun was setting and Light yawned. Then the temple came into view.

"Can we explore the temple in the morning?" Light yawned.

"I'm afraid we cannot wait." Lira came to a halt at the edge of shadow.

"Why not?" he asked.

"The dakorians are already here," Lira replied, pointing to the hulking figures ascending the steps.

Chapter 13: The Hidden Chamber

"They haven't been here long," Jeric said, eying the temple.

"They're still placing guards," Lira agreed.

Light yawned again, obviously not interested. "We should have brought Shadow for the night work."

"There's *always* night work," Water said, his tone amused.

Light shrugged wearily. "Doesn't mean I have to enjoy it."

As they talked, Lira scanned the temple with augmented vision. The structure was set atop a small, oddly shaped hill. Rather than a simple mound, sheer walls ascended for fifty feet, ending with a flat top. Almost perfectly round, it looked like a squat turret.

Stairs ascended to the top of the hill, where the temple occupied the entire summit. Gardens and lofty trees had once graced the exterior, but the obscure location had discouraged patrons from visiting, and it had gradually fallen into disrepair. Jeric had mentioned it was abandoned and it looked borderline decrepit.

The temple contained a circle of pillars, each taller than the last as they spiraled to the center, where a towering pinnacle rose above the center of the hill. A spiral roof ascended to the center pillar, and the windows between the pillars showed an interior with sweeping staircases and fine walls, most of which had been stripped of anything of value.

Dakorians flanked the stairs, with others at the top of the stairs and stationed around the summit. Others moved inside, their torches a steady, unwavering light. Lira frowned at the sense of familiarity, and wondered why the temple would seem memorable.

Wylyn.

Her hand clenched into a fist at seeing the krey woman, and she recalled failing to kill her on Grenedal. Jeric sidled up to Lira as the vestiges of sunset faded on the horizon. Lira resisted the surge of irritation, but he was examining the building with a keen eye.

"You said it was once a krey outpost?" she asked.

"That's what I believe," he said.

"You believe?" she asked, raising an eyebrow.

His grin was faint in the darkness. "The krey have not lived on Lumineia for thirty thousand years. My assumptions are based on rumor, myth, and legend."

"So you don't know," she said flatly. "Is there something you *do* know?"

His smile widened and he pointed to the hill. "I know that hill is not a natural formation."

"You think the Verinai built the hill to support the temple?" Water asked, glancing to Jeric.

Lira's eyes widened. "The hill doesn't support the temple, the temple hides what lies beneath."

"And what is that?" Light asked.

"A Gate Chamber," she breathed.

The shape was unmistakable. Throughout the Empire world Gates were used for the lower houses to travel. All looked the same, with a distinctive circular wall and a pointed roof that led to a spire. The construction and maintenance of a Gate was costly, and only the wealthiest had personal Gates capable of traveling across the Empire. This particular location had likely been built without Ero's knowledge, and rock had been placed above and around the ancient building to hide the chamber. The center pillar likely contained the beacon.

Lira's gut clenched. She'd banked everything on the idea they had time on their side, but if a functional Gate resided beneath the temple, their quest would be over before it began. Already the sounds of crashing came from within the temple as the dakorians sought to discover its secrets. It was only a matter of time until Wylyn realized her goal lay beneath her feet.

"Is the Gate still active?" Light asked with a yawn.

"We need to get inside," Lira said, her voice tense. "If they find an active Gate here, Wylyn won't need to build one."

"How can we get in without being noticed?" Water asked. "Shadow always does the infiltration work."

Lira looked to the base of the hill where a pile of boulders leaned against the cliff. It looked random, as if a piece from above had broken free and fallen. But there was no hole in the hill above. She stabbed a finger to the mound.

"There," she said. "That's where the entrance should be. We might be able to get in before they realize what they're standing on."

Without waiting for an answer, she hurried through the shadowy trees. It appeared that half the dakorians were present with Wylyn. If Lira was discovered, Wylyn would seek to eliminate the threat, and this time there was no place to flee.

Lira reached the edge of the tree line and looked upward, to the dakorian soldier standing directly above the pile of boulders. She scowled and eyed the gap, but there was no way they could cross the twenty feet of moonlit grass to reach the hidden entrance.

"Light?" Water asked.

"I'm on it."

Light rubbed his eyes and stepped out of the trees. Lira gasped and reached out, but Water caught her hand. "There's an advantage to being made of magic," Water murmured.

Light strode across the gap, pointing skyward. With every step a transparent shield appeared, expanding with him until he'd reached the opposite side and attached to the wall. Like an invisible roof, it seemed to bend the light like water, warping it around the path. Abruptly she realized Light had made it so the view remained unchanged from above.

"My lady," Water said, motioning to the path.

She snorted, annoyed that she would feel attraction at such a time. She eased from the gap and into the open, and when the dakorian did not look down, she crept across the open stretch of earth to the pile of boulders. Water joined them and Jeric lowered his voice.

"Our passage seems barred," he said, pointing to the boulders. "I don't suppose you have a key?"

"I do," Water said.

He reached down and pressed a palm against the earth. Droplets of water immediately seeped from the soil. The drops merged and pressed into the gaps of the boulders, rising, expanding. More water rose into view, filling the gaps between the stones and gradually pushing them apart.

At a faint grinding of stone, Lira winced and shot a look upward. The dakorian was leaning down, his expression one of suspicion. He made a hand signal that she recognized, and she realized they were out of time.

"They're on their way," Lira warned.

"Almost there," Water said, his voice strained.

The boulders lifted and moved, forming an expanding tunnel. Lira spotted movement at the stairs and poked Light in the stomach. He lurched awake, and at Lira's direction, cast another false light wall on that side. The weird glass stretched across the gap as dakorians appeared, taking shape just as Tardoq appeared.

"Thirty seconds until they're here," she hissed.

"Not enough time," Water said, his face tight with the effort to lift the boulders. "We'll have to go now."

The boulders had lifted enough to form a small tunnel, revealing the bottom of a large, white door recessed into the hill. Jeric dived through and Lira followed. Then Water kicked Light and he clambered through the gap, moving far too slow for Lira's liking.

106

The movement of the boulders had shifted the dirt, creating tiny gaps that allowed her to see the approaching dakorians. The foursome had their hammers ready, their pace slow as they searched the exterior of the hill. Twenty feet from the light wall that hid Water . . .

"*Go*," Lira growled.

Water hardened the liquid supports and dived into the opening, worming his way through the tiny tunnel as the boulders shifted above him. Lira caught his hand and yanked him into through as the stones settled, closing off the hole. She all but punched Light and he started.

"*The illusion*," she hissed.

"Right," he said.

He reached out and Lira heard a faint pop, and guessed the mirage had been extinguished. Then she held her breath, not daring to move as the dakorians appeared on the opposite side. They came to a halt and moved about, scanning the boulders, but the cracks were dark. Tardoq hefted his hammer as if he was about to strike and Lira retreated to the door—but a shout from above drew Tardoq's attention and he departed. A moment later the others did as well.

Then Light began to snore.

Water clamped a hand over Light's mouth just as the last dakorian turned. Lira grimaced as Light struggled in Water's grip, the movement silent in the darkness. The dakorian returned a step, just as a rabbit burst from a hole in the boulders and darted away.

The dakorian snorted and departed, and she breathed a sigh of relief. Then she spun to Light and leveled an accusing finger at him. He shrugged apologetically. Lira turned to Jeric, and found him petting a rabbit before the image disappeared into his ring.

He smirked and Lira wondered how many secrets the elf possessed. Then she turned to the door and examined it with interest. Nearly fifteen feet tall and pure white, the barrier was smooth to the touch except for the symbol of a Gate at the center. A ring split by a spike rose from the center, its interior a shade of purple.

107

She stepped to the side where a small, square panel extended from the door, and passed her hand across it. A glimmer of light appeared before flashing orange and disappearing. She frowned and did so again, with the same result.

"It's been sealed," she whispered.

"Why?" Jeric asked.

She shook her head and pulled a small, spiderlike object from a pouch at her side. Placing it on the display, she touched a symbol and the legs of the object pressed into the material, illuminating with dim light.

"Every lock has a key," she said.

The spider flickered a few colors before going dark and the color changed to blue. In a whisper of air, the door slid to the left, allowing them entry into a short tunnel. Lira felt a sense of foreboding as she crossed the threshold, the lights automatically glowing to life.

The group advanced inside, with Jeric releasing a low whistle at what lay before them. Pristine white walls circled the gigantic chamber, with the ceiling rising to a point that extended into the center pillar of the temple above. A forty-foot arched opening sat in the center, the space beneath like fractured glass, reflecting Light and Water into a myriad of positions and shapes. Illumination came from everywhere and nowhere, as if the very air had been infused with power. The majesty of the space was undeniable, but that was not what drew the eye.

Trash lay strewn about—bits of equipment, scraps of metal, and chunks of the krey building material known as seracrete, all layered in dust. To the side, a curving staircase descended from view, but the barrier that would have blocked it had been ripped open, the metal torn and snapped, ripped from its hinges. More light came from a subterranean level and she heard the gurgle of water. Then she spotted the walls and saw where all the debris had come from, a dozen pockmarked gouges in multiple places, the walls scored and blackened, as if someone from within had been attempting to escape. With a start she realized the truth. Someone had been trapped inside the Gate chamber, and a clatter of sound indicated they were still present . . .

Chapter 14: The Invited

A *screech* of a moving chair came from below, accompanied by the rushed footsteps of a solitary figure. Lira spun to the gate that had evidently been destroyed from within, the pieces falling into place as she barked an order for her companions to brace themselves.

The Gate Chamber had been used as a prison, and the quantity of rust on the twisted metal of the gates suggested that, at one time, the occupant had been confined to the lower levels of the outpost. The prisoner had probably managed to escape and figured out a way to use the Gate to send the message that had brought Wylyn.

A figure ascended the steps and came to a halt. Tall and thin, he was dressed in a regal cloak and rich tunic, obviously new. His eyes were a dark grey, and glinted with slumbering power—not unlike the fragments. He came to a halt and released a low chuckle.

"Draeken," he said. "You are not supposed to be here yet."

Water and Light exchanged confused looks and spoke in unison. "You know us?"

The man's lip curled into a sneer and sparks ignited on his palms, his clothing flickering transparent and revealing threads of water and earth in his body. Lira instinctively retreated a step as she realized the man was a guardian—a powerful one.

"You have no idea how long I've wanted to speak to you," he said, his voice calm, calculating. "Yet to my surprise you appear." His eyes flicked to Jeric and he gave a tiny nod, as if he understood why. "Still, I am grateful I will no longer have to hide."

"Who are you?" Water asked.

The man flashed a dark smile. "I am your creator."

Light's eyes were wide and open. "But Guildmaster Elsin created us—"

"With *my* help," the guardian said.

The glint in his eyes was almost madness, but it was too controlled, too triumphant. Lira swallowed and eased back again, glancing to Water for support. He, too, had gained a measure of doubt, but it was Jeric's caution and that sent fear into her belly. She'd never seen him worried.

"I was her first attempt to create a guardian with multiple magics," he said. "But she called me unstable and locked me up here. By the time I escaped, the Verinai had been destroyed, and I sought survivors. I found you." His lips curled into a sneer. "But another was raising the fragments of Draeken, and I knew you would not trust me. And so I waited until the time I could fulfill my promise to Elsin."

He began to stalk around them, like a predator that had cornered its prey. "She was my love. And when we discovered the guardian charm, I insisted I be the one to attempt the magic. Such pain it caused . . ."

He passed a hand over his face and Lira cast an air blade. The guardian was dangerous, and she sensed the burning hatred, the desire for revenge. A glance revealed the shock on Water's face, and she knew he hadn't known of the creator's existence.

"Who *are* you?" Water asked.

"Serak of Verisith," he said, and flashed a disturbing smile. "Father of guardians."

Serak's voice reverberated inside the Gate Chamber, the dark timber seeming to overlap and merge until it elicited a shudder. Lira had faced countless threats in her life, but the guardian Serak inspired terror.

"I think we should depart," Jeric said, his smile lacking the characteristic amusement.

"We have to destroy the Gate," Lira said. "Before the dakorians find the door . . ."

All heads turned to the door as a grinding of boulders echoed beyond. "Too late," Light said, yawning. "I told you we should have waited until morning."

Serak's gaze was fixed on the door, and he seemed to be ignoring them. As he advanced toward the exit, Water stepped to Lira and pointed to their feet, lowering his voice to a murmur.

"I can sense a well beneath the citadel," he said. "It connects to an underground reservoir. If I can undermine the floor . . ."

"It will bring the entire structure down," Jeric finished. "I like it."

"Don't forget we're inside," Lira said.

"Light," Water said, but he'd fallen asleep again. Water reached over and slapped him, hard. As he sputtered awake Water stabbed a finger at the floor. "Come with me. You need to find us a way out. I'm going to bring the building down."

"We'll hold them off," Jeric said.

As Serak came to a halt before the door, Water and Light slipped behind him and descended the stairs. When they were gone Jeric reached to the strap across his chest and withdrew the two hilts. With a snap of his wrist, water flowed out and shaped into aquaglass swords. Lira hardened her air blade.

"He's unpredictable," he said, tilting his chin toward Serak. "I don't like it."

Lira snorted a laugh. "Really? *You* don't like unpredictability?"

"Not in others," Jeric said.

They retreated behind the guardian just as the floor trembled, followed by a muffled crash. Then the door slid open and dakorians flooded the chamber. Serak watched them enter, seemingly unperturbed by the outlanders' appearance.

Wylyn stepped into view and regarded the father of guardians. "You must be Serak."

"I see you received my invitation," he said.

Lira felt a chill as Wylyn smiled. "I did indeed. You have my gratitude."

Then Wylyn caught sight of Jeric and Lira and smirked. She motioned to Tardoq and the dakorians split up, several drifting around Serak and advancing on the pair. Others moved to the Gate, and Lira scowled, retreating a step.

"Kill them," Wylyn said.

"Not yet," Serak said.

Wylyn scowled at the order, but Serak turned and raised his hands. Lira dived away—but her body froze. Her limbs refused to move and of its own accord, her body turned to face Serak. She cast strength and tried to break free, but her entire body was bound in place. Then her feet slid forward, scrapping the floor as she fought the movement. In her peripheral vision she spotted Jeric similarly bound, also sliding towards Serak and his disturbing grey eyes.

A current of water poured through the open door and shaped into a spike pointed at Lira's heart, the water turning to glittering aquaglass. Another spike pointed at Jeric. Inch by inch Lira felt her body come closer to the spike, and knew Serak meant to impale them both.

"I feel the water in your blood," Serak said, his voice deathly calm. "And it now belongs to me."

Her fear mounting, her anger exploding, Lira fought with every ounce of will but her body refused to respond. The shard of aquaglass came closer and closer, and Wylyn folded her arms, her gaze filled with anticipation as she watched the Lira slide closer to the spike. She motioned to the dakorians and they moved away from Lira and stepped to the Gate, obviously intent on repairing it.

The spike touched her chest and pressed into her armor, driving into the thick material. It became hard to breathe, the effort increasing as she felt the armor begin to give way. She knew that, when it did, the spike would tear through her body. . .

A hole exploded into view near the wall and a geyser of water rose into the air. Instead of falling back to the ground, it sharpened and drove into the floor, piercing it and disappearing from view.

At the sudden appearance of the magic, Wylyn's eyes widened in shock. Serak glanced that way, releasing Lira and Jeric from their bounds. Lira swung her air blade with all her might, shattering the aquaglass shard before leaping into the air. Casting stepping stones to aid her flight, she cast wings of air and leapt high, soaring around the top of the chamber.

"She's flying!" a dakorian shouted in surprise.

Lira cast a spear of air and dropped to the ground, using the fall to drive the spear into the back of a dakorian at the Gate. Badly wounded, he still spun and swung his hammer. She launched herself into a long back flip as the hammer came down where she'd stood.

Hammer blasts flew at her and she ducked and weaved. Distantly she was aware of another geyser of water, and then another, and realized Water was shattering the supports of the floor, intent on collapsing the entire structure.

Gouts of water detonated across the floor, rising and crashing into the floor again, shattering supports and flooring, tearing them apart one hole at a time. Lira dived to the floor and used the explosions of water to hide her approach, and then slashed her sword across the neck of a dakorian. It spun at the last moment and caught her blade, throwing her aside. She managed to keep her sword and landed on her feet, casting strength to deflect the incoming hammer. Then she rotated and drove her sword upward, beneath the bone armor.

She flashed a grim smile at the mortal blow, even dying he struck her with the back of his hand, sending her skidding away. Another dakorian appeared, his hammer falling toward her chest—and landing on Jeric's sword.

He released the hilt and sent it spinning around the shaft of the hammer, the hilt smashing into the dakorian so hard the horn snapped, the bone tumbling away. The soldier growled and reached for the hilt of Jeric's sword, but the weapon turned on him, morphing into a face and claws that ripped into the dakorian's armor, gouging the bone and

113

drawing blood. The dakorian recoiled and threw the hilt aside, but it leapt back into Jeric's hand, who darted in, evading the meaty blows to land his own, a brutal strike through the chest plate, forcing the dakorian back.

All around was mayhem. Wylyn was shouting at her soldiers to take the Gate outside, but the floor was trembling, and an entire corner caved in, taking the wall with it. Tardoq barked an order and the dakorians converged on the Gate, attempting to wrest it from its moorings by brute force. Lira saw her chance and cast a thunderstorm.

Clouds formed in the ceiling above, the driving wind pulling the water from the geysers. The clouds darkened and rain began to fall. Wind shrieked across the chaotic battlefield as geysers continued to tear through the floor. Lira caught a glimpse of Wylyn and Serak retreating to the door. Serak clearly possessed a great deal of water magic, but he made no move to stop the destruction. Their eyes met, and she had the insane thought that Serak had orchestrated the entire moment.

Lira gritted her teeth and reached to the clouds, intensifying the storm until lightning crackled and thunder boomed. Dakorians sought to reach her but a geyser exploded into view, cutting them off. She felt a surge of gratitude and knew Water was watching over her. Then she leapt off the ground. Snagging a fallen dakorian hammer, she cast a quartet of air stones as she sprinted to the top of the Gate.

The dakorians had managed to break the bonds and had lifted the Gate, but she reached the top and cast a needle of air on the base of the hammer's handle. Just as she leapt over the top of the arch, she plunged the weapon into the keystone of the arch, the shaft sinking into the Gate.

A hammer appeared and slammed into her back, knocking her from the Gate. She cried out and just managed to catch herself before she struck the floor. But the damage was done, and she felt blood seeping from the wound. Tardoq stalked forward and reached out, his hammer flying into his grasp.

"And so the slave dies," he snarled, hefting the weapon.

"Not yet," she said defiantly.

She turned and focused her gaze on the hammer at the top of the Gate . . . and the lightning crackling in the storm above. His eyes widened and he roared an order, but it was too late. Drawn to the hammer, the lightning pulsed, striking the hammer and plunging into the Gate.

The Gate shattered.

The *boom* was deafening inside the confines of the chamber, and the Gate blasted apart, the pieces tearing through the nearest dakorians and cracking the floor all the way to the walls. The already unstable floor began to crumble in a groan of grinding stone and steel. Lira caught a glimpse of geysers, lightning, and thunder as the dakorians fled. She spotted Wylyn's fury as the krey woman was dragged through the entrance. Then Jeric scooped Lira into his arms and raced away—but the floor crumbled beneath them. The rising lake reached up to engulf her and suddenly she was underwater.

The temple, the hill, the remnants of the Gate Chamber, all of it crashed into the sudden well of water. The dakorians scrambled for safety as the colossal groan filled the air. The pillars of the temple came down, the great stones and walls crashing into the Gate Chamber, the entire hill collapsing. When the boulders and broken pillars of the temple finally lay still, the sounds of chaos came to an end.

Nothing emerged.

Chapter 15: The Titan Chamber

Elenyr, Mind, and Fire departed Cloudy Vale and took their journey north, to Herosian. The capitol city had been built near the end of the Mage Wars, with much of the construction completed by the Verinai prior to their fall. Since then, the city had grown significantly, with villages and settlements surrounding the city proper.

High walls circled the city, the stones bleached white by the sun. Buttresses extended up to the battlements above, where soldiers patrolled. Dwarven-crafted ballistae further reinforced the city walls, adding to the formidable city.

Elenyr and her companions approached the city from the south, passing through endless tracts of farmland as they followed the large highway. Horses grazed in corrals, their owners laboring to train the steeds. Cattle ranged in the outer fields, the large herds feeding on lush grass that thrived in the region.

"King Porlin may not be present," Mind said, motioning to the castle rising behind the city walls. "The Talinorian Games began yesterday."

"We can find out easily enough," Fire said.

Elenyr stepped around a cart carrying two children to reach the guards permitting entry. The quartet of soldiers recognized Elenyr and waved them through, and Elenyr passed beneath the thick walls to reach the city.

Elenyr motioned to the captain and the man approached. Although not all the city guard knew Elenyr and the fragments, most recognized them as mercenaries that completed bounties for the crown. Elenyr frequently dispersed her portion of the coin to the guards that assisted her, a fact that led to a wellspring of loyalty from the common soldiers.

"Erina," the captain said with a nod, calling her by the name Elenyr had been using for the last decade. "Do you need assistance?"

"Where is King Porlin?"

"At Stormwall for the games," the captain said with an apologetic look. "But I'm sure the captain of the guard would be able to assist you. Would you like me to dispatch a messenger . . .?"

"No, thank you," Elenyr said. "We'll find him."

The man inclined his head and departed, and Elenyr turned toward the castle. When they were out of earshot of the city guard, Fire released an irritated grunt.

"We'll have to track the king down."

"Perhaps we can find another source of information while we are here," Mind mused.

Elenyr frowned as she realized his intent. "The Assassin's Guild? We aren't exactly on the best of terms."

"You *did* kill one of them," Fire said with a smile.

"I was his target," Elenyr said. "What did you expect me to do?"

Mind merely grunted. "You could have gotten answers. We don't know who took the contract on your life."

"He was a master assassin." Elenyr rubbed the scar on her shoulder where the blade had pierced. "I didn't have much choice."

The assassin had lured her to a meeting by donning the persona of an old friend. When she'd arrived the assassin had struck. She'd phased to ethereal, but the blade had been enchanted with lightning magic, and even in her ethereal form, it had cut deep.

"Perhaps we can even discover the identity of the lightning mage," Mind said.

"It's been eight years," Fire said. "Why did they not send another assassin?"

117

"If they wanted to complete the contract, they would have sent another by now," Elenyr said. "Mind is right. The assassins have connections across every kingdom. They could help us locate Wylyn."

"There's just one problem," Fire said. "We don't know the location of their guildhall anymore."

"I do," Mind said. Elenyr raised an eyebrow. He shrugged. "I may have picked the memory from the last assassin I encountered."

Elenyr swept a hand forward. "Then by all means, lead the way."

Mind inclined his head and then took the lead, guiding them into the city. The city was the largest on Lumineia, its wide streets making it feel even larger. Towering trees added shade and beauty to the streets, while shallow streams trickled their way under roads and walkways.

Shaped like a circle, Herosian was broken into rings, each marked by a road and a smaller wall. The castle comprised the center, while the first ring contained the military. The larger homes and opulent fortresses of the nobility comprised the second ring, while the third and fourth contained all the commerce, taverns, and inns. The last three circles were filled with homes, the poorer living further from the city epicenter, their homes interspersed by factories and mills. Indeed, many defined their status by the ring in which they lived.

Passing through the seventh circle, the trio worked their way through the crowd to reach the rings of commerce. As they passed the wall of the fourth ring, the buildings gained a marked shine, the shops containing jewelry and fine linens, many of which were enchanted. Renowned swordsmiths displayed their wares, the streets free of urchins, while nobles of the kingdom rode in gilded wagons. The tinkling of laughter by courtesans mingled with the exuberant laughter of men partaking at the tavern.

As they approached the military circle, Mind veered off the entrance road and followed the circular road that curved around the third district wall. One man spotted Elenyr and his eyes gained a glint of desire. He approached with a swagger in his step, but Elenyr met his gaze. The man blinked and swallowed before veering away, feigning ignorance.

She spotted Fire's grin. "Does something amuse you?"

"Just wondering why you turn all men away."

"I don't have time for romance," Elenyr said.

"You have nothing but time," Mind countered. "Unless you still have feelings for Jeric . . ."

Elenyr grunted in irritation. "Where's the entrance?"

Mind flashed a faint smile, as if Elenyr had confirmed his suspicions. Then he turned and ducked into a garden of a large estate. Avoiding the guards, he guided Elenyr and Fire to a small structure that bordered the third circle wall. The opposite side would be much more austere, the military circle lacking the trappings of the circle of nobles.

Mind reached the structure and motioned them inside, the interior containing tools for maintaining the estate's gardens. The small room smelled of soil and steel, and equipment hung from nails on the walls. The building leaned against the city wall, and the builder had apparently decided to forego building the rear wall, leaving the stones of the third city wall visible.

Mind reached up and counted down and left before pressing one stone. It slid into the wall with a whisper, and Mind pressed other stones, each sliding into the wall before locking into place. The order was apparently important, because Mind mumbled to himself as if counting. Then he reached up and pressed the last stone, and light flowed from the crack.

The light glowed and reached to the other stones, the shape becoming the symbol of the assassin's guild, two blades touching at the tip, hung above a skull. A third dagger was just visible, the hilt protruding from the skull, the blade showing beneath the jaw.

The image glowed, and then faded, and the section of wall swung inward, providing a view of the inside of the wall and a staircase descending from sight. Elenyr inclined her head to Mind as she stepped inside.

"Well done," she said.

"Assassins always think they guard their minds," he said. "But their thoughts are easy to find."

"Do you read everyone's mind?" Fire asked.

"Not yours," Mind said, unconvincingly.

"And me?" Elenyr asked.

"Never," Mind said, a little too quickly. As the door swung shut behind them he seemed to notice her look, and shrugged. "Sometimes. But you actually do guard your memories."

Elenyr smiled at the defensiveness in his tone, pleased that she'd managed to disconcert him after his comments about Jeric. "Be on your guard. Do not forget these are master assassins."

"There are seven of them and three of us." Fire flexed his fingers, calling fire that illuminated his expression. "I'd say they're outnumbered."

Elenyr chuckled but did not disagree. Since Mind could feel the presence of another mind, she motioned him to the take the lead and fell into step behind him. The staircase descended below the city and then intersected with what looked to be an ancient sewer. Now dry, its stones had aged, but it still carried a trace of rank that made Elenyr wrinkle her nose.

Out of fear of discovery, the assassins moved their guildhall every few generations. Elenyr had seen most of them since her days as high oracle, especially those located close to one of the capitol cities.

Three thousand years past, one assassin had built his guildhall in the dwarven realm. Another had chosen to hide in the ruins of an old Verinai village. Most assassins, however, chose to build near a seat of power, and preferred the capitols. Then the tunnel turned—not toward the city, but toward the castle, and she frowned at the sense of familiarity.

"I've been here before," Elenyr murmured.

They came to a halt, and Fire motioned to the tunnel. "When?"

"With Shadow," Elenyr said. "We came to meet with the Assassin's guild fifteen centuries ago."

"So they're reusing an old guildhall?" Mind asked, glancing to Fire.

"Looks like it," Fire said. "What will we find?"

"A secret lost to time," she said.

They exchanged a confused look, but Elenyr stepped in front of Mind and led them down the corridor. Now that she recognized the direction, she strode with purpose, guiding them beneath the military circle of Herosian. The tunnel turned downward, heading deeper. The tunnel was lit by ensconced orbs that gave light only when they passed, the tunnel fading to darkness in their wake. Then they reached the end of the cavern and Fire sucked in his breath, murmuring a curse of astonishment.

A massive cavern was situated directly beneath the castle of Herosian, the enormous pillars on the exterior supporting the foundations of the castle. As large as the fortress above, the cavern was lit by twelve giant symbols placed around the exterior of the room, each a symbol of the twelve common magics.

Blue light filled the space, revealing an underground river flowing through an opening on the northern side, feeding the lake at the base of the cavern. A large island rose from the center of the hidden lake, and on it stood a small castle.

Much newer than the cavern, the fortress contained seven towers, each dedicated to one of the assassins of the guild. A massive statue stood at the center of the castle. At least fifty feet tall, the statue was of a knight, it's sword larger than the assassin towers. Although the cavern was ancient, the statue looked new, the stone lifelike, the muscular torso of the statue showing every curve of flesh.

"The assassins didn't build this place," Mind said, and nodded to the statue. "And unless I am mistaken, that is a titan."

"It is," Elenyr replied. "It and the cavern were built at the end of the mage wars, by the Verinai."

Mind frowned. "You once said the Verinai built the titans beneath the castle at Herosian. They used this chamber?"

"They did." Elenyr pointed to the statue. "Titans were sentients of magic so mighty it took ages to complete. The Verinai used four to destroy my home."

"And that one?" Mind asked, motioning to the statue.

"That's the original titan," she said. "Draeken may be the last of the Verinai, but that titan is the last thing built by your people. Be grateful it will never rise."

"Why?" Mind asked.

Elenyr's gaze was hard. "Because I killed it."

Chapter 16: Assassin Council

"How did you kill a titan?" Mind asked.

Elenyr spotted movement outside one of the towers and motioned them to silence. "A tale for another time. Just know it cannot be awakened."

"So we only have seven master assassins to contend with," Fire said.

"Perhaps not all of them are here," Elenyr said.

"They are," Mind said, his eyes narrowing. "It looks like we have interrupted a meeting."

Elenyr squinted, and made out the group of men and women entering the structure that formed the titan's footstool. A quick count revealed they were all present, and their black clothing was ceremonial, suggesting Mind's guess was accurate.

"Let us learn what we can," Elenyr said. "Split up. Mind, go to the door and see if you can listen to their thoughts. I'll come from beneath and see what I can hear. Fire, get into position where you can come quickly if we have need."

"Done," he said.

The end of the tunnel connected to a spiral staircase that descended to the cavern floor. Other entrances were visible on the exterior of the cavern, and Elenyr marked their location in case they needed a quick escape. Then she descended the stairs and crept her way across the bridge of aquaglass to the assassin island. Nodding to the fragments, she phased to ethereal and dropped into the stone.

The ground looked solid from above, but to her ethereal eyes it looked like smoke. Patches of denser stone were interspersed with dirt and pools of water from the lake. She could see all the way across the island, the foundations of the assassins' personal towers a darker tint than the rest of the ground. Beneath the ground she moved more by will than force, and her body glided forward, drifting beneath the courtyard that separated the towers from the titan's footstool.

She caught a glimpse of movement and spotted Mind advancing to the entrance of the chamber, where he came to a halt at the door. Elenyr continued to advance until she hovered in the rock beneath a triangular table of black stone. The seven assassins were gathered around it, while the woman at the head was speaking. Elenyr willed herself upward, rising until her head surfaced above the floor. She lifted free and crouched beneath the table, listening to the woman speak.

"I know you dislike such a summons," Guildmaster Loralyn said. "But circumstances in recent weeks have changed."

"I'd been stalking a contract for six months," one replied, his tone irritated. "Surely this could have waited."

"It could not," Loralyn said.

The guildmaster, a human woman, had been the head of the guild for only a few years. Elenyr knew very little about her except that she had once served in King's Guard in Griffin, the youngest to ever become a high captain. Then suddenly she and her sister had disappeared. Ten years later, she and her sister had assassinated a duke in the very kingdom they'd once sought to protect.

Elenyr knew the remaining five, but only by name and deed. Two were elves, one was a dwarf. One was a gnome gifted in anti-magic— his specialty the assassination of mages. The last was a man named Gendor, the Blade Ghost. He too had come from a king's guard, only he'd been under King Numen in Erathan. Discharged for excessive brutality, he'd returned and slaughtered his commanding officers. All of them. Then he'd joined the Assassins' Guild.

"The krey have returned," Loralyn said, ending the growing complaints.

"The ancient race?" her sister, Lorica, sounded shocked. "When?"

"Three weeks past," Loralyn exclaimed.

Elenyr identified Lorica by her voice, but knew her by another name. With a cloak that spread into great white wings, the woman had gained a reputation as the Angel of Death. Feared by the nobility yet loved by the populace, she was the most well known assassin the guild had seen in centuries, and the bounty on her head exceeded even that of her sister.

Elenyr felt a familiar tug at her consciousness, and realized Mind wanted to speak to her. Loosening her mental barrier, she permitted him into her mind, and the fragment's words came from nearby.

The sister didn't know.

What about Gendor? Elenyr asked.

His mind is closed to me.

Keep trying.

Questions bubbled up in the chamber and Loralyn slammed her fist onto the stone, bringing them to silence. "We do not know their purpose, but they are quickly gaining allies. There are those who have awaited their return and they have begun to gather."

Elenyr frowned. She'd heard rumors of a group that worshiped the krey, but thought they were just rumors. Perhaps there was more truth than she realized. Then Lorica shifted her feet, nearly kicking Elenyr, and Elenyr leaned away from the boot.

"We should kill the krey," Lorica said.

"Why?" an elf asked, his tone scornful. "They are no threat to us."

"Sister?" Loralyn asked, her tone puzzled. "Why do you think we should kill the ancients?"

"We all know the stories of the Dawn of Magic, and the krey are a threat to everything. If they have returned, they will seek a return to the power they once had."

"How could you know that?" Gendor scoffed.

"Because all crave the power they lost," Lorica said.

Elenyr caught the note of hatred in Lorica's voice. It was obviously suppressed, but Lorica hated Gendor, and the current of emotion ran deep. Elenyr wondered why he deserved such animosity.

The elf across from her shifted in his seat. "Our youngest member speaks with wisdom."

"I think we should ally with the krey," Gendor exclaimed, eliciting a stunned silence.

"Why?" Lorica demanded.

"Because if they return to power, we could benefit," he said. "The contracts could be very lucrative."

"At the expense of the people," Loralyn said.

"Of course our guildmaster sides with her sister," the dwarf, Thorg, exclaimed with a derisive grunt. "Gendor is right. We must ally ourselves with the krey."

"I am the guildmaster," Loralyn said. "And as guildmaster, I carry the burden of knowledge. Every past guildmaster has shared their secrets in our archives, and you have no idea how dangerous the krey can be."

"I don't care about the archives," Gendor growled. "I care about profits."

"Is that why you have been accepting contracts without my approval?"

Loralyn's tone had turned dangerous, the mood in the chamber darkening in an instant. Elenyr watched as several blades were drawn beneath the table, the whisper of steel on leather only heard by her. Elenyr eased her own weapon free, careful to remain ethereal.

"I don't know what you're talking about."

"Do you take me for a fool?" Loralyn demanded. "I order a contract refused, and then weeks later they are dead."

126

"Coincidence," Gendor said.

"I think not," Loralyn said, tossing what sounded like a memory orb and a handful of parchment on the table. Whatever it showed elicited a round of gasps, indicating it proved Loralyn's claim.

"Is this true?" the elf demanded.

"You would betray the guild?" another growled.

Gendor began to laugh. "Does it matter? Ever since I sent Holden to kill the Hauntress, you've been suspicious of me."

Elenyr's hand tightened on the handle, and she struggled with the urge to rise through the table and strike at the man. He was small, but he possessed inhuman strength, and she reminded herself to remain cautious.

"So you admit it?" Loralyn pounced.

"Of course," Gendor exclaimed. "You pick and choose contracts, discarding most, until we hardly hunt at all."

"We kill for honor," Loralyn said, also on her feet. "Not for greed."

"Your antiquated idea of our craft is laughable," Gendor exclaimed. "We are paid to kill, to hunt and draw blood."

"Yet we only kill those who merit death," Loralyn said. "You know our creed."

"And I *despise* it."

The rancor in Gendor's voice echoed in the chamber. Elenyr again stayed her hand, forcing herself to listen as Loralyn drew her blade. The reverberation of her longsword coming free sounded like a gauntlet being dropped to the ground.

"I should kill you where you stand," she said. "But tradition grants you a choice. Do you wish to fight me to claim the guild? Or leave in disgrace?"

127

Elenyr risked lifting her face through the table, catching a glimpse of the assassins in the chamber. Gendor was too confident for her liking, his expression a sneer as he regarded the guildmaster.

He was small, his body at odds with the story of inhuman strength he seemed to possess. Yet he was not a body mage, that much Elenyr knew. He stood with his arms folded, his grey eyes conveying the utmost scorn.

Loralyn had stepped away from the table, and stood with her blade out and ready, her features hard. She was aging, yet still beautiful, her blond hair going silver. Lorica, a younger image of her sister, glared at Gendor, her expression oddly triumphant, as if she'd waited for this moment.

"You have served your purpose," Gendor said, finally drawing his blade, an ugly knife with two side prongs.

Elenyr considered her course of action. She could wait and watch Loralyn kill Gendor, but that would mean Elenyr would never learn who had sought her life. And if Gendor killed Loralyn, the guild would be against her for decades. Making her decision, she gathered herself and ascended.

Gendor came to a halt when Elenyr rose through the table, and the other assassins scrambled to retreat. Elenyr held her sword low and ready, fixing Gendor with a cold glare. Green smoke cascaded off her body, her cloak and cowl partially ethereal. The man regarded her with irritation.

"You are interrupting a private council, Hauntress."

"You should thank me," Elenyr said. "I just saved your life." She turned to Loralyn. "I apologize for the intrusion."

"No apology needed," she said, her eyes on Gendor. "I know one of our number was given a contract on you, but I assure you, I did not issue it."

"I believe you," Elenyr said. "And unfortunately, before you begin your duel, I would ask your permission to challenge him myself."

"Me?" Gendor asked. "You wish to challenge me?"

Elenyr smiled, the grim expression causing the other assassins to retreat. Elenyr stepped off the table and glided around the assassins, her blade rising as she closed the gap to the Gendor. To his credit, he remained in place, his expression calculating.

"Do I have your leave?" Elenyr asked.

Loralyn inclined her head. "He acted outside the creed of this guild. You are welcome to him."

Elenyr raised her sword and pointed it at the man. "Who issued the contract on my life?" Elenyr asked, her voice gaining a dark timbre.

Gendor regarded Elenyr like she was a mild irritant. His eyes maintained the calculating look, as if he were attempting to solve a difficult puzzle. Elenyr fleetingly wondered if he was the lightning mage that had crafted the sword for the failed assassination.

"It is fortunate that you have chosen this moment to come," Gendor said. "For it means you will die with the others."

"Us?" Lorica asked. "You mean to kill us all, alone?"

Elenyr, Mind's voice cut into Elenyr's thoughts. *We have a problem.*

I'm a little busy.

You're about to get busier.

Instead of words, Mind sent an image, a fuzzy glimpse of Mind's vision as he retreated behind an assassin tower. Elenyr's eyes widened when she spotted dozens of shadow figures rushing across the bridges to the island, their blades reflecting the light.

Gendor stabbed a finger at Loralyn. "You adhere to these pointless traditions, keeping our number small, selecting only a handful of contracts, all while we are meant to rule. While you've been cautious, I've built an army of assassins, and it's time this guild joined a new era with the krey."

Dozens of black garbed figures burst through the door and flanked Gendor, their matching blades drawn. Each wore a silver mask, the

129

features bland and sharp, meant to terrify. The insignia on their shoulders indicated they served a single master.

"Hauntress, at least you lived to see my Bloodsworn." Gendor's smile turned triumphant. "We have worked from the shadows long enough."

The assassins looked between Gendor, with two joining Loralyn and Lorica. The other two, Thorg and the other elf, joined Gendor without hesitation, suggesting they were already part of the Bloodsworn.

"Fire," Elenyr said, raising her voice.

Gendor snorted. "You think to threaten me with flames?"

"It wasn't a threat," Elenyr said. "It was a summons . . ."

Chapter 17: The Bloodsworn

Outside the council chamber, Fire stepped off the assassin tower and fell to the ground. He landed and struck the stone, blasting fire in all directions. Those in the doorway were caught in the explosion, the flames knocking them into the council chamber, the Bloodsworn tumbling into each other, their clothes burning.

The elven assassin with Gendor reached outward and the lake rose up, flowing into the chamber and extinguishing the flames, the water bursting into steam. By then the two ranks had closed and Elenyr had reached Gendor. The man smirked and the dagger elongated, stretching to become a sword.

She drove her blade towards his chest but he knocked the sword upward, spinning and striking her right flank. She phased to ethereal, intent on letting the weapon pass through her body. At the last moment the blade sparked with power, lightning crackling up the blade. She realized her mistake too late and flinched—but the weapon came to an abrupt halt next to her waist, parried by Loralyn from behind Elenyr.

Elenyr darted to the side as Gendor scowled, the surprise of his weapon's lightning magic spoiled. Loralyn locked eyes with the betrayer and stepped into Elenyr's place, motioning her aside.

"He's mine."

Elenyr realized they were beyond answers and inclined her head. "As you will."

Lorica and the other two assassins fought on the opposite side of the table, the Bloodsworn driving them back by sheer numbers. Fire stood in the doorway, singlehandedly preventing other Bloodsworn from entering. Mind watched his flank, his thin sword cutting into the ranks of Bloodsworn.

Elenyr plunged into the ground and flew across the chamber to rise behind the pair of Bloodsworn battling Lorica. Elenyr turned solid and swung her weapon, the blade cutting deep. As they fell, she spun, deflecting a sword and then striking a third Bloodsworn with her free hand. Her sudden appearance left them in shambles, and the remaining attackers fell beneath Lorica's sword.

Across the room, Thorg and the water mage had cornered the elf, and the mage stabbed her with a spike of water as the dwarf slew Lorica's remaining ally. Lorica growled and charged, with Elenyr at her side.

"Your sister is a fool," Thorg growled. "But I suppose it runs in the family."

The dwarf slammed his fists together and fire burst apart, forming two barbed shields. He twisted and threw the first, but Lorica ducked, allowing the spinning shield to pass above her. It spun into the wall and plunged deep, carving a line into the stone.

"Thorg," Lorica snarled, "I'll gut you for this."

"Not if you are dead," Thorg said.

The elf cast a whip of water and swung it at Lorica's feet, coiling it about her ankles. Just as she leaned back, Elenyr leapt through Lorica's sword, phasing ethereal and then solid on the other side, her own blade slicing through the whip. She drove into the elf as Lorica charged Thorg.

"You are not part of this," the elf said, her whip morphing into a snake.

"I am now," Elenyr said.

She deflected the snake and leapt in, but steam from the fire morphed into a dozen swords, all driving for her body. Elenyr phased to ethereal and they passed through her. The elf snarled and raised her blade, but Elenyr's sword edge passed through her ethereal throat. The elven assassin whirled—to find Elenyr's sword at her heart.

"You chose the wrong side," Elenyr said. "Care to make another choice?"

132

The elf snarled and deflected Elenyr's sword, but instead of attacking Elenyr, she spun and charged Lorica, locked in a duel with the dwarf. Seeing her intention, Elenyr leapt across the gap and shouted a warning.

Lorica spun, her sword rising to deflect the elf's blade, the motion leaving her open to Thorg. Elenyr passed between them and turned corporeal just before reaching the dwarf, her blow sending him tumbling into the entrance corridor. When Elenyr turned, she watched Lorica twist beneath the aquaglass blade and plunge her sword into the assassin's heart. The woman's scream echoed in the chamber, drawing Gendor's gaze.

The room was in shambles, the chairs and table rent by the fury of conflict. The Bloodsworn lay where they had fallen, while only Thorg remained standing with Gendor. Hundreds of Bloodsworn remained outside, but they could not pass Fire and Mind, who barred the opening. Evidently realizing his reinforcements could not be reached, Gendor whirled and sprinted to the exit.

"Mind!" Elenyr cried.

The fragment spun and raised his sword, but Gendor leapt to the wall and used it to push off, allowing him to soar over Mind and Fire. Landing hard, he darted out of the opening and joined the Bloodsworn in the courtyard. Thorg opened a hole in the ground and disappeared, a moment later the stone spitting him out beyond Mind and Fire.

The assassin sisters and Elenyr charged the doorway, joining Fire and Mind. Hundreds of masked assassins were arrayed against them, their blades reflecting the light. Gendor smirked as the assassin sisters joined Elenyr.

"Your army will die with you," Loralyn snarled.

Gendor released a mocking laugh. "Only two of you remain. And even with the Hauntress, you cannot stop me, or the master I serve."

"Do you ever stop talking?" Fire wiped the blood from a cut on his cheek, flames licking at his fingers.

Gendor glowered at Fire and raised his hand to reveal a small, spherical object. He touched a rune on its surface and it glowed to life. Then he tossed it toward Elenyr, his sneer one of disdain. Gendor and his Bloodsworn retreated, the soldiers tossing other spheres onto the ground around the council chamber. They all glowed into life, growing brighter by the second.

"You are a relic from a dead age, Hauntress," Gendor said. "And it's only fitting you die by another ancient weapon."

"Go!" Elenyr barked. "Inside!"

The group sprinted into the council chamber and Fire summoned a wall of flames, closing off the doors and forming a barricade. The spheres outside detonated together, the explosion ripping into stone like it was kindling.

The walls of the council chamber were built to support the titan's weight, but it absorbed the brunt of the blast, the stone cracking, the supports giving way. The ceiling began to cave in, great stones falling inward, smashing the council table into chunks of polished stone.

"Above you!" Loralyn cried, shoving her sister out of the way as a stone came free.

Lorica tumbled in the dust as the stone landed on Loralyn, knocking her to the ground. "Loralyn!" she cried.

Fire leapt to the stone and with a burst of fire, pushed it out of the way. Lorica scooped her sister up and the group sprinted for the entrance as the entire ceiling gave way. Last in line, the ceiling dropped on Elenyr, and she passed through the tumbling rock in ethereal form, bursting through the dust to join the others.

Dead Bloodsworn killers littered the ground, and two of the explosive weapons had detonated in their ranks, leaving a pair of craters. Gendor had left the dead where they had fallen, and the battlefield lay strewn with their dark bodies, the silver masks covering their features. Then a cracking of stone drew their eyes.

She looked up and watched as the titan, its footstool broken, teetered, and then fell to the side. Its waist slammed into an assassin

134

tower, crushing it to rubble as it crashed its way to the ground, splashing into the lake before finally coming to a halt, half submerged.

"Sister." Lorica's voice was barely a whisper as she set Loralyn on the earth. She snapped to look at Elenyr and the fragments, tears in her desperate eyes. "Do any of you have healing magic?"

"We do not," Mind said quietly.

Lorica cradled her sister as she died, and Loralyn reached up to grasp her hand. "You must rebuild the guild," she said. "The assassins must continue."

"I can't do it without you." Tears wet the dust and blood on Loralyn's chest. "I'll get you to a healer. There's enough time."

But there wasn't, and Elenyr grimaced in helplessness. Gendor had planned his strike with great care, all but eliminating the assassins in a single stroke. The grief on Lorica's features was palpable, and reminded Elenyr of the other assassins that had been buried beneath the titan's footstool. They had been the woman's family, and in a matter of minutes she'd witnessed their betrayal and slaughter.

Elenyr's thoughts turned to her losses, the family and friends she'd seen die in the Mage Wars. Witnessing Lorica's raw grief cut deep, and Elenyr recalled the agony of loss. Her eyes flicked to Fire and Mind, both soberly watching Lorica, and Elenyr imagined the pain of losing her sons. Her heart clenched in her chest, and she looked away, trying not to imagine kneeling over the body of a fragment.

Loralyn smiled up at her sister. "You have always been the strong one," she whispered.

Lorica grimaced, the tears flowing faster. "That's not true and you know it."

"Rebuild the guild," Loralyn repeated, her voice fading.

"Gendor's guild is too strong," Lorica said.

"It is not the Bloodsworn you must fear," Lorica said, her eyes flicking to Elenyr. "It is his master. Be wary, for the Order of Ancients has risen . . ."

135

Loralyn's body relaxed in death, and Lorica screamed her rage, the primal sound reverberating in the chamber. Elenyr reached out and placed her hand on the woman's shoulder, but Lorica jerked free of Elenyr's grip.

"You must leave."

"We can help you against the Bloodsworn," Mind said.

"Your help got my sister killed."

Elenyr glanced to Mind and saw him grimace. With no other recourse, Elenyr motioned them away, and they retreated back the way they had come. Elenyr paused when they had ascended the stairwell to the corridor, her eyes settling on the figure of Lorica leaning over her fallen sister.

"She died saving her family," Mind said.

"That is what family does," Elenyr said quietly.

"Are the Bloodsworn still present?" Fire asked. "I have no wish to see both sisters perish this day."

Mind frowned, his eyes gaining the faraway look that indicated he was using his magic. "I feel no other minds present." His gaze flicked to the titan, and then back to Elenyr. "No mortal minds, anyway."

"This was no accidental strike," Fire said. "Gendor was ready to destroy the Assassin's Guild. We just happened to be here."

"If we hadn't, Lorica would be dead," Mind said.

Elenyr noticed the frown on his features. "What else did you sense?"

Mind hesitated, and then motioned to the refuge. "I caught the thoughts of another. "I can't be sure, but it could have been Shadow."

"What would he be doing here?" Fire asked.

"If he did not reveal himself, he had a reason," Elenyr said.

136

"So you'll just leave him with Lorica?" Mind asked. "In the state she's in, I wouldn't be surprised if she killed him."

"Shadow has his task. We have ours." Elenyr turned away from the chamber and ascended the sloping corridor. "We learned what we came to learn. And it appears Wylyn has discovered allies."

"The Order of Ancients?" Fire asked. "I've never heard of them."

They both looked to Elenyr, and she sighed. "There have always been rumors of people that believe the ancient race will return. I never gave credence to such a myth."

"A myth just destroyed the Assassin's Guild."

"What are you saying?" Elenyr asked.

"That Gendor doesn't serve the Order. He's a member."

Elenyr was nodding. "Then it appears Wylyn is not our only threat. Let us hope the kings know more about the Order, for if they are large enough to eliminate the Assassins, they are large enough to aid Wylyn's rise to power."

Elenyr didn't say what she really feared. Gendor had all but admitted that he'd ordered the contract on her life. If he was a member of the Order, it meant the Order knew about Elenyr. And the fragments. As they left the fallen Assassin's Guild behind, she realized the attempt on her life may not have succeeded, but it had informed their foes that Elenyr had a weakness.

Lightning.

Chapter 18: Lost to the Deep

In a cavern deep underground, a stream flowed out of a crevasse in the wall, gurgling into a lake. The sound reverberated off the confines of the cavern, a quiet echo that did not disturb the denizens that called the cavern home. The sounds had existed for centuries, untouched, unchanged. Then the water cut off, gradually diminishing as if the stream had suddenly dried up.

Deep hawks fluttered in the sudden silence, their agitation mounting. Lizards skittered across the beach to the streambed and sniffed about, and then fled when the stone around the crevasse cracked. Another crack appeared, and another, the pressure behind the wall mounting by the second.

Boom, the wall exploded outward, stones and boulders falling down the slope and splashing into the lake. A sphere of water bounced out of the new hole, and was carried on the stream into the lake, where it floated like a giant bubble. Then it popped, dropping four figures into the lake.

Exhausted, Water plunged into the freezing lake, the cold piercing his clothing and sinking into his skin. He surfaced and sucked in a breath, casting about to ensure his companions were with him. Wearily, he swam to the edge and pulled himself onto the beach, collapsing in relief.

Iridescent mushrooms and vines clung to the walls and ceiling, casting the large cavern in blue and green light. Grey spotted lizards flitted away from him, eager to protect their eggs from the sudden intruders.

"I can't believe you got us out," Light exclaimed, yawning.

"To be fair," Jeric said, emptying the water from his boots. "He is the one that dropped a mountain on us."

"And you have our gratitude," Lira said.

Her smile warmed Water's heart, and he hoped he was not turning red. "You told us to destroy the Gate, so we did."

"No thanks to me," Light said morosely. "I'm just so *tired*."

"You'll feel better when we get to the surface," Lira said. She leaned against a rock and wiped a hand across her clothes, the wind gradually drying her armor, the action causing her to shiver.

"Light," Water said, "think you can get a fire going?"

"With what?" Light asked. "It's not like we've got any wood down here."

"The mushrooms will burn," Jeric said, pointing to the iridescent stalks.

Water stood and sliced several off. Then he gathered stones and placed them in a ring. He too was shivering, and felt lethargic and slow. Light pulled from the cavern's light and focused it on the pile of mushroom stalks, sending flames blossoming upward. Instead of orange, the flames were a bright blue.

Water smiled in relief and sat next to the flames, warming his hands. Lira did the same, her smile illuminated by the sparkling fire. She glanced at him and saw his shudder, and then cocked her head to the side.

"I wouldn't think you'd be cold."

"Only Fire is resistant to cold," Water said wryly. "The rest of us feel the chill."

"It's times like these I miss his ugly face," Light said, clearly miserable.

"He has your face," Jeric said, taking a seat next to Water.

"And yet he's the ugly one," Light said, a faint smile on his lips.

They shared a laugh and then Lira gestured to the hole in the cavern wall. "I'm impressed you got us out alive. The pressure must have been tremendous."

Water recalled the moment the Gate Chamber and the temple had collapsed into the reservoir. Great stones had plunged into the water and sunk, giving Water only seconds to pull his friends into a sphere that would keep them safe. Then the rocks had piled on top of them, the sheer weight all but crushing Water's magic.

With great care he'd shifted the boulders until they had access to an opening at the side of the reservoir, which dropped into an underground stream. The current had carried them for hours before striking the wall at the edge of the cavern, the water building up pressure until it shattered the barrier.

"I wasn't about to let such a beautiful companion drown." Water realized how forward his words were and flushed. When he looked back she held his gaze, and nodded in gratitude, warming his chest more than the fire.

"I'm inclined to camp here for the night," Jeric said. "I think we're close to a dark elf city and they would have heard our exit."

"You think they heard the stone breaking?" Water asked, motioning to the gaping hole in the wall.

"They have sound magic that allows them to listen to everything," Jeric said. "In a day or two they will find us and lead us out."

"Why wait?" Light complained. "I miss the sun."

"Do *you* know the way out?" Jeric asked.

"No," he said, looking to Water with hope.

Water gestured to the underground stream. "I could follow that back to the surface, but we know what waits for us at the other end."

Light looked to Lira, but she shrugged helplessly. "I haven't been on Lumineia in centuries. You expect me to know what lies underground?"

Light groaned. "And what if the dark elves do not come?"

"They will." Jeric spoke with such confidence that Water was inclined to believe him.

"We wait," Water said, and when Light scowled, he added. "Two days. Then we venture out on our own."

Light reclined next to the fire with a groan, obviously intent on sleeping for the next two days. Jeric withdrew a string and began fashioning a fishing pole. Water regarded him for several moments and then motioned upward.

"When did you meet Elenyr?" Water asked.

"She has not told you?"

"She does not share her tales of love with us," Water said.

Light grunted in irritation. "She's overly protective of those secrets."

"I wonder why," Lira said with a laugh.

"I met her in my youth," Jeric said. "I was devilishly handsome and she was captivating. Of course she had a sword on my throat, so I was rather distracted."

"What did you do to incite her ire?" Water asked.

"A misunderstanding," the elf said with a dismissive wave. "She thought I was with the bandits she'd come to punish, but I was merely a merchant seeking their ill-gotten goods."

"To return them?" Lira asked, raising her eyebrow.

"Of course," he replied, fastening the hook. "For a profit. Bandits steal, and the nobles paid me to retrieve their wares. It's a delicate balance."

"I can see why she mistook you for a bandit," Water said.

"The next time we met was far more interesting," Jeric said, his eyes sparkling with amusement. "She and Shadow were hunting a thief

141

from the Thieves Guild who had resorted to murder on several occasions. They needed help tracking him down."

"What was your price?" Lira asked, a frown creasing her forehead.

Water hid a smile as he realized the woman still held ill feelings toward the elf for telling the dakorians the location of the temple. Unperturbed, Jeric leaned back against a rock and continued crafting his fishing rod.

"I said a kiss on the cheek would suffice," he replied.

"I don't believe she kissed you," Water said with a snort.

"Not that time," he said with a broad smile.

Water and Lira exchanged a look. Water wasn't sure what to make of the elf. He was clearly devious, but he couldn't be sure if his cunning was for their benefit or not. Before he could decide, Jeric stood.

"I'll be back with a meal."

"I could bring the fish to you," Water said.

"Where would be the fun in that?" Jeric asked. He winked and strode away, ascending a small outcropping of rock before dropping his line.

"I want to hate him," Lira said softly, "but I find him rather intriguing."

"I as well," Water said.

Lira yawned, and Water gestured to the ground. "You should sleep."

She shook her head. "I need a bath."

"Didn't you already have one?" he asked with a smile, pointing to the lake.

"No," she said.

She gathered her things and stood, going the opposite direction from Jeric. She disappeared behind a boulder and a moment later tossed her tunic on top of the rock. Water stared into the flames, his thoughts on what they'd learned in the Gate Chamber.

Several minutes later he heard her hiss in pain. On his feet in an instant, he darted to the boulder. Keeping his eyes averted, he sought for the threat, but she was closer than he thought, and he caught a glimpse of her bare back.

She hissed again, and tried to bandage the wound on her shoulder blade. He turned away, uncertain how to respond—offer aid, or retreat before she spotted him? He sought to withdraw but she turned, and their eyes met.

"Since you're here, mind helping me place the bandage?"

"I'm sorry," he said hastily. "It sounded like you were in pain."

"Are you going to help or not?"

He nodded, and closed the gap. With great care, he helped wrap the bandage across the wound. It was a makeshift cover, but he was highly conscious of her bare back, and his hands fumbling to fasten the dressing. Then he noticed the marks on her back and his eyes widened. Scars marred her skin, white and ugly, stretching from her shoulder to her waist.

"How did you get burned?" he asked.

She donned her shirt, covering the scars before tightening her belt. "Ero's experiments."

"*Ero* did this to you?" he exclaimed.

She held his gaze. "Ero was not always benevolent," she said cryptically.

"Yet you trust him now?"

She nodded. "With my life."

She turned and strode away, leaving him to his confusion. Try as he might, he could not fathom how she'd come to forgive anyone for such an act, let alone work beside him. With a start he realized he knew very little about what had happened in the Dawn of Magic, and wondered if he would ever know.

For the next two days they waited, and Water spent much of the time talking to Lira. He found her fascinating, and it seemed she found him fascinating as well. Light, predictably, slept most of the time, while Jeric seemed content to fish or read the book from his pack, *The Dragon's Sleep, ways to extend your life beyond the grave.*

Water enjoyed the time, and on several occasions, walked with Lira around the lake. He often wondered about Lira's scars. She remained guarded, so he did most of the talking, and filled Lira in on the events of the last few thousand years.

When rescue finally came, Water was loathe to depart. The sounds of boots came from a tunnel on the opposite side of the lake, and Light roused in an instant, eager to leave what he'd come to call his crucible. All four turned and looked upward to the host of caves dotting the far side of the cavern. Out of the largest, a figure appeared, but it was not who Water expected.

He'd expected a scout, a dark elf garbed in the traditional gear of a hunter. But the dark elf standing in the opening wore a silver mask and a black robe. For several moments the four stared at the newcomer until another appeared at his side. This one was a soldier, but not like those Water had seen in the army. He wore matching dark armor, a bare sword in his hand. Then another appeared, and another, the soldiers filling the opening.

"I don't think they're friendly," Light said.

"They wouldn't be," Jeric said, and Water noticed he had drawn his weapons, turning them into a large shield and a sword.

"You know who they are?" Water asked.

"Many regard them as a myth," Jeric said wryly. "They were a legend, a story to frighten children."

The robed figure in the mask raised a hand and pointed at them, and without a word the dark elves leapt from the opening, a silent flood of armored soldiers. They raced down the slope and across the water, their boots splashing on the surface of the lake, sending ripples toward the banks. Water's eyes widened as he saw how many soldiers had come for them.

"Who are they?" Light asked, casting a faint, curving blade from the light in the room.

"The Order of Ancients," Jeric said.

"The what?" Water asked.

"They worship the krey," Jeric said. "Have since the Dawn of Magic. They believe our lives were better under the ancient race, and want them returned to power."

"You think they are here on Wylyn's order?" Lira asked, drawing her sword.

"For Wylyn!" the robed figured bellowed.

Water exchanged a look with Light. "I think that answers that."

Jeric swished his sword as if eager for the battle. "Make sure one is left alive. We're going to need someone to guide us out of here."

Chapter 19: Churning

The Order swept across the lake, a dozen, a hundred, and still they came. The foursome spread out, placing the wall at their backs while Water and Lira took the center. Water grimaced, wishing they were above ground. There wasn't much light down here and Light would be far weaker than he would on the surface.

"How have we never heard of them?" Light asked, rubbing his face as if to wake up.

"It's a secret order," Jeric said. "They have members throughout every kingdom and army."

"The Order must have figured out the ancients have returned," Jeric said. "Or Serak is part of them."

"It's hard to imagine he isn't," Water said.

"Don't let them get behind us," Lira said, gesturing to the wall behind them.

Water recognized that among the four, and in a battle on the lake, he would be the strongest. Light was weakened and Jeric was an unknown quantity. He'd seen Lira in battle and her skills were impressive, but he doubted she had the ability to fight so many at once.

The dark elves were halfway across the lake, sprinting on the surface as if it was flat stone, sending ripples away from their footsteps. Water guessed they wore water boots, the soles enchanted to turn water solid. Without the lake as a barrier, Water and his friends would be sorely pressed. He pointed to the boots of his friends and water trickled up the slope, binding to the soles of their boots, giving them the same ability.

"What are you doing?" Jeric asked, watching the blue light condensed around his boots.

"If they can run on water, it's only fitting we can as well."

"I love it when you do this," Light exclaimed, growing excited.

"How much control do you have over water?" Lira asked.

He heard the touch of hope in her tone and looked to her. "What do you have in mind?"

She flashed a grim smile. "We are at a beach," she swept a hand at the sand and dirt beneath their feet. "I think we need some waves."

He realized what she meant and grinned. He leapt into the water and waded up to his waist, and then began to push himself along the bank. His body pressed against the water like the prow of a ship, and he reached out, gathering threads of water, pulling them along with him. More and more he grasped the liquid, the water churning in his wake.

The strain mounted and he growled, forcing himself to accelerate as he towed boatloads of water, willing it to come with him, to follow his path. White capped waves appeared in his wake as he rotated around the charging dark elves. A small contingent came for him, but the lake had started to rotate.

The dark elves raised a dozen crossbows and fired, but he was moving too fast, the bolts striking the wave at his back. Still he pushed, driving his body around the edge of the lake. The army had all exited the tunnel except for the robed leader.

Water pushed even harder, speeding around the exterior, circling back to his friends just as the leading ranks of dark elves reached the shore. He caught up the water and raised a shield, catching several bolts as he blasted by. The waves in his wake caught the dark elves and carried them along. They fought to keep their balance and several failed, plunging into the water only to be swept into the current.

Several raced up the wave and leapt over to land on the beach. Lira, Light, and Jeric engaged the forerunners, but they were forced to retreat as the lake expanded its borders. The center of lake dropped, the water pushing to the banks and rising.

The dark elves were in shambles, with most spinning around the exterior, many struggling to swim in the churning water. Others raced

147

backward, calling for aid, for direction, and the leader in the mask paced in the tunnel, barking orders that were lost in the din.

One dark elf was sucked into the turmoil of Water's wake. He fell into the water and the current sent him crashing into the wall, the brutal impact of armor and stone echoing over the groaning lake. And still Water accelerated.

He whipped around the exterior of the lake, each rotation faster than the previous one, each turn pushing the lake to greater speeds. He spotted his friends as he swept by. The beach was nearly gone, so they'd retreated to the mouth of the stream, fighting on the rocks, their blades clashing with the dark elves'. The dark elves that fell were picked up by the expanding lake and dragged along the rocks, drowning as the lake crept up the walls.

Jeric kept a wide shield and turned the other hilt into a spear. He spun and twisted, arcing the bladed weapon to strike at the dark elves, driving them back, towards the expanding lake. Light stood at the rear, pulling the light from the cavern to fight, hurling his curved weapon at the line of dark elves, forcing them to duck to avoid the spinning blade.

Lira darted about, her agility active as she danced across the uneven surface, never turning a stone. A dark elf lunged for her and she swept to the side, the blade passing within inches of her shoulder. She kept the rotation and elbowed him in the stomach before rotating back and catching the extended arm. Pulling the soldier to her, she leaned forward and smashed her forehead against the dark elf's face. Dazed, he was helpless as she yanked his sword from his grip and hurled it into another dark elf. Then she kicked him into the expanding tide and he was dragged across the rocks, his shouts quickly falling silent.

The borders of the lake had risen thirty feet, the water turning with frightening speed. Water sped by the robed figure, now just twenty feet above him, and couldn't resist smirking at his foe. The leader came to a halt, her eyes boring through the mask.

"You cannot stop the krey from rising!" she shouted.

"You cannot stop us!" Water called back. Then he noticed the dark elves.

Most had retreated to the center of the lake. They stood on the water that was mostly smooth, allowing it to carry them around a slow circle. Their weapons were at the ready but they made no move to advance toward the outer edges of the lake, where the hurtling speeds were more dangerous. Water realized they were biding their time, hoping he would tire.

Coming around the lake towards his friends, Water leapt from his path and released his magic. He landed on the rocks behind the last dark elf, distracting him so Jeric could dispatch him. As the body fell Jeric used his spear to point to the lake.

"You put them in a cage," he said. "Now what do we do with them?"

"Too many to fight," Light said, leaning against the wall for support.

Water noticed he had several injuries. Lira had a cut along her arm and her armor on her stomach was damaged. Jeric had a wicked gash along his shoulder to which he calmly pressed a bandage.

"We don't need a victory," Lira said. "We just need a guide."

"Perhaps we could get some answers as well," Jeric mused, pointing to the masked leader still in the tunnel.

"Then get ready for a ride," Water said.

Jeric grinned and took the lead, jumping onto the water. He'd braced his body well and didn't lose his balance as the water swept him away. His excited shout reverberated off the interior of the cavern. Light shrugged and followed, and Lira jumped onto the spinning lake with Water.

Water landed on the surface of the spinning lake, the current yanking them around the exterior of the cavern. He had to lean away from the wall to keep from being launched into the stone, and he ducked a protrusion of stone that nearly took his head.

They streaked around the exterior and Jeric leapt, changing his sword to a whip that he used to catch the rock. The lake carried him past the protrusion and yanked him upward. He flipped in the air and landed in the mouth of the masked one's tunnel. Surprised by his sudden appearance, she went down from a quick blow, and Jeric moved to bind her hands.

The dark elves howled in dismay and charged, abandoning their previous patience. They sprinted up the slope, fighting to keep their balance as the water carried them around the cavern. The smarter ones timed the rotation, allowing them to get close enough to wield their hand crossbows.

Water raised a wave to absorb the blows and then used a surge of water to launch himself off the surface of the lake. He alighted in the tunnel. Lira landed at his side and bled away her momentum before coming to a stop.

"That was exhilarating," she said with a laugh, ducking as a volley of crossbow bolts clattered off the wall.

Light jumped for the tunnel but fell short. He managed to bounce off the wall and land on his feet, but the water continued to slow, carrying him towards the horde of dark elves. He had time to cast a pair of swords before they closed the gap.

"Stay here," Water said.

"Not a chance," Lira said, dropping down with him.

They landed on the spinning water and sprinted to Light. Water cast his favorite staff and sprinted across the water, racing with the current to strike at the pack of dark elves. Water spotted the blades cutting into Light's body and anger pooled in his belly.

"Have you no *shame*?" he roared, his voice gaining a dark timbre.

He called on the lake and great jaws appeared. As large as a wagon, they widened, the teeth sharpening into shards of aquaglass. Dark elves scrambled away but the jaws clamped shut, devouring a foursome about to strike Light's back.

With Lira at his side, Water attacked the remainder. Their blades spun in unison, working in tandem as they cast aside the dark elves. In the heat of combat Water glanced to Lira, feeling a unity he'd never felt with anyone. Lira slipped through a gap, slicing a dark elf's leg and allowing Water to leap over the falling dark elf. Water cast a shield and bashed another, sending him tumbling into her blade. Their eyes met and she smiled, obviously feeling the same kinship.

They collected Light and retreated, fleeing before the horde of dark elves. Water reached down and cast a quartet of giant horses, leashing them to the edge of the lake. Then he gave them a single purpose. To run. With the water at their chests they charged, pushing the water around the exterior as Water had done, and the lake continued to churn. Water then cast a pillar to lift himself and his companions to the mouth of the tunnel.

"That will give us a few hours," Water said as the dark elves howled anew, falling and tumbling about.

Lira nodded in approval, and Water noticed a glint in her eyes that went beyond respect. "Well done," she said. "I think I just may have to keep you."

"Can we *please* go to the surface now?" Light exclaimed.

"Lead the way, princess," Jeric said, poking the masked dark elf.

She scowled and turned into the tunnel. Water and the others fell into step behind the captive, and the woman led them away from the cavern. As the turn in the tunnel took the spinning lake from sight, Water realized their foes were mounting, and they were still no closer to stopping the krey.

Chapter 20: The Ear

Water stepped into the sun and breathed a sigh of relief. The dark elf had sought to lead them the wrong way—twice—but Jeric had a knack for discerning the truth, and for manipulation. The dark elf scowled and came to a halt when they reached the surface.

Light leapt out of the cave, pushing past Water and launching himself skyward. He flitted about like an excited sparrow, drinking in the illumination until his skin veritably shimmered, and his cry of delight echoed over the water.

The cave exited onto a short, rocky beach that bordered the great Blue Lake, the water stretching to the horizon, sparkling in the late morning sun. Clouds floated in the sky, fluffy and white as they drifted east.

Water looked back and saw the dwarven mountains rising in the distance, marking their location as several days east of the Gate Chamber where they'd been buried. He nodded in satisfaction and turned to Lira, who smiled as she watched Light exult.

"The sun on Lumineia always seems brighter than other worlds," she exclaimed.

Jeric joined them and stooped to lift water from the lake, drinking the cool liquid. "Someday I'd like to see another sun," he said.

"Answers first," Water said, turning to the bound dark elf.

"We had a deal," she said. "I brought you here, and you release me."

"I never said *when* we'd release you," Jeric said with a smile.

From behind the mask her eyes glowed with hatred, and Water reached for the mask. The elf tried to evade but Water caught the edge and pulled it from the dark elf's head. The woman staring back at him was furious.

"You have no idea what the krey are capable of," she snarled.

"And you do?" Lira retorted.

"The krey once controlled all life on Lumineia," she exclaimed. "They gave us everything, even the magic we call our own. And we rebelled against them."

"What do you know of it?" Lira said, her voice gaining an edge.

"Our memories are longer than the surface races," she spat. "And we have not forgotten what they did for us. When the krey rise again, you will see for yourselves—if you join Wylyn."

"That's not likely to happen," Jeric said with a laugh. "The foe you face is the Hauntress."

The dark elf's eyes registered a flicker of recognition and then hardened. "Even she can be killed."

Water frowned as he recognized the expression. There was something about the dark elf that was familiar, but he couldn't quite place where he'd seen her. Still, his memory twinged, wanting to remind him of a past connection.

"Tell us about the Order," Jeric said.

"I will speak nothing," she said haughtily. "No matter how much pain you inflict upon me."

"We'll see about that," Lira said, drawing a short dagger.

"No need to get sharp," Jeric said, tapping the dagger away. "The lady merely needs some encouragement."

The dark elf sneered. "You think you can get me to talk with your words?"

"Of course," Jeric said. "The question isn't even which tactic to use, only which I will find most amusing."

The dark elf scowled, but Jeric regarded her like he would a fascinating puzzle. Water watched him, confused and curious about the elf's demeanor. He was a wanderer with a passion for the exotic, probably the very reason he was attracted to Elenyr. The dark elf had refused to give her name or identity in the Deep and he doubted she would now. But Jeric had a strange way of getting what he wanted.

As Jeric continued to study the dark elf, Light cavorted in the water, sprinting about until wings sprouted on his back and he soared into the air, his peeling laughter sending a group of birds squawking and soaring away.

The dark elf glanced at Light and then back to Jeric before fidgeting. "I do not care for your silence. Do what you intend and be done with it."

"You are one who has served the krey your whole life," Jeric said. "Yet you live by another name, a face the world sees. Do you keep your true allegiances hidden out of fear? Or envy?"

The dark elf spit and leaned towards Jeric but Water put a hand on her shoulder, keeping her in place. "You think to understand me?" She straightened, her demeanor haughty again. "You know nothing."

The words clicked in Water's memory and he blinked in surprise. Was it really her? If so, it explained exactly how she'd come to know about the disturbance in the cavern—and prevented others coming in her stead. Wary of disrupting Jeric's direction, he glanced to him, but Jeric bore a slight smile on his face.

"Princess Melora," he said, offering a mocking bow, "second daughter to the crown, and likely never to sit on the throne."

"My sister is a fool," she snapped. "She does not deserve to lead our people."

"And you do?" Jeric asked, sweeping his hands towards the mouth of the cave and the lake beyond. "You have betrayed your people, and secretly joined an Order that follows the darkest of purposes, to enslave the people you are oathbound to protect."

"My people are vile," she said. "They squander their freedoms in riotous living, and have forgotten the old ways."

Jeric sniffed, his expression lit with scorn. "And you don't understand the new. Your people are evolving, princess. What you despise, they view as happiness, and you would rob them of it."

"They cannot stop us," Melora sneered. "Even my mother has no understanding of our Order, or our might."

"Might?" Jeric scoffed. "Your paltry army below? You wouldn't last a day against an army of dwarves, let alone the rock trolls or humankind."

"The Order has members in every city, guild, and government. Captains in the army, princes, even a king. By now they know the krey are here, and they accept the gods the people have forsaken."

"You lie," Jeric said. "There could not be so many."

"More than the entire rock troll race," she boasted, "and we even have a handful among them."

Water recalled Bartoth's comments, and wondered if he was a member of the Order. The rock troll had displayed the same pride, the arrogance, as if he'd known a secret Water could not understand.

Jeric began to laugh at Princes Melora, his tone one of derision. Water glanced at Lira and found her expression amused, but neither spoke. Jeric seemed to poke and prod at Melora's pride, his words like a knife that nicked and cut, forcing her to turn and retaliate, each time providing another glimmer of truth.

"You are beautiful," Jeric said.

The sudden shift caused her to blink in surprise. "I don't . . . why would you . . ."

"Do your lovers know that your beauty hides a vile soul?"

Pink rose into her grey skin, and then her features contorted with anger. She lunged at Jeric. Water restrained the dark elf before she could

155

break her bonds but she fought against him, forcing Lira to catch her other arm.

"I'll kill you," Melora snarled.

"I guess they don't," Jeric said, amused. "And your family? Do any of them know your secret?"

Melora strained against them and refused to speak. But her silence only served to delight the elf, who leaned back and folded his arms, tapping his chin in thought. After a moment he nodded as if he knew the truth.

"Do you crave death?"

"Of course not," she said with a snort. "I'm just—"

"But you support Wylyn," Jeric reasoned. "And she wants to destroy what Ero and Skorn created."

"Your thoughts are meaningless to a member of the ancient race," she said. "And I look forward to the day you kneel before her. When that day comes I will be the one to cut out your heart."

"You're an insect," Jeric said, his tone mocking. "She would never tell *you* her plan."

"I know enough," Melora retorted.

"Like how she's building a Gate?" Jeric asked.

"It's only a matter of time until the tower is lifted again," she sneered. "Then you will discover your place."

"The krey seek dominance, and you wish to provide them with slaves."

"They *are* the dominant race," Melora growled, heat touching her cheeks. "They *deserve* their slaves."

"And the Order?" Jeric asked. "Will they not be slaves?"

"Never," she growled. "Wylyn has issued a decree and we accept. When the world is hers, we will command the slaves—we will command *you*."

Melora's chest heaved and her eyes spit fire at the impudent elf. Then Jeric stepped back and brushed off his sleeves as if he'd just completed a difficult labor, his smile becoming wry when he turned to Water and Lira.

"The Order has made a deal with Wylyn," he said. "They are to serve them, and believe the krey will accept them as slavemasters, servants to the new world order."

Melora flushed as if realizing how much she'd said. "I never said—
"

"The Order numbers over five thousand but less than ten," Jeric continued. "Her claim about them surpassing the rock trolls is an exaggeration, but based on what we saw, it is not too far off."

Melora sputtered, her eyes wide in disbelief and shock, the truth evident in her dismay. Water hid a smile and glanced to Lira, who seemed to have gained a measure of respect for the elf. But Jeric wasn't finished. He motioned to the ground at their feet.

"Her older sister probably doesn't realize Melora is part of the Order. Melora is too impulsive and quick to anger to be in command of the Order, but not resentful, meaning whoever is in command has a high rank or a great deal of power, someone she would respect."

"And the tower?" Lira asked.

"I cannot say," Jeric said, and Melora looked relieved for a moment. Then Jeric met her gaze. "But I wager she speaks of an ancient structure, and there cannot be many capable of rising."

"You know nothing," she snarled.

"You told me *everything*," Jeric said.

His smile practically dared retaliation, and she lunged at him, breaking free of Lira's grip and knocking Jeric to the cave floor. Melora struck at him with her bound fists, her fury only heightened by his

157

mocking laugh, causing her to scream even louder. Water and Lira hauled her off—but she pulled a knife from a sheath on Jeric's chest and sliced her bonds. She slashed at Lira before sprinting back into the tunnel. Water took a step after her but heard the whistle of a blade and raised his hands, catching the knife in his palm.

He winced and retreated, and when he looked again she was gone. Grunting in irritation, he yanked the knife from the wound, spilling blood down his sleeve. He turned back to Jeric. The elf stood and dusted himself off, his expression pleased.

"That was more fun than I anticipated," he exclaimed.

"You *let* her go," Water accused.

"Of course," he replied. "I did give her a promise."

Lira frowned. "You have a strange sense of honor."

Jeric smiled and reached out to accept the knife from Water. "Shall we?" he asked. "I suspect it's time we regrouped with Elenyr."

"You'd like that, wouldn't you," he said.

Jeric grinned and swept his hands wide. "Just because my interests are aligned with that of our purpose, does not mean I have nefarious intent."

Water snorted and called out to Light, who flitted to their side in an instant. "What would you have me do on such a fine day?" Light asked.

"It's time we part ways," Water said. "Light and Jeric can find Elenyr and inform her of what we've learned."

"You're not coming?" Light asked.

Water motioned to Lira. "Lira and I should return to Erathan and speak to King Numen about the Order."

"Do not forget that Melora said one of the kings is part of the order," Jeric said. "Perhaps even its leader."

"We can trust King Numen," Water said. "And hopefully, he will have some answers."

"Then this is farewell," Jeric said, clasping his hand.

Water looked to Light but he was already crafting a boat out of sunlight, the hull taking shape on the water. Obviously eager to depart, he clambered aboard and cast a sail of light, one that brightened and shimmered.

"Be cautious, Light," Water called, but the fragment had begun to sing, his voice so loud that it was impossible for him to hear Water's warning.

Jeric grinned. "I'll take care of him." He then inclined his head to Lira and jumped aboard. In moments the ship sped away, Light's laughter carrying across the surface of the lake. When it died Water abruptly felt shy, and swept his hand to Lira.

"Shall we?"

Her smile was faint. "We shall."

Suddenly conscious that he was now alone with his beautiful companion, Water reminded himself to keep his senses, and then followed her up the slope. Their foes were gathering, but right now the problem seemed distant, and Water only had eyes for Lira.

Chapter 21: The Strange Master

Lira pondered the ramifications of what they'd learned as they worked their way south. She'd come to Lumineia hoping to put an end to Wylyn quickly, but now the path to victory was murky and fraught with unseen foes.

Despite her worries, her heart was light, and she often found herself examining Water's profile. The more she knew, the more she was drawn to the fragment, and she frequently had to remind herself that when her assignment was complete, she would be leaving Lumineia.

A day's journey from Heth, the road curved down to the beach, where a long bridge connected the mainland to an island on Blue Lake. Backed by water to the horizon and just feet from the kingdom of Erathan, the island was not owned by Erathan. Rather, it contained a village outpost of the Azure people.

The thousand islands of the Azure nation dotted the center of the great Blue Lake, and the Azure people had called it home since the Dawn of Magic. Dark skinned and formidable on the water, they built ships for every kingdom, and were renowned as the greatest artisans of wood.

The village contained a shipyard, with four great vessels under construction. All bore the seal of Erathan, and Lira assumed the village did most of their work for King Numen, or the people of Erathan. As the sun set, the pair crossed the bridge and entered the village.

Instead of walls and a roof, huge tree trunks leaned against each other to create homes and halls, forming the supports for the structures that were all roof. Finely crafted shingles lined the roof all the way to the ground, broken only by recessed glass windows. A dozen such structures circled a giant gathering hall, the tavern becoming the meeting place of the village. The blacksmith, shipbuilder's hall, and farmer's hall ringed the main structure, all having their main doors pointed to the great center building. Finely carved wooden sea creatures adorned the outer wall, and great beams extended above to carry the flag of the Azure nation.

Legendary for their hospitality, the Azure people welcomed them through the gates, which were built of large poles that sank into the walls, the gears clanking to permit them entry. Soldiers smiled, and the chief himself met them at the gathering hall.

"I am Chief Barbith," he said, offering a bow. "Welcome to our village."

"You have beautiful homes," Lira said.

"Not as beautiful as our ships," Barbith said with a hearty laugh. "But then, little compares with the curves of a sleek vessel."

Barbith ushered them inside the gathering hall, calling for food and drink. The room was fifty feet across, the sharply angled walls ascending to the peak above. Other logs supported the second floor, the beams carved into runes and stories, the wood stained with a dark oil. A long counter fronted the kitchen while a set of stairs ascended out of view.

"Welcome to Fishhook Shipyard," Barbith said. "Will you be staying long?"

"I wish we could," Lira said, "but we must depart for Heth in the morning."

"Then please," the chief said, "enjoy our fare and the warm beds above. We make our coin from the ships, and have no need to charge the people that visit."

Barbith motioned to a young woman and she approached with a pair of keys. Lira accepted a key to her own room and nodded her gratitude to the giver, a girl that couldn't have been older than fourteen. Unlike the other barmaids, she wore pants instead of a dress, and carried both a bow and a curved sword on her hip.

"Are all Azure youths so well armed?" Lira asked.

161

The young woman shook her head and walked away. Seeing the exchange, Barbith approached and lowered his voice. "Rune lost her parents in a winter gale," he said. "Since then she cares naught for our craft and instead trains with the old weapons master, Sentara."

There was a note of disapproval in his sad tone, and Lira wondered how much was due to the girl's craft, or her disdain for the work of her people. Rune obviously disliked serving in the gathering hall, her expression one of stoic resignation as she carried drinks to the fishermen and families sitting about the hall.

Rune then appeared with plates of rice and fish fried in butter. Herbs had been added and the scent made Lira's mouth water. She'd sampled fare throughout the Krey Empire, but little compared with the flavors of home. She and Water expressed their gratitude and approval, but Rune simply left, drawing a sigh from Chief Barbith.

"The girl will be the death of me."

"How well does she fight?" Lira asked, her eyes on the way the girl moved. Lithe and graceful, she moved like a predator among the peaceful flock of villagers.

"I wouldn't know," Barbith said. "It has been some time since we have known combat, and I've never seen her train."

"You said there is a weapons master?" Water asked.

"Sentara," Barbith said absently. "But she is old and her mind is in shambles. I wish my grandfather had never taken her in."

"She is not of your tribe?" Lira asked.

The chief shook himself as if he'd just realized how much he'd spoken. "My apologies, I didn't mean to speak so frankly. Please, enjoy your evening."

He left them to their food, but when he was gone Water lowered his voice. "What do you see in the girl?"

Lira turned to him. "Do you feel the isolation?"

He frowned. "What do you mean?"

"We call it the Curse of the Ageless," she said. "We see the world turn but we do not turn with it, and so we feel alone."

"An uncomfortably familiar sentiment," Water said.

Lira looked to Rune. "It is easy to forget that many feel as we do."

"But she has a home," Water said, motioning to the room, "and family. Why would she feel alone?"

She flashed a sad smile. "Too often we hide our true self from those we call family, and live a life of loneliness."

"And what do you hide from the Eternals?" His smile was soft, a quiet challenge to the share the truth.

"I've known you for a month and you wish me to reveal my deepest secrets?"

"You're right," he said with a firm nod. "I'm a day early. You can tell me tomorrow."

She laughed and settled in to eat. As they talked and ate the delicious fish, Lira found her resolve weakening. Water may have been a being of magic, a fragment of a powerful guardian, but he had a soul, one she found attractive. He had an appealing sense of humor, and his sense of honor was without peer.

Shortly after they finished, a bard made his way to the fireplace situated at the rear of the hall and began to sing. Gifted with the magic of music, the man sang with an inviting quality, and Lira was drawn into the tale of battle and love, of a warrior departing from home to join a crusade.

The song rose and fell, becoming a crescendo that gradually filled the room with images of mighty war steeds charging a battlefield. The cavalry rode through the room, leaping a table to the delight of the children huddled beneath. Lira knew it was all an illusion created by the magic of song, yet could not deny the stirring of excitement.

The horses galloped through the far wall and the song changed, gaining a mournful note as a lone soldier returned, his weary horse carrying him over mountains and through valleys. He boarded a ship and stood at the prow, his gaze fixed on the horizon. Rain fell, so realistic it seemed to patter across the tables before the sun shone again, and a house rose up in the center of the gathering hall, the golden walls rising to fill an empty section of floor. Fireflies appeared to flutter around the room, glimmering in a room suddenly growing dark.

The soldier approached the door and it was flung open, his wife and children leaping into his arms. The song swelled and Lira realized tears were in her eyes, the scene so moving that she instinctively reached for Water. Their hands intertwined, and suddenly the hope was not an illusion.

The soldier entered his home, a triumphant arrival accompanied by friends and family, the song becoming an invitation, a challenge that couples in the gathering hall accepted. They leapt through the illusion and began to dance, spinning as the bard sang of a life shared with a love.

"Would you care to dance?" Water asked.

She turned to find him on his feet and shook her head. "I haven't danced in ages."

"Then it's overdue," Water said.

He caught her hand and pulled her to the floor, spinning her into an embrace. The music swelled anew and she was caught up in the enchantment. A part of her knew the moment was just an illusion, but not all of it, and as she looked into his deep blue eyes she marveled at the heat in her chest.

A burst of thunder echoed but the storm sounded distant, and she smiled, feeling a sense of home she had not felt since her youth. She wrapped her arms around Water's neck and drew him close, a smile on her lips . . .

The door crashed open, startling the bard. His song faltered and the illusions evaporated, all eyes snapping to the figure standing in the opening. The storm had arrived and rain poured on her form, but she didn't seem to care. Slight of figure, she looked ancient, her white hair tied back and layered down her back. The old woman glared at the room, her eyes searching, hunting.

"Sentara?" Rune called, threading through the crowd to reach her. "Is something amiss?"

"There are guests," she demanded, stepping into the hall, oblivious to the pained looks exchanged by the villagers.

"Sentara," Chief Barbith said, stepping to her side, his voice conciliatory. "There is no need for such hostility."

"Where are they?" she demanded.

"Here," Water said, striding forward with Lira. "Do you need—"

The woman spotted Lira and raised a hand to Water. She crossed the gap inhumanly fast, a sword appearing in her hand. Lira instinctively cast an air blade but Sentara's weapon was already on her throat.

"Sentara!" the chief cried. "You cannot think to attack a guest!"

"You do not know who she is," Sentara growled.

"I'm merely a traveler," Lira said, subtly casting speed.

Sentara closed the distance so fast that Lira flinched. "I know who you are," she spat, and then lowered her tone. "You are an *Eternal*."

Shock bound her tongue, and Sentara took her silence as a confirmation. Water stepped to intervene, but she threw him a look that stopped him in his tracks. Then Sentara leaned forward and whispered to Lira.

"Do not be so quick to ally yourself with Elenyr," she said, her voice a harsh murmur that only Lira could hear. "For a dark power lurks in the fragments, and they cannot be trusted."

"How do you know of . . ."

But the woman was already gone. Whirling, she strode from the room and departed into the night. Rune cast a look to Lira before the girl departed as well, leaving Lira to her confusion. The chief approached and spoke with Water, but Lira watched the door, wondering about the identity of the mysterious woman.

Chapter 22: King Numen

The next morning, Water met Lira in the tavern for a morning meal. Throughout the breakfast of bread and fish eggs, an odd combination that Water did not care for, they spoke of Sentara. Lira had shared with him what Sentara had said, and he'd admitted he'd never seen the woman.

"You really don't know her?" Lira asked.

"I don't," Water said. "But from what you say, I would wager she knows Elenyr."

Their speculation yielded no truth, and shortly after, they departed Fishhook for the road. Water half expected the ancient woman to attack them, but neither she nor Rune appeared. Once they had returned to the road, the conversation turned to what they hoped to learn from the king, and Water tried not to think about how they'd almost kissed the previous night.

"Will the king see us?" she asked.

Water nodded. "He's a friend, as was his father. We helped quell an insurrection from a group of mercenaries three decades ago. King Numen was just a boy at the time, but he bore witness to the battle."

"What happened?" she asked.

"A group from the outer villages demanded lower taxes," Water said. "The king refused, but offered to let the leaders of the group examine the kingdom's records, so they could see for themselves that the taxes were needed."

"A generous offer," she said.

"Indeed," Water said. "We were asked to be present for the negotiations. Unfortunately, a cousin to the king had backed the group, and used the negotiation to attempt to kill the king, and his son. Fire and I stopped the attack, but the battle left dozens dead. We saved King Numen's life."

"Which explains why he's a friend."

At her request, he continued to share tales of his assignments for Elenyr until they crested a rise to see the city. Coming from the north, the river split to either side, feeding the two waterfalls that flanked the city. Heth sprawled across the flat section of rock between the two rivers.

The road descended from the forest and across the plateau, connecting to a bridge that spanned the eastern river. The sun was high over the Giant's shelf and the golden light filtered into the city. The city was newer than the other capitols, its buildings lacking the refinements of other cities. Most of the roads were just the bare stone of the cliff, while the structures were fashioned from brick and mortar.

When they'd entered Heth to meet with Jeric, the sun had been setting, the growing darkness an invitation for those that craved anonymity. This time, he and Lira entered the city in the early morning, and the crowds were largely absent. Those still present stumbled about, their eyes faded, jugs of hard ale in their hands. Trash lay strewn in the streets, and a handful of harried soldiers sought to clean the mess.

The surface of the cliff was barren, but many trees had been planted, their limbs young and failing to provide shade against the mounting heat. Water led the way to the throughway that pointed to the river's junction.

The castle was not overly large, it's walls built of wood supported by stone. What it lacked in strength it made up for in beauty, the wood carved and burned with fire to depict past kings in battle. The contrast to the state of the city was striking.

Lira frowned in disapproval. "The king lives in splendor, while the people live in squalor."

"This is actually better than it was," Water said. "King Numen has loosened the heavy taxes his father levied, and uses what he cans to

167

improve the city. In time, he hopes to make Heth as beautiful as Herosian or Ilumidora."

They reached the gate and the guard sent a messenger to the king. Shortly after, they were permitted inside the gardens. Lush and vibrant, the greenery surrounded the courtyard, the walls of which held banners of the king, a storm over a rising sword. To Water's surprise, King Numen met them outside.

"River!" he exclaimed, using the persona Water had been using for the last two decades. "To what do I owe the unexpected visit?"

"Your majesty," Water said, "I hope you are in good health."

"I am," he said, clapping Water on the shoulder. Then he caught sight of Lira. "And who is this vision of beauty?"

"A friend," Water said. "She is accompanying me on my current assignment."

"Come," King Numen said. "We should speak inside." The king paused and handed a sealed envelope to a messenger. "See that it's delivered within the hour." Then he motioned Water to follow.

Dressed in a regal purple cloak and fine linens, King Numen looked every bit the ruler. His dark hair had just begun to silver above the temples, while his dark eyes lit with amusement. His smile came often and easy, gaining him the name "The Charismatic King." He was also built like a soldier, his body lean and powerful. He frequently carried a sword and trained with his guard, a fact that endeared him to his people.

"You must be hungry from your journey," he said. "My servants have leftover roast boar that we could sneak from the kitchen." He winked slyly.

"No," Water said. "Unfortunately we have come on a grave matter. May we speak in private?"

"Of course," he said.

The king turned down a side corridor and descended a turret to reach the bottom level of the fortress. Then he led them down a short corridor to a door flanked by two guards. The other side of the hall had windows that overlooked a courtyard. Passing them by, he stepped into the room and aside, smiling as he motioned to his office.

"I hope you enjoy the view."

Water's eyes widened. Although underground, the room had windows that overlooked the city. The sun rose in the east, the light cascading on the vast forest below. It felt like they were a hundred feet off the ground, sitting in the highest turret of the castle.

"We're not in a turret," Water said. "How is this possible?"

"Man may be known for being clever, but elven magic is always inventive." King Numen nodded in satisfaction. "They planted a tree in the turret above, and threaded roots all the way to here. It allows me to be more protected without losing the view. You can even see the guards outside my office."

He pointed to a window in the side of the keep, through which Water spotted the two guards they'd seen outside. One fidgeted, scratching his backside before straightening, the motion noticed by his companion, who frowned. King Numen chuckled.

"Even knowing about my window, they still forget I can see them."

The king made his way to the circle of chairs set beside the hearth at the back. All were carved by hand and bore the mark of the kingdom, the symbol the same as the banner. He settled into his chair and motioned to them.

"I do hope you have a tale for me."

Water exchanged a look with Lira. "What do you know of the Order of Ancients?" he asked.

"A harmless group of discontents," the king, said, waving his hand.

"They attacked us in the Deep six days past," Water exclaimed. "They had legion strength."

The king frowned. "That's not possible."

"We were forced to flee."

169

King Numen shook his head, gesturing to Water. "You and your companions are powerful—beyond powerful. How many could rival your might?"

"The Order is real," Water said, leaning in. "And they are working with the krey."

The king gestured in dismissal. "I heard rumors that the krey had returned."

"Rumors based in truth," Water said. "I've seen them with my own eyes."

The king's amusement faded as he regarded Water. Then his features turned serious. "If what you say is true, then we are in danger, for the Order has been preparing for the return of the ancients since the Dawn of Magic."

"How have they not been discovered?"

The king's brow was furrowed in thought. "Their members are supposedly scattered across every race and station, with many in the noble houses. There's even rumors that a king was once involved." He jerked his head and swept his hand to them. "And you think they are searching for the krey?"

"Worse," Water said. "We think they are already allied."

"How many members are in the Order?" Lira asked.

"Dozens? Thousands?" The king shook his head. "No one knows. What I can tell you is that if they exist, they have been preparing for thousands of years for this moment. They probably already know every threat that can stop them."

"You think they know who I am?" Water asked.

"You said they attacked you," the king said wryly. "And they were prepared for your power."

Water leaned back in his seat, struck by that idea. He'd assumed the Order had found them at the underground lake at Wylyn's request, but what if they had already been hunting the fragments?

He had the image of thousands of men and women going about their daily business, their secret signs given only to each other, their meeting held without the knowledge of kings or guilds. They knew the enemies of the krey, and the krey had come. The Order had risen to claim the krey as their rulers, and the fragments were all being hunted. He grimaced, wondering if it was just his imagination, or if there was truth to that idea. He resisted the urge to look over his shoulder, but the feeling of being watched would not be so easily shaken.

The king rubbed the goatee on his chin. "What do the krey want?"

Hesitant to reveal the truth, even to a friend, Water said, "We are still uncertain."

The king leaned against the hearth. "Last night a village was attacked by what the people claimed to be strange rock trolls. A survivor reached the city this morning, claiming one of the attackers was a krey."

"Where?" Lira asked.

"Southern Erathan," he said. "Close to the coast."

"What did they want?" Water asked.

"They wanted a location of a mine in the dwarven kingdom," the king said. "What is most disturbing is that the city had a dwarven blacksmith, and the dwarf had recently returned from visiting his kingdom. It was almost as if the outlanders knew the dwarf possessed the knowledge they sought. One among the rock trolls was reportedly a strange looking human with purple eyes."

Water exchanged a look with Lira and knew she was thinking the same thing. It seemed the Order was helping Wylyn find Serak, while Wylyn's son was searching for the material to rebuild a Gate.

Water rose to his feet. "We should go to the village. Perhaps we can pick up the trail there."

"I sent a contingent of guards to return with the villagers," the king said. "If you wish to speak to the survivors, I'd suggest you talk to a woman named Grena. She seemed to know the most, but she insisted on returning to her home. You'll have to find her there."

171

"We will," Water said. "And thank you."

He clasped the king's hand, and the man nodded. "Send word when you discover the truth. If the krey are truly returning, my kingdom will stand with you."

"Your bravery is admirable," Lira said, inclining her head in respect. "But let us hope it does not come to that."

"Ero be with us," the king said.

Water managed to hide a smile and stepped around the chair. He stepped to the door and glanced to the window, expecting to see himself step out of the door. But his hand froze halfway through turning the handle. Through the enchanted window he could see the exterior of the door he was about to exit.

"Where are your guards?" he asked.

King Numen looked up, his eyes falling on the window. He frowned and strode to the edge of the room to peer at the exterior of the office. He shook his head in confusion and looked to Water, his eyes lacking the usual smile.

"They would not willingly leave their posts."

Lira leaned in and pointed. "That's blood on the wall."

Water spotted the splash of red and realized the men outside were likely dead, the attackers just waiting for them to emerge before striking. They would not wait forever, and if they could strike the king in his own castle, they had planned with care.

"Who would attack you here?" he asked.

"I have no threats of such magnitude," Numen said.

"The Assassin's Guild?" Water asked.

King Numen shook his head. "I've spoken to Guildmaster Loralyn recently, and she would not accept a contract on my life."

"Then who has come for you?" Lira asked.

"Perhaps they are here for you," King Numen said. "You came asking questions about a powerful organization. It's possible they do not want to be discovered."

A flicker of movement at the edge of the window drew Water's eyes, and he spotted a figure dressed as a guard stride into view. He took up position next to the door while a moment later another stood on the opposite side of the door. But they were not the same guards as before, and they betrayed a nervous air.

King Numen growled and reached for the sword hanging from his belt. "Make sure to leave one alive. I want answers."

"Wait," Water said, raising a hand to stop the king from stepping into the ambush. "Let me go first. If they strike at me, we know they are here for us. If they do not, I will pass beyond them and . . ."

"*No,*" King Numen said, his eyes widening with horror. "They aren't here for you."

"How can you tell?" Water asked.

King Numen pointed to another spot of the keep, also visible through the window, where two men dressed as guards were wrestling with a girl. Bound and gagged, the girl fought like a lion, but the guards dragged her from the chamber.

"They have my daughter," King Numen said.

Without another word, he leaped to the door and wrenched it open.

Chapter 23: The Dark Dwarf

The king dived through the door, leading with his sword. The false soldiers were ready, but not for an enraged father. Numen parried the expected strike, lifting the sword and ducking under to avoid the second sword. Then he turned and leveled a crushing blow with his free hand, sending one to the floor. Twisting, he knocked the second sword high before charging, slamming the man into the wall. As he groaned and crumpled, Numen leapt down the hall.

Other soldiers appeared and filled the end of the hallway. Water stepped into the open and sprinted after the king, passing the two groaning men on the floor. Lira caught up and ran at his side.

"They are all in guard uniforms," she said. "How do we know which is against us?"

"If they try to kill you," Water said, "they're probably against us."

Lira grinned and they accelerated to catch the king. Ten feet from the line of soldiers, a dwarf stepped into the open and leaned down. With a gauntlet of bright steel, he struck the floor—cracking the floor of the corridor from end to end.

The floor split open, the two sides of the floor parting. Water jumped to the side but the floor receded, and all three of them fell into the chamber beneath, which proved to be a prison cell.

Water alighted on his feet but the king landed hard, crying out as he twisted his ankle. Lira landed at his side, all three looking up as the floor sealed above them, the thick stone closing and healing like a wound.

"Where are we?" Water asked.

"Prisoners brought to see the king are kept here," the king said, his face a mask of pain, anger, and fear. "The walls and doors are reinforced with enchantments. Get me up. I need to find my daughter."

"Why would they take her?" Lira asked.

"I don't know," he said, rising and limping to the door. "But the men outside my office door did not strike to kill. Their blows were meant to incapacitate."

"So they want you as well," Water said.

Water joined him at the door. The prison cell was like any other, a box with no windows that contained a bed and a privy. The door was wood overlaid with iron, with only a tiny window allowing visibility into the hall. The thudding of footfalls echoed, but Water guessed they would be foes. The dwarf had dropped them into the cell on purpose, likely to place the king in a contained area, out of sight.

"We need to get out of here," Water said.

"The door is barred," the king said, slamming his hand against the door in futility, his face red with anger and fear.

"Allow me," Lira said.

She stepped to the door and cast a spike of air. The charm fit around her hand like a pointed gauntlet, the air hardening into a blade. Then she cast strength and reared back, slamming the weapon into the door.

Wood snapped and sparks burst from broken enchantments, and the door cracked down the center. Lira leaned back and struck again, blasting the door into shards of wood and broken metal. Sparks and tongues of flame passed around the opening as enchantments died.

Water stared in awe. The dust settled around Lira as she dismissed the gauntlet, the swirls of air tugging at her hair. Then she noticed Water's expression and raised an eyebrow. Realizing he was staring, Water managed to find his voice.

"If I ever go to prison, I want you at my side."

175

She snorted in amusement and led the way through. As the smoke cleared soldiers appeared at the north end of the corridor, presumably the only way out. Other cells lined the space, all locked, the silence from within suggesting they were empty.

"Stay here," Water said to the king. "We'll handle the guards."

King Numen cursed and tried to shove his way past them. "I'm not leaving my daughter."

Water reached out and restrained him. "We'll get your daughter, but you are injured, and we cannot stay with you."

An order was barked and the group of attackers charged. King Numen scowled at his choice and his voice gaining a desperate edge. "Don't let them take her."

"We won't," Water replied.

Water started forward, drawing on the moisture in the air to shape an aquaglass staff. The transparent weapon hardened into a blade as fine as dwarven steel, and he used it to point upward.

"You take the high route," he said.

"Done," Lira said.

She cast a line of air stones and surged up them, the last two attaching to her feet and swinging her upside down. Water charged the soldiers beneath her, ducking a swinging sword and slicing through the man's armor. He cried out and fell, but Water was already beyond him. He slapped a sword away and slammed his fist into the woman's stomach, knocking her into the wall.

The falsely clad soldiers struggled to defend themselves against Lira's sword above and Water's staff beneath. Some parried Lira, leaving an opening for Water. Others chose to engage Water, allowing Lira to strike from above. She plunged her sword into their necks as she soared above them.

In perfect unison, Water and Lira charged down the corridor, leaving dead and wounded on the floor. Nearing the end, a man raised a spear and sought to stab Lira, but she caught the end of the shaft and dropped to the ground. Casting strength, she lifted the man off the ground and slammed him into his companions. Then she cast speed and leapt into their midst.

They cried out in fear, her blade cutting them apart before they could retaliate. Water leapt to the wall, bonding the soles of his boots to the stone with a brief burst of ice. From there he swung around the raging battle to reach the two captains at the back. Both snarled and reached toward Water, but he parried a blade high and stepped between them.

The woman on the right reared back with a sneer, and drove her sword into Water's chest—but Water morphed his body to liquid. The blade passed through him and stabbed the woman's companion. The impaled man stared in shock at the sword passing through Water's body and piercing his own.

"What *are* you?" the woman in front of Water cried, her eyes wide with horror.

Water stepped forward, sliding the blade through what would have been his heart if he was still flesh. The woman yanked her sword free and retreated, desperately swinging her sword again, the blade splashing through Water's elemental form.

"Who are you?" Water demanded. "Why do you seek the king?"

The woman stumbled on the stairs, her fear mounting. "I don't know . . ."

Water stepped forward and leaned down. "I am an elemental lord, and even the water in your body will answer my will."

He reached forth his hand as if he would pull the blood from her flesh and she panicked. "The Order wants the king because—"

A dagger spun past Water and plunged into the woman's chest. Her eyes widened in shock, and then dimmed in death. Water spun to see a new group of the enemy at the other end of the corridor. They held an unconscious King Numen as they dragged him into a cell.

"Lira!" Water shouted.

She looked up, briefly registering surprise at Water standing with a sword through his body, and then spun. She dropped the last of her adversaries and then charged, but the dwarf stepped out of the cell and raised his fists. The floor answered his summons, rising into a wall that blocked the whole corridor.

Water grasped the sword in his chest and ripped it free, and then morphed to flesh. Sprinting the length of the corridor, he reached the wall just as Lira cast her spiked gauntlet again, the blow shattering the barrier and allowing them past.

They reached the last cell and darted inside, only to watch helplessly as the hole in the ceiling sealed anew, closing off the image of the sneering dwarf and the unconscious king being dragged off.

Water grimaced and turned away. "We need to get up there before the king disappears."

"Was that a sword through your body?" Lira asked as they sprinted back down the corridor and leapt over the fallen dead. "How are you unharmed?"

"All the fragments except Mind can turn into an elemental form," Water said. "In such a state we can only be harmed by an opposing magic."

"Did the woman speak of the Order?"

Water sprinted up the steps and through the open doorway, stepping into the courtyard. "Apparently we are not their only foes."

He didn't like the deeper implications of the kidnapping. The king was an ally, and taking a sitting monarch would throw the region into turmoil, especially Erathan. But why? What did the Order have to gain from such a public action?

They raced across the courtyard and out the front gates, diving into a full battle. Soldier fought soldier, confused captains barking orders. Unable to discern friend from foe, Water reached for the stream flowing through the garden, and the creek burst from its banks, rising into a wave that knocked soldiers to the ground. The wave split around Water and Lira, and wherever it went, the figures were left bound and struggling in the puddles left behind.

"Let them sort it out," Water said, spotting the dwarf dragging the king out the front gates and into the street.

He and Lira raced after, following the dwarf and his companions through alleys and side streets. Just as they closed the gap, they reached the eastern branch of the river. Water turned a corner around a warehouse and spotted the king being loaded into an aquaglass boat. His daughter was at his side. She spotted them and began to struggle, but a woman put a knife to her throat and she went still. Her terrified eyes locked on Water and he charged the river.

The elf at the helm of the ship spotted them and reached to the river. The river flowed up and over, sealing the edge of the aquaglass boat. The ship pulled into the current and sped away as Water and Lira reached the bank. Water skidded to a halt and reached for the ship, and it lurched to a standstill, the water passing around it, forming an eddy.

"Can't hold it for long," Water said, gritting his teeth. "Not with that elf driving the current."

"I'll get to the ship," Lira said.

She stepped onto an air stone and sprinted away from the shore—but a shadow passed over Water and he glanced back—to see the dwarf stepping into view. The stone on the bank rose up around him, covering him in a goliath charm. When it hardened, he was the size of a rock troll, and a giant hammer grew out of his hand.

"Lira!" Water shouted.

She reversed and darted back, raising her sword to block the stone hammer. Her strength stopped the blow, but the dwarf expertly spun, his feet making the ground shudder as he attacked from the opposite side.

Water ducked the hammer, but the dwarf had cast a second hammer, this one rising from the ground. The first was blocked by Lira, the second landed on Water's side. The blow knocked him sprawling, shattering his attempt to hold the ship. The vessel leapt way and dropped into the river, disappearing from sight. The dwarf raced along the bank and leapt into the water, the river swallowing him from sight.

Water's vision cleared to see Lira kneeling at his side, his blood on her hands. A look of relief passed over her face and she helped him rise. He groaned, but managed to regain his feet, his eyes searching the river.

"Are you well?" she asked.

"They were prepared for us," Water said, holding his side as he growled. "They were prepared for *me*."

He looked to the end of the river, but the ship was gone. Even with him and Lira present, the Order had kidnapped a king, and already the cries went up from the city. Water grimaced in pain, wondering how the Order was staying ahead of them, the emotion quickly followed by anger and regret. He'd failed to protect King Numen, and now the king's family was in the hands of the Order.

Chapter 24: Stormwall

Elenyr dismounted her horse and patted its flank. The stable boy accepted the reins and guided the mount into the stables, while another accepted the steeds from Fire and Mind. Fire turned away and rubbed his backside.

"I hate horses," he said.

"How can you hate horses?" Mind asked.

"I can create a horse out of fire," he grumbled. "One that doesn't leave me hurting."

Elenyr hid a smile at Fire's discomfort. "People tend to notice when you ride a fire steed," she said. "And it's attention we do not need, especially now."

Fire grunted in annoyance and stretched. "I still prefer my own mount."

"I prefer a fire mount as well," Mind said, "but it doesn't mean I can't appreciate a fine horse."

They'd reached Stormwall three days after departing Herosian, arriving as the sun set. Exiting the stables, they entered the packed streets and worked their way toward the sea shore, their passage slowed by the crowd.

Stormwall sat on the southern edge of Blue Lake, the city shaped like a crescent moon, wrapping around a small cove. The city was new but growing quickly, showing additional taverns, inns, and meal halls since Elenyr's last visit. Stormwall had few permanent residents, most of them warriors that trained with the mercenary guild that owned the arena.

Tens of thousands flocked to the city for the yearly games, the inns and taverns now swollen with guests. The rest of the year the city was host to many soldiers, warriors, and hunters that came to train with the Bladed, the legendary warriors that owned Stormwall. Soldiers from throughout the kingdoms came to learn from the Bladed, while others came hoping to join their illustrious ranks, a challenge made difficult by their number.

The Bladed were comprised of exactly one hundred, each assigned a number that corresponded to their rank. Dressed in dark blue uniforms with a splash of silver on the shoulder, the Bladed displayed their number above their heart, and Elenyr spotted 67 speaking to a crowd outside an inn.

The behemoth barbarian towered over the woman fawning over him, a sight that made Fire sniff in disdain. "Mind is a greater swordsman than any of them."

Mind almost smiled and shook his head. "I've had quite a bit more time to master swordcraft," he said, and then glanced to Elenyr. "And I've been trained by the best."

Elenyr privately approved him for his modesty. Mind had been training with a sword for five thousand years, and his skill was without peer. Still, the men and women in the Bladed were legendary for a reason.

A swell of noise came from the arena, the shouts indicating the end of a conflict. Merchants on both sides of the streets called out their wares, their merchandise adding a savory scent to the scene. Children raced about, while entertainers of every type sought to garner attention. Elenyr spotted a dwarf that she and Water had seen on their journey back from the north, his coin-operated machines drawing many of the youths.

Elenyr passed through a gap and reached the gates to the arena. Bordered by squat turrets that doubled as homes for the Bladed, the gates were open, allowing spectators to stream through. Elenyr paid their entrance fee, a meager four coppers each, and then walked to the back of the benches.

A high wall surrounded the cove, the barrier manned by those apprenticing with the Bladed. The Bladed didn't perform regular guard duties, and they walked among the spectators, or helped prepare the warriors attempting to fight in the arena.

The stands themselves were fashioned of rough wood and stone, some sections sporting a roof and cushioned seats. All were full, and Elenyr had to ascend a few steps to get a view of the arena.

An island of aquaglass floated on the still surface of the cove, the transparent surface scarred from thousands of duels and battles. Benches and raised stands lined the shore, allowing the spectators to witness the events.

On the opposite side of the cove, waves lapped through the gap in the shore, a short channel of water leading to Blue Lake. A large wall formed a barrier to east and west, preventing the waves of frequent storms from entering the arena.

The arena floor itself floated on the center of the cove, and was large enough for a dozen warriors to battle. Two bridges allowed combatants to enter. The strict rules of combat usually prevented death, but injuries were common. Elenyr looked to the top of the arena wall, where a series of ornate huts overlooked the stands, providing a premium view of the duel.

She spotted the one reserved for the royals of Talinor, but it was empty, causing her to frown. The king was supposed to be there, so why was he not watching the arena? She turned to Mind and he nodded.

"I'll see what I can learn."

With Mind's memory magic, he was the most adept of the fragments at getting answers. Often he had not even needed to ask a question, and merely had to listen to the thoughts of guards to find the truth.

"I'm not familiar with those two," Fire said, motioning to the current duel.

Two pairs of warriors battled on the arena, and they couldn't have been more different. One side had two dwarves, both armored and

183

bearing giant axes. Their foes were thin—an elf and a mage—both covered head to toe in bright, enchanted cloaks that shimmered in the light.

The elf had two aquaglass swords, while the mage carried a shield of light attached to a chain. As Elenyr watched, the mage hurled the shield at one of the dwarves, the weapon striking his chest plate and driving him backward. The mage yanked on the chain and the shield spun back into his hand, a burst of laughter escaping his lips.

The swell of noise from the crowd made it clear the dwarven brothers were favorites, but the two odd warriors were quickly gaining a following. The elf with the blades darted in, evading the dwarven axe with ease, and landed a dozen blows on the dwarf's armor, the ringing matching the music played by a renowned bard. Laughter erupted among the crowd, contrasting with the scowling of the dwarves.

The two dwarves charged, fire spilling off their axes as they sought to trap the elf and the mage on the edge of the arena. Both the mage and the elf were laughing, the sound coming from their cowled features. The mage leapt into a high flip, sailing over the dwarf, his cloak billowing behind him. Then he spun and hurled his shield, knocking the dwarf sprawling.

"They look familiar," Elenyr said.

"They sound familiar," Fire added.

The second dwarf had trapped the elf at the edge of the arena, and sought to drive him into the water. With four bodies at the edge, the arena began to tip, the enchantments lifting the opposite side out of the water. The elf slid backward, eliciting a groan from the audience. If he fell in, he would not be permitted to re-enter the arena.

Then the elf leapt forward, kicking off the dwarf's helmet and flipping over his head. He called out to the mage and the mage cast a ball of light the size of a wagon. It fell onto the arena, echoing as it struck the edge, tilting the already tipping arena ground. Teetering at the edge, the dwarf was bounced into the water, his shout ending as he went under. The second one desperately spun his arms and balanced on the edge, but the elf advanced and poked him in the chest, sending him over.

The sphere of light faded and the arena righted itself, and the First Blade, a rock troll named Mox, strode out onto the platform. The large warrior carried an enormous axe on his back, the tattoos across his torso, arms, and face a fearsome list of all his kills. But his smile was broad as he gestured to the victors.

"A most interesting victory by the Beacons of Light," he said, his voice booming over the cheers. "The Bearded Brothers are eliminated."

The dwarves glowered as they waded out of the cove, their armor dripping wet, their flaming weapons sodden. The Beacons of Light danced about, cavorting in their victory. Elenyr frowned as she watched the mage move, almost too fast for man or elf . . .

"No," she breathed, recognizing his motions.

Fire began to chuckle. "Is that . . .?"

Mox motioned to them and they removed their cowls, revealing Jeric and Light. Jeric was obviously well known, and his appearance elicited a swell of noise, men shouting in praise, women calling his name, waving to gain his attention.

"What are they doing here?" Fire asked.

"They should be with Water," Elenyr said, annoyed that Jeric was here, annoyed that Light was with him, bus mostly annoyed at the surge of attraction. To her extreme annoyance, Jeric spotted her and smiled.

The elf bowed deeply, and Elenyr scowled. Fire glanced her way and raised an eyebrow. "You can't avoid him forever."

"I can if he's dead."

"What even happened between you two?" Fire asked. "I thought you were in—"

"Don't say it," she said. "The man is an insect."

"That's not what you used to say."

She glanced his way and found Fire struggling not to laugh. Then Light spotted Elenyr and his face lit up. Abandoning the arena, he

185

sprinted to the edge and leapt twenty feet to the shore, eliciting shouts of praise from the crowd. Light didn't notice the noise, and wove through the crowd to reach Elenyr.

"We hoped to find you in Herosian!" He jumped about, his evident excitement unable to be constrained.

"Care to explain why you're in the arena?" Elenyr asked, folding her arms.

Light's expression turned guilty. "Jeric said we had enough time for a quick match, and you know how much I like to duel."

"It's true," Fire supplied. "He does."

"And you listened to Jeric?" Elenyr ignored Fire.

"His argument was very persuasive," Light said.

"I'm sure it was," Elenyr sniffed.

Jeric stepped into view and clapped Light on the back. "He's built for combat. He deserves a chance to prove it."

"Jeric," Elenyr managed to convey all the scorn and disdain into the single word.

"Elenyr," he said, unperturbed. "It's been a few decades."

"Not long enough," she said.

"I think you need some time together," Fire said. "Light? Let's find Mind."

Elenyr jerked her head. "You should stay."

"No," Fire said, a laugh on his lips. "I think we should go."

"Why?" Light asked quizzically. "They just got here, and there's a lot we need to tell them."

"You can tell me on the way to getting a roast turkey leg," Fire said.

"Really?"

Elenyr's protests were ignored and the two fragments left for the cooking fires. She watched them go, her irritation mounting. Then she spun and walked away. Undeterred by her dismissal, Jeric jumped to catch up.

"We have much to discuss."

"I'd rather hear it from Light."

"Elenyr."

The softness to his voice caused her to turn, and for the first time his expression was serious. She regarded him for several moments, the people gliding around them, the crowd ignoring the apparent tension.

"I'm sorry," Jeric said.

Elenyr held his gaze, but saw a different city, an inn where she'd waited. Four days she'd sat alone. Then she'd gathered her things and departed, leaving her heart behind. She shook her head to Jeric.

"I'm sorry too," she said.

"Elenyr," he said. "I don't want us to end like this."

"Why?" she said. "Why does it matter now?"

His features reflected an inner conflict and then he grimaced. "Because I'm dying."

Chapter 25: Beacons of Light

Elenyr's thoughts spun, her emotions in turmoil. Guilt came first, a burst that faded into anger. It had been forty years since he'd failed to appear, and he'd wasted all that time. Last was sorrow, a bitter emotion as she realized she was going to lose him.

"How?" she asked.

"The healers couldn't say," Jeric said with a shrug.

"How much time do you have?"

"A few months, or years." He flashed a faint smile, his eyes sparkling with amusement.

Her eyes narrowed. "You're not really dying," she accused.

"I am," he said, indignant. "Every day, I lose a day of my life. No telling how soon the end will come."

She raised a hand to strike at him, the surge of anger surprising, and not helped by his laughter. She wondered how she'd ever thought him amusing, and imagined dropping into the earth in front him, leaving him staring at where she'd disappeared.

"I shouldn't be surprised at your lying," she said. "You're very good at manipulation." She turned and strode away, forcing him to catch up.

"Come now," he said, laughing. "I said I'm dying, which I am. I'm nearly nine hundred years old, even if I have the good looks of my second century."

She glared at him, annoyed that he did speak the truth. "If you helped the fragments, then I no longer need you. I am just here to meet with the king."

"The king won't be back until tonight," he said, too quickly.

Elenyr turned on him. "You knew we were coming here," she accused.

"Guilty," he said. "Light said you were going to Herosian to meet with the king, and I knew he was going to be in Stormwall. Since you had yet to arrive, I convinced Light to enter the arena."

"You shouldn't have manipulated him." Elenyr frowned in disapproval. "He could have killed those dwarves."

"He's just a kid," Jeric said.

"He's five thousand years old," Elenyr said.

"Still a kid," Jeric replied. "And he *loves* to play."

"True," Elenyr admitted.

"I miss the fragments," he said. "How are they doing?"

"They mature slower than normal men," she said, "and yet I still find myself unprepared for them to be on their own."

Elenyr wanted to ignore him but the words came out. She wondered if his skill at getting people to talk had been innate, or gained through his travels. Most elves preferred to stay in the elven forests, but Jeric had a craving for adventure that would not be satiated.

There had been a time that she'd enjoyed that sense of adventure, and the memories were tinged with fondness. She'd traveled with him numerous times, their bond growing with every conflict, until she'd fallen in love.

She looked away, abruptly aware of their position in the middle of the crowd. They stood close to the entrance doors of the arena, and she spotted Fire and Light at the cooking fires, purchasing roast meat and dwarven fire ale. The next arena event had begun and shouts filled the benches. She sighed, and resigned herself to his presence.

"What news do you have to share?" she asked, walking towards an alcove in the wall where they would have a semblance of privacy.

189

Jeric outlined the events in Erathan, the Gate Chamber, and the battle at the underground lake, and Elenyr listened with growing concern. She'd known the Order existed, but never imagined it had united to such a degree, or gained such a foothold. But who was their master?

"Water and Lira are probably meeting with King Numen as we speak," he said. "Or perhaps they are kissing in an alley somewhere."

Elenyr smiled at the idea of Water falling for the Eternal. The woman certainly had her charms, and Water obviously found her attractive. But Elenyr's thoughts were dominated by the Order, and Wylyn. It chilled her to realize how close they'd come to locating a functioning Gate.

"And you?" he asked. "Surely you did not simply stop in Herosian. Any events I should know about?" he blinked innocently.

"Do you already know?"

He shrugged. "I may have heard whispers about a fissure in the Assassin's Guild."

"How do you know so much about everything?" she asked, half exasperated, half admiring.

"Friends talk," he said. "And I happen to have a lot of friends."

"Many of the female variety," Elenyr said, spotting a pair of women that had noticed Jeric. They batted their eyes and offered sensual postures, waving to him like Elenyr was not even there.

Jeric smiled at them, sending them into fits. When they departed Elenyr shook her head, wondering how she'd fallen for such a rogue. Gritting her teeth, she watched the women flit away.

"They're just friends," he said.

"I've heard that before," she said.

"I was always faithful to you," he said.

"Except when you didn't show up," she countered. He frowned, but before he could speak she changed the subject. "How much do you know about the Order?"

"They're dangerous," he said, "but until now, they've been content to hide in the shadows. "Now that the krey have returned, they've taken a much more active role."

"How many in their ranks?"

"Four legions, I would guess," he said. "Maybe five. But they have people in every guild, every army, every kingdom. I wager they even lurk among the Bladed."

"But what will they do?" she asked.

"Serve the will of the krey."

"That's disturbing," Elenyr replied.

"Do you know of an ancient tower that could rise?" Jeric asked.

Elenyr shook her head. Elenyr watched the current arena combatants through a gap in the benches. Both women, they fought with short, spiked blades, drawing shouts from the spectators. It was an open event, allowing anyone to enter. The games were simple and varied, and the people loved the chance to view such a contest.

"The krey view us as slaves," Elenyr said. "And for us to be free threatens the entire Krey Empire."

"Then Wylyn will seek to remove the threat, while also turning a profit."

Elenyr noticed a Bladed woman catch Jeric's eye and give a subtle hand motion. Jeric twisted, a casual motion that could have been him just shifting his feet, but it also hid his hand, allowing him to return a signal.

Elenyr frowned and motioned to the woman as she departed. "What was that about?"

"The king has arrived."

Jeric stepped from the alcove and Elenyr looked to the king's viewing chamber. The portly monarch was indeed sitting down at his chair. King Justin of Griffin was also at his side. The two monarchs were obviously well into the ale, their faces turning a shade of red, King Porlin's laughter robust.

"Why did a Bladed give you the message?" Elenyr asked, lowering her tone.

"A friend," he replied, working his way through the crowd to the royal viewing chamber.

Elenyr recalled the woman's expression, the casual deference she'd paid to Jeric. It had been subtle, but her behavior had been that of a subordinate carrying out an order, not a friend helping a friend.

"What aren't you telling me?" she asked.

Jeric grinned and shook his head. "Don't you have a king to speak to?"

Elenyr scowled at the deflection, but they'd reached the guards. After a quick conversation, Elenyr and Jeric were led into the viewing chamber. She felt a tug on her consciousness and glanced to the spectators nearby, spotting Mind sitting with Fire and Light. The three seemed content to wait, their smiles making it clear they wanted Elenyr to stay with Jeric.

She grunted in irritation but opened her thoughts enough that Mind could view what was occurring, and then stepped through the curtain to greet the kings. Both raised their glasses to Elenyr and smiled broadly.

"Erina!" King Porlin said. "Join us. The competition has been particularly thrilling today." Then his eyes lifted to Jeric and brightened. "And Master Jeric! Your gift is most appreciated." He tapped his glass and sipped, making it clear the gift had been of the drinkable variety.

"Most generous," King Justin said, nodding in gratitude.

The two kings couldn't have been more different. King Porlin was a large man, broad like a barrel. Lazy and prone to amusements, he favored everything in excess. But he was more intelligent than he appeared. He kept his kingdom in order, and his generosity was legendary.

King Justin was a soldier. The second son of his late father, he'd not been fated to take the crown, and instead had been a general in the military, proving his worth in combat many times over. When his older brother had died from illness, he'd become the crown prince, and later the king. On the exterior he seemed just and honorable, but Elenyr knew him to harbor a streak of cruelty that rarely showed itself to outsiders.

"As much as I would like to enjoy the games," Elenyr began, "I come on a most serious matter."

"Nonsense," King Porlin said, gesturing to the contest about to start between a cowled rock troll and a trio of sand trolls. "We cannot have talk of such weight on such a night."

The sun had begun to set, casting the arena into shadow. Large light orbs ignited, glowing in the gloom, flooding the stands and the floating arena floor with light. The combatants fought in the deepening darkness.

"Of what do you speak?" King Justin asked.

"The ancient race has returned," Elenyr said.

"Word is there are only two of them," King Porlin said with a dismissive wave. "I've dispatched a contingent of cavalry to find them. Their handful of outlanders will not last long."

"So the rumors are true?" Justin asked, a trace of anger appearing in his voice. "When did you intend on informing me?"

"After the games," King Porlin said. "Minor inconveniences need not be discussed during festivals."

He shouted to the battle when the rock troll picked up a sand troll and flung him clear out of the arena, the troll landing in a heap on the shore next to the benches. The other two sand trolls sought to flank their opponent, but the hooded rock troll remained in place, lazily spinning his hammer.

"The krey are dangerous," Elenyr said. "But the true danger lies in their allies, the Order of Ancients."

"Just a myth," King Porlin said.

"The Order is no myth," King Justin said.

"You know of them?" Jeric asked.

The king nodded, his expression dark. "The day before my departure to the games, I found a dagger stabbed into the wall above my bed. It had a few drops of blood on the blade, and a note informing me that the Order of Ancients required my obedience, or it would cost me the throne. I dismissed the threat, but then discovered a small cut on my son's arm. He said he'd woken to find the injury, and assumed it had come while he'd been sleeping."

"The Order infiltrated your castle?" King Porlin's smile had faded.

"It seems so," he replied. "I ordered an increase of the guards and an immediate search, but found no sign of the attacker."

"That's why you brought your family to the games," King Porlin said.

King Justin's expression was dark. "Indeed."

We have a problem.

Elenyr blinked in surprise at the mental intrusion and looked to Mind. The three fragments were on their feet, staring intently at the battle being waged in the arena. The rock troll had defeated the second sand troll and was stalking the third, his hammer spinning, the troll scrambling to escape.

Then Elenyr noticed what Mind had spotted. The rock troll was clad in a cloak and cowl, revealing only his hands. For a rock troll to hide the tattoos of his Sundering was odd enough, but the strange shape to his helmet was distinctive, almost as if there were two horns pointed downward . . .

She sucked in her breath and stepped to the edge of the viewing balcony, watching as the rock troll caught the handle of the axe as the troll attempted to strike, and ripped the weapon from his hands. Then he kicked the unfortunate troll off the arena. A Bladed stepped on the arena floor and gestured to the victorious troll.

194

"For our final open duel of the night, our victor proves to be the Unnamed!"

The rock troll turned to the Bladed—and swung his hammer, smashing him in the chest hard enough to break bone. The Bladed fell in a heap, his lifeless body broken. The shocking kill silenced the crowd, and then the rock troll ripped the cowl from his head, tossing the cloak aside to reveal the bone-plated armor, the horns descending from his skull. He was not a rock troll at all.

He was a dakorian.

Chapter 26: The Broken Crown

The dakorian's appearance drew fearful shouts from the audience, with many recoiling in terror. Soldiers rushed to the shore of the cove while Bladed appeared from all directions, weapons clearing sheaths, the glint of steel bright in the torchlight. Heedless of the army gathering against him, the dakorian sneered.

"Slaves of Lumineia," he called, raising his hammer and the stolen axe. "I am a dakorian, soldier of the Krey Empire. I am here to proclaim the return of your masters. Those you call the ancient race have come, and in time, all will kneel at their feet. Your time of freedom is at its end."

Spectators retreated up the benches, calling out in fear, staring in horror at the outlander. He turned toward the royal viewing chamber, using his hammer to point at the two kings now standing beside Elenyr. The dakorian sneer caused King Porlin to flinch.

"Your thrones are made of stone and wood, artifices of false power. In the coming days you will face a choice, to relinquish your kingdoms, or be buried with those foolish enough to fight. Your kingdoms are naught. Your lives are naught. The lands you call your own do not belong to you. Tremble, kings of men, for your rulers demand your loyalty . . . or your lives."

The dakorian reared back and hurled the troll's axe, the weapon spinning end over end toward the kings. Both recoiled in fear, too slow to evade the weapon. Elenyr was on the far side, helpless to stop the weapon—but a large hand reached from the shadows of the room and caught the axe, the blade stopping inches from King Porlin's belly.

Mox, the First Blade, stepped into the open and handed the axe to King Porlin like it was a trophy. Then he turned to the dakorian and drew the much larger axe from his back. When he spoke his voice was calm.

"You killed one of mine," he said.

The dakorian glanced to the Bladed, who still lay at the edge of the arena. "He's just a slave."

The First leapt the wall at the front of the platform and advanced toward the edge of the arena, the people and soldiers parting for his passage. He hefted his axe, setting it into a spin that emitted an eager whine, the weapon's magic spilling flames across the curved blade.

"I think you'll find we are not the slaves you claim us to be."

The dakorian sneered as the rock troll advanced across the bridge, the gathered crowd glancing between the two massive combatants. Elenyr made to follow but Jeric caught her arm, holding her back.

"He can handle the dakorian," Jeric murmured. "We have another problem."

Elenyr followed his gaze to the crowd, where dozens of men and woman were slipping unnoticed into the benches. Clad in black robes, they worked their way toward the ring of soldiers lining the shore of the cove.

Elenyr realized the tactic in an instant. The dakorian had drawn the people's attention, while the Order planned to strike the backs of the Bladed. Renowned for their weapon skills and honor, the Bladed were admired by many in all the armies—and their destruction would strike fear across Lumineia. With the people riveted on the approaching duel between Mox and the dakorian, they didn't notice the Order passing among them, their anonymity like armor, their daggers approaching the backs of the Bladed.

"We have to stop this," Jeric said in a rush as the two leapt from the viewing chamber.

"There are too many," Elenyr said. "So we'll have to draw attention to them."

She joined Mind, Fire, and Light, who had descended the benches and stood on the shore. Elenyr stabbed a finger to the nearest member of the Order, a woman creeping up behind a Bladed, and called to Light.

"Light, take the shadows!"

Light smiled and reached for the torches blazing around the arena, the light bending and twisting, morphing into columns of illumination that landed on the Order members. One by one, they all found themselves standing in a pool of light.

The crowd saw the robed figures with blades pointed to the Bladed. They reared back, shouting in fear. The Bladed turned and spotted the attackers just feet from them. Screams rent the night air as the Order and the Bladed closed in battle, the people fleeing in terror. The dakorian and Mox clashed into each other, the titanic battle going unnoticed as the Bladed fought for their lives.

"What do we do?" Light asked.

"Protect the people," Elenyr said, spotting more Order members attacking the fleeing crowd.

Elenyr cast Mox a look before leaping into the chaotic battle. Townsfolk and merchants milled about, screaming, while black clad Order members unleashed their blades upon them. Soldiers and Bladed fought, the conflict spreading into the raised benches.

Elenyr left the soldiers to fend for themselves and sprinted into the crowd. The melee prevented her companions from reaching the attackers, but Elenyr lifted her cowl and became the Hauntress, green smoke cascading off her body, flowing into her dark cloak. Then she turned ethereal and passed through the masses.

She reached an Order member about to kill a mother protecting her children. Elenyr turned corporeal just long enough to strike, and then she was gone, already reaching the next. Order members fell to her blade as she passed through the crowd, clearing the way of attackers so the innocent could flee the arena.

Light and Mind took the right flank, the two working in tandem to cut down the attackers. The Order, their attention elsewhere, didn't see them coming, their bodies falling to the ground as the pair swept around the arena.

Jeric and Fire went the opposite direction. With his flaming sword in hand, Fire darted into the fray, striking at the mages in the ranks of the Order. Bursts of light and fire illuminated the night, and smoke filled the scene. A portion of the wall was on fire, but the Bladed did not flee, their discipline absolute.

Elenyr reached the arena gates and the last of the Order fell to her blade. When she turned back, the people fled around her, some calling out their gratitude but most fleeing, their fear too bright to realize she had saved their lives.

All at once the conflict was over, the din of battle ending as quickly as it had come. Innocents flooded out of the arena until only a few stragglers remained. Bladed and apprentices slew the Order members that did not flee, and all eyes turned to the furious duel in the arena.

The rock troll swung his axe upon the dakorian, but the warrior blocked with his hammer before twisting, using the end to strike the rock troll in the skull. The First Blade rocked back, and the hammer swung across his body, the spikes in the head cutting deep into the troll's flesh. But Mox rolled with the blow and used his own axe to knock the hammer upward.

He darted into the opening, feinting to the side before reaching up and grasping the dakorian's left horn. Twisting his body, the rock troll yanked the dakorian to the arena floor, where he landed brutally. The dakorian expertly rolled away, but not before the rock troll dealt a glancing blow, his flaming axe cutting through the bone armor to draw blood.

The dakorian rose to his feet near the center of the arena, a scowl on his features. A trace of disbelief flickered in his eyes, as if he thought the rock troll's survival beyond possibility. Then the dakorian noticed the dwindling battle and retreated a step. With a growl, he slammed his hammer into the arena floor, the shaft piercing the aquaglass and sending cracks outward. Then he whirled and sprinted to the edge of the arena. Of the litany of scars on the dakorian's body, one stood out, a dark burn across his leg.

Mox gave chase, but the dakorian reached the end and dove into the cove water, disappearing through the gap in the storm wall. Shouting in praise, Kings Porlin and Justin descended to the arena and strode to the rock troll.

"Well done," King Porlin said.

"Indeed," King Justin said, sheathing his sword. "Without you, the attack would have been victorious."

Bleeding from a dozen wounds, the rock troll turned and strode to the hammer. Motioning to it, he said, "This wasn't an attack they intended to win."

Elenyr joined the fragments and Jeric on the arena. "I agree," she said. "They wanted damage and fear, not destruction."

"They failed in both because of your presence," King Porlin said. He wiped sweat from his brow, his hands shaking. "You have our gratitude."

Elenyr's gaze swept the abandoned arena. Bodies of the wounded were being tended by healers, while Bladed, apprentices, and Talinorian guard helped those with smaller injuries. The Order dead lay scattered about. Then Elenyr noticed the wounds on Mox's body, the volume a testament to the tremendous duel.

"Why did he flee?" Elenyr asked.

"He was here to deliver a message," Mox said, pointing to the dakorian hammer.

He shifted, allowing them to see the hammer. The shaft had been plunged into the center of the arena, the weapon scorched and blackened from his battle with Mox. At the top, two broken halves of a golden circlet were smashed into the metal.

A broken crown.

"King Numen's crown," Elenyr said, recognizing it.

"They have killed him," King Porlin said, his tone filled with shock.

"They wanted to threaten us," King Justin growled. "To let us know we can be killed."

Jeric strode into view, his eyes softening as he glanced to Elenyr. "They wished to sow discord," he said, nodding to Elenyr. "But that was not their only intention."

"Of what do you speak?" Mox asked.

"As we fought the Order, a ship viewed the conflict." He motioned to the gap in the seawall, where the barrier allowed a view of the moonlit sea. "They wanted to test us, to see for themselves how much of a threat we pose."

"The dakorian is a match for my kind," Mox said, motioning to the wound on his chest. "And now they know it."

As they debated the purpose of the attack, Elenyr stepped free and motioned to Mind. The fragment followed her to the edge of the arena, his expression curious. When they were out of earshot of the others, Elenyr lowered her voice.

"Do you think the kings are in danger?"

"Not yet," Mind said, frowning in thought. "I think Wylyn wants the people to be afraid, and the Order will gain followers, mark my words."

"What did you get from the minds of the Order?" she asked.

"They are men and women that have lost much," he said. "They believe they have been wronged by their nations, by the people, and they think the krey will deliver them to their rightful place."

"Any indication on where the krey are hiding?"

"I caught a glimpse of a krey outpost," Mind said. "There were dark elves present, and from Light's description, Serak was there as well."

Elenyr tightened her jaw. "That's the second time we've seen a connection between the Order and the dark elves. Perhaps we go to them for answers."

Chapter 27: Burned

Erathan was in an uproar, the streets of Heth filled with soldiers. It took hours for Water and Lira to finish explaining to the captain of the guard, an unappealing woman that asked incessant questions, how the king had been kidnapped. It took all of Water's skill to ward off her suspicion, and still the woman wanted Water and Lira to remain in the city for further interrogation.

Water did learn one thing from the conversation. The dwarf that had attacked them was well known for his criminal acts. He'd robbed and murdered his way across the kingdoms, an act that would have earned a hefty bounty, except he didn't have one.

"You know him but do not hunt him?" Water asked.

"Someone pays the bounty before it can be issued," the woman said. "We call him the Dark Dwarf, and suspect he is a member of the Assassin's Guild. He was seen entering the city shortly after you arrived, and he left a horse bearing Herosian colors outside the city."

Water and Lira exchanged a look, and he guessed she was thinking the same thing. Someone was paying to keep the Dark Dwarf's actions from coming to light—someone powerful. In light of what they had learned about the Order, and his presence when the king had been taken, it appeared that the Dark Dwarf worked for them.

"Where can we find him?" Lira asked.

"If I knew that, I wouldn't be talking to you," the woman retorted.

Another soldier appeared and captured her attention, and the woman jerked her head in dismissal. Water and Lira strode away, leaving the castle behind. Lira began to speak but Water motioned her to silence until they were outside the fortress walls.

"The Order has powerful members," Lira said.

"We do not know if the Dark Dwarf is part of them, or works for them," he said. "But if he is an assassin, I suspect his name is Thorg. Elenyr has spoken of the Assassin's Guild members and he would match the description. What is disturbing is that the assassins have a very strict code, which it seems Thorg is not obeying."

"It doesn't matter," Lira said, her tone harsh. "We need to eradicate them."

Water cast her a sharp look. "We do not slaughter."

"Tell that to the Mendelen."

He'd never heard the name, but her tone was dark, her features forbidding. Hesitation bound his tongue, and the two departed the city in silence. They used the descender to reach the lake below the Giant's Shelf, and then a boat carried them to the forest.

The miles passed without a word, the Giant's Shelf fading behind them. Water cast about for a topic but the rigidity to Lira's features did not lend itself to conversation. He desperately wanted to ask about the Mendelen, but feared inciting her to greater wrath.

"Can we go back to dancing?" he finally asked.

She snorted in disbelief and glanced his way. "You don't understand."

"What do you mean?" he asked. "I understand that I enjoyed dancing with you."

"There are things I cannot tell you."

"So you didn't enjoy dancing?"

After a moment she met his gaze. "I cannot deny that."

"That's good to hear," he said with a smile.

"You don't have to look so smug."

"Me?" Water asked, feigning ignorance. He ducked under a branch. "I would never be so smug."

She shoved him and he laughed, the tension passing. But Water had seen the depth in her gaze, of anger, of loss. Lira had demonstrated courage and valor, a conviction that went beyond any woman he'd known. But this was the first time he'd seen fear in her eyes.

They worked their way south and west, towards the village King Numen had said was attacked by Wylyn. Lira did not speak about the Mendelen or her fears, and Water did not press the topic. He'd gotten a glimpse of a haunted memory within Lira, and yearned to know what she feared.

He wondered what had led to her pain, what tragedy had driven her to become an Eternal, to fight for Ero, the one that had given her the magic she possessed. But patience was a virtue gained by one free of time, and so he waited.

They camped in the trees, and Water cast a quartet of entities to stand guard. Despite his fatigue, sleep was slow in coming, and he pondered the revelations about the Order until deep into the night, his thoughts inevitably returning to Serak. He hoped by morning Lira's mood would lighten, but she spoke little throughout the day. And the next.

He tried to tell himself it wasn't because he found her attractive, that it was just out of duty. But the harder he tried, the more he found himself stealing looks at a woman that made his heart feel alive for the first time. He yearned to understand, to see what she held back, and to be the one to offer solace.

The road wound its way south and then split to the west. They passed a handful of travelers, but the road was empty. The days passed in snippets of conversation, and during the lulls in conversation sound came from their boots scraping across the road, an endless rhythm that did not seem to lull Lira's dark mood.

"Are all the krey ageless?" he asked, three days after departing Heth.

"All," she said. "Eons ago they figured out how to perfect their bodies. They do not age or contract disease. Their bodies do not wear after time, so they simply continue to live."

"And the dakorians?"

"They are one of the races the krey have conquered," she said. "The krey reward their most loyal with a perfected form, and they then become ageless. Those with four serrations on their horns are high captains, and earned that honor. Tardoq, Wylyn's personal guard, is one such, and I believe he's over ten thousand years old."

"So what's the oldest krey you've met?" he asked.

"Some are considered new, and have lived for less than a thousand years. Others have lived for tens of thousands, even more."

He swept his hand to the empty road. "It is a hard thing to imagine a life without end."

"Not so hard," she said.

"What's it like, living so long?"

"At first it feels like a curse," Lira said. "You miss those you love, your family, the place you call home. But as you spend more time with other ageless it becomes normal. The days bleed into years and centuries, and one day you realize you no longer see an end to your existence."

"But the krey can still be killed."

"I have killed many of them," she said. "And many dakorians."

"The krey do not fight?"

"They use the dakorians," she said. "Or constructs."

"Constructs?"

She motioned to him. "You are a being of flesh blended with magic. A construct is the same, flesh bonded to powerful energy, giving the wielder incredible power. Constructs come in many forms, but they are all deadly. Think of them like a glove for a soldier's mind, a powerful body the soldier can use for a short time."

With the sun filtering through the trees, illuminating the shaded road, all seemed at peace, and the conversation about the krey made him feel closer to Lira. He wanted to ask more pointed questions, but hoped that simply talking would help her open up.

"What about you?" she asked. "What was your life like, in the beginning?"

"Not much to tell," he said wryly. "Draeken fractured the first time he tried to use his full power, and I remember standing in the sun before we merged back together." He winced at the memory. "Elenyr managed to get Draeken to separate and train us on our own. She hoped we would master ourselves, allowing Draeken to master the fragments."

"And after?" she asked.

He heard the curiosity in her tone and hoped it meant her mood had softened. "The first few decades were brutal, and we caused a great deal of damage. If our protector was anyone but Elenyr, they would have been killed. Over time we managed to control our magics, and then Elenyr began to take us into the world."

"You must have been eager," she said.

"You have no idea," he said. "Shadow managed to sneak out a few times, and he was lucky he didn't kill anyone."

"So she took you outside your refuge one at a time?"

Water nodded, recalling a yearning to be the one chosen, and jealousy when he was not. Looking back he realized they were probably much like children, despite their age, and it had taken many years before Water had accepted Elenyr's wisdom.

"Our excursions were small at first," Water said. "But we gradually dealt with more pressing matters. Elenyr was very careful, and planned each excursion to test and strengthen our discipline."

"What did you do?"

A flutter of something soft brushed across his face and he brushed it away. "I studied with water mages and built buildings. I even spent time as a guard."

She grinned and motioned to him. "Your magic is formidable, and you did guard duty?"

"That's what Shadow said," he replied. "But Elenyr wanted us to see that magic was more than just fighting. She wanted us to see all that could be created, not just what could be destroyed. I helped build forests and enchant rivers through cities. I also helped stop a few floods."

"And Fire?" she asked. "Surely there is little he can do besides destroy."

"He used fire to shape wood and forge great structures. He's the best artist of us all."

"An artist?" She shook her head. "I would never have thought." She wiped at her cheeks, brushing aside what had fallen on her face.

"Mind helped to negotiate treaties and train soldiers while Light filled villages with illumination. Shadow—when he could control his sense of mischief—used his magic to create special weapons the guards could use against thieves and brigands. Of course, he was frequently the one that *caused* the trouble, but they didn't know that."

"They are your family," she stated.

"We are brothers first and fragments second," Water said, a small smile on his face. "And each of them has saved my life many times over. Our magic may be strong, but it is when we are united that we are truly powerful."

He brushed at his face again, irritated by the smog. Lira chuckled. "I cannot imagine such a bond. Do you always agree with the fragments?"

He burst into a laugh. "Hardly. Do you not occasionally feel an internal conflict? Imagine that conflict split between two beings. We once had a feud endure for more than a year, and I think Fire still has the scar from Light."

"Light did the damage?"

207

"Fire may have the anger, but Light has the rage." He recalled the fury of the fragment in their early years. "And trust me when I say, do not steal his cheese."

"Oh?"

He smiled. "Fire wasn't the only one to get scars from Light."

She brushed at her face, and this time he looked up. .The air was full of dust, the particles floating down to settle on them. Confused, he reached up and caught some on his hand. It looked like snow, but was grey rather than white.

"Ash," he said.

They exchanged a look and she nodded. "We're here."

The road curved around the trees and the village came into view. Water slowed, but his caution was unnecessary. Homes and shops had been reduced to smoking beams, the wood turning white, ash rising with scattered plumes of smoke.

They advanced onto what had once been the main road through the village, but had to pick their way over the remains of the stables. Beams had collapsed, the supports falling into the road, wisps of smoke curling around them.

The blacksmith shop was in ruins, the home behind it nearly unrecognizable. Water sucked in his breath when he saw the shape in the ash where a body had lain, and then spotted the others, all signs of the slaughter visible by the tracks in the ash.

"Erathan soldiers retrieved the dead," he said.

When there was no response, he turned to Lira and found her with her hand over her mouth, her eyes filled with horror. It was the look of someone seeing a memory, the present eliciting a haunting past.

"What's wrong?"

She didn't seem to hear him, her features rigid, her eyes wide as she took in the ash falling like snow, drifting through the air to settle on her clothes, the still smoking wood of homes, and the scorched ground.

"Lira," he said, an urgency to his voice.

He took a step toward her but a sound nearby made him spin. Already on edge, he cast his water staff and scanned the village for the danger. It came again, and Lira sucked in her breath. She wiped at her eyes and then stood with him, both realizing the same thing.

They were not alone.

Chapter 28: Lira's Gate

Instantly on guard, Water and Lira faced the source of the noise. The seconds passed and no one appeared, but Water kept his attention focused outward, his thoughts on the possibility of a trap. Had the dakorians done all this just to draw them in? It seemed improbable, and yet he could not dismiss it outright. The Order had kidnapped a reigning monarch, and it seemed they'd been a step ahead from the beginning. They'd proven their power.

The sound repeated, a shuffling of feet through the ash, of a beam succumbing and falling, the impact muffled by the soil. They were not the sounds of an attacker, so Water advanced through the devastated village until he spotted a flicker of movement.

The woman knelt in a destroyed building, sifting through the rubble and ash. Wearing a homespun dress, the cloth now stained black, she seemed intent on locating an object, and did not hear them approach until Lira coughed.

Spinning to her feet, she woman faced them, a small knife in her hands. She shifted between pointing the blade at Water and then at Lira, her eyes wild. Lira raised her hands to placate the woman.

"We are not here to harm you," she said.

The woman stared at them suspiciously, her eyes moving over and around them, searching for more. But there was just the ash falling through scattered smoke. She kept the blade up, her hands quivering.

"Who are you?"

"King Numen sent us," Water said. "We hunt those who attacked your village."

"Demon trolls," the woman spat. "They had horns like a beast."

"Were you here?" Lira asked.

The woman seemed to realize she still held a blade pointed at them and straightened before tucking the knife into a tiny sheath on her waist. She nodded to Lira, and her eyes swept the ruined structure where she stood.

"This was my home."

"You must be Grena," Water said.

The woman stared at the ash at her feet. "The soldiers took the dead and brought me to Erathan. I returned as soon as I was able."

"Can you tell us what happened?" Lira asked.

"There were four of them," Grena said, her voice haunted. "They walked into the village and demanded to know the location of a dwarf. They picked up the dwarven blacksmith like he was a child. Others rose up to fight, but we were no match for them. They spoke of us like we were pests to be exterminated."

"What did they want?" Water asked gently.

"They wanted answers," Grena said. "But when they had them, they wanted blood."

Water glanced to Lira and lowered his voice. "Why would they do that?"

"Dakorians are taught that man is a lesser form of being," she murmured. "To them, these people would have been a herd of beasts."

"But wanton slaughter?" Water asked. "We don't just kill beasts for sport."

"You don't understand," she said, turning to him. "They shed blood as easily as we breathe, and love to fight, to kill."

Appalled, Water gazed on the village, the families destroyed, simply because the dakorians enjoyed killing. Anger rippled through him and he turned to Grena. The woman was on her knees again, brushing ash off a memory orb.

211

A light mage had captured an image of a young boy and placed it inside the glass orb. Smiling impishly, the boy stared into space, his eyes dancing with delight. Grena cradled the orb to her chest, tears wetting the black stains on her cheeks.

"When you find them, will you kill them?" Grena's voice was surprisingly strong.

"We will," Lira said.

Grena stood and pointed south. "They spoke of returning to Keese, of a guild of thieves called the Ravens. After watching the village burn they departed in that direction."

"You have our gratitude," Water said.

The woman turned away, and Water and Lira withdrew. They left the disturbing village behind and returned to the road, but the daylight had lost its luster. Even after they'd gone far enough to avoid the falling ash, he still felt stained.

"Do any dakorians have a sense of morality?" he asked.

Lira didn't answer, and he glanced her way. Lira's features were dark, her hands clenching and unclenching. Yet it was the same fear she'd displayed before, prompting him to reach out and touch her arm.

"Don't," she said, flinching. "Don't touch me."

"I'm sorry," he said.

They'd come to a halt, and she stared into the woods. But he could tell she still faced the village, her eyes still seeing the ash and fallen buildings. He wanted to reach out to her, to embrace her, but she stood so rigid she trembled.

"It's happening again," she said quietly.

"What's happening again?"

She stabbed a hand back toward the village. "The krey, the dakorians. This is what they do. They destroy all freedoms, enslave all men and women."

"We can stop them."

She rounded on him, her eyes flashing. "Do you know how many have said that? How many have died for their beliefs?"

"I don't," he said. "But I know we can."

"You really think our magic is enough to stop them?"

"It's done so already," he said. "We've fought the dakorians and survived. We've fought the Order and survived. They are not so different from the many foes we've brought to justice."

"You don't think they are different?" she challenged.

"Wylyn is just another tyrant that needs to learn humility," he said.

"Do you know what the krey do to get more slaves?" She stepped in, so close he could see the flecks of green in her blue eyes. "They take a few thousand men and women and put them on a world much like this one. Then they let time and the nature of man work. Several thousand years later they return and harvest millions. There is always a rebellion. It is always destroyed."

"Like the Mendelen?"

She stared at him and he held his breath, wondering if he'd pushed it too far. The seconds passed but he did not speak, and finally she grimaced and looked away. She clenched her eyes shut, and for a moment she looked utterly vulnerable.

"There is something you should see."

She withdrew a small mirror from a pouch at her side and lifted it to a tree. The glass poured to the ground and flowed up the trunk, shaping into a large arch that reflected them standing in the road.

"Is that a Gate?" he asked.

"This Gate only works on Lumineia or in the Hall of Eternals," she said. "Will you come with me?"

"Where does it lead?"

213

"You'll find out," she said, and offered her hand.

He glanced between her hand and the Gate, and then reached for her hand. After her anger, he expected her grip to be rigid, but her fingers were soft and trembling. He realized she was about to show a piece of herself, but the dark tinge to her gaze left him with a sense of foreboding.

"I am yours," he said.

She nodded and then pulled him through the Gate. Stepping through the mirror was not unlike falling into water, the liquid passing over his skin and clothing, yet he was left dry as he emerged on the opposite side.

He coughed at the dust in the air, and then shivered, the cold piercing his clothing and settling into his bones. They were in a cave, the dim light a shade of red that came from outside. He spotted her wrapping a cloth around her features and he did the same, allowing him to breathe. Then he followed her to the mouth of the cave.

They stood near the summit of a small mountain, providing a view that stretched for miles. The landscape was barren and hostile, an endless expanse of rock, dry riverbeds, and billowing clouds of dust. Then he saw the ruins.

On the far side of the valley sat the remains of a mighty city. Time had been unkind, wearing away the vestiges of the buildings until they'd gained a weariness, a resignation to their fate.

The city could have housed the entire population of Lumineia, and stretched across mountains and valleys, expanding so far it touched the horizon. Some buildings towered over others. Others were fallen. Even broken, they were as tall as mountains, their reflective exterior long since gone dark.

He squinted and spotted the damage in the city. Like a great knife had been plunged into the earth, a black gorge carved through the earth. Buildings and streets were gone, others falling into the abyss. Some buildings were cut in two, the interior exposed to the elements, as if a great weapon had pierced the city, plunging into its heart.

"What is . . ."

The wind swirled, parting for a moment and allowing a view of the sky. His eyes widened in shock, for the city extended into the heavens. Huge and decaying, more buildings floated above, bits hanging off, the rubble about to fall. Many hung low in the sky but some remained high, kissing the clouds as they resisted the pull of the earth.

The sun was descending into the sky, casting the region in a reddish hue. Through the floating buildings he spotted a moon—and then a second moon, and a third. Two were crescents while the third was full, the sight robbing him of speech.

"We're not on Lumineia," he breathed.

"We are not."

He cast her a look and then returned to examining the sky. "I thought small Gates could not travel between worlds."

"That is true," she said. "But we are close to Lumineia, and my Gate draws power from the Hall of Eternals to travel to this one destination."

"What is this place?" he asked.

"Renara," she said, and then pointed to the city. "That's Herikelenis, the capital city. The rest of the world looks much the same, now."

She stepped to the side of the cave and pressed a faintly glowing rune. A dome of light appeared, seeming to flow from the stone and rising up like a giant bubble. The scenery changed, color filling the canvas.

Trees and grass appeared, buildings straightened and sealed. Mighty rivers flowed and ships were visible on its surface. Other trees grew, their trunks a strange, glowing green, their branches bending upward rather than hanging down.

The sky turned a deep blue, the floating buildings shifting to gain an order, an organization that implied an architect. Balconies extended from buildings, flying vessels departing from them to carry men and women to distant destinations.

"This place is breathtaking," he said.

She flashed a sad smile. "It was. Thousands of cities once dotted this continent, all flourishing under a single government, the people electing a Governor Prime, a woman that had the respect of all. They were at peace."

"Why did you bring me here?" he asked.

"Lumineia is my home," she said, "but here was my heart. It is also the place of my greatest failure."

"What happened?" he asked, a trickle of foreboding seeping into his gut.

"The krey," she said simply, and reached for the rune again. And the image began to change . . .

Chapter 29: Renara

An object appeared in the sky and grew larger as it approached. Two other vessels appeared, and their appearance sparked panic among the populace, the people screaming as they fled. Large weapons were activated, launching beams of fire and light at the arrivals, but the ships emerged unscathed.

One glided through the smoke and Water got a full look at the ship. It resembled a longsword, with an extended, flattened hull made of a bright silvery material. At the rear, two stubby wings extended to either side, the stern shaped like a hilt. Weapons opened up and beams of light lanced into the earth.

Lira watched the destruction with wooden eyes. "The krey had seeded Renara thousands of years before, and came to collect the crop of new slaves. The Mendelen were the soldiers of the people, and they fought with valor and courage, but it didn't matter."

Water clenched his hands into fists, helplessness and anger spilling into his veins. The defenders fought, but their cities, their armaments, were for nothing. The krey were far more powerful, almost lazy in their attack.

A second ship landed and unloaded a small army of dakorians. Led by two soldiers of pure light, they waded into the city, driving the people out. The soldiers of light killed the defenders and leveled buildings, their might rivaling deranged guardians from the Mage Wars. One carried a weapon that cut a structure down like it was wheat, the blade in his hands slicing through stone and steel.

"Constructs," Lira said. "Those are helmed by dakorians."

"They are the machines you spoke of?" he asked.

"A most deadly machine," she said.

The people were subdued and another krey vessel landed. Large doors were opened and people were herded into the opening, where a Gate stood waiting. Many fought. All died. Those that accepted the krey passed through the Gate, their wailing filling the smoke-laden air. And ash rained down from the sky.

Many of the buildings in the sky were falling, their structures in flames. Beneath, families were forced into long lines, their captors showing no mercy. The Mendelen soldiers were cut down with such ease that the people stopped fighting. With heads bowed, they abandoned their homes to become krey slaves.

The image came to a halt, and Lira motioned to the city. "Millions dead. Billions captured."

"All for slaves?" he asked, heat rising in his voice.

"All for slaves," she repeated.

"Why were you here?" he asked. He turned to her, unable to watch the image any longer.

"This was my first assignment as an Eternal," she said, her eyes on the image. "I joined them, lived among them. I was supposed to locate the krey spies and kill them before they could report back. I completed my assignment and thought the world safe."

"You stayed," he realized.

"I fell in love," she said. "His name is difficult to pronounce in our language, but he was everything to me. We built a home, a life, and I allowed myself to think the krey would never come. I asked Ero to release me from my vow."

She passed a hand over her face. "Ero and I argued. He warned me the krey would come, but I thought it would be distant, centuries into the future. I married my Mendelen captain, and for the first time since the Dawn of Magic, I was truly happy.

"You cannot imagine what life is like exploring a new world," she said, her eyes distant. "The people are different, the culture even more so—and yet they are all the same. Fathers and mothers watching their

218

children, homes built and loved ones lost. The race of man is remarkably resilient, and always prone to curiosity."

"Did you have children?"

"Three," she said. "All girls."

She smiled, the softness to her expression reminding Water of Elenyr. All at once his perspective shifted. He'd viewed Lira as a young woman because of her appearance, but she was one who had endured much, and lost much.

Lira spoke of her girls with sadness and resignation, indicating they had long since perished. He did not ask how, but suspected they had died when the krey had arrived. The loss had evidently cut into her soul.

He asked about her family and friends, and she spoke of them as if they were still living. Her words were halting at first, as if she'd never shared the tale. But as the minutes passed, the words came easier. She touched the rune on the wall, and the image returned to before the krey arrival, to when the world was at peace. Then she pointed to strange beasts, describing their near sentient natures, and telling of how one of her girls had owned one as a pet.

She pointed to the area of their home, a small farm on the outskirts of the city. He squinted, and just managed to make out the building on the top of a hill, the structure tall and regal, with a section floating off the ground.

Water listened to her speak of her life on Renara, and saw beyond her story. She was an ageless, but while on the world she'd believed she could live a life free of the Empire. Even if the krey had never come, she would have witnessed her husband wither and die, her daughters become adults before they too succumbed to age.

"Do you regret starting a family?"

She shook her head. "My time with them was worth any cost," she said, and then her voice hardened. "But the krey will pay the greater price."

"Why do the Eternals not destroy the Empire?" he asked.

"Would that it could be so easy," she said. "You could sooner move an ocean with a bucket."

"So that's Ero's plan?" Water asked. "Keep Lumineia hidden from the Empire?"

"That is all we can do," she said simply. "None in the Empire know of Lumineia's existence or location. If they did . . ." She swept her hand at the still frozen image.

"Did you fight when the krey came to Renara?"

"To protect my family," she said. "I failed."

"Who did this to Renara?" he asked.

She shifted the image back to after the battle, and froze the illusion where Water could see a ship on the ground. Near the stern of the vessel was a symbol, a strange rune. It had two sharp curves like claw marks, and a single dot above the left curve.

"That's the symbol for Wylyn's house," she said.

"*Wylyn* did this?"

"Her house is incredibly strong," Lira said. "I doubt she was here personally, but they were here on her order. Renara was owned by her house, and when the time came, she sent her forces to retrieve her property. The people would have been sold in weeks."

He struggled to contain his mounting anger. Witnessing what the krey had done to Renara filled him with a desire to tear down the Empire and free those enslaved. But one glance at the ships was enough to bring caution.

"What happened after the battle?"

She touched a rune on the wall and the image accelerated until all the people were gone. The ships withdrew, and then rained fire from the heavens, devastating everything that remained, destroying forests and rivers, until the entire planet was desolate, and the light of the mirage drained into the ground, leaving the sober reality.

"This is the fate that awaits Lumineia," she said. "This is what the world will look like. And all of our magic will be for nothing against the Krey Empire."

"*If* Wylyn opens the Gate," he said.

"Yes," she said. "And I cannot let it happen again. Not to Lumineia. I failed to stop Wylyn's arrival, and if I fail again . . ."

On impulse, he reached out and gathered her into his arms. "You are not alone this time."

He expected her to pull away, but she leaned against him, her head on his neck, her arms around his waist. He could feel the strength of her body, yet now she was not the warrior, she was a woman afraid for the loss of her home.

He looked over her shoulder at the desolate Renara, and shared in her ache. To witness such a fate would leave a scar, and he now understood her reaction at seeing the destroyed village. She'd seen a glimpse of the future if she failed to stop Wylyn.

His thoughts were drawn to Lumineia, to his friends and family. If the krey invaded, the fragments would fight, but he'd seen the might of a construct, and wondered if even Draeken could survive such a duel.

A cold resolve settled into his chest. The people did not know the threat they faced, could not understand the danger Wylyn posed, but he and Lira would stop at nothing to protect them from Renara's fate.

Abruptly Lira retreated. "I'm sorry," she said. "I shouldn't have . . ."

"I don't mind," he said, and flashed a faint smile. "But now that I know what we face, we need to return and find Wylyn. She is vulnerable until she opens a Gate."

"But where do we go?" she asked.

"To the Ravens," he said. "We can get more information from the thieves."

"You really think we can find Wylyn?"

221

"We can together," he said, offering his hand.

She accepted it, and this time with a firm grip. Still close, he could feel the heat from her body, and a yearning to draw closer. A flicker of desire appeared in her gaze before she released her hand and stepped toward the rear of the chamber. She reached into her pocket and activated the Gate.

"Can I ask why you created a Gate to come here?" he asked.

"Sometimes I need a reminder," she said, and her eyes lingered on him. "A reminder not to get attached."

"How many have you brought here?" he asked.

"You are the first." She activated the Gate and it flowed across the wall.

"Careful," he said, stepping past her. "I'm easy to get attached to."

She snorted and looked to the ruins of Renara. Then she turned and stepped with him back onto the empty road. She deactivated the Gate and pocketed the mirror, and he breathed deeply of the air. It carried a tinge of smoke, reminding him of the proximity to the village.

As they took their journey south he stole frequent glances at his companion. They spoke little, but it seemed she was lighter than she'd been before, and there was an openness about her that implied a connection had been forged. But that openness brought a tightening to her jaw, and he saw the determination in her gaze.

His thoughts returned to Renara often, and as they walked among the trees he imagined fire raining down from krey vessels, burning the trees to ash. He saw smoke billowing up from their cities, of men and women carted off like cattle. The resolve in his chest turned into fire. He would not let that happen.

Chapter 30: An Unexpected Ally

Water and Lira worked their way south and crossed the Blue River into Talinor. At first, both carried the weight of what they'd seen on Renara, and Water found his optimism had been sapped. But with the sun shining and Lira as his companion, the burden of what he'd witnessed gradually faded, so by the time they reached Keese, his gaze was fixed on what lay ahead.

They reached the city of Keese in the waning hours of the day, the dark clouds heralding a storm. They'd set a grueling pace and both were tired, the sight of the city a welcome reprieve from the road. As they approached the city, his gaze lifted to the city wall, a new addition.

Built of white sea stone, the wall circled the coastal city. Strategically located close to the river leading to Blue Lake, and bordering a natural cove, the city of Keese didn't need the wall to protect from without. They needed it to protect against threats from within, and many of the patrols watched the streets.

"During the mage wars, Keese was a hive of corruption," Water explained. "It was so rampant that the king all but abandoned it to the thieves and mercenary guilds. Since then, Talinor has been fighting a quiet war with the thieves and brigands. Many have gone into hiding, but they still harbor a grudge against the king, and skirmishes are frequent."

"And the Ravens?" she asked.

"A rival to the Thieves Guild," he said. "They are more mercenaries than thieves, and are willing to steal, destroy, or kill for a price. They've been battling the Thieves Guild for the last twenty years."

"And you think they are allied with Wylyn?"

"The Ravens know everything that happens in the region," he said as they entered through the city gates. "But we'll have to find them first."

"You don't already know where they are?"

"Shadow probably does," he said. "But they move a lot to keep the guards from finding them."

"So where do we start?"

He flashed a smile. "We need to get robbed."

"How do we do that?"

"We have to get married."

She burst into a laugh and leaned close. "I'd need a ring for that."

His heart thumped in his chest but he managed to stay focused. "Exactly."

She raised a confused eyebrow, so he turned north and explained his plan. Shortly after, they were exiting an elven glass shop, and she sported a very realistic looking ring on her finger. It glittered like a diamond, but at a fraction of the cost. Now dressed in the garb of minor nobles, they departed the wealthy section of the city for the north side.

Shaped like a crescent moon, the city followed the curve of the coast. The south end contained the Duke's small castle and the homes of the wealthy. Upscale merchants also found a home in the south. The center of the city was all waterfront, with ships arriving and departing from throughout Lumineia. The northern curve of Keese had been claimed by the remnants of the thieves and thugs, and guards only entered in large numbers.

As they worked their way through the cobblestone streets, the buildings took on a seedier look, the white stone being replaced with aged wood and stones stained black. The people too, gained a grungier air, with many looking at them with greed in their eyes.

"So we just wait?" she asked, eying a pair of young men sitting outside a tavern.

Water resisted the urge to punish them for their leering looks. "It shouldn't take long."

A woman stepped out of an alley and blocked their way. "Seems to me the two of you are lost." She flashed a smile, but absent the teeth, the expression did not lend itself to comfort.

"Just looking for someone," Water said.

"Can we help?"

Water turned as a small knot of men appeared behind them. Four in number, they sauntered close, and one tapped the hilt of his dagger. "Perhaps you need an escort."

"No escort needed," Lira said.

"Then I'm afraid you'll have to pay the toll for your passage," the woman said. She drew a dagger and used it to clean her fingernails.

"Actually, you might be able to help us," Water said. "We'd like to find the Ravens."

The woman laughed. "Foolish questions from foolish men." She jerked her chin to her companions. "Take everything they have."

Water cast his water staff and struck the ground, sending a wave of frost blasting outward. The ice spread up the bodies of the four behind and the woman in front, freezing them where they stood. Shouts rang out from the bystanders nearby, and most beat a hasty retreat.

One of the men cursed and Water turned to find a thief with a sword extended towards Water's back. His arm, frozen and covered with ice, would not budge, and the man shouted profanities. Water merely smiled and stepped to the frozen woman.

"You did offer aid," he said. "And we'd like to accept."

"I'll gut you like a fish," she sneered, struggling to free her hands, the dagger still poised to clean her nails.

"The ice takes time to melt," he said, and glanced to the dark sky. "Even if it rains. You can remain and gain a chill, or tell us what we want to know."

"Or I can do more than make you cold," Lira said, her tone hard as she placed her sword on the woman's chest. The sound of the blade scrapping across the ice sounded harsh in the street, and the woman grimaced.

"What do you want with the Ravens?"

"Information only, I assure you," Water said.

The woman glanced between them, her breath coming in frozen puffs of air. She shivered and then relented. "You can find them in a tavern on the docks, the Shark's Tooth. Ask for Wenta."

"You have our gratitude," Water said, releasing the charm and melting the ice for all five.

The men collapsed to the earth, shivering and cursing. To her credit, the woman remained on her feet. "We helped you," she said. "Some payment is in order."

Water and Lira exchanged an amused look at the woman's boldness, and Lira plucked her ring from her finger. "The price of your information," she said, and tossed it to her.

Water and Lira strode away, and didn't turn when the woman shouted, "But it's a fake!"

"That was more fun than I anticipated," Lira said.

"They might stab us in the back, you know."

"That's what makes it exciting," she said. "But I think their fear will keep them in check."

"I'm just glad it didn't take long," Water said, yawning.

"Is the great guardian tired?" she teased.

"Aren't you?" he asked.

She feigned indignance. "I never get tired." She began to yawn but stifled it, and he stabbed a finger at her lips.

"I saw that."

"You saw nothing," she said.

Water grinned and stepped out of the northern district. They headed west to the waterfront and then, after a few inquiries, headed south. As the sun set they reached a surprisingly lavish tavern.

The Shark's Tooth sat on a pier over the water, allowing ships to dock just feet from its door. Large and boasting a wide balcony on the second floor, the tavern hosted many minor nobles and ships' captains, the savory scents wafting from the doors indicating the meals were a major draw.

A giant shark hung above the door, its jaws open as if it sought to devour the door. The beast would have been huge in life and inspired no less awe in death. Mages had trapped the flesh in a thin layer of aquaglass, preserving the beast and giving it a visceral look. Still in their noble attire, Water and Lira were ushered inside.

The inside of the tavern was no less lavish than the exterior, with smaller sharks hanging from the ceiling. Glasses clinked and conversation was lit by laughter. The scents coming from the kitchens made his mouth water, and he craned his head to see a plate of spiced fish being served to a ship's captain.

"I expected something less . . ."

"Rich?" he supplied.

"Why would the Ravens have a presence in such a nice tavern?" she asked, and pointed to the guard captains sitting at a table.

"The Ravens are not traditional thieves," he said. "And rumor has it, their founder was once a member of the Thieves Guild."

"But they are not members of the Thieves Guild?"

"The Thieves Guild trains their members well," Water said, lowering his tone as they took a seat by the window. "They do not accept just anyone. They have rich traditions that date back to before the Mage Wars. They only steal from those with excess."

"And the Ravens?"

"Rumor has it the Ravens are led by a woman who scorned the restrictions of the guild, and wanted to steal from all. She drew away some of the guild's members and started her own. It didn't take her long to destroy the Thieves Guild in Keese, and Shadow has said they seek to destroy the guild completely."

"Sounds like an angry woman."

"She's dangerous," he said. "Even more so because only the Ravens know her identity, and those caught have been surprisingly loyal, keeping the secret to the grave. Be on your guard. If Wylyn or the dakorians are here . . ."

"I know," she said. "So perhaps we should maintain the persona of a married couple."

"I think I need a ring," he said.

She grinned at his repetition of her words and reached across the table to take his hand. Even though he knew it was just an act, he couldn't help the thrill of excitement that burned in his chest.

"Maybe we should eat first," he said. She raised an eyebrow, and he added, "Once we reveal ourselves to the Ravens we might not get a chance to eat."

"Who am I to argue with such logic?"

He smiled and motioned her to an empty table. As they ordered food from the pretty barmaid, he scanned the room, making note of any he thought could be a threat. But none of the people seemed likely to be a thief, or even a member of the Order.

They talked as they ate, but it seemed she had the same thoughts as he. The fish was divine, a distraction that commanded attention. Perfectly seasoned and fried, the meal washed away any lingering taste of dried nuts and cured meat, the only food they'd had the last few days.

Although the food was delicious, he found his thoughts drawn to Lira, and the last tavern they'd stayed in, when a certain bard had played music that had nearly brought them to a kiss. Although music was absent, this meal felt more intimate, and her smile suggested she felt the same.

Just as they were finishing, he began to wonder if the thief in the north district had given them false information. He savored the last bite and settled back into his seat, scanning the tavern for anyone that might be Wenta.

"We can't just ask about the Ravens," he said, eyeing the soldiers at a nearby table.

"Perhaps the barmaid?" she suggested. "She seems to know the patrons well."

The barmaid was already approaching, but before Water could beckon her closer, she set a key onto the table. "Your room has been paid for," she said. "I think you'll find the accommodations to your liking."

"Wait," Water said, surprised by the overture. "Who paid for the room?"

"He said he was a friend," she said.

"What did he look like?"

"Dark hair, a little shorter than you, and he was handsome," she said, and then flushed, her eyes flicking to Lira and back. "He actually looked a lot like you."

Water glanced to Lira, but she shrugged in confusion. Water thanked the woman and she left. Collecting the key, he dropped coins on the table and rose to his feet. They threaded their way through the tables to the stairs at the back. Instead of going up, they went down, into the sea.

The aquaglass walls were beautiful, allowing a view of the fish and undersea coral. Then they reached the underwater corridor, the walls, floor, and ceiling all transparent, a faint glow allowing a view of the sharks swimming above them. Water glanced in both directions as he reached the door bearing the number on the key, and then unlocked it.

He glanced to Lira and found her with her air blade in hand. Nodding, he cast his staffblade and then unlocked the door. He swung it open and stepped inside, spinning to scan the entire room. But there was only one occupant.

Lounging in a chair with his feet on the desk, Shadow flashed a smile. "Hello, brother, what brings you to Keese?"

Chapter 31: The Fragment of Shadow

"Shadow," Water said with a laugh.

He dismissed his staff and stepped forward, Shadow rising to embrace him. When they parted Shadow bore a wide smile on his face and rotated to face Lira. He took her hand and kissed it.

"I hope my brother has been treating you well."

"He has," she said.

"Not as well as I could, of course," Shadow said with a sniff. "But he'll do."

"What are you doing here?" Water asked.

"Still looking for the ancient map," Shadow said. "I've tracked it to Keese and happened to spot you in the tavern."

Water shared their tale, including encountering Serak and the battle with the Order underground. He finished by describing the kidnapping of King Numen and Grena, the woman that had told them to come to Keese.

"So you think Wylyn is with the Ravens?" Shadow asked.

"Do you know where they are?" Lira motioned upward. "We were told to speak with Wenta."

"She is a low-level informant for the Ravens," Shadow said. He rubbed his chin in thought. "Since we both want the Ravens, perhaps we can help each other."

"What do you have in mind?" Water asked.

"The Ravens and I are not friends," Shadow said, "but I need time in their archives, undisturbed."

"How do we help with that?"

Shadow's smile was too smug for Water's liking. "I need you to get caught. While they interrogate you, I can sneak in and find what I need. Then I'll help you get out."

"I get my answers, you get yours," Water said cautiously.

"An interrogation usually involves sharp objects and blood," Lira said.

"They won't know who you are," Shadow said smoothly. "I need ten minutes, no more. The Raven won't be so hasty to harm you."

"And if she realizes I look like you?"

"You would be so lucky," Shadow said with a laugh, stepping to the door. "Just feign ignorance. You're good at that."

"Where are you going?" Water asked.

"I have my own room," he said. "And there's only one bed here. I guess you'll have to share."

Water flushed. Shadow smirked. Then he disappeared. When he was gone, Water motioned to the floor. "You can have the bed, I'll take the floor."

"That's very kind of you," Lira said.

She claimed Shadow's chair and turned to face the windows. From floor to ceiling, the windows provided a stunning view of the underwater coast. Fish swam about and sharks hunted. Colorful coral was visible on the rocks beneath, and an octopus was just discernible.

"Do you trust Shadow?"

"With my life," he said. She raised an eyebrow and he allowed a small smile. "He likes mischief, but he would never put us in harm's way. Why?"

"I just get the feeling he isn't being entirely truthful."

"You get used to that."

232

She chuckled. "Yet you still trust him?"

He hesitated, and examined the conversation. Shadow had been evasive, but that could have just been Shadow being Shadow. Still, he knew Shadow well enough to know that if he withheld information, it was always for a reason.

"We can trust him," he said.

Lira measured the confidence in his gaze and then inclined her head before facing the window. For a moment they were quiet, and Water tried not to think of the bed sitting just inches from them.

"I'd forgotten all that magic could do," she said, motioning out the window. "A group of mages probably built all these rooms in a matter of weeks. On Renara, such an undertaking would have taken years."

"Do you think magic could defy the Empire?"

She cocked her head to the side and looked to him. "You're still thinking about Renara."

"I can't get the image out of my head," he said. "It just makes me wonder what it would take to stop the Empire from ever doing such a thing again."

"Lumineia is not ready to fight," Lira said. "But one day, when the people stand united and magic is harnessed, perhaps we can do what so many could not."

"And the Eternals?" he asked.

"Will stand with Lumineia," she said.

He nodded, his thoughts drifting to the future. When Wylyn was found and dealt with, he wondered if he would be permitted to join the Eternals. The prospect thrilled and terrified him, but he lacked the courage to ask.

"We should get some sleep," Lira said. "It appears we are going to be captured by the Ravens tomorrow, and I'd like to do it well rested."

She slipped into the privy to change, and he discarded his nobles' clothing. Once comfortable, he unrolled the small bedroll from his pack and lay down. The light orbs dimmed and a moment later Lira's bare feet padded to the bed, followed by her groan of delight as she slipped under the covers.

"This is shockingly comfortable," she said.

"I'll have to take your word for it," he said.

Her head poked over the edge of the bed and she smiled. "Thank you for letting me have the bed. I'm not used to someone taking care of me. It's nice."

He sat up and smiled. "You really thought I'd make you sleep on the floor?"

Her eyes softened and she leaned in, brushing her lips across his. The contact was brief but sent lightning into his toes, his blood beating in his skull and hands, which suddenly felt hot and sweaty.

He swallowed, but she'd already withdrawn, the bed creaking as she settled in for the night. His heart pounded against his ribs and he forced himself to lay down. He didn't speak until he could trust his voice.

"What was that for?"

"We were married," she said, the smile evident in her tone. "It's only fitting you get a kiss out of it."

He smiled, and rotated to face the wall of aquaglass. Lit by exterior light orbs, the sea was alive with silent motion. Although he lay on the floor, he'd never been so comfortable, and he fell asleep watching the fish swim past their room.

***

The next morning they dressed and departed the room. Once again armed and dressed for combat, Lira did not speak of their kiss from the previous night. Realizing she was guarded once again, Water tried to focus on their task.

Shadow met them in the tavern, yawning as he took a seat. He plucked a seared potato from Water's plate and tossed it into his mouth. Motioning a barmaid for his own meal, he leaned forward and spoke in low tones.

"The Raven's current guildhall is in the home of a noble," he said. "You'll reach it through the sewers, while I'll come from above. Once inside, you'll need to get caught, allowing me to get into the archives. Once I have what I need, I'll help you escape."

"This isn't going to make them your friends," Water said, fending off Shadow's hand as he tried to take another bite.

Shadow cast a thread of darkness that curved around Water's hand and skewered a bite. The thread retreated and Shadow caught the food. He flashed a smug grin and then accepted his own plate from the barmaid. When she was gone, Water stabbed his fork through two of his potatoes, stealing them back.

"I don't need them to be my friends," Shadow said. "Besides, the Raven has other information I seek."

Water frowned. "I thought you were just going to get the map."

"That too," Shadow said.

He flashed a smile and then began to eat, and Water glanced to Lira. Instead of angry, the woman seemed amused, and he wondered if she'd just resigned herself to trusting Shadow. Shadow ate quickly and the group departed the Shark's Tooth.

Once outside, Shadow winked to them. "Good luck."

He disappeared into the crowd, and Water could have sworn a woman joined him at the last moment. As he disappeared, Water came to a halt on the waterfront. He laughed lightly and motioned east.

"Ready? I don't think Shadow will get us killed."

"You *hope* Shadow won't get you killed," she corrected.

He grinned and the two set off, winding their way into the city to the alley Shadow had indicated. The overcast sky heralded rain, and lightning crackled in the distance. Normally Water liked a good storm, but this time it set him on edge.

They ducked behind a building and found a rusted grate atop a hole in the ground. Removing the cover of a sewer drain, they dropped into the storm sewers beneath, and Water used a thread of liquid to return the grate to its former position.

As a coastal city, Keese frequently endured raging gales, the rainwater dumping off roofs and flooding the streets. The water sluiced off the streets and into strategically placed drains that funneled the water back to the sea.

Damp and smelling of mold, the tunnel gradually ascended with the terrain, rising toward the eastern side of the city. Water took the lead and guided them up the slope, the angle of the tunnel heading toward the Duke's castle.

Their boots splashed through the water in the base of the drain, and he guessed it had rained some the previous night. Muffled thunder echoed down to them and the soft patter of rain came through another storm drain.

"Looks like we're going to get wet," Lira said.

"It shouldn't be far now," he said, stepping around the water pouring through a drain.

The level of water continued to rise at their feet, ascending up their boots as the storm mounted above. Thunder rumbled, and a flicker of light signified more lightning. The rushing of feet signaled the people were seeking shelter.

They reached the side tunnel Shadow had described and followed it to a dead end. Water counted the stones and found one that seemed darker than the rest. He looked to her and she cast her sword, and then he pressed the hidden trigger.

The wall swung inward, allowing them into the darkness beyond. In the gloom he sensed a large space, the basement of a noble's manor. He squinted, but could not make out anything in the darkness. The darkness to the space gave the room a chilling air, and he shivered. Then he spotted movement and came to an abrupt halt.

A figure stepped from the gloom and came to a stop twenty feet away. Tall and robed in silver and black, the man was one they'd seen before, and Water cast his staff of water as he spoke his name.

"Serak," he said. "I take it the Order is working with the Ravens?"

"The fragment of Water," Serak said. "I'm glad you followed my invitation."

"What invitation?" Lira asked cautiously.

"From Grena," Serak said with a smile.

Water bared his teeth as he realized the woman had been a ruse, a feint intended to draw Water and Lira to Keese. His anger rose as he understood the truth, the village had been destroyed—not by accident—but by intention, to give Grena the chance to trick Water and Lira.

Another figure appeared at Serak's side and Water retreated a step when he recognized the Dark Dwarf. Clad in black steel, Thorg carried the insignia of earth and fire on his chest, and he raised his hands to Water and Lira.

Flames exploded from the ground. As thick as Water's wrist, the flames arced upward and separated to become bars, the flames so bright he felt the heat through his clothing. The blast of light revealed two dakorians and dozens of Ravens in the room, along with more members of the Order. They were arranged on barrels and crates, and sitting on the stairs, all looking to the cage of fire.

The bars had not been cast on a whim, the forged fire requiring time to cast and prepare. Their presence indicated the cage had been crafted for a specific purpose, to trap someone vulnerable to fire. Shadow may have wanted them to get caught, but this was not by accident.

It was an ambush.

237

Chapter 32: Father of Guardians

Serak regarded them with a look of triumph, his expression indicating he did not wish to kill them. At least not yet. The window of opportunity might be sufficient for Shadow to find the archive and return. Still, Water surreptitiously examined the bars of fire, the barrier spitting sparks.

"An attempt to escape would be lethal," the Dark Dwarf rumbled.

"Maybe we're just here to talk," Water said, and motioned to Serak. "Is that not your intention as well?"

A ghost of a smile appeared on Serak's face and he approached the cage. "You are the fragment of Water, a guardian of integrity and honor, unlike your brothers."

Water bristled at his tone. "You presume to know me?"

"I know all about you, and the other fragments." Serak began walking around the cage. "In your first millennium you killed a bandit named Balir in his camp south of Griffin. Twenty years later you, Fire, and Elenyr helped quell the Urdia rebellion."

Water scowled. "How do you know this?"

"The next century you accompanied Elenyr and Mind to negotiate a treaty between Talinor and the new kingdom of Erathan. An assassin appeared, and the three of you successfully defeated him."

On it went, Serak describing Water's life as if he'd been there, picking it apart, the events he'd participated in, the conflicts he'd resolved—even the clothes he'd been wearing. He spoke of events from a thousand years ago and events from his first century, of events in the north and the south, the east and the west. Times when he'd failed and times he'd succeeded. The telling left Water angry and uncertain.

"How do you know these things?" Water demanded, rotating to keep the guardian in sight.

Serak came to a halt after circling the cage, a flicker of irritation on his features. "You must understand, for many of the conflicts, you were the resolution." He smiled. "I was the cause."

Water stared at him, and suddenly saw a different face, a man standing beside a rebellion leader, or the guard at the assassination of a king. The features were altered but not so much they were unrecognizable. Serak had been following the fragments for ages, using conflicts to elicit a response.

Serak smiled at his shock. "Did you never wonder why attacks occurred, always while you were present? Did you not question why events were resolved?"

His questions recalled a conversation Water had once had with Mind, where Mind had wondered much the same thing, and suggested a foe was working against them, seeking to test their abilities, their strengths, their weaknesses. Water had thought the idea absurd, but an invisible foe had indeed been working from the shadows, always hunting, always watching.

Water struggled with a rising fury as he realized he faced an ageless adversary, one that had orchestrated combats, just to test the fragments. How many had died because of Serak? How many pawns had perished because of Serak's game?

Wars, rebellions, battles, Serak had been the unseen adversary, fanning the flames of anger until they became an inferno. And for what? Water clenched his fist at the realization that he'd been manipulated.

"How many have died because of you?" Water growled. "Thousands? Tens of thousands?"

"Dragons do not mourn the loss of the insects they crush—because they are greater beings."

"And you think we're greater beings?" Water growled, his voice rising. "That innocent people deserve to die?"

239

His body trembled with a desire to strike at Serak, and it took all his willpower to resist. Never had he felt such hatred, never had he felt such a desire to kill. Both emotions surprised him, but they roiled inside him like a living beast, prowling against his skull just as he prowled inside the cage.

"You cannot make us believe you've been the source of every conflict the fragments have resolved," Lira said, placing a hand on Water's arm.

"Of course not," Serak said. "I did not have to be. A nudge here, a word there, and the nature of man was escalated."

"*Why?*" Water asked.

"I was the first," Serak said. "You were the last. Between us, we are the only guardians that have retained our sanity, which grants us a singular opportunity."

"An opportunity with the krey?" Lira asked, her voice full of scorn as she pointed to the dakorians lurking in the shadows at the edge of the room.

"Indeed," Serak said. "My beloved knew much about the krey, and knew the day they returned would spell the end of everything. The people would be enslaved and taken away, our lands destroyed, our world left desolate."

His hands clenched and he felt the need to reach for the bars. He recognized the action might be lethal, but a darker thought had surfaced. With such anger in his chest, he could imagine ripping the cage to pieces, using the burning shards to slaughter Serak and everyone present.

Including Lira.

The cage held him bound, but he was not afraid of being trapped, or the captor. Instead it was a fear of self that stayed his hand. Water's eyes flicked to Lira and caught the tension in her face, her expression finally cooling his rage. As the sheen of black faded from his eyes he seemed to regain his senses, and he realized just how close he'd come to seeing the slaughter become reality.

"Few know of these things," Water managed to say.

"And for good reason," Serak said. "If the people knew the truth, they would tear themselves apart. Still, their fate awaits, and the krey have returned. The day has arrived, and perhaps in a matter of weeks a krey armada will appear in our skies."

"You *invited* them," Lira growled.

"I did," he said. "So I could be present when they return. If I had not, the krey might have returned after I had perished, and the world would not be ready."

"We will stop them," Water said.

The Dark Dwarf rumbled a laugh, the sound dripping with scorn. "You cannot stop them."

Lira stepped to the edge of the cage. "You have no idea what we're capable of."

"Even if you could," Serak said, his expression amused, "they will come again. Perhaps not in a year, perhaps not in ten, but one day, they will arrive. It is inevitable."

"And so you stop fighting?" Water challenged. "Just accept your fate?" He shoved his darker impulses aside, burying it beneath a reminder of his purpose.

"I'm picking a side," Serak said. "You and I are unique, and the krey value what is unique."

"Have you forgotten that, to the krey, men are slaves?"

Serak took a step forward, his eyes lighting with triumph. "But we are not men."

Water realized what Serak intended and glanced to Lira. He expected an expression of scorn, but it was worry that creased her forehead, suggesting there was truth to Serak's words. Serak didn't want to *stop* the krey. He wanted to *join* them.

"Think of it," Serak said, approaching to the limit of the fire bars. "We are ageless just like them, yet we have power they do not know. They will want us. They will need us. To fight against them will only lead to ruin, and you will witness the death of your fragment brothers one by one, until all are slain, and you finally perish, alone."

Serak's words were persuasive, a whisper of truth that had led many others to spark the conflicts Water had resolved. He noticed Lira's doubt, her eyes on him, and knew she questioned his resolve. By asking him to betray his brothers Serak had made a mistake, and despite the surge of darkness, Water began to laugh.

The sound rolled out of him, mocking and scornful. Serak folded his arms as Water continued to laugh at the absurdity of the suggestions, and the Ravens in the room shifted, the Order members scowling. The dakorians sensed the spark of conflict and drifted forward, hefting their hammers.

"You picked the wrong fragment," Water said. "Mind, Shadow, or maybe Fire would have been tempted, but even they would have refused. You really think we'd fight to defend the people of Lumineia, and then abandon them? If Wylyn opens a Gate, the krey will destroy the Eternals, and the woman at my side has more strength than you have ever seen. You actually thought I would cast her aside to join you?"

"You don't understand," Serak said. "Staying with them will only invite their doom. Joining me is the only chance you have of saving those you care about."

"Trust you to save them . . . or trust them to save themselves." Water shook his head. "The choice is easy."

He spotted a flicker of movement at the back of the room, a flicker of darkness that entered and dropped off the stairs, avoiding the Ravens on the steps. It disappeared into the shadows behind a group of Order members.

"I had hoped that time would provide you with wisdom," Serak said, his features dark. "But as you said, perhaps Mind will accept what you have refused."

242

"He won't." Water began gathering the moisture from the ground and air, pulling it through the bars, careful to keep the liquid from burning up. "He will choose family, same as I have."

"I have seen knights of honor fall to their darkest impulses," Serak said, "and kings betray their people. All that is required is the proper motivation."

Water's smile was gone, and he approached the fire bars until he felt the heat on his face. "No gold or price, no offer of security, no pain, loss, or manipulation will *ever* get me to betray my family. You have studied me for ages and think you know what I will say, but you know nothing."

Water spotted another flicker of movement, and noticed a pair of Ravens were absent, as if they'd disappeared. Another Order member was also gone, and one had a pink smile painted on his helmet. The burly soldier with a full beard stood with arms folded, oblivious to the garish alteration to his expensive armor.

"They all say they will not change," Serak said. "But all metal bends in the fire, and I assure you, the fire is just beginning."

"You wish me to kill them?" the Dark Dwarf asked.

"No," Serak said. "Not yet. But give him a scar."

The Dark Dwarf grinned and raised his palms. Water retreated to the center of the cage and gathered his magic, but chains erupted from the bars and wrapped around his wrists. He sought to break free but they went taught, pulling his arms apart. Lira yanked her sword free and struck the chains, the impact sending sparks onto them both.

The Dark Dwarf reached his hand outward and gathered heat into his palm, shaping it into a long rod with a symbol on the end, the symbol of Wylyn's house, two curves with a dot on the upper side.

A brand.

"So you know your master," he said, and extended the brand through the bars.

"Before you mark me there's something you should know."

"What's that?" Serak said, raising a hand to stop the Dark Dwarf.

In response, Water unleashed every drop of moisture he'd gathered, expanding it into a wave that struck the bars of the cell. The water burst into a plume of steam that spread outward, obscuring everyone from view.

Out of sight, Serak's chuckle was mocking. "Your attempt to escape is woefully disappointing."

"I wasn't trying to break free," Water said, eyeing the brand that extended from the mist. "I just wanted more darkness."

There was a moment of silence and then Serak barked an order for light. Too late, a large shape climbed from the shadows and released a delighted snarl. Men and women scrambled backward from the massive creature, their shouts drowning out Serak's words. Huge and terrifying, the creature seemed a thing of nightmares, and one woman shrieked that it was a demon. Then the beast charged and the room dissolved into chaos.

Chapter 33: Brothers United

Water caught a glimpse of a large creature tearing through the room. It roared, the sound filled with menace, yet to Water's ears, it sounded like laughter. A man screamed as he was thrown over the fire cage, his body flitting through the mist before slamming into the far wall. A Raven tumbled away, knocking into the Dark Dwarf and sending them both into the shadows.

Lira snatched the branding iron before it could fall out of the cage. She placed the tip of the branding iron on the chains that held Water bound. Sparks exploded from the contact, but the branding iron proved stronger, the chains giving way. She jumped to the chains holding his other hand and did the same. Just as Water burst free, Thorg stalked into view.

"You will not escape so—"

A giant clawed hand appeared behind him and wrapped around his torso. Pure black, the hand was like smoke, but it picked him up and launched him across the room, his body bouncing off the stairs and colliding with one of the dakorians.

Giant jaws appeared in the gloom and chomped on the second dakorian, the soldier howling and smashing his hammer into the beast's head. Then the beast launched the dakorian at the cage of fire. The armored body crashed into the bars, its bulk cracking several before the dakorian bounced off and struck the ground, burn lines on the bones of his back.

Smaller creatures of shadow burst through the darkness, jumping to women and pulling their hair, tearing into the clothing of the men, and clawing at feet. Women shrieked and men howled, the sound tinged with Shadow's delighted laughter.

"We need to get out of here," Lira said. "Shadow can't take them down alone."

He spotted flickers of light as Serak shouted for illumination. The mist was clearing as well, and with each spark of light Shadow would lose power. In moments, whatever beast he'd decided to become would disintegrate, leaving him vulnerable.

"Give me a moment," Water said.

He turned and faced the tunnel they had entered. Dropping to one knee, he placed his fingers on the floor and closed his eyes, reaching through the room, beyond the wall, and to the storm drain beyond. The storm had picked up and water churned through the drain, turning white as it crashed its way toward the sea.

A faint smile crossed his lips as he felt the power. Breathing it in, he bent the current to his will. In the drain outside the room, the rainwater surged up and turned, pushing down the tunnel to the secret entrance, colliding with the stone barrier. The wall shuddered at the impact and spurts of water cascaded through cracks. Water summoned more and more, pushing against the wall, willing it to break.

He sensed the mist clearing, burned away by the rods of fire. The chaos of the room faded as Shadow lost strength and Serak regained control. Beneath it all Water heard a cracking of stone and rose to his feet.

Serak stepped to the cage and laughter nearly robbed Water of his magic. The guardian's features were painted bright orange, his hair spiked in one direction, like a beast had licked his face, the saliva holding the hair straight upward. Paint dripped down his face and onto his body, staining his fine tunic.

"You'll pay for that," Serak growled.

"Not before you do," Water said.

Serak's eyes flicked over Water's shoulder, widening as he spotted the water streaming through the cracks in the wall. Water gathered all his might and forced the water against the wall, and it shattered. Rocks scattered through the room as a ten-foot wave exploded into the

246

basement. The water engulfed the cage, bursting to steam and cooling the magical barrier, the fires succumbing to the torrent.

Water held his hand to the wave, splitting it to either side until the bars disintegrated. Then he caught Lira about the waist and let the current carry them into the chamber. A dakorian appeared and brought his hammer down on Water, forcing him to dive to the side.

Lira went the opposite way, landing in the middle of a group of Ravens. Swords swung at her but she cast her blade and deflected the blows in a ring of steel—and then struck back. Men and women crumpled and fell away.

Water landed next to the dakorian and used a burst of magic to make him stumble. Then he sent a thread of magic up to the hammer, leashing it and bringing it down on a woman charging from behind.

Water stumbled when the ground opened up beneath him, and he heard the Dark Dwarf advancing on him. He used the water scattered across the floor to flood into the hole and lift him out before it could close. Then he rode the wave directly at his attacker. The dwarf raised a flaming axe but Water leapt into a flip that carried him over. Landing behind Thorg, Water yanked the wave into the spinning dwarf, knocking him sprawling and extinguishing his hammer.

More soldiers appeared from the shadows. Realizing they could not stay and fight, Water summoned every bit of water from the storm drain and pulled it to himself. The current picked him up and carried him to Lira, where he caught her about the waist and banked toward the stairs. He spotted Shadow and sent a hand of water out. The fragment leapt aboard, the trio riding the wave as it carried them up the stairs to the door. Shadow's taunting laugh echoed in the chamber as the wave carried them through the door. Water caught a glimpse of Serak as they escaped.

The water from the storm drain parted around him, as if afraid to touch his form. He stood with his arms folded, his voice silent as Water slipped from his grasp. No orders were given, and he simply stood there. Water could have sworn the guardian smiled.

"What's with all the paint?" Lira asked as they hurtled up the stairs. "You could have just fought them."

"Anyone can fight," Shadow said. "But it takes a true master to be remembered by his foes."

Water sent them up the stairs and shaped the current into a fist, blasting through the door at the top. They burst into a room of fine tapestries, elven-made carpets, and golden chandeliers. Water winced when the wave ripped through them all, carrying them across the room to the hall beyond.

Raven guards appeared with weapons drawn, and Water banked to the side, angling down the corridor and around another bend. Arrows flew towards them but Lira raised a hand, the wind sending them scattering into a cabinet, shattering glass and dishes. Spotting the doorway, Water shaped the front of their wave into another fist and they exploded into the open.

Wind and rain assaulted them as they flew into the street. White cobblestone and finely crafted seastone greeted them, the rich nobles standing under overhangs, staring in shock as they streaked by. Water banked into an alley and split the river, one turning into a bubble that curved down to the next street, the other sending them up to a roof.

The trio landed on the roof as their ride splashed on the roof tiles. The angled roof extended across the home, but a rooftop garden had been constructed, rainwater clattering off the roof and flowing into cunningly built tubes that fed the flowers beneath. Water ducked into the garden as Ravens sprinted through the alley, rushing to catch the now empty water carriage.

Breathing hard, Water motioned to the disappearing river. "That should keep them occupied until we are out of Keese."

"Well done," Shadow said, brushing water off his arms.

"Couldn't have done it without your aid," Water said, nodding his gratitude.

Shadow bowed and swept his hands wide. "I live to serve."

"I thought you lived to play," Lira said.

"That too," Shadow said.

Lira was drenched, her hair in disarray, her clothing sodden. But there was a smile on her face as she dismissed her sword. Water gestured to her and sucked the water from her clothes, sending rivulets of moisture onto the floor of the rooftop garden.

"I can do that," she said.

"I know," he said with a smile.

She smiled and thanked him before stepping to the edge of the garden. She leaned to the edge of the falling rain and peered into the street, where soldiers and shouts rang out. More Ravens appeared, rushing down the alley before they disappeared.

"Serak was ready for us," she said. "He was ready for Water."

"I thought the same thing," Water said. "That cage would have taken a year to build, and multiple mages."

"But Wylyn has only been here for a few months," Lira said.

"It appears Serak planned to trap you before Wylyn appeared," Shadow said, nodding to himself.

"In the Gate Chamber," Water said, recalling their conversation when they'd met Serak. "He did say he wasn't ready to meet us." Then he noticed Shadow's expression and frowned. "Did you know it was a trap?"

Shadow grinned. "Perhaps."

"I could have been branded," Water growled.

"We got what we needed," Shadow said. "And it was a pleasure to see you so furious."

"*You* got what you needed," Lira said, her expression tight with disapproval. "And we paid the price."

"You were *supposed* to get caught," Shadow said. "And you did get the chance to speak to Serak. From what I heard, you learned a great deal."

"You lied to us," Water said.

"Serak would have noticed if you were prepared," Shadow said. "You aren't very good at assuming a different persona."

As much as Water wanted to argue, he knew Shadow had a point. Serak had been studying them since their first years, and would likely have noticed a change in behavior. Serak had also revealed a great deal, so perhaps the risk was worth it.

Shadow seemed to notice his fading anger and took that as approval. "It's been a pleasure, brother, but my assignment awaits. Have fun with Lira."

He winked, his tone making Water flush. "Where are you going?" Water asked. "Did you get the map?"

"Do you even know me?" Shadow asked with a snort of amusement. He reached into a pouch and tossed it to him. "Something came up—I'll meet up with you later."

Then he stepped to the edge of the roof and leapt off. Water watched him disappear into the street, again joining the woman Water had spotted on the docks the previous day. A sour chuckle escaped his lips.

"I've known him for thousands of years, and still he surprises me."

"Did you see the woman he was with?"

"I don't know her," Water said. "But she looks like a warrior. She may even have been a Raven. Shadow has always had friends among such people."

"I suspect you have friends among the knights and honorable nobles."

"Why would you say that?'

She joined him at the edge of the garden. "Because we get along with those that mirror our attributes."

"Is that so?"

Her gaze was soft. "Always."

"Still, I'm sorry Shadow got us into that."

"I'm not."

Water turned to Lira and found her smiling. "Why?"

"He was right. And we did get answers."

Water spotted a group of Ravens appearing on the streets below and pulled her away from the ledge. Surrounded by flowers, the air filled with rain, and still hunted, he found his companion more beautiful than ever.

"Were you tempted?" she asked.

By Serak's offer?" He shook his head. "Not even for a moment."

Her comment reminded him of their adversary, and his smile faded. Serak was a patient foe, one that had waited and watched for ages. He'd planned the moment in the Ravens' guildhall with great care.

"Why is there doubt in your eyes?"

"I don't doubt my choice," he said. "I doubt his. Serak had been plotting for millennia, and would have planned that moment with great care."

"And?"

"So why pick me?" he asked.

Lira frowned. "As you said, you are the least likely to accept his offer."

"Serak knew I would refuse," Water realized.

"So why did he still invite you?" she asked.

The question reminded Water of Serak's smile as they departed. It was disconcerting to feel like they were several steps behind, and disturbing to know that Serak was already allied with Wylyn. He'd invited her to Lumineia, and now issued an offer to Water to join. Serak was a dangerous adversary, one that left him with a lingering worry as they departed Keese. The threats were mounting, and it was time to unite with the others. He just hoped they weren't too late.

Chapter 34: Willow

"Do you think she will meet with us?" Light asked, his voice eager.

Elenyr hid a smile. "Willow will be here."

They'd left Stormwall six days past, and traveled east and south to a small settlement in the hills of northern Talinor. Little more than a tower and a collection of structures, the outpost sat under a long overhang of rock, the trees further shading the outpost walls.

Arches of stone connected the tower to the stone behind it, allowing those within a quick escape into the cave. For most, the cave would have been a dead end, but for those who occupied the outpost, it was the entrance, for the outpost was owned by the dark elves.

Built a century before, the outpost allowed the dark elves to sell their exotic wares on the surface. Many had been against allowing the dark elves a presence in Talinor, but the king had permitted them use of the location, and it had quickly flourished, with many merchants seeking dark elf weaponry and enchanted items.

Elenyr and her companions had arrived and been permitted to stay in the inn outside the outpost walls. Reserved for guests of the underground race, the inn was built in their style, the stone glowing with underground plants each night. It was evening, and the walls were lit with silver, blue, and green branches, the trees growing inside the structure.

They'd been waiting two days for Willow, a captain in the dark elf army. Elenyr had met her two centuries ago, when she, Light, and Shadow had traveled into the Deep in search of a criminal that had fled below. Elenyr had been impressed by Willow, but Light had been enchanted, and sought many opportunities to see the woman.

She noticed the amusement on Mind's and Fire's faces, but Light didn't see their smiles. Veritably bouncing on his feet, his eagerness was obvious as he watched the door. Jeric leaned over with a smile.

"I take it he favors the girl?"

"A great deal," Elenyr murmured.

"I can hear you," Light said, and then grinned. "But I can't deny it."

"How long has it been?" Fire asked.

"Twelve years?" Light didn't seem certain.

"She could be married," Mind said. Light looked to him in shock, but he shook his head. "Probably not."

The door opened and a dark elf woman stepped inside. Short and thin, she did not look intimidating, but she'd proved to be an accomplished weapons master, even if her favored weapon was unusual.

She carried no visible blade, but her body was covered in tattoos, every inch of visible skin inked with various blades, axes, even tools. A whip curled around her bare stomach while the back of her left hand showed a long dagger, the tip extending up her arm. A short sword marked her hip, the weapon disappearing below her skirt to show the blade on her thigh. The curve of a crossbow extended from her back and onto her ribs. On anyone else, the ink would have been ornamental, but on Willow, it was an armament.

Unlike most dark elves, she did not tie her hair, and let it hang free to the middle of her back. Her grey skin was flawless, her almond eyes creasing with delight when she spotted Light. Before she'd taken two steps into the inn, Light bounded across the space and engulfed her in a hug, and then planted a kiss on her lips.

Jeric grinned. "Now that's a greeting."

"Light's never been good at controlling his impulses," Mind said, his expression disapproving.

Light and Willow parted and she smiled up at him. "Hello, bright one," she murmured.

254

"I missed you," Light exclaimed. "And Mind thought you were married." He cast a glare at Mind.

"What if I was?" she asked.

"Are you?" Light asked, his voice shocked.

"No," she replied, a ghost of a smile crossing her features.

Light looked relieved.

Elenyr approached the woman and greeted her. "Thank you for coming."

"When I informed the queen of what you'd learned, I was ordered to meet you," she said.

"An order?" Jeric asked. "So she believed us about her daughter."

Willow nodded. "Mothers know their daughters, and the Princess Melora has been very secretive of late."

"What will the queen do with her?" Fire asked.

"Princess Melora had disappeared," Willow said. "I suspect she is with the Order."

Elenyr motioned them all to the table. "We have much to discuss, and you must be tired."

Willow nodded her gratitude, but instead motioned toward the door. "Actually, another would like to speak with you."

"Oh?" Elenyr asked. "Who?"

Willow's eyes swept the group, and then flicked to the dark elves sitting at the table nearby. A handful of humans and a trio of elves were also present in the tavern, all merchants. Elenyr had seen their caravans outside and guessed them to be genuine, but Willow's caution suggested the mysterious person wanted privacy.

"Elenyr, would you accompany me?" Willow asked.

"Of course," Elenyr said.

Light took a step forward, but Willow's expression turned apologetic. "Only Elenyr."

His face fell, but Fire clapped him on the shoulder. "I'm guessing you'll get to see her again."

"I'm certain of it," Willow said.

Light brightened, and Elenyr followed Willow from the inn. As she did, she noticed Jeric and Mind bearing matching expressions of concern. Then Mind's thoughts tugged at the corner of her consciousness.

It could be a trap.

Not if Willow is here. Elenyr said.

She could be an unwitting pawn.

Answers first, Elenyr said, glancing his way as she stepped outside. *But keep the link open.*

She sensed his nod of agreement, and then turned her attention to Willow. The woman was quiet, not prone to outbursts of emotion or affection. Elenyr had only ever seen her favor Light, and for the first time, questioned the purpose of her attention.

She scowled when she realized she was doubting a friend. Willow had always been honorable, and never displayed a hint of disloyalty. The Order had infiltrated a great deal, but their reach was not infinite.

"These are troubling times," Willow said softly.

"Indeed they are," Elenyr said, privately deciding that she should continue to trust Willow until she gave reason to remove that trust. "Did you know about the Order?"

"I did," she said. "Unlike the criminal guilds, the Order kept quiet, and did not attack anyone. For that reason, most in the Deep considered them harmless."

"Most?" Elenyr caught the connotation.

Willow glanced her way. "The Order approached me."

Elenyr came to a halt, and the elf rotated to face her. "When?" Elenyr asked.

"A few decades past," she said. "When I was appointed to my captainship."

"They sought to recruit you," Elenyr guessed.

"They did recruit me."

Elenyr retreated a step and palmed the hilt of her sword, but Willow offered a faint smile. "Joining the Order was not my choice."

"They forced you?"

"No," Willow said. "The order came from above."

Elenyr's first thought was that Princess Melora had ordered Willow to join the Order. But the Order of Ancients wanted only loyal in their ranks. So if she had not been manipulated by the Order, that left only one explanation.

"Your queen ordered you to accept."

Willow inclined her head, and then resumed walking toward the gates of the outpost. She lowered her voice as they passed in earshot of the guards, and murmured a warning.

"The Order has ears everywhere," she whispered. "Even here. Wait until we are inside to speak."

Elenyr nodded to let her know she understood, and then smiled to the guards. As they passed inside, Elenyr sent a quick thought to Mind, but asked him to keep the information private, for now. The possibility of having an informant on the inside of the Order could change everything, and she didn't want to risk an Order member hearing of Willow's role because the fragments spoke of it in the tavern. Willow had only spoken the truth outside the outpost, a strategic location chosen for its lack of potential listeners.

The outpost wall extended in a half circle, wrapping around the collection of warehouses which sat next to the tower. Between the warehouses, a tower connected the ground to the overhang of stone.

Behind the turret, a second wall, thicker than the first, extended from the sides of the tower to the mouth of the cave, allowing dark elves to enter and depart the turret without fear of attack. Since the tower's construction, it had been attacked a handful of times, and each time the thieves had been left wanting.

They passed warehouses stocked with foodstuffs and exotic spices from the Deep, as well as weapons crafted by dark elf swordsmiths. They passed into the shadow of the overhanging rock and then entered through the bottom doors. The interior of the turret was more lavish than it had been the last time Elenyr had visited, with glowing trees growing up the walls, the limbs providing beauty and light to the space. At the center, another tree stood, the trunk rising through the floor above.

Willow led the way to the tree and the bark opened, revealing a recessed space inside. Large enough for a small group, the space in the trunk rose up through the center of the tree, the magic silent as the wood carried them aloft.

"This magic is from the surface elves," Elenyr said.

"Our queen has forged a treaty with our surface cousins," Willow said. "And we have traded magics, benefiting us both."

"I was not aware you had signed an accord," Elenyr said.

"Until more of our people are ready to accept the surface dwellers as more than an enemy, our treaties must remain secret."

The answer was simple, but spoke volumes. The queen had pushed vigorously to allow just the one outpost, and many of her people thought the dark elves should remain in the Deep. If they knew their queen was signing treaties, there would be riots.

"Does Princess Melora know of the treaty?"

"She does," Willow said.

Elenyr heard the current of disapproval and realized the dark elf warrior did not care for the princess, another note in Willow's favor. Elenyr was grateful Willow was on their side. She would have hated having to fight the woman.

The ascender came to a halt and the trunk opened, allowing them into the topmost chamber of the tower. The canopy of the tree flowed across the ceiling, clinging to the stone, the limbs glowing a faint blue. The room was open all the way to the walls, where darkened windows allowed a view of the cave in the back, and the outpost and outer inns in the front.

The floor was all stone, and contained an assortment of tables, couches, and chairs. The receiving hall could have housed fifty, and it had, on the occasions the dark elves hosted leaders of the merchant guilds. On the eastern side of the room, the chairs were arranged in a circle so that many could gather to speak. Despite the size of the chamber, it lay empty, with only a single occupant standing at the front window.

Dressed in a gown of purple silk, the woman was intimidating. She was tall for a dark elf, her body trim and muscular. She showed no obvious blade, but Elenyr suspected there would be at least one hidden in the folds of her gown. Her black hair was turning silver, the braids lying down her back to her waist.

Elenyr glanced at Willow but the soldier stood by the tree, so Elenyr advanced alone. She approached and joined her at the window, and the woman finally turned. Elenyr had suspected her identity the moment she'd walked into the room, but blinked in surprise.

"I expected the queen," Elenyr said.

Princess Aranian, first daughter of the dark elf kingdom, stood before her. Her features were tight with regret and worry, the expression one of a heavy mantle. Elenyr had seen that look before, when a prince became a king.

"What happened?" Elenyr asked.

"My sister has taken my mother," Aranian said. "And I need your help to get her back."

Chapter 35: A Royal Request

Elenyr studied the woman, and saw that the Princess Aranian's despair was real. Elenyr didn't know the princess as well as the queen, but respected her for her wisdom and poise. She'd taken after the queen in looks and temperament, and many of her people regarded her as a royal. But she was still a dark elf, and secrets were currency for the underground race.

"You never trust members of the surface race," Elenyr said. "Least of all with such a dangerous truth. Why ask for my aid?"

"The Order of Ancients has spread among my people," she said. "And there are few I know I can trust."

"And you trust me?" Elenyr's expression was doubtful.

"I trust Willow," she said, her eyes flicking to the soldier. "And when she received your message, she swore I could trust you and your companions."

Elenyr glanced Willow's way, but her features were inscrutable. Willow's loyalty was not surprising, but the princess must be desperate indeed to turn away from her own soldiers, especially the elite guard.

"Why not send the Hand?"

The queen's Hand consisted of five warriors sworn to obey the queen. Like wraiths in the Deep, they used intimidation and assassination, ending disputes that had potential to become lethal to the royal family. Many regarded them as a myth, but Elenyr had fought beside one, and knew just how dangerous they could be.

"I did," the princess said. "They did not return."

"You think they were killed?" Elenyr asked in surprise. She didn't think anything could kill them.

"I believe they have joined the Order."

The prospect was even more deadly. If the Queen's Hand had truly joined the Order, very little could stop them. It also explained why the princess had come to Elenyr for aid, for if the most loyal of the queen's guard could be subverted, anyone was suspect.

"The Order has grown bold since the ancients appeared," Elenyr said. "And they are gathering strength."

"We thought them to be harmless," Aranian said. "Now they pose the greatest of threats."

"How much do you know about the Order?" Elenyr asked.

Princess Aranian flashed a faint smile. "They have always had a presence in our kingdom, and for most of our history, they did not hide their allegiances. They spoke of the peace the ancient race provided, and attempted to persuade the people to seek their return. Those that grew overzealous were imprisoned, but for the most part, they gathered in peace."

"You speak of them like they were a religion."

"They worship the ancients," she said. "Not unlike the Church of Light that worships Ero, or the Cult of Skorn that worships Skorn."

Elenyr hid a smile. Most did not know that Ero and Skorn were members of the ancient race, and churches still worshiped them as gods. But the way the princess spoke, it was almost as if the Order of Ancients among the dark elves were not connected to those on the surface.

"What changed?" Elenyr asked.

"After the Mage Wars, when the oracle bloodlines were extinguished, they slipped into obscurity. We do not know why."

"Perhaps they found a new ally," Elenyr said.

The princess frowned. "You know who they are?"

"I do now," Elenyr said, and detailed what Light had said regarding their encounter with Serak.

"This guardian," Willow said. "He is powerful?"

"He is," Elenyr said. "But the true threat is his cunning. He has managed to avoid detection for thousands of years, suggesting a malevolent patience."

"And he has joined the Order?"

"I am uncertain as to his role," she said. "From what you describe, it would appear his influence has led to the Order withdrawing from the public eye."

The princess glanced to Willow and inclined her head, a mark of permission. Willow then stepped forward. "What I am about to share is known by only a few within the Order, and the last one to speak openly endured weeks of agony before they killed him. If you know this truth, they will hunt you."

"They already hunt me," Elenyr said. "And I'm not so easy to kill."

Willow inclined her head. "After the Mage Wars, Serak took control of one of the Order factions on the surface. Over the next hundred years he gathered and united all the factions, including those in the deep. With that unity, he brought them to focus, and gave them a purpose: to stop waiting on the ancients to return, and to discover a way to bring them here. From what you speak, they have finally been successful."

"We are fortunate there are only two krey," Elenyr said. "If they had brought their full might . . ."

"Indeed," the princess said. "But Wylyn's arrival has emboldened Serak and the Order, and they are shedding their anonymity."

"Do you know what they intend?" Elenyr asked.

"Not yet," Willow said.

Elenyr considered what she'd learned. The dark elves had confirmed Serak to be their foe, and knowing the enemy was the first step in victory. Still, they had now kidnapped not one, but two monarchs, and threatened the others. Doing so would invite retaliation from all the kingdoms. Why?

"Wylyn is the true threat," Elenyr said, thinking aloud. "And I believe the Order is attempting to draw attention away from the krey. The surface races are already in turmoil, and the kingdoms are in chaos. It has already hampered our efforts to find the krey."

"Will you not offer aid?" the princess asked.

Elenyr stared out the window and spotted Light pacing outside the outpost. The fragment kept looking up at the tower as if he knew about the discussion, and she wondered how long he would wait before barging through the gates.

"Do you know Wylyn's location?" Elenyr cast over her shoulder.

"I do not," Willow said. "But I know she is on the surface."

"And Serak?" she asked. "Is he in the Deep?"

"Also on the surface," Willow said. "He does not often come below."

"Good," Elenyr said, an idea forming in her mind.

"You have a plan," the princess said.

Elenyr turned back to her. "We need to find Wylyn and Serak, and you need to find your queen. I think there's a way we can get both."

"How?" Willow asked.

Elenyr pointed to Light. "My companion has seen Serak."

"So?" the princess asked.

Willow's eyes glowed with excitement. "I see what you intend. May I retrieve him?"

Elenyr nodded, and the princess made a confused gesture of agreement. After Willow departed, the princess pointed to Light. "Why would it matter if he'd seen Serak?"

"How much do you know about my companions?" she asked.

"You travel with five mages," she said. "They are talented and share odd kinship with each other."

Elenyr hesitated, wondering if she could reveal the truth. But under the current circumstances, they needed to unify against a common enemy, and Elenyr had to trust someone. Besides, Elenyr got the impression that Princess Aranian spoke the truth.

"They are fragments of a single guardian," Elenyr said. "And each contains a fragment of power."

The princess regarded Elenyr with surprise on her features. "So the light mage?"

"Is a guardian," Elenyr said.

As she spoke, Elenyr watched the princess closely. Fear appeared in her dark eyes, an obvious response to learning of the fragment's identity. The guardians during the Mage Wars had wreaked havoc on every nation, their madness killing thousands, including their masters. And one was about to enter the room.

The princess wrestled with the fear, but it faded to resolve. Elenyr mentally nodded her approval. The princess did not have a choice, and she'd come here for aid. She needed Elenyr and her companions.

"My mother occasionally spoke of you," the princess said, her eyes on the trunk of the tree, where Light would soon appear. "As did my grandmother. Yet you look like you have not aged a day."

"There are those in this world that have lived many lifetimes," Elenyr said.

"Like Serak?"

"We are not like Serak."

"That is my hope," the princess said, "for if my faith is misplaced, my people are doomed."

"I am not unlike you," Elenyr said. "I fight for my family, my sons, and those I love."

The princess glanced her way, her features uncertain. "How risky is your plan?"

"Very," Elenyr said. "But I think it's our best chance at finding our foes, before they multiply any further."

A whisper of sound came from the trunk and the door swung open. Light bounded into the room, crossing the space faster than seemed possible. He reached Elenyr and came to a halt, words tumbling from his lips.

"You were talking forever," he complained.

"Light," Elenyr said. "What we talk about here cannot be spoken of to anyone."

"Except my brothers."

"Of course," Elenyr said with a smile. "But what I'm going to ask you to do will be very dangerous."

"Is it necessary?"

"I believe it is."

"Then what do you need?"

"Do you remember what Serak looks like?"

"Of course," Light said.

"Can you look like him?"

Light shrugged—and his features began to change. The light warped and bent, shaping across his features, lengthening his nose and darkening his eyes. His hair lightened, and his lips gained a cruel twist. The princess gasped when Light became their foe.

"It's not possible," she breathed.

"He is a guardian," Elenyr said, as if that answered her doubt.

The princess stared at Light in shock, and Elenyr understood why. The complexities of a face made it difficult for mages to replicate. Even experienced mages took many years to create a false image of another, and even then, it did not last long. Then the princess realized Elenyr's intent.

"You wish to send him to the Order?" Aranian guessed.

"With Willow," Elenyr said. "She knows the Order, and he can look like their leader. Together, they can get the answers we both seek."

"You want me to travel into the Deep?" Light's features returned to normal, his frown one of doubt. "My power is limited underground."

"You are the only one capable of becoming Serak," Elenyr said.

"Shadow can bend his features," Light said.

"Not well enough," Elenyr said. "But when he returns, I will dispatch him to your aid. But time is not our ally, and you can do what none of us can."

Light's expression was uncertain. "I will be vulnerable."

Elenyr grimaced. "And that is why this is a risk. But you will not go alone." She hesitated, and then impulsively added. "Jeric will accompany you."

"The elf?" the princess asked. "Why?"

"Because he is a master at discovering truth that others wish to hide," Elenyr said.

She did not say that she wanted Jeric to help protect Light. Elenyr knew the danger of the assignment, and still felt a measure of conflict regarding Jeric. Sending him with Light would help the assignment, while giving Elenyr time to figure out what she wanted from him.

"If you trust him," the princess said, "then I do as well."

Elenyr inclined her head and then motioned to Willow. "Willow will also be your companion."

"Willow?" His face lit up, and then he scowled. "But will she not be in the same danger?"

Elenyr couldn't resist the smile at Light's concern for Willow, and then explained how the soldier had infiltrated the Order. When Elenyr finished, Light regarded her with the most sober expression Elenyr had ever seen.

"I understand," he said. "As you said, this is necessary."

Elenyr stepped close and embraced the fragment, lowering her voice so only he would hear. "Come back alive."

"I will," Light said, hugging her back.

When they parted, Elenyr had a lump in her chest. Light was one of the stronger fragments, but in temperament he lacked wisdom, and Elenyr was asking him to don a dangerous persona. If he perished because of her . . .

Elenyr jerked her head and turned to Willow. The woman understood her question before she could ask. "I will keep him safe."

"I cannot keep the truth from people for long," the princess said. "You have only days before the people learn their queen has been taken. When they do, the people will demand answers."

Willow's features were fixed. "We will not fail."

Elenyr had sent the fragments to face countless threats, but never had she sent one into such danger, and as Light departed with Willow, she wondered if it was the last time she would ever see him.

Chapter 36: Seeking Wylyn

Water and Lira left Keese and set a grueling pace east. The storms continued, and Water used the moisture to craft a pair of steeds. With rain battering them, they raced across the countryside. Water only paused long enough to cast a jungle cat, one that would track Elenyr and deliver a message. It disappeared into the storm, its body bounding from view. Water could only hope it would find Elenyr somewhere in Talinor.

Water sensed a rising urgency. With Shadow's map in hand, they finally had a chance of locating Wylyn. There was always the chance that she and her son were not in one of the ancient outposts, but he suspected that Elenyr was right. He'd known enough nobles to know that once they grew comfortable with their station, they loathed living in squalor.

They pushed themselves until weariness overcame Water, and then camped in a small stand of trees. Water cast a bubble with his remaining strength, the dome shielding them from the storm, and allowing them to sleep.

Water sank into slumber, the fatigue of using so much magic in the last week pulling him into unconsciousness. His dreams were filled with Lira and their kiss, the image fading as she departed to rejoin the Eternals. And he said farewell.

He woke up, groaning at the sun in his eyes. Lira, standing at the fire, looked up and smiled. "About time you woke up."

"How long was I asleep?"

"A day."

Water lurched to his feet. "Why didn't you wake me?"

"You're attractive when you're sleeping."

He flushed. "We need to hurry."

"I know," she said. "But when we find Wylyn, we're going to need our strength. You won't be any good if you're exhausted."

Her words had logic, but it still irritated him that he'd been sleeping so long while Wylyn continued to expand her influence in Lumineia. For all he knew, she'd finished preparing the Gate and the krey were already on their way.

"Rest easy," she said, seeming to sense his tension.

"How can you be so calm?"

"I'm well fed," she said.

"How?" he asked.

She turned and revealed a plank of wood with bread, cheese, and a jug of ale—none of which had been present when he'd fallen asleep. She smiled at the surprise on his face and pointed north.

"When the storm ended I tried to wake you, but you slept like a child. Then I spotted a farm and decided to get us a meal."

"You left me alone?" he asked.

"Of course not," she said. "I left you a sentry."

He spotted a small creature with four arms clinging to a tree above. It had a head that resembled a snake, and intimidating fangs. It was the first time he'd ever seen her cast an entity out of air, and he raised his eyebrow as he took a seat by the fire.

"Why do you not cast entities?"

"Honestly, I'm not very good. I use them mostly for sentries, but in a fight, I'm better with my blade."

He still felt the same urgency, but one bite of cheese reminded him that he was also hungry. Deciding that she'd done well under the circumstances, he settled in for the meal, and savored the bread.

Without the storm, he could see that the trees they'd chosen for their camp were situated adjacent to a creek. Sunlight streamed through the branches, the streams of light illuminating their small camp. The trunks provided enough shade to feel cool, but he caught glimpses of the surrounding countryside.

They'd crossed most of Talinor during the storm. To the east he spotted the forest of Orláknia, home to the elven nation. Farms dotted the hills nearby, and from the architecture he guessed they were also elven.

"The races are very different than I remember," she said.

"How so?" he asked.

"They were more distinct in my day," she said. "Now, the blood of the races has become mixed."

"Love has no nation," he said.

"True," she said. "But nations do not always permit such a union."

"What do you mean?"

"I will show you," she said.

He picked up his food and followed her to the edge of the trees. From there, he could see the farm she'd visited. He'd expected elves and was not disappointed, but then he spotted the mother, and she was human.

The woman scolded her sons, their muddy clothes indicating they deserved the punishment. But the mother's words were tinged with affection, and it was obvious she loved the two boys. In the fields, the father used a flicker of plant magic to tend to the field of wheat, while an older daughter aided in the planting.

"Are such unions not frowned upon?" she asked.

"By some," he said.

Her eyes were on the mother and her boys. "The Krey Empire cares nothing for human families, and few children are raised knowing both their parents. Strong children are sold like the people here would sell cattle."

"Why do you share this with me?"

She turned to face him, her blue eyes intense. "Because even when these families are ripped apart, other mothers take these children in, and fathers raise those that are not of their blood. Race and age do not matter."

Water read the mixed emotions on her face. She hated the krey, and loved the race she fought for. But this time there was something else in her eyes, a determination that had been absent before.

"You want to fight the Empire," he guessed.

She flashed a determined smile. "Ero believes we cannot face the Empire, that we can only protect Lumineia from discovery. Until now I thought he was right."

"What changed?"

"You."

"How did I do that?"

Lira pointed to his chest. "I've seen what you can do, and you've made me think we can overthrow the Empire." She seemed to shudder at her treasonous words.

"How?" he asked, thinking of Renara. "How can we possibly defeat such a foe?"

"I don't have all the answers," she said. "That's what I'll have you for."

She laughed and turned away from the farm, forcing him to keep up.

"Are you saying you want me to be an Eternal?" he asked.

"I want you to be an Eternal . . . with me."

He realized what she meant and caught her hand. She came to a halt and turned to him, but the amusement was gone. Instead it was a glitter of desire in her eyes. He tentatively leaned into a brief kiss.

"Is that a yes?" she asked.

"I don't know," he said. "I would have to leave my brothers."

"Will you consider it?"

"I will."

She smiled again, her amusement returning. "Wylyn first. Then we talk."

He couldn't resist the smile on her face. "Agreed."

The two gathered their supplies. She dismissed her entity and he used the stream to cast a new pair of steeds. Feeling much more hopeful than before, he led the way into the elven forests, and he frequently imagined a future with Lira at his side.

They worked their way south and west, heading for Cloudy Vale. She made no attempt to speak of the Eternals, and he realized she was content to wait. As much as he wanted to dream of a future as an Eternal, his thoughts turned to Wylyn, and then Serak.

He wanted to dismiss Serak's claim, but there was too much truth in his words. But it was his motivations that Water questioned. Why had he revealed himself to Water, to give an offer he knew Water would refuse? Even more, what did he really want out of the fragments?

When Lira asked, he reluctantly shared his concerns, but she reminded him that they couldn't afford to get distracted, and steered the conversation back to Wylyn. He knew she was right, but he couldn't quite shake the feeling that their true adversary was Serak.

They ascended the hills and then climbed into the mountains until they reached the entrance to Cloudy Vale. He dismissed the water mounts outside one of the secret entrances and opened the door in the cliff. They ascended through the tunnels to the refuge, and he wasn't surprised to find it empty.

The sun was setting on the refuge, the light fading from yellow to orange. Eager to explore the map, Water went straight to Elenyr's archives, and strode through her receiving hall to the interior library.

"She won't mind you inside her home?"

"We all use the archives," he said, and then flashed a faint smile. "But don't damage the books. Shadow learned that lesson the hard way."

He ascended the steps to the platform with the fireplace and laid a fire. Then he used a phoenix feather to light the fire, the feather igniting the wood with ease. She spotted the feather and raised an eyebrow.

"Is that what I think it is?"

He nodded. "A gift from the Ancient, father of phoenixes."

"I didn't realize you knew the firebirds," she said.

"Elenyr has many friends," he said.

As the firelight filled the room, he withdrew the map from his pack and set it on the table. Lira touched the rune and it came to life, light glowing from within. But instead of examining the map, she manipulated the runes until the light flowed from the object, rising into a ten-foot sphere that resembled Light's map when they had departed Cloudy Vale.

"Impressive," he said.

"The krey may not have magics, but their machines are sophisticated."

"Don't let Light see this," he said. "He would be jealous."

She grinned and touched the runes, activating points of light across the globe. "This is all the krey outposts."

"Not all of them," Water said, pointing to an empty spot on the map.

"We should assume the map is incomplete," she said, striding around it. "The question is, how can we find out which location is Wylyn's refuge?"

"This," he said, sweeping a hand at the library. "We can find out which have been destroyed by disaster or war. That way we can narrow it down until Elenyr arrives."

"How long will it take?"

"The cat I sent to her will continue running until it finds her," he said. "But it could take a few days. For now, we've got a lot of work to do."

He nodded to her and they dived into the archives. He pulled down a number of historical archives, and they searched the records, eliminating locations on the map one by one. The hours passed in near silence, broken by moments of excitement when finding information on a krey site.

They worked deep into the night and then retired, both sleeping on couches in the library. The next day they continued their search, the discoveries growing further and further apart as they went deeper into history.

They ate and slept, the search consuming them both as they sought to find Wylyn's refuge. Water tried to resist the doubt that Wylyn was in none of them. It was always possible Serak had prepared a place for the krey, but he doubted Wylyn would let the guardian take the lead, and she would be prideful. He hoped.

Four days after arriving at the refuge Lira dropped a book onto the table, the thud drawing his attention. He looked up from his own archive and leaned back to see her through the pile of books.

"Giving up?"

"We haven't found anything since yesterday," she said, pointing to the glowing map in irritation. "And there are still dozens of locations she could be at."

"The others will know more," he said. "I'm sure of it."

"And if they don't?"

Her voice carried a trace of worry. He rubbed his eyes and leaned back in his chair, contemplating where they could go with the knowledge they'd gained. Ultimately, he realized there would be only one choice.

"I guess we start searching them all."

"A slow endeavor," she said.

He rubbed his neck. "We'll have to see what Elenyr has to say."

"When she gets here."

"She already is," Elenyr said.

Water heard Elenyr's voice and stood, smiling when he spotted Elenyr, Mind, and Fire entering the archives. Wending his way through the piles of books, he reached her and nodded in greeting.

"I see you got my message," he said. He craned his neck for Light, but he was not present. "Did Light not find you? Where's Jeric?"

"They have gone to another assignment," Elenyr said.

Water noticed the conflict written on her face, and realized there was more to the tale. Worry and doubt flashed across her face before her features smoothed, and Water realized she worried for both of them.

"And Shadow?" Elenyr asked.

Water gestured to the krey map. "We met up with Shadow in Keese. He got the map but said he had another matter to attend to."

He briefly detailed what they had encountered on their journey north and then to Keese, finishing with the conversation with Serak. Then Elenyr motioned to Mind, and the fragment shared his own tale. When Mind had finished, there was a scowl on his face.

"We have learned much," Mind said, "but I find the revelations to be disturbing."

Fire frowned and sank onto a couch before picking up a plate containing a crust of bread. "Where exactly did Shadow go?" he asked. "It's not like he has another assignment."

"It's Shadow," Water said with a shrug. "Who knows."

"He offers aid in his own way," Elenyr said, her features dark. "The more pressing matter is Serak. It seems impossible that such a powerful adversary has gone undetected by us for so long."

Water saw the anger on the woman's features, and realized it came from guilt. Elenyr had always planned with care, but none of them could have anticipated an ageless foe, one willing to operate from the shadows.

"One foe at a time," Mind said, striding to the map and examining it with interest. "Right now we need to find Wylyn. Any progress?"

Water turned to the map. "We've eliminated some of the locations, but we're hoping you know more."

"We don't," Fire said, clearly annoyed.

Mind swept a hand at the piles of books. "What have you learned?"

"That there are plenty of krey sites," Water said. "I fear we may have to search them all."

Elenyr's eyes were on the map. "Actually, I think I know exactly where Wylyn is hiding . . ."

Chapter 37: A Daring Plan

"You do?" Fire asked, surprised.

Elenyr nodded, her thoughts returning to the dakorian that had fought the First of the Blades. Of all the injuries, one had stood out, one that had not come from the duel. Her confidence mounting, Elenyr turned to Mind.

"When we witnessed the dakorian fight Mox, did you notice anything unusual?"

Mind frowned. "A burn on his leg. The injury did not come from the duel."

"Did you recognize the burn?" she asked.

"What does this have to do with Wylyn?" Water asked.

Elenyr turned to Fire, whose eyes had gone wide. The fragment seemed lost in thought, but Elenyr saw his expression as one of recognition. She called his name, and Fire started. He motioned to the map.

"The burn came from a dragon."

"How can you know that?" Lira asked.

Fire snorted. "I've caused more burns than anyone alive. Burns from magical fire are distinctive, as is an injury from a dragon. The dakorian had endured dragon flame within the last week."

Lira reached up to the map and caught the sphere of light with her hand, rotating the globe. "Do the dragons still live in the south?"

"They do," Elenyr said, but her attention was on the map.

The entirety of the kingdoms comprised the northern side of the continent, with a large swath of land to the south. Dominated by mountains, jungles, and canyons, the southern region had never been explored, and for good reason. It was already inhabited.

Known as the Dragon's Teeth, the mountain range south of the Evermist swamp extended for hundreds of miles. Dragon kind had lived in the land since the Dawn of Magic, and few ventured north, a fact for which the people of the kingdoms were grateful, even if they did not know the cause.

"There," Elenyr said, pointing to an outpost in the center of the Dragon's Teeth. "It's the only krey outpost south of the Evermist. It has to be here."

"A dangerous choice," Mind said. "The dragons are as likely to kill us as Wylyn."

"Perhaps," Elenyr said, and considered revealing the truth. "But I think it's more likely Wylyn made a deal."

"With whom?" Water asked.

Elenyr considered her answer. Certain truths on Lumineia were known only to the high oracle. If she spoke now, the fragments would possess the knowledge, as would Lira. But if Wylyn was there, the fragments needed to understand. Making her decision, Elenyr spoke.

"What do you know of the dragons?" she asked.

"They never stop growing," Water said.

"And we learned the Dragon's Sleep from them," Fire said.

"And their culture?"

Water shrugged. "They are territorial and prone to quarrel."

Elenyr motioned to the map. "There are actually three types of dragons, and each keeps to themselves. The fire breathers are the ones we usually associate with dragons, and they are the gold, red, and brown dragons. The elementals are a second type, and breathe frost or lightning. They are the blue and white dragons. Blacks are a type of their own, and possess acid breath that can melt through steel armor.

"How does this matter to us?" Mind asked.

"Because the three factions of dragon kind are not divided," she said. "And they, in fact, have a ruler."

"They have a king?" Fire asked.

"They do indeed," Elenyr said. "And the king maintains order. All dragons fear the king, for he is the strongest of all."

"So the most dangerous," Fire said.

"Exactly," Elenyr said. She then stepped to the map and pointed to the krey outpost, positioned in the center of three gigantic mountains. "This krey outpost was one of the first from the Dawn of Magic, but since then it has been occupied by the king."

"How do you know so much about the outpost?" Lira asked.

"Because I've been there."

"You've been to the throne room of the king of dragons?" Mind asked.

The surprise in Mind's voice brought a smile to Elenyr's lips. It was not often she managed to shock Mind, and she enjoyed the moment—especially because she was about to surprise him again.

"At the close of the Dawn of Magic, a treaty was made. The dragons got the south, and the races got the north. The northern edge of the Dragon's Teeth became the border, and dragons were not permitted to come north. Every generation, the high oracle traveled to the king and confirmed the treaty."

"But why do they obey?" Mind asked. "Surely they are as strong as the races."

"Not against an oracle," Lira said, and Elenyr motioned her to continue. "The oracle's farsight is a powerful weapon against the dragons, and the magic of the races is formidable as well. The dragons

279

could do tremendous damage, but a full-scale war would likely result in their demise."

"You met with the king to confirm this treaty?" Mind asked.

"When I was high oracle," Elenyr said.

"So why would Wylyn choose such a location?" Fire asked. "It is remote, and inaccessible to the populace, but the dragons could kill her easier than we could."

"The outpost would be accessible to other outposts through the Gates," Lira said.

"Which would explain how easily they've traveled," Water said, nodding to Lira.

Elenyr noticed a glint in Water's eyes that she'd never seen, a softness, a closeness. Lira shared the same, and Elenyr wondered how close the two had become. Was it possible for a fragment to fall in love?

"I still don't see why Wylyn would make her home with the dragons," Fire said. "They are volatile, powerful, and lethal."

"Much like Wylyn," Lira said.

"Are dragons present elsewhere in the Krey Empire?" Water asked.

Lira shook her head. "They are unique to this world. As are the phoenixes, the moordraugs, and the reavers."

"Lucky us," Fire said, his tone sarcastic.

"So Wylyn arrived on Lumineia, and then it appears she encountered the dragons." Mind spoke slowly. "How would she react? The dragons would have recognized her as a krey, and . . ."

"Seen an ally," Elenyr said with a nod. "Of any race, the dragons are the most respectful of the ancients."

"Just how many allies does Wylyn have?" Water exclaimed.

"Too many," Fire said.

"So you think she is there?" Lira asked.

"I think it's worth a try," Elenyr said.

"Then we should gather the fragments," Fire said, rising to his feet. "I'll dispatch messengers for Shadow and Light."

Elenyr raised a hand and Fire stopped at the door. "Light cannot be reached," she said. "And if Shadow is occupied, we should not interrupt."

"You're saying we go on our own?" Mind asked, and shook his head. "If Wylyn truly has made a friend of the king, then we need all the support we can get."

"We'll have it," Elenyr said. "And I think it's time Wylyn saw what the fragments are capable of."

"Draeken?" Fire asked, his voice incredulous. "Every time we unite, we can't sustain it."

"There will be only three of you," Elenyr reasoned, "and we cannot wait for the others."

Elenyr watched Mind, gauging his reaction. Mind scratched his chin, his brow furrowed in thought. With three fragments joined, Draeken would be more powerful than the three fragments apart, and it would give them an advantage.

But could Mind hold it together? The question was written on his features. Elenyr saw his consternation and knew the fragment feared becoming Draeken. Mind's eyes flicked to Fire and Water.

"Do you think it's time?"

Fire nodded and stepped forward. "Let's show them the magic they face."

Water seemed uncertain, and Elenyr noticed he glanced to Lira. Was it possible he now wanted to be apart? From the beginning the fragments had yearned to be whole, but lifetimes apart may have changed that. Then the fragment gave a curt nod and motioned to Mind.

"If you believe we can hold together, then we can."

Mind regarded Water and then agreed. "We are ready."

"Then we depart in the morning," Elenyr said. "Prepare yourselves, and convene at dawn."

Fire nodded and then departed. After looking to Elenyr, Water and Lira left together. When they were gone, Mind approached Elenyr where she stood watching the map. For several moments there was silence until Elenyr sighed.

"You fear Draeken."

"I fear his power," Mind said. "We have yet to control him successfully."

"Even with only three?"

"It is easier with three fragments," Mind said. "But when we combine there is something in us that wants to get out."

She frowned and turned to him. "You've never said that before."

Mind grimaced and looked to the hearth. "There's a part of Draeken in each of us, and the more that comes together, the stronger he becomes."

"You think it's weakness to admit a fear?" Elenyr asked. "We all have fears. We all have fragments of ourselves that make us weak."

"Not like this," he said.

"Exactly like this," Elenyr said.

He raised an eyebrow at her suddenly harsh tone. She smiled and pointed to a tapestry hanging between the bookshelves. She'd woven it herself shortly after becoming the Hauntress, in memory of the threads of the future she'd once seen. It depicted a scene of battle, with smoke and fire rising in the background. A general with a mighty spear sat on a horse, the mount rearing back, arrows reaching for his body.

"General Jarvin," Mind said. "He was a good man."

"When you knew him," she said.

He frowned. "What do you mean? He led the Griffin army in the great Talinorian War. Even outnumbered, he preserved both kingdoms when they would have perished."

"You did not know him in his youth," Elenyr said. "In my closing days as an oracle, prior to the mage wars, I met with Jarvin's mother. She wanted to know of her son's life, and I saw that scene in Jarvin's future." She pointed to the tapestry. "But I also foresaw a man of devious appetites."

"I didn't know that."

"Few did," she said. "After the Mage Wars, he grew to manhood and fought his demons. He did not prevail, and spent many nights answering the beckoning call of harlots. When his wife discovered his infidelities she left with their children, and shortly thereafter he lost every copper he possessed. I found him on the streets of Terros, a beggar."

"And he grew to that?" Mind asked, gesturing to the tapestry.

"I was no longer an oracle, but I told him what I'd foreseen when his mother came to me. Just knowing what he could become changed him, and he fought his demons again. Over ten years he became a master with the spear, rose through the ranks of the Griffin army, and even saw the return of his family. All know his feats on the battlefield, but his true victory was the mastery of self."

Mind examined the tapestry with new eyes, and then nodded. "And you think I can master Draeken?"

"You are the eldest fragment," Elenyr said. "Lead them, and neither Wylyn nor Draeken will be greater."

"Thank you," Mind said quietly. "You have given me much to ponder."

He turned and departed. Elenyr watched him go, and then looked back to the tapestry. Her story had been true, but in the end, General Jarvin had once again fallen to his weakness, leading to his ultimate demise.

283

She sighed and turned away from the reminder of her time as oracle. For the first time in a long time, she regretted her choice to become the Hauntress, and wondered if she could have done more as an oracle.

Chapter 38: Draeken

"Are you ready?"

Water nodded and tried to keep the surge of excitement from showing on his face. The other fragments were equally as fidgety, with even Fire falling silent. Water glanced to Lira and noticed the curiosity on her face. Their eyes met and he read the concern on her features. She was worried for him. He gave her an assuring nod.

"We have two days to the outpost," Lira said. "Why are you going to become Draeken now?"

It was the morning after their decision, and Water and Lira had talked deep into the night. He knew he should have rested, but for the first time he was reluctant to merge with Mind, and worried that doing so would erase what he'd become. And remove his feelings for Lira.

"Mind?" Elenyr asked, motioning to him to answer.

"We'd rather fail here than outside the outpost," Mind said.

Water flashed a faint smile. "It's rather destructive."

"That's an understatement," Fire said with a grunt.

They had gathered in what had once been the meal hall of the refuge, a vaulted chamber that extended into the cliff adjacent to Elenyr's home. It was the strongest room in Cloudy Vale, and had proven before that it could bear the brunt of Draeken shattering.

Cut by magic, the vaulted stone supports merged into the ceiling, the arches intricately detailed and scorched by fire to add contrast. The tables were long gone and the space was open. Early morning light streamed through the large windows set against the cliff face, the light augmented by the bracketed light orbs that hung from the ceiling.

"One thing before we depart," Lira said. She reached to her wrist and tapped a rune on the band there. Images flowed upward, creating a figure the size of a dakorian, its body layered in bone. Horns extended from its skull, the ends serrated, but not naturally, as if they had been marked by hand.

Bone covered much of its body, a natural protection that eliminated the need for armor. Its resemblance to a rock troll was uncanny, except for the eyes, which burned with a haughtiness that did not match the rigidly disciplined rock trolls.

"This is Tardoq," Lira said. "Wylyn's Bloodwall. Where she goes, he goes, and he's the only ageless of the dakorians here."

"What does that mean?" Fire asked.

"The life span of a dakorian is around five hundred years," she said. "But the ones that attain a captainship through loyalty are given a gift, and their bodies are perfected. Tardoq is several thousand years old, and has trained his entire life. He's smart, vicious, and strong. Like all dakorians, he uses an impact hammer in combat. Every impact powers the weapon, and the power can be fired like an arrow, to devastating effect. Water has seen it before, but in the hands of Tardoq, the weapon is truly lethal."

Fire's expression glowed with anticipation, but Water was not so confident. They'd fought countless foes but this was different, and Water noticed Elenyr's sober expression, and recalled their conversation of the previous night.

"What are we waiting for?" Fire asked, clenching his fist and letting fire trickle down his forearm. "Let's get going."

"As soon as you are ready," Elenyr said, and she raised an eyebrow to Lira.

"I'm not leaving," she said.

Water wanted to protest, but the woman folded her arms. Seeing she would not be moved, he relented, and then stepped to Mind's left. Fire took up a position on his other side, while Mind reached out and placed his hand on Fire's shoulder.

Cracks blossomed across Fire's flesh, fire spilling forth until the cracks widened and consumed his form, his body turning elemental. Then the flames flowed upward and swirled around Mind's arm, sinking into his skin.

The fire bled away from Fire's body, his features losing their form, until he resembled an entity. Mind clenched his jaw as his flesh brightened, his veins turning red, cracks appearing in his flesh and spilling flames. Then the last of Fire's body faded, the flames extinguishing.

Mind's body seemed to pulse with power, and then the light dimmed and he reached for Water. Casting Lira a final look, Water relinquished his will, and his body turned elemental. His consciousness seeped up the magic on Mind's arm, sinking into his flesh, adding to the power within.

Like a sudden fever, heat filled Water's mind, Fire's simmering determination adding to Mind's methodical thoughts. Fire's interests, likes and dislikes, even Water's attraction for Lira sank and blended into a single consciousness, until Water's individuality blended with the others and the last of his elemental form sank into the new body . . .

Draeken smiled as the sensation of power filled him, of strength tinged with a simmering heat. Fire's mind was now merely a series of emotions and ideas that were all but indistinguishable from his own. Water's thoughts were also gone, leaving a legacy of attraction for Lira, an emotion stronger than expected.

For a moment the dissonance rose inside, and Water threatened to burst apart. But Draeken controlled his breathing and his body stopped pulsing, the powerful magics finally beginning to settle. He still felt Water's touch of doubt, of worry that he would not get to be his own person. Then it too faded, and Draeken straightened.

He drew in a long breath, relishing the feel of power in his blood, of the three magics merged as one. He felt the absence of Shadow and Light, and yearned to be whole. A genuine smile crossed his face as he turned to Lira.

"It's a pleasure to meet you."

He was pleased to notice a slight pink light her cheeks, the heat only noticeable to one with fire magic. It was not the first time Draeken had been attracted to a woman, but this felt different. Both of them were ageless, and any sort of connection had much larger ramifications. But the attraction left him conflicted, as he recognized that only a part of him desired Lira.

"I am well," Draeken said. "No breaking apart today."

He actually felt bound, more stable and powerful than he had on previous attempts, and he felt a deep craving for more. He wished Light and Shadow were present, and imagined how much power he'd have when all five were merged.

"Is Water in there?" Lira asked.

"He is part of me," Draeken said.

"You look . . . different," she said.

Elenyr gestured to him. "Draeken does not look like the fragments. The features are similar, but he is the combined version of all of them."

Lira seemed distant, and Draeken felt the need to reassure her. Recognizing that it came from Water's sense of honor, he smiled and reached out to touch her arm, a subtle gesture that bespoke Water's thoughts. Lira gave a tentative smile.

"Are you okay?"

"Ready for a fight," Draeken said. "I can remain together until the battle. Then we'll see how much control I possess."

Elenyr eyed him with cautious eyes. "Then let us be going," she finally said.

Instead of taking the tunnel north, Elenyr led him to the south exit, a rarely used corridor that led into the barbarian region. The secret tunnel culminated in a shallow cave several miles away from the refuge, where they took their journey into the high meadows of the southern mountains.

Trees and forests dotted the slopes, rising up the peaks until the height prevented such growth. Flowers and brush were abundant, as was the wildlife. Butterflies and bees flitted about, their insatiable desire to explore taking them across the field. Streams swollen with melting snow cascaded through trees and over cliffs, plunging down escarpments in sprays of white. In the distance, a plume of smoke rose from a barbarian village.

"Tell me about the Eternals," Draeken said.

"You have the memories of the fragments," Elenyr replied, brushing her fingers across the high flowers. "And you know they protect Lumineia."

"I know what they do," he said, irritated by her evasive answer. "But I do not understand who they are."

He sifted through his memories and found Water's visit to Renara. He threw Lira a sharp look, surprised to realize that one of the fragments had departed Lumineia, even if it was for a short time.

"You took Water to Renara?" he asked.

She winced, and Elenyr raised a questioning eyebrow. Lira briefly related how she'd taken Water to Renara, and the tale of the events on that world. When she was finished, Elenyr shook her head.

"I cannot imagine bearing witness to such an event," she said. "You have my sympathy."

"Time eases all wounds," Lira said quietly.

Draeken suppressed the burst of irritation over Lira taking Water to another world. He disliked her influence on Water, and sensed his growing attachment for the woman. She was a dangerous intrusion to the fragments, especially after what she'd said about Water becoming an Eternal.

He recognized that without the tempering effects of Light and Shadow, his anger was quicker to surface, but he did not suppress the emotion. It brought a sense of clarity that he wished to preserve. Still, he needed answers.

"Did you really invite Water to be an Eternal?" he asked. He kept his voice light, his anger in his chest.

"The Eternals protect Lumineia from the Krey Empire," Lira said, her gaze guarded. "The Empire is larger than you can imagine, and poses a more dangerous threat than any bandit or war."

"How many worlds?"

"Millions," she said with a shrug. "All owned by one of the krey families."

"And mankind?" he asked.

"Slaves," she said.

"None are free?" Elenyr asked.

"Rebellions are crushed," Lira said. "Quickly."

Draeken considered all the relics they'd seen of the krey, the race the people of Lumineia called the ancients. Buildings, structures, strange artifacts, all were present, all vestiges of a civilization that had lived during the Dawn of Magic. Draeken had seen strange ships, ones that legend spoke of flying through the air. Other buildings were fashioned of materials even the dwarves could not identify.

Draeken looked to the sky, at the sun rising in the east. He'd studied the stars with Elenyr and knew Lumineia rotated around the sun. Around other suns must be other worlds, all filled with krey. He frowned at the image, disliking the idea of so many enslaved to the Empire.

"It is a hard thing to understand," Draeken said.

"It is," Lira said. "But it is a dangerous truth, one the people of Lumineia are not ready to receive."

"Many still think the sun is their god," Draeken said, recalling one of Mind's memories.

Elenyr smiled faintly. "And all of this is what the Eternals protect," she said, sweeping her hand at the mountain meadow.

"And magic?" Draeken asked. "The krey do not possess it?"

"They cannot," she said simply. "And none in the Empire have it. The few krey that know about us want to destroy us because we are a threat. Small as we are, we could destroy the very fabric of their Empire."

"How?" he asked.

"Their slaves are human," Elenyr said. "They have the very same potential as we do, and if they gained magic . . .?"

Draeken felt a chill. "There would be war."

Chapter 39: A Dragon King

Draeken pondered the revelations about the Eternals as they journeyed south, through the barbarian mountains and into the Dragon's Teeth. Set apart from the kingdoms of elf, dwarf, human, and barbarian, the great range extended for hundreds of miles of wild forests and mountains rich with gold and silver. Or so the tales said. No government ventured past the Evermist swamp to claim the region.

Every type of dragon and reaver called the region home, the sentient beasts constantly at war. The few explorers that survived a journey into the mountains witnessed devastating battles between rival dragons, and great bones heaped up where ancient dragons had fought.

"Be on your guard," Elenyr said as they entered the pass at the southern end of the charted world.

The pass lacked a road or sign, the passage rough, the ground free of horse tracks. The absence of civilization would have felt exciting, but another object stood in the center of the pass. As tall as Draeken and bleached white from the sun, the object was easy to identify. A giant tooth. The dragon fang extended from the ground, a chilling warning of what lay beyond.

They reached the end of the pass and descended into the valley. Lush trees filled the base of the valley, while large meadows contained herds of animals. The mountains on the opposite side contained large caves that looked down on the valley, and had a view of the pass. A flicker of motion within the caves drove them into the trees, and a moment later a white dragon burst from an opening.

The ice dragon flapped for altitude and soared around the valley, its great wings shimmering in the sunlight. Draeken had seen a handful of dragons in his life, but never one so large. It banked towards the pass and soared above them, and Draeken and his companions hid in the brush, awed by the majesty of the creature.

Scars littered its body, claw marks from battles with other dragons, teeth marks from where it had been bitten on the neck. The white scales were cracked and broken, tinged grey along the nape of the neck. Draeken frowned as he saw the signs of age.

"He's old," he murmured.

Elenyr nodded. "A sentry to guard the pass," she said. "Those are his flocks."

Draeken followed her gaze and spotted a group of cattle in a clearing next to a bend in the river. The dragon released a low growl before soaring down to its flocks, plucking a pair of cows like they were mice and carrying them back to its lair.

"How many dragons are there?" Lira asked.

"More than we wish to meet," Elenyr said. "But we need to keep moving. The longer we remain in the Dragon's Teeth, the longer we risk being discovered."

They returned to the game trail and followed it down, but veered off the path and ascended into a pass on the opposite side of the valley. As always, Elenyr's footsteps were silent, and he sought to do the same.

They exited the valley and entered a stretch of mountains. There they camped for the night in a tiny cave, foregoing the fire in case any beasts would come searching for them. He suggested they travel at night, and use magic to hasten their travel.

"Do you wish to encounter a black dragon?" she asked. "They hunt at night, their breath an acid that melts through solid steel armor."

Draeken looked down at his leather tunic and imagined acid eating through to his flesh. "I think the cave is rather comfortable," he said.

She smiled. "That's what I thought."

"What if we are too late?" Lira asked.

"We won't be," Elenyr said.

Draeken and Lira exchanged a look, and in her gaze he saw a reserve that had been absent in Water's memories. It wasn't fear exactly, but suspicion, and as Draeken reclined to sleep, he wondered what she saw in him.

They rose the next morning and pushed through the mountains, frequently diving from sight when a winged figure passed above. Draeken heard the sounds of a battle, the snarls and roars like distant thunder. Many times they found tracks of silver reavers, suggesting they were in their territory.

"The krey outpost lies at the peaks," Elenyr said, pointing to a trio of towering mountains.

"That looks like a dragon's home," Draeken said, spotting the caves near the summit.

"That's the outpost that became their throne room."

Lira pointed to the caves. "You think that's where Wylyn entered Lumineia?"

"It doesn't matter where she arrived," Draeken said. "It only matters where she hides."

Despite her earlier refusal to travel at night, the sheer cliffs and plunging ravines made passage difficult, so they traveled at night, allowing Lira to cast air stones across ravines and dense forests.

A journey that would have taken normal men a month to traverse, they crossed in two days, reaching the trio of peaks that marked the pinnacle of the Dragon's Teeth. At every step they saw more signs of dragons or reavers, a river torn apart, a forest scorched black, a clearing containing the decaying body of a great golden beast.

When they reached the base of the largest peak, Draeken gazed upward, shocked by the size of the behemoth mountains. Caves dotted the exterior, and he noticed certain types of dragons favored one mountain over another.

The fire dragons of red, gold, and grey lived in the largest mountain of the trio, while the elemental dragons lived in the second. The third was home to the black dragons, their dark bodies avoided by the others.

294

"Where's the outpost?" he asked.

"Up there," Elenyr said.

"How are we supposed to climb past the dragons?" Draeken asked, eyeing the dozens of beasts draped on overlooks.

"Through this," Elenyr said.

She stepped through a pair of trees and pointed to an archway built into the stone. Strange runes adorned the keystone, with other symbols down the sides. Instead of housing a door, the space inside the archway was solid stone.

Elenyr stepped forward and touched the most prominent rune set on the right side—and the archway glowed to life. Draeken nodded as a silver liquid seeped from the stone and formed into a mirror.

A dragon bugled in the distance, and Elenyr nodded. "They know we're here."

"But is Wylyn waiting on the other side?" Lira asked.

"Only one way to find out," Elenyr said, and stepped through the mirror, disappearing from sight.

Draeken shook his head. For a serene old woman, Elenyr had more courage than anyone he'd ever met. He glanced up at the dragons, the small group folding their wings and diving toward the Gate. Lira cast him a look and leapt through the portal.

He cast his favorite weapon, a spear of fire. Then he readied his magic and stepped through the Gate—into darkness. The moment he appeared Elenyr stepped to the side and pressed a rune, extinguishing the Gate.

"Hurry," she said. "They will not like the intrusion."

The fire of Dreaken's staff illuminated the room, a small chamber with stairs at the back. Instead of stone, the walls and stairs were white tinged with swirls of blue, giving the room a regal feel. Elenyr was already darting to the stairs, her ease of familiarity reminding him of what she'd said about the king of dragons.

"Why did you never tell me of the king?" he asked.

"Oracles have secrets for a reason," Elenyr whispered back.

"Even from me?" he asked.

She paused and cast him a long look. "Even from you," she said quietly.

"We're wasting time," Lira said.

They worked their way through a short series of rooms and corridors before reaching another set of stairs, allowing them to ascend to another level. The light was dim but got brighter the further they climbed, and shortly after, they came to a stop at a towering archway that opened onto an enormous space.

The cavern sat in the hollow between the three peaks. A massive roof connected the three peaks, the material white and blue, the arches curved and graceful. Wind blew through a trio of giant openings set across from each other. Large enough for several dragons to pass with ease, the openings permitted sunlight to spill into the interior, but the light failed to pierce the abundance of shadows beneath the roof.

"I don't see any sign of the krey," Lira whispered.

"They have to be here," Elenyr said, stepping to the edge of the darkened stairwell.

Is that Elenyr I hear? a voice rumbled.

Draeken scowled against the sudden surge of fear. The voice was like the very voice of the mountain, vast and deep and gravelly, the voice of an ancient being that knew its place, and did not know fear.

Fires blossomed into view, the flames bursting from an enormous golden dragon. Draeken flinched, but they were not directed at him. Instead they ignited the stone across the rim of the ceiling, filling the room with light to reveal a pair of red dragons also present, the trio perched on ledges surrounding the enormous space.

"*It* is *Elenyr*," the dragon said, its voice mocking. "*Do come out. It's rude to hide from your host.*"

Draeken glanced back down the stairs but realized the dragons had probably already blocked the exit. If they stayed put, a dragon could breathe fire into the opening and turn the staircase into an oven hot enough to melt flesh from bone.

Elenyr glanced his way and then straightened. Then she strode into the vast cavern. Draeken and Lira fell into step beside her. In his entire life, he'd never felt such fear as when he gazed upon the King of Dragons. The well of power rose within him, crushing the fear with a burst of defiance.

The cavern was enormous, easily twice the size of Talinor's entire castle, large enough to house a dozen dragons on the wide perches set around the chamber. Sunlight spilled through the dragon doors, and Draeken spotted the ground far below.

The gold dragon dropped from the largest perch, the stone of which was covered in gold and silver, all melted with dragon fire into swirls of beauty and violence. Its landing on the stone seemed to make the mountain shudder, and Draeken looked up a hundred feet into the whirling eyes of the king of dragons.

"Thistikor," Elenyr said. "Where is your father?"

Dead, the dragon said, humor threaded into the mental voice. *I'm sure you saw the body on your journey. Who is your companion? He reeks of power.*

Elenyr ignored the question. "I hunt a group of dakorians," she said. "And the krey that leads them."

Draeken noticed her rigid posture, her sword in her hand. He got the impression she'd expected to find Thistikor's father, a more amiable dragon, if that was possible. But the current king set her on edge.

Wylyn said one would come, the gold dragon said. *But I did not think it was you. You should be dead.*

"My life was extended," she said.

Indeed. The dragon snorted. *I am pleased to see you.*

The trace of anticipation in his voice caused Draeken to bristle, his staff brightening in response. But Elenyr kept her cool, only her knuckles going white. Before she could speak, the dragon bent its neck, bringing its enormous head down to Elenyr's level.

"Do not break the treaty," Elenyr warned.

The dragon's chuckle sounded like a roar, and the two reds dropped from their perches, their claws tearing furrows in the stone as they closed off the other two exits. Draeken sensed the trap snapping shut and shifted away from Elenyr, giving them space to fight. Lira did the same on the opposite side.

They offered me a new treaty, the dragon rumbled. *And the terms are much better.*

The great dragon shifted, allowing Draeken a view of an opening on the opposite side of the chamber. A solitary figure stood in the opening. Although they had never met, Draeken recognized her immediately from Water's memories.

Wylyn.

Chapter 40: Adversaries

Tardoq, Serak, and Relgor appeared in the opening behind her, but Wylyn advanced across the space alone, her pace methodical, her gaze never leaving Elenyr. Tardoq scowled and spun his hammer, as if he hated being left behind. Serak watched with dispassionate eyes, while Relgor watched with interest.

A little shorter than a human, Wylyn had greyish skin, her eyes a mixture of purple and black. Her ears were slimmer than human but her features were more angular than those of the race of man, more pointed. Dressed in a blue tunic with strange buttons and whirls, she also wore what resembled a dress, the curve of the hem raised up the side, revealing a stretch of leg.

She passed the dragons as if they didn't matter, the great beasts parting for her like she was the god the Order believed her to be. The sight brought a curl to Draeken's lips. Wylyn spotted the expression but her eyes flicked back to Elenyr. Then she came to a halt, well short of where Elenyr could strike.

"Elenyr," Wylyn said. "Or do you prefer being called the Hauntress?"

"I have many names," Elenyr said. "And I don't want to hear any of them from your lips."

Wylyn released a low chuckle. "You are not an Eternal, yet you protect Lumineia just the same. Why?"

"Why do you attack it?' Elenyr countered.

"Because it's mine," Wylyn said, sweeping her hands outward. "The land, the water, the air . . . the people. All of it is mine."

"You call them yours?" Elenyr asked, her voice gaining an edge. "You may own worlds, but you understand nothing. Freedoms can be taken, but free will must be yielded."

"There is truth to your words," she said. "But all men ultimately yield to the Empire. Is that not true, Lira?"

Lira bristled and took a step forward. Draeken stepped to her side and caught her arm, holding her in check. Wylyn smirked at her response and gestured to Elenyr, her voice turning amused.

"I have learned a great deal about you since my arrival," Wylyn said. "An oracle turned Hauntress, a warrior without peer, and one capable of passing through the very stone. You are an impressive adversary."

"You are not the only one that has learned," Elenyr said. "You are the head of the ninth most powerful house in the Empire, a member of the second tier, a royal, and a woman that commands an army so vast that we are just a handful of rodents to you."

Wylyn inclined her head in agreement, and then looked to Draeken. "Your companions are equally as impressive, especially Draeken, a victim of the guardian charm, now fragmented into five separate beings. All unique. All powerful."

Draeken scowled at the tone of greed that seeped into the woman's voice, like he was a commodity to be owned. Wylyn didn't flinch as fires curled up Draeken's arms, and merely looked on in interest. In the background, Tardoq struck his hammer on the floor, powering the weapon.

"After all the millennia that you have lived, did you ever wonder what your death would look like?" Draeken shaped the flames into a blinding sword and pointed it at her. "I wager you never thought it would come at the hands of a human."

"No," she said. "I did not." But her amusement remained as she turned to Lira. "The reckless Eternal. I admit I know less about you, but only because Serak's knowledge does not extend to the Eternals."

"At least one secret remains private."

"I applaud the Eternals for what they have done," Wylyn said. "You have kept Lumineia hidden from the Empire far longer than any rebellion before you. But that time is at an end. Will you fight the battle that cannot be won? Or fight the battle that you have a chance of winning?"

"Every battle can be won," Lira spat.

The king of dragons released a snort, smoke billowing up from his nostrils, his voice piercing Draeken's thoughts. *I told you they would not listen.*

"I am not your enemy, Hauntress," Wylyn said, her features darkening. "And it would be wise to hear my offer."

"Then speak," Elenyr said.

Draeken turned to her in shock, but Elenyr did not take her eyes off the woman. Lira appeared equally surprised, but Draeken had never seen Elenyr agree to listen to a foe, least of all one with such power. Then Elenyr opened her thoughts to him, and he sensed her words like a whisper in the corner of his mind.

Know your enemy, she said.

He realized her intent and recognized the wisdom behind it. They had spent months tracking Wylyn, and they had found her in a room with three mighty dragons. All their foes were gathered into a single room. Whatever was said could prove useful.

"Lumineia is fallen," Wylyn said. "It's only a matter of time until we build the Gate and the people are taken."

"As slaves," Lira snapped.

"Yes," Wylyn said. "But not all slaves are equal, and the people of Lumineia possess incredible abilities—abilities that make them valuable."

"There's no way the Empire would let them live," Lira scoffed. "They would fear magic spreading to the other slaves."

"True," Wylyn said, "and they could be slaughtered—unless I speak to the Empress on your behalf. If I do, the Empire can preserve your races that they may be owned by the royal houses. They will live a life of luxury, while we study what brought about the change in their bodies."

"You want to experiment on us?" Draeken asked.

Wylyn scowled at the disdain in his voice. "It is a better offer than you will get at the hands of the Empire."

Lira trembled with rage. "How *dare* you speak such things as if they are good for these people."

"You are all slaves," Wylyn said. She was obviously trying to restrain her anger, but a tinge of red ignited in her eyes. "Your only choice is how you will live the remainder of your lives."

Elenyr raised a hand to stop Lira from surging across the gap. The dragons had sensed the rising tension and begun to pace, Thistikor sitting on his haunches, smoke rising from his open jaws, his multifaceted eyes spinning with excitement.

"And what do you and your son get out of this arrangement?" Elenyr asked.

"We reap the benefits, of course," Wylyn said, her voice still carrying an edge. "My house would be responsible for you not breeding with the others, and that will require significant cost." She smiled. "We can't have more magic spreading."

"*I'll rip your throat out,*" Lira snapped.

"And Serak?" Elenyr asked, ignoring Lira and glancing to the guardian in the door behind her. "What of him?"

"I have already promised him a place at my side," Wylyn said, glancing to the father of guardians.

"I supposed the dragons received a similar deal."

We get to keep the world when you are gone, Thistikor said, his mental voice low and dangerous. *Along with a number of slaves as new stock for ourselves . . .*

Draeken's anger mounted, and he gauged the distance to the nearest red dragon, his blood seeming to boil with magic. But Elenyr's laughter brought his anger to a halt. Low and mocking, Elenyr's amusement caused Wylyn to flush.

"My apologies," Elenyr said. "I should not find amusement in your ignorance."

"I've lived for eons," Wylyn said stiffly. "My knowledge far exceeds your own."

"Without question," Elenyr said. "And so you see my dilemma at discovering a subject of which you are so oblivious, that you do not even know you are ignorant."

"And what is that?" Wylyn asked acidly.

"You truly believe that you've chained the race of man," Elenyr said. "And believe them incapable of defeating the Empire."

Wylyn sneered. "They lack the courage to—"

"Indeed, you have come to believe," Elenyr continued as if Wylyn had not spoken, "that they are lesser beings. And yet this race will be the undoing of your Empire, the end of your rule, your very lives. To bring us into the Empire will not be the end of our race . . . it will spell the end of yours."

Elenyr's voice had gained an almost prophetic timbre, and Draeken found himself in awe. Facing a trio of mighty dragons and the head of a powerful krey house, she was the one commanding attention.

"You would rather die?" Wylyn challenged.

"If the choice is to live as slaves or die free, we refuse both," Elenyr said. "No tyrant, king, or even Empress will *ever* strip us of our willpower. You want the people of Lumineia? I dare you to try and take them. You will die at their feet."

Elenyr's challenge faded into a ringing silence, and Wylyn stared at Elenyr in shock. Draeken got the impression the woman had never been spoken to in such a manner, and that it was the first time in Wylyn's life that she met someone—especially one she viewed as a slave—speak with such authority.

The dragons had begun to fidget again, and Draeken spotted a few wings flitting past the opening, as if other dragons had been summoned by the king. Elenyr had gotten Wylyn to admit several truths, but she'd refused her offer with such force that there would not be another, and Draeken sensed the impending battle.

"You are a fool," Wylyn spat. "When the tower rises and my world Gate is opened, I will enjoy killing you with my own hands."

"I welcome you to try," Elenyr said, drawing her blade.

Wylyn regarded her with contempt. "I had hoped you would see reason, that you would convince the remaining kings to accept my rule. It would have spared many lives. Now, their blood will be on your hands."

"Their blood will be on the hands of their killer," Elenyr retorted. "And that certainly won't be me."

Wylyn eyes were a deep red now, the black swirling with burgundy and blood. She swept her hands to the waiting dragons and they rose to their feet, their wings unfurling. She smiled, the expression dark and forbidding.

"Just remember, Hauntress," she said. "I did give you an offer."

Elenyr raised her sword to Wylyn. "The day will come when you stand on the precipice of victory, and see the slaves you so disdain destroy every shred of your hope. On that day you will die with a heart filled with disbelief."

Wylyn shook her head and muttered a curse in a foreign language. "Unfortunately, you will not live to see any future, because I cannot let you live. My dakorians were sorely disappointed they did not get to claim your lives, but the dragons are indeed eager."

We are not your dogs, Thistikor said. *But on this we can agree. I am eager to kill this one.*

"Goodbye, Hauntress," Wylyn said. "I hope your ending is one of fire and pain."

"You first," Elenyr said.

Elenyr burst into motion, sprinting across the floor toward Wylyn. The krey woman stood firm, her expression one of disdain as Elenyr closed the gap. But the king was also in motion, and it reared his head, air rushing into its maw. The great golden dragon dropped its head to the floor and opened its jaws, forcing Elenyr to turn and face the king. Draeken and Lira dived away but Elenyr wasn't fast enough, and the mountain of flames poured from the jaws of the huge dragon, engulfing the Hauntress in a searing blast of dragon fire.

Chapter 41: Draeken's Power

The torrent of flames was thirty feet high, and poured into the tunnel where they had entered, filling the breadth of the opening and splattering to the sides, spilling across the floor. Draeken sprinted out of reach, and caught a glimpse of Wylyn disappearing into a tunnel on the opposite side. There was a flash of silver light as a Gate opened, and the woman disappeared. Relgor and Serak followed, and Tardoq sneered before he too departed. Then one of the red dragons darted into Draeken's path and its jaws opened.

Draeken skidded to a halt and summoned his own fire, a wall of solid flame that hardened just as the dragon unleashed its power. The blast of dragon fire was not as large as Thistikor's, but it was twice Draeken's height. It struck the wall and exploded outward, cascading to either side.

Draeken gritted his teeth as he held the shield and looked to where Elenyr had stood. The king cut off its fire and reared back, releasing a thunderous roar of triumph. The wind from the dragon entrances gradually cleared the smoke, revealing scattered fires.

And Elenyr.

Unharmed in the midst of the fire, she stood with a look a fury on her face. She held her blade low and ready, while the fires burned through her ethereal form. The King's roar ended abruptly when he spotted his adversary unharmed.

What magic is this?

Elenyr advanced through the flames, green smoke billowing out from her form and shaping into the cloak and cowl of the Hauntress. Then she stepped free and flicked her sword, her words an ominous snarl.

"Your father was smarter."

She charged, and the dragon reached down with its jaws, snapping shut on her body. But she'd phased to ethereal and passed through the huge teeth. Then she leapt and sliced across the dragon's foreleg.

Dragon scales were renowned for their rigidity, but with the blade turning solid when it was already inside the flesh, it cut deep, spilling dragon blood onto the floor of the cavern. The king roared its pain, drawing the surprised attention of the two reds.

Draeken smirked as he watched the king fight the Hauntress, his giant form whirling and snapping, attempting to catch her while she was in solid form. It was a deadly game, for if he did, Elenyr would be killed in an instant.

Dragons dived toward the entrance, but Lira cast a trio of cyclones, the tornados whipping the interior air into a frenzy as they churned for the openings, the shrieking wind preventing the dragons from receiving reinforcements. It left Draeken facing two red dragons. By himself.

The dragon had ended its assault on Draeken and turned its head toward Thistikor, obviously uncertain if he should assist. Draeken made the decision for him, and changed his wall of fire into a ballistae, the fire reshaping at his will. Drawing heat from the pools of dragon fire, he augmented the bolt until it changed from yellow to orange, the heat sparking across its length.

The dragon swiveled back to Draeken, its multi-faceted eyes whirling in surprise at the giant weapon at his feet. It took one step forward and Draeken fired, the bolt piercing the dragon's body just above a foreleg.

The dragon issued a horrendous bellow. It stumbled back and collided with the wall next to the south opening, blood spilling from the wound. It clawed at the bolt with its other foreleg, and ripped it free of its body.

A great thundering of feet signaled the approach of the second red, and Draeken spun, gathering the flames on all sides, shaping them into a large torso, legs, and head. The dragon snarled as Draeken shaped his body into a giant soldier.

The dragon's claws dug into the ground and the dragon released a blast of fire, intent on burning Draeken to ash. But Draeken opened the golem's mouth and swallowed the fire, using it to expand his body, filling his body and adding an armor of white flames.

Now standing as tall as the red dragon, Draeken swept his hand out and cast a ten foot sword. Facing a soldier as large as it was, the dragon actually retreated a step, partially unfurling its wings and snarling a warning. Within the midst of the flames, Draeken raised his sword and charged.

They collided in a blast of sparks, the dragon snapping at Draeken's throat, but Draeken raised his arm and caught the jaws on his forearm, using his sword to slash across the dragon's body. Scales clattered to the floor as the sword cut into the dragon's torso. Snapping at Draeken's mangled arm like a ravenous wolf, it sought to break through his guard.

"You may be a dragon," Draeken snarled, "but you are just a beast."

He plunged the flaming sword into the dragon's body. The beast opened its jaws to howl, and Draeken leveled a crushing blow with his fist, striking the dragon in the face. Teeth broke loose and clattered to the floor, and then Draeken struck again, and again, pummeling the dragon with punishing blows. Then he reached for the blade and yanked it free.

The dragon recoiled and swung around, smashing its tail into Draeken's legs, knocking him to his back. He lost his grip on the sword and it skittered away, the flames dissipating into smoke and cinders. The dragon's muscles clenched as it caught Draeken's arm and forced it away, and the beast sought to drive its jaws into Draeken's body, ripping apart the armor around his tiny form.

Draeken roared and used a fiery fist to strike the dragon in the skull. Its head snapped to the side and Draeken struck again. Blood dripped from its eye, and then Draeken caught the beast's horn and yanked, tossing the roaring dragon aside.

Draeken rose to his feet, his body spitting fire and sparks, half his armor torn to shreds—and the second red struck his flank, knocking him into the wall. Its jaws clamped on the head of Draeken's golem and snapped back and forth.

"You want a bite?" Draeken growled, and released his hold on the golem's head. "You're not going to like the flavor."

Unprepared for the sudden release, the dragon tumbled backward— just as the head detonated, knocking the dragon into a wall, where it crashed through the stonework into a reservoir of water beyond. Obviously intended to provide water to the outpost, the water was tainted green and reeked of mold.

The dragon rolled free and spotted Lira, just a few paces away. It lowered its jaws, and a surge of fear filled Draeken's chest. He reached for the liquid in the reservoir. The wave flowed up and crashed on the dragon, wrapping the water around the dragon's jaws. Legs appeared in the water reached out. Other legs solidified as the water morphed into a clamping spider that struck the dragon repeatedly. More arachnids appeared and swarmed the wounded dragon, latching onto its legs, wings, and tail.

It rolled and clawed, its roars muffled through the bindings on its jaws. Draeken caught a glimpse of Elenyr still battling the King, its great body bleeding from dozens of tiny wounds, darkening its bright scales. Beyond them, Lira nodded her gratitude as she struggled to keep the cyclones in place, the tornados barricading the dragons that sought entry. One swooped for a gap, but the wind gusted, knocking the great beast into the wall, where it tumbled from sight. But Draeken saw the toll the magic was taking, and Lira's features were strained, her face lathered in sweat.

A burst of movement caused Draeken to spin. He caught a glimpse of a dragon's maw and just managed to catch the jaws of the second dragon, the fireflesh of his large fingers spitting sparks as the dragon chewed. The beast snapped and snarled as it sought for Draeken's chest.

The dragon's charge drove Draeken back, toward the edge of an opening, where a tornado churned just feet from him, the wind tearing at Draeken's fireflesh. Draeken braced his feet, his golem slowing as they approached the drop, and with all his might and magic he brought the dragon to a halt.

Real and enchanted muscles strained to keep the dragon at bay, and the beast lunged and snapped, bringing all its legendary strength to bear on the headless golem. Inside the golem, Draeken glanced back and saw the endless drop below, the sight eliciting a spark of fear that nearly extinguished his golem. Then he sneered and cast a spike from the water beneath the enraged dragon.

Nearly invisible beneath the dragon's bulk, the shard of dark green liquid grew, its point sharpening as it extended to the belly of the beast, gaining an angle that aimed for its heart, the idea drawn from Water's encounter with Serak.

Draeken's power rose, his anger spilling into strength that allowed him to drive the beast backward a step. The dragon thrashed, its claws gouging the stone, the motions laced with a desperate surprise. Draeken tightened his grip on the dragon, his fury reaching a breaking point.

"I am Draeken," he shouted. *"Lord of magic, god of guardians. And even dragon kind will KNEEL AT MY FEET!"*

Draeken reversed his grip and yanked, pulling the dragon toward the opening, impaling the dragon on the spike, the spike piercing its body all the way to its back. Its horrendous roar indicated a mortal wound.

Draeken clung to the beast's head as it thrashed its death throes. Pinned by the spike of aquaglass, the dragon's body hung down the mountainside with Draeken clinging to his horns. The wind snapped at Draeken's cloak, while soaring dragons spotted him and dived. The lead dragon closed its jaws on the golem's leg, and Draeken released the golem. He jumped free of the golem and caught the horn of the thrashing dragon with his bare hands.

As other dragons dived for him, Draeken used the spikes on the beast's neck to ascend back to the great cavern. He jumped free of the beast and tumbled to his knees, just as a trio of blue dragons sought to land, their claws reaching for him.

The tornado dodged to the side, spinning around Draeken so closely that he felt his clothing tear from the wind. Then the cyclone bashed into the lead dragon, the wind shoving its wings and sending it tumbling into its companions.

Draeken looked to Lira and nodded his gratitude, and she flashed a tightlipped smile. Then she was forced to retreat as the king's duel with Elenyr spilled more fire in her direction. Draeken rose to his feet and advanced on the remaining red dragon, his surge of anger dissipating into a cold resolve.

The second dragon clawed the last of the spiders from his shredded body, but instead of attacking, it dived for an exit, escaping past a tornado into the relative freedom of the sky. But its roar was not of dismay, and the call was answered by dozens of other throats. Realizing they were about to be overrun, Draeken started toward Elenyr, stumbling as fatigue swept across his body.

As fragments, he'd faced many enemies that were a true threat, but never as Draeken, and the sensation of weakness was new. He gritted his teeth and used the lingering pools of fire to gather his power, adding water to the mix.

The king clawed at the wall where Elenyr had disappeared into the stone, tearing away great chunks in the cavern as it roared its fury. Although Elenyr was a fraction the golden dragon's size, she'd hurt the king, and the host of bloody furrows bore testament to her fortitude.

Abruptly Elenyr burst from the wall above the King and fell towards his snout. The king saw her at the last moment and reared back, but she landed on his nose and aimed her sword at the dragon's eye, her blade a scant finger-width from the King's right iris.

The great dragon froze, its entire body trembling in rage. Elenyr clung to a scale with one hand, her other holding the sword where she could blind the beast. Her cloak was torn and green blood darkened her body, but her face beneath her cowl was bright with a disturbing calm.

"How long would you survive with just a single eye?"

Draeken saw the consternation in the dragon's whirling eyes. If he tried to fling Elenyr off and failed, his life was at an end. Perhaps not now, perhaps not tomorrow, but unable to see an entire flank would leave him vulnerable, and the rest of dragon kind would terminate his reign.

You dare to—

311

"Yes I *dare*," Elenyr shouted, her voice a righteous timbre. "If you or your kind *ever* threatens to break the treaty, I will see you extinguished from this world."

Muscles bunched in the dragon's body but its head did not move. *You are no longer the high oracle*, the dragon snarled. *You do not have the authority to speak on behalf of the races.*

"My blade is my authority," she said, her voice rising. "King or commoner, demon or dragon, you will not defy the treaty. If you continue to break your oath, I will return upon your head a hundredfold the violence you wreak upon the kingdoms, and strip you of your title and life so another may reign in your stead. Your bones will rot next to the corpse of your father and all will speak of the foolish king of dragons."

The seconds bled away as the flapping of wings approached, and suddenly dozens of dragons filled the openings, blasting through the cyclones. The shattering of the magic sent Lira to her knees. Draeken turned to face the nearest group of dragons, filling his hands with magic just as the king voice thundered in his head.

The treaty stands, the King bellowed. *The krey are no longer our allies. This oath I speak is bound by my reign, and all will abide.*

Elenyr withdrew her blade and dropped through his jaws to land on the floor. Without looking back, she strode to Draeken. He fell into step beside her as they walked through the parting dragons and past the corridor to the Gate chamber. It was shredded, the stone still burning, the finely cut granite coated in ash and smoke. Passing it by, Elenyr led them to the south ledge, ignoring the dragons parting for the small trio. Limping, Lira joined them.

Feeling the weight of the dragon's eyes, Draeken stepped off the edge and fell, holding Elenyr's hand as they plummeted out of view. Elenyr kept a firm grip on him while letting her sword turn partially ethereal. Stabbing it into the cliff, she slowed their descent until they reached a rocky crag from which they could descend. Only then did Draeken look up, and spotted Lira with wings of air floating down beside them, looking all the while like an angel.

"How many could face down the king of dragons?" Lira asked.

Elenyr snorted and winced before lifting her cloak to reveal bloody furrows down her side. "Not unscathed."

"We should have killed the king," Draeken said.

He reached up to the wound across his shoulder, grimacing as his hand came away bloody. The dragon's teeth had dug into his flesh, and now that he looked at the wound his head swam. Every touch of his shoulder heightened the pain and he growled.

"I'm made of magic," he said. "So why does it hurt so much?"

"If you live, you can bleed," Elenyr said, using a strip of cloth to bandage his arm. Then their eyes met. "We are ageless," she said. "Not immortal."

Draeken looked up to the dragon peaks. He'd trained his entire life to fight threats to the people of Lumineia, and escaped death countless times—but never as Draeken. Today he felt different. Today he felt vulnerable.

Chapter 42: Divided

Water groaned as he separated from Draeken. He fell to his knees, his first thoughts of pain. Fire and Mind separated behind him, and Water heard Fire's growl as he too registered his new wounds.

Water gingerly took a seat at the log next to the fire and examined the wound on his shoulder. The dragon that had clawed its way through the fireflesh had gotten close enough to tear into his body, but Water was lucky. The wounds were shallow.

"Here," Elenyr said, offering her water skin. "You need to clean the wound."

The concern in her voice prompted Water to look up at her and offer a fleeting smile. "I'll be fine."

"I know," Elenyr said.

She returned the smile with her own and then stepped to Mind, giving him the bulk of her attention. Fire had already stepped into the small fire in the center of the clearing, grimacing as the flames burned across his own injured shoulder.

Throughout the exchange, Lira sat silently next to Water. Her injuries were minor, but without her, the outpost would have been overrun with dragons, and they would all have perished. Water caught her eye and she nodded her assurance, but there was a rigidity to her posture that indicated she was not well.

They had departed the Dragon's Teeth and reached the pass with the giant tooth. Fatigue and injury had finally brought them to a halt in the valley on the north side of the pass, where Elenyr had built a fire and tended to their wounds.

"Elenyr," Mind said softly. "You have your own injuries."

"I'll be fine," she said.

"Can I help?" Lira asked.

Elenyr glanced her way and nodded. "Get Water to the stream." She used her chin to point to the gurgle of water nearby.

Lira helped Water to his feet. He wanted to refuse, but her touch sent a shudder into his skin that briefly overpowered the pain. They worked their way down a shallow gulley and Water spotted the sheen of flowing water in the darkness. He stepped to the bank and waded in, breathing a sigh of relief as he brought the water across his flesh, using his magic to begin healing.

"You use water to heal, and Fire uses flame, what does Mind use?"

Water sank into the stream up to his neck. "He's the only one that cannot heal with an element," he said. "His injuries will have to heal the old-fashioned way."

"What's it like being Draeken?" Lira asked.

"It's difficult to explain," Water said. "If any one of us joins with Mind we become Draeken. When all are joined our mind is whole, and our strength is . . . significant, but there is only one consciousness."

"But what happens to you?" she asked.

"We are part of the whole," Water said with a shrug. "All the fragments have the aspects to their personality and together I think we're relatively normal. Any experiences we've had when apart are merged into a single memory."

"So Mind now knows everything we did together?" she asked.

He flashed a faint smile. "Are you ashamed of the kiss?"

She shook her head and looked away. "It's just disconcerting to feel like anything we share will be shared with another."

"Mind doesn't keep the memories," Water admitted.

She splashed the water at him, and he laughed. "You knew I was worried."

"I knew nothing," Water said with a mischievous smile.

"Your healing is making you bold," she said.

"Perhaps," he admitted.

Her smile faded. "Where do the shared memories go?"

Water checked the wound on his shoulder, pleased to see the flesh beginning to knit, giving a strange itching sensation. "I don't know," he said. "There's still a lot we don't know about Draeken. Not yet."

"But you give up yourself to be joined," Lira pressed.

Water smiled at Lira's confusion. She sat on a boulder at the water's edge, their hands almost touching. The proximity spoke to a rising attachment, or that was Water's hope. With moonlight streaming through the trees, she looked more stunning than ever.

"The fragments are drawn to each other," Water explained. "When apart, none of us feel completely whole. I imagine if you lost your sense of amusement and fun you would feel the lack."

"Is that Light?" she asked. "The sense of fun?"

Water glanced north, toward where Light had departed. "He has a greater portion than the rest of us."

"Before me, did you ever think about leaving the others?" Lira asked. "Just living your own life?"

Water had in fact considered that fate, but always come to the same conclusion. The fragments were all connected. How could one—especially he—consider abandoning Draeken. To do so would forever deprive them of Water's personality.

Water grimaced as he imagined how his absence would weaken the rest of them, alter their collective thoughts. Together the five balanced each other's desires, wants, and darker inclinations. Mind craved power, while Fire had a temper. Shadow's sense of mischief frequently resulted in real damage. Even Light had a darker side, and occasionally struggled with bouts of fury.

316

Water alone seemed mostly free of such darkness, and without him, all the rest would be weakened. He recalled how many times he'd been the moral compass that had helped them make choices when the others had fallen to their darker impulses. They also helped curb his own darker inclinations, which his conversation with Serak had brought out.

Her question also reminded him of her invitation to join the Eternals. It was an invitation she'd extended to him, not to Draeken or the fragments. Then he recalled how she had looked at Draeken.

"You do not like Draeken," he stated.

She regarded him for several moments. "I don't trust him." She laughed to herself. "Which doesn't make sense, because I trust you, and you are part of him."

"You would have liked him even less if he'd lost control," Water said.

He winced as a fragment of dirt was pushed out of the wound, and lifted his shoulder to watch the sliver exit his flesh. Using water to heal was always preferable to healing the normal way, and he recalled Elenyr making him heal from a cut in his youth. It had taken weeks, and he'd never complained about injuries again.

"I must admit, watching you fight a pair of dragons was exhilarating, but Draeken has a vicious streak."

He looked away, uncomfortable with where the conversation was headed. Draeken had killed a dragon in battle, but the act was tinged with brutality, tarnishing the victory. The anger was an unsettling reminder of Water's own rage in Serak's cage.

"Draeken has yet to learn control," Water said quietly.

She regarded him for several long moments. "His power is . . . disconcerting."

"I'm just glad we survived," he said. "And without you blocking the doors, we would not have."

"I didn't know what else to do," Lira said. "When Elenyr disappeared in the king's fire, I thought she was dead."

317

"Elenyr has a way of surviving," he said with a smile.

"As does Wylyn," she said sourly.

"We'll find her," he said.

He reached out and placed his hand on hers. She met his gaze and nodded, and he wondered if she was thinking of Renara, and the family she'd lost. Lira was a warrior, but the scars of her life refused to be buried.

The last of his skin closed and he rose from the stream. As he stepped free, he pulled the moisture from his clothes and joined Lira, who stood as well. She ran a finger across his now smooth skin, her touch eliciting a shudder.

"I've never seen you so injured," she said, her voice worried.

"Everything can be killed," he said softly.

She reached up and put a hand on his cheek, and then leaned into a kiss. The contact spoke volumes of the fear she'd felt, of the worry, and something deeper. He wrapped his arms around her and sought to reassure her.

When they parted, her expression was irritated. "I don't like the effect you have on me."

"I think you do," he said.

She pushed his shoulder, making him wince. Then she smiled and they ascended the slope, reaching the fire a moment later. As they resumed their seats, Fire stepped free of the flames, equally as healed. Mind stared into the campfire, holding the bloody bandage on his shoulder.

Elenyr glanced to Water and he nodded, indicating he was well. Then Elenyr turned to the others. "I know we are injured, but it's a time of decision."

"And suspicion," Fire said. "Wylyn knew we were coming."

"What are you saying?" Water asked, confused by his accusation.

"What we're all thinking," Fire said. "It was a trap, and someone we trust is on her side."

"Who?" Lira asked. "The only people that knew we were coming are those in this circle."

"It wasn't one of the fragments," Fire said, glaring at her. "And it certainly wasn't Elenyr."

"You're saying it was me?" Lira asked, her voice cold.

Fire filled his hand with flames. "I think you're a traitor."

Chapter 43: A Brother's Request

"This is absurd," Water said. "We can trust Lira."

"Says the one falling for her."

Water flushed, and shook his head. "I've fought with her for months. I think I know her by now." He threw Elenyr a pleading look, but she did not intervene.

Taking her silence as confirmation, Fire stabbed a finger at Lira. "If you betrayed us I'll—"

"It wasn't her," Mind said.

"How can you say that?" Fire demanded, rounding on him.

"Because it's true," Mind said. "We were led there, but the trap started long before we walked into the outpost."

Relieved for Mind's support, Water motioned to him. "What do you mean?"

Mind grimaced as he leaned against the trunk of a tree. "Water and Lira were guided to the destroyed village, where an Order member sent them to Keese. There they met up with Shadow, who retrieved the map, which in turn led us to the southern outpost."

Water gained a new level of appreciation for Mind, and his gift for strategy. He'd seen what Water had not, and recognized the unseen hand of their adversary. Water then recalled Serak's smile when they fled.

"This doesn't feel like Wylyn is pulling the strings," Water said slowly. "I think Serak was the one that orchestrated our coming south."

"If he truly has been watching us for so long, he has his own plans," Mind said.

Fire scowled. "We should have killed her."

"Do you mean Wylyn now?" Lira asked. "Or do you still speak of me?"

Fire stared at her, and then looked into the trees. "I'm sorry I accused you," he muttered.

"You got an apology out of Fire," Water said. "Well done."

"I'm man enough to admit when I'm wrong," Fire said, obviously stung.

"I'm still waiting for an apology for when you singed my eyebrows off," Water said. "Both times."

Fire grinned. "That was Light."

Water shook his head in amusement and glanced to Lira, but she did not seem to be offended. Fire's temper was always close to the surface, but Fire trusted Mind. Lira settled back into her seat and nodded to Fire, a subtle acknowledgement of his apology.

"The question is, what do we do next?" Elenyr asked.

"We enforced the treaty," Mind said, his voice distant, as if he were examining the events of the conflict through the lens of larger tactics, "And we learned a great deal about Wylyn."

"We were defeated," Fire said.

"We survived and we learned more about our adversary," Mind said. "That is our victory. And now Wylyn knows that even the dragons fear us."

"Wylyn also fears Elenyr," Lira said.

"Me?" Elenyr asked in surprise.

"You brought her to silence," Lira said. "I've never seen anyone do that—not even another krey."

"We've put her on the defensive," Water agreed. "Now we must press the attack."

"She's going to be harder to find," Mind said. "She knows who we are and that we can track her."

"She mentioned a tower," Water said, looking to Elenyr. "Did you understand that part?"

Elenyr shook her head. "I would assume it's an ancient structure, but I don't know what she intends." She raised an eyebrow to Lira, but the woman shook her head.

"They raised many towers, and I didn't live on Lumineia for long."

"Perhaps we could ask Ero?" Water asked.

"He is unavailable," Lira said.

"Why?" Water asked. "What could be more important?"

"The day before we arrived here, two Eternals were caught attempting to steal the plans for a new warship, one that could scan for life across the galaxy."

"They would find Lumineia," Mind said.

Lira nodded. "Ero is using his influence among the houses and sending another team of Eternals to aid in their escape."

The truth that they were on their own settled into the group, and silence persisted for several moments. Since Lira's arrival, Water had assumed that if their situation proved dire, Ero would send more Eternals. Now he understood that what they struggled to thwart was just one of the threats against Lumineia.

"Perhaps if we cannot find answers in the past, we can find answers in the future," Mind said.

"The oracle," Fire said, nodding. "Senia will help us, and now that we know about the rising of a tower, she can look for that in our future."

"A wise strategy," Elenyr said, nodding in approval.

A thought occurred to Water and he frowned. "Would Wylyn seek to harm Senia?"

"I doubt it," Lira said. "The krey have sought to find a way to see the future for millennia. I believe she will fear what Senia can do. I suspect Wylyn will want a larger army before going up against an oracle."

"Nevertheless," Fire said. "It would be best to warn Senia of the current threat."

"Then it's time we part ways again," Elenyr said. "I will travel with Mind and Fire to the oracle's refuge. And since Wylyn has her dakorians, we need our own strength. Water and Lira can go north, to the rock trolls."

Water met Elenyr's gaze, and realized she was sending him to the rock troll kingdom for a secondary reason. He was the only fragment to never visit Astaroth, and even facing such a conflict, she thought of her sons. He gave a tiny nod of gratitude, and she smiled in turn.

"Traveling with Mind will be slow," Fire said.

Mind scowled. "I am well."

"You will be," Elenyr said.

Mind's scowl deepened, and Water felt a twinge of guilt that his healing took so long. Then Mind pointed to Fire. "Perhaps he is right, and there is another assignment he could pursue before meeting with Senia."

"What are you thinking?" Elenyr asked.

Before he could finish, a low snarl came from the darkness, and all were brought to their feet, weapons in their hands. Then a sleek black cat padded from the shadows, its cough sounding a like a laugh as the dark flesh faded in the firelight.

"Shadow," Fire spat. "I hate his messengers."

The cat padded to Elenyr and deposited a small note in her hands before dissipating. Elenyr read the note, her expression darkening until she nodded to herself. Then she looked to Fire and motioned east.

"It appears your path has been given to us. Shadow is in trouble."

"When is he not in trouble?" Fire asked.

"When has he asked for aid?" Mind countered.

Water was nodding. "It's true. Shadow does not often ask for help."

"Then it's decided," Elenyr said. "Fire will join Shadow."

"Doing what?" Fire asked.

Elenyr flashed a faint smile and showed the letter. "Shadow claims he has Relgor cornered. He just needs someone who can do some damage."

"Then count me in," Fire said with a smile.

Water looked around the campfire, pleased to feel a sense of hope. Wylyn may have escaped, but the battle was just beginning. In the last few months they had been fighting ignorance, reeling from each new group of foes. But now they knew where to fight, and Wylyn had witnessed what the fragments possessed.

Wylyn had lost dakorians, and her Order was no longer secret. In revealing themselves, they'd sought to gain the advantage, but doing so had stripped their anonymity, giving the fragments what they most wanted. Someone to fight.

The hunt was about to begin.

Epilogue: Light and Shadow

"I sent your message," Shadow said, wiping blood from his mouth. "Will you let her go?"

Serak inclined his head. "I will spare her life as agreed. But I admit I'm surprised. I did not think you would feel compassion for another's pain."

"I'm surprised as well," Shadow said. "Surprised that anyone thought you attractive enough to love. Tell me, was she blind? Or just desperate?"

Serak reached to the rune on the bars, and the illumination in the cell brightened. Shadow cringed away from the brilliance and raised a hand, but the effort was futile. The bars, the floor, even the walls and ceiling were all imbued with light, burning away every patch of shadow, and burning his flesh.

Stripped to his waist, the light scorched his chest and face, splitting lines and causing blood to drip to the floor. Shadow grimaced and began to laugh, the sound low and mocking, daring him to brighten the room further.

"I like long walks on the beach."

"You won't like this one," Relgor said, stepping into view.

The krey stood as tall as Serak, his body lean, his black eyes turning with a trace of gold. His smile suggested the coloring meant he found pleasure in Shadow's pain, and Shadow managed to make a rude gesture to the krey, and then laughed again.

Relgor did not take his gaze from the cell. "You have no idea how much you are worth," he said softly. "With you and your fragment brothers, I will even be able to buy a marriage into the empirical line."

"You cannot trap us all," Shadow said.

"Actually I can," Serak said.

He reduced the illumination in Shadow's cell, not enough to create darkness, but enough so Shadow wasn't bleeding. Then Serak stepped to the center of the circular chamber and touched a rune on the pedestal.

Four walls descended into the floor, revealing four additional cages. One crafted of bright blue flames, the other absent of all light. The third was built of water so cold that frost vapors curled off the aquaglass wall. The last was a traditional cell, with hardened steel and mithral walls. Serak smiled at Shadow's expression.

"You see, I've been preparing to cage you for thousands of years, ever since I found the Gate chamber and sent a message to Relgor."

"I thought you sent the beacon to Wylyn," Shadow said.

"That's what my mother thinks," Relgor said, his smile turning smug.

"You lied to your mother?" Shadow feigned indignation. "How beastly of you."

"I wonder if your buyer will cut out your tongue," Relgor said. "Or maybe he will enjoy your crassness. Either way, it won't matter to me. I will already have my reward."

"You cannot cage what you do not understand," Shadow said.

Serak swept a hand to him. "I've spent my entire existence studying you. And there is nothing you can do that would surprise me."

"We shall see," Shadow said.

Serak regarded him for several moments and then motioned to the only entrance into the cell. "Come, Relgor. We must prepare for Fire's arrival."

"Enjoy your final days of life," Shadow called. "You won't like how they end!"

Serak and Relgor departed, leaving Shadow in his glowing cell. He listened to their footfalls diminish. Then he stepped to the bars of his cage and leaned against them, examining the other cages.

He always appreciated how much men divulged when they thought themselves in power. Shadow had learned more in the last few minutes than he had in the last few months. Plus, Shadow would have the benefit of removing their smug expressions soon enough.

"Your plans are good," he murmured, a faint smile spreading on his face. "But my plans are better . . ."

By Ben Hale

—The Shattered Soul—
The Fragment of Water
The Fragment of Shadow
The Fragment of Light
The Fragment of Fire
The Fragment of Mind
The Fragment of Power

—The Master Thief—
Jack of Thieves
Thief in the Myst
The God Thief

—The Second Draeken War—
Elseerian
The Gathering
Seven Days
The List Unseen

—The Warsworn—
The Flesh of War
The Age of War
The Heart of War

—The Age of Oracles—
The Rogue Mage
The Lost Mage
The Battle Mage

—The White Mage Saga—

Assassin's Blade (Short story prequel)
The Last Oracle
The Sword of Elseerian
Descent Unto Dark
Impact of the Fallen
The Forge of Light

Author Bio

Originally from Utah, Ben has grown up with a passion for learning almost everything. Driven particularly to reading caused him to be caught reading by flashlight under the covers at an early age. While still young, he practiced various sports, became an Eagle Scout, and taught himself to play the piano. This thirst for knowledge gained him excellent grades and helped him graduate college with honors, as well as become fluent in three languages after doing volunteer work in Brazil. After school, he started and ran several successful businesses that gave him time to work on his numerous writing projects. His greatest support and inspiration comes from his wonderful wife and six beautiful children. Currently he resides in Missouri while working on his Masters in Professional Writing.

To contact the author, discover more about Lumineia, or find out about the upcoming sequels, check out his website at Lumineia.com. You can also follow the author on twitter @ BenHale8 or Facebook.

www.ingramcontent.com/pod-product-compliance
Lightning Source LLC
Chambersburg PA
CBHW020906200626
46814CB00001BA/202